Among the Poppies

by
J'nell Ciesielski

SMITTEN
HISTORICAL ROMANCE
LIGHTHOUSE PUBLISHING of the CAROLINAS

AMONG THE POPPIES BY J'NELL CIESIELSKI
Published by Smitten Historical Romance
an imprint of Lighthouse Publishing of the Carolinas
2333 Barton Oaks Dr., Raleigh, NC, 27614

ISBN: 978-1-946016-48-5
Copyright © 2018 by J'nell Ciesielski
Cover design by Elaina Lee
Interior design by Karthick Srinivasan

Available in print from your local bookstore, online, or from the publisher at:
ShopLPC.com

For more information on this book and the author visit:
http://www.jnellciesielski.com/

Brought to you by the creative team at Lighthouse Publishing of the Carolinas:
Eddie Jones, Shonda Savage, Karin Beery, Pegg Thomas, Brian Cross, Judah Raine, Jennifer Leo

Library of Congress Cataloging-in-Publication Data
Ciesielski, J'nell.
Among the Poppies / J'nell Ciesielski 1st ed.

Printed in the United States of America

PRAISE FOR *AMONG THE POPPIES*

Ciesielski's debut pays tribute to those who gave their lives for their country, and those who stood with them, and highlights the ambulance corps drivers, a group that isn't mentioned in many novels of this period. The reader is transported back in time and made to feel a part of this tale.

~**Leslie L. McKee**
RT Bookreviews Magazine

What a debut! J'nell Ciesielski ignites the pages with a captivating, out-of-the-box heroine and a kind-hearted, by-the-book hero in this World War I romance of changing times, shakable lives, and a steadfast God. With tedious detail and heart-wrenching descriptions, Ciesielski takes the reader on a journey through the hospitals, trenches, and frontlines of France, giving us not only a view from a solider but also the rare perspective of women who dared enter the devastating world of war. Friendships are challenged and formed, faith is tried and strengthened, hearts are broken and healed, and romance is found and forged through the fires of The War to End All Wars. This novel sweeps beyond the glitz and glamour of the Edwardian Age and draws a realistic tale of love, loss, war, and dreams. The heroine was delightful and the hero a fitting match. A beautiful story.

~ **Pepper D Basham**
Author of the *Penned in Time series and Just the Way You Are*

World War I history comes to life in debut author Ciesielski's *Among the Poppies*. With the talent and skill of experienced authors, Ciesieskli brings to the pages the challenges, fear, bravery, and heroism of those who fought in one of the world's most troubling times. Humor, wit, history, and romance brim through a story that is enlivened with characters facing familial obligations, societal restrictions, and the chasing of dreams as their world falls apart in war-torn France. *Among the Poppies* is not only beautifully written but beautifully told by an author who clearly loves the time period and honors with her words those who fought for freedom.

~ **Marisa Deshaies**
Acquisitions Editor of Bling!
At Lighthouse Publishing of the Carolinas

Among the Poppies has all the ingredients for a great read. A feisty, strong heroine, a handsome soldier hero, riveting World War I history, and romance to melt your heart make this a story you don't want to miss.

~ **Ann H. Gabhart**
Bestselling author of *These Healing Hills*

"From page one, the characters pull you in and keep you reading! J'nell Ciesielski pens her story with beauty and skill."

~ **Roseanna White**
Bestselling author of the *Ladies of the Manor*
and *Shadows Over England* series

With *Among the Poppies,* Ciesielski exhibits her mastery of the historical genre. With whip-smart dialogue, a strong female message, fluid turns of phrase, and characters at once relatable and inimitable, this sweepingly romantic and impeccably researched novel is one of the finest examples of Great War fiction I have read in an age.

~ **Rachel McMillan**
Author of the *Van Buren* and *DeLuca* series

Introduce a dashing, heart-thrilling Captain to a chauffer's daughter set on adventure and helping The Great War efforts and you have sparks! Add witty dialogue, swoon-worthy tension, heroic intentions, and then the vivid descriptions of turn of the century England and war torn France ... and you have J'nell Cielsielski's well-crafted, enchanting, debut novel, *Among the Poppies*.

~**Dawn Crandall**
Author of the award-winning series, *The Everstone Chronicles*

For my dad, who taught me that stubbornness can be a good thing. I think you'd be proud.

Acknowledgments

Thank you to my agent, Linda S. Glaz, for taking a chance on a girl who likes to wrap her romances with an adventurous bow.

My editors, Pegg Thomas for loving my story enough to want to share it with the world, and Karin Beery for shining it up like a diamond. Who knew *The Lord of the Rings* could bring out just the right amount of sparkle?

Kathy Rouser and Anne Evans for taking the precious time to hunt for missing plot points, overbearing secondary characters, and those pesky commas that I can't seem to control. And to Kim, my magical unicorn of a muse, where would my stories be without you?

My mom for all those childhood trips to the library to feed my imagination, for giving me a love of historicals and always encouraging my writing even when I came home from school with a love story between a trash can and an apple core.

My little girl who teaches me a lesson in forgiveness, unconditional love, and grace every single day.

Bryan, my ever patient and understanding husband. You've put up with a lot over the years between trench outlines in the living room, impromptu hand-to-hand combat demonstrations, and the constant stack of warfare books for a little light reading at night. Not once have you batted an eyelid. You are the firm ground upon which I stand and stretch upward to grasp my dreams.

I can never fully express my full gratitude to the men and women who have gone before us in sacrifice for country, love, family, and freedom. To the men and women of today who stand on the front lines and the families they leave behind, you are the true heroes.

CHAPTER 1

Great Malvern, England 1915

"No, no. Like this. You must tie it off with a bow."

"Oh, yes. You are quite correct, Edith. The bow is indeed what this bandage needs."

Gwynevere Ruthers crushed her fingers together in the folds of her navy wool skirt. *If he's bleeding to death, he's not going to care about a stupid bow.*

Like a flock of hens, the ladies of Great Malvern gathered around the bedside and clucked over their impractical handiwork.

"The Red Cross nurses are satisfied with merely a knot, but I think the bow gives it that extra finishing touch," Mrs. Shearing said as she glided to the head of the bed. A cool smile of self-admiration tilted one side of her thin mouth.

Gwyn's hand shot into the air.

Mrs. Shearing's smile flattened. "Do you have a question, Gwyn?"

"Doesn't a bow have a higher probability of snagging something and pulling free, as opposed to a knot?"

The hen pack's eyebrows rose in surprise. As one, they turned to their leader with wide eyes.

"You may double knot it before the bow if you feel so inclined." Mrs. Shearing sniffed. "The artistry of a bow is not to everyone's taste."

Gwyn bit her tongue. She hardly thought the soldier in the next bed would care much for artistry as he waited to be bandaged. Hopefully, he wouldn't have Mrs. Edith Shearing, the prominent banker's wife, in his ward.

Gwyn glanced around the hospital room at the other small groups of volunteers. Dressed in their sturdy clothes and white aprons, the women practiced head bandaging, stopping sucking chest wounds, and checking for broken bones. All while her group tied pretty bows. "I think we should try splinting again," Gwyn blurted out.

Mrs. Shearing's pale forehead creased like dried parchment. "We did that last week."

"Yes, but we could try with other objects. Things we might find on a battlefield if supplies are limited, like branches, belts, odd bits of leather. I once read the American cowboys used dried animal hides to—"

"You are *not* wrapping me in a dead animal. I'd rather bleed to death." Their 'patient,' Miss Cecelia Hale, sat up in bed, crossed her bandaged arms over her cream lace blouse, and scowled. "Besides, not one of us will be going anywhere near a battlefield."

"Every week, new units of women are forming in war areas in Belgium, France, and Malta." Excitement at the possibility bubbled inside of Gwyn. "After that second battle at Ypres, they need us more than ever."

Cecelia rolled her eyes. "Oh, G. You read too many newspapers."

"I just think it's a good idea to be proactive and learn all we can while we still have time."

"Are you afraid the war will end before you have the opportunity to patch up some Tommy?"

"I've read that the hospitals are filling faster than they can find places to keep the wounded. They're shipping them further into the country, and Great Malvern could be next."

Cecelia fluffed one of the cotton strip bows at her wrist. "It's nothing more than news fodder and editors trying to sell more papers."

"Miss Hale is right." Mrs. Shearing sniffed through pinched nostrils. "It's nothing to overly concern us. The war will be over by Christmas."

Gwyn clamped her fingers together in frustration. "That's what they said last year."

Mottling red in the face, Mrs. Shearing's mouth popped open, but Sister clapped her hands together. "Excellent work for the day, ladies," she said. "Tomorrow, we will go over head traumas and instrument sterilization. Please clean your workstations and store all unused items back in the cabinet."

"Get me untangled from this mess." Cecelia held her bandaged arms out to Gwyn. "My fingers are going numb from all these bows."

"One thing I can say for these decorative little additions is that they're easier to undo than knots." After extracting Cecelia from her bindings, Gwyn took a quick inventory of the scissors, linen strips, cotton swabs, water bottles, and iodine-soaked gauze littering the worktable and bed. "What a mess."

"Those old peahens think they're too good to clean up." Cecelia huffed at the women's retreating backs as they grabbed their fancy hats and hotfooted out the door. She fluffed her velvet ribbons back into order, after having been smashed down with bandages. "Just because they have one servant at home. One. As if that's anything to brag about."

Gwyn placed the scissors and iodine bottle on a metal tray. "Not everyone is the daughter of a baron and blessed with seventy servants like you, CeCe."

"All the more reason they should help with cleanup. If I can do it, so can they." Cecelia snatched a discarded roll of gauze and attempted to roll it. Thirty seconds later, she threw it down. "Why do they make these so tricky?"

If they hadn't been childhood friends, Gwyn would have had her fill of Cecelia, the daughter of the Baron of Somerset, long ago. But friends they were, or as friendly as a lord's daughter and his chauffeur's daughter could be past the age of braids and knee-high skirts.

Picking up the gauze, Gwyn rolled it with a few quick twists of the wrist and tucked it beside the rows of bandages on the tray. Throwing the spoiled materials into the rubbish bin, she put the tray in the storage cabinet and shut the door. "All done. Let's get out of here."

Only too happy to leave the overwhelming smell of bleach and carbolic lotion behind, Gwyn grabbed her hat and burst through the front doors, inhaling the spicy autumn air. Late afternoon sun filtered through the towering alder trees' yellow, orange, and red leaves like light piercing stained glass. Closing her eyes, she tilted her head back and let the warmth bathe her face.

"That's how you get freckles," Cecelia said behind her.

Gwyn's eyes popped open, a mischievous grin curling her mouth. She passed through the hospital's wrought iron gate and turned down the lane leading home. "You mean, that's how *you* get freckles."

Cecelia made a face as she adjusted the brim of her velvet and ostrich feather hat over her milk-white skin. "If I had your lovely rich brown hair instead of this unfashionable strawberry blonde, then I could forget my cover as often as you do, but, alas, the Fates have shunned me from kindness."

"You know better than anyone how fickle fashion is, so take heart that blonde will be all the rage in just a matter of time."

"As it should. Though I shall never have your height."

"Be grateful for never having to answer how the weather fairs from up here. Or have your ankles constantly flash because your hemlines are too short."

"At least yours don't drag behind you like some old stuffy Victorian dowager's train from last century." Cecelia tapped a gloved finger against the brim of Gwyn's straw hat. "Speaking of fashion, you need to add a new ribbon to that. Pale pink and fraying ends won't do. Not to mention it being three years behind fashion. Add it to the trunk of dresses I'm donating to the orphanage. Maybe they can use it for a doll."

Gwyn swooped down and plucked a bright red leaf from the

ground. "Are they fraying? I hadn't noticed."

"Of course you haven't. Your nose is stuck in a book half the time, and the other times it's covered in axle grease. You need to pursue more ladylike habits if you want to snag a man."

"Like running?" Gwyn wiggled her eyebrows.

"He can't catch you if you're running."

"Who says I want to be caught?"

"If you don't, you'll spend your life living above your father's garage. Or worse, as an old maid."

"At least then I won't have anything tying me down to hearth and boring routine. I could travel the world, see the things I've only read about, taste exotic foods." Gwyn twirled the crisp leaf between her fingers, the color blurring faster and faster. "A life of adventure and freedom, just as the Stinson School of Flying promises."

"I cannot believe you've applied to a flying school halfway around the world. Where is this place again?"

"A little town in Texas, America. San Antonio, I think. Doesn't that sound exotic? The landscape is said to be ideal for flight, and it's the only school in the world offering pilot licenses to women. Think of all the good things I could do with a pilot license for the war effort, like mail delivery or dropping off supplies to remote hospitals." Dropping the leaf, Gwyn patted her pocket and her mother's list protected within. Places Mum never got to visit, but Gwyn would soon. A pilot's license would see to that.

"Is that what all that talk was about in there? Women going to the front lines just for a lark?" Cecelia shook her head. "You've always had an adventurous streak longer than the Thames, but facing down the guns of the Kaiser is something else entirely, G."

"Helping our boys is hardly a lark."

"But you can help them right here, or in London, where there's running water and hot meals to come home to."

"I'd endure a few cold baths and mushy porridge for a small taste of exploration." A chilled breeze stirred along the dirt lane, ruffling Gwyn's long skirt, the latest hand-me-down from Cecelia. "Can you imagine what it would be like to break past this island's borders, sail over waters charted for thousands of years, and step foot on foreign soil while helping our fighting boys at the same time?"

"I don't think about it. My mother likes to remind me that it is my father's job to think for me, and someday it will be my husband's." Cecelia's pert nose scrunched up. "Which reminds me, I'm late for the party."

"Another benefit?"

"The Oxfordshire and Buckinghamshire Infantry needs more fundraising, and my mother is precisely the hostess to pull money from the purse strings of all her rich friends." Cecelia tugged her beaded jacket closer as wild leaves tumbled their way. "But it's also an opportunity for her to play matchmaker for me with one of the local officers. My question is, if he's such a catch, why haven't I seen or heard of him before?"

"Maybe he's not so much a catch, but more of a last-minute contingency."

"I bet he's bald."

"Or too fat to sit on a horse." Gwyn giggled as Cecelia's face sagged further. "And talks with his mouth full."

Cecelia groaned. "Of course none of that matters as long as he's rich and well connected, or so I've been taught. You are so lucky your father doesn't use you as a trading card."

Not knowing what to say, Gwyn merely nodded. Dear Papa. The kindest and most understanding man she had ever known. Though he never silenced her dreams, he did struggle to keep her feet on the ground from time to time. "He would love to see me settled and cared for. I know he worries about me being alone."

They stopped at the turnoff to Clarendon Downs, the ancestral seat of the barons of Somerset. Straight ahead, down the poplar-lined drive, stood Cecelia's massive sandstone house, shining like a jewel in its velvety green surroundings. To the left, a long, winding dirt-packed alley led to the servants' entrance and garages. Gwyn's way home.

"I'll tell you what," Cecelia called as she started down her sun-dappled lane, "if the Mr. Officer I'm scheduled to meet tonight doesn't work out, I'll send him your way."

"Thanks ever so much."

"And remind your father to bring the extra straps for the trunks. I told the orphanage I was bringing two, but I found more shoes in the bottom of my wardrobe last night."

Gwyn raced down the pebble-strewn path that dipped behind the great house, calling hello to the kitchen maid as Gwyn ran straight into the garage. Musty oil, metal tools, and worn leather permeated the air. She scanned the area until she spotted her father's feet sticking out from underneath Lord Somerset's Renault.

"Hello, Papa."

"I thought that was you stampeding in." A greasy finger pointed from behind the wheel well. "Hand me that wrench there."

Plucking the tool from its wooden toolbox, Gwyn squatted and placed it in his waiting hand. "What are you working on?"

"One of the lug nuts shook loose. Too many potholes from last week's rain."

Gwyn eyed the toolbox. Her fingers itched for a solid task after the bow-tying lesson. Removing her hat, she tossed it on the workbench. "Can I help?"

"Almost … done … there. That should do it." Wiggling free from underneath the car, he leaned on one elbow and pulled a stained rag from his pocket to wipe his hands. Bright green eyes, the same as hers, shone out from the grease smudged across his face. "How was your class today?"

"Enlightening." Grabbing the wrench, she wiped the head with a cloth and placed it back in the toolbox. "I learned how to tie bows."

"Bows?" Papa sat up. "That Shearing woman still taking things into her own hands?"

Gwyn rearranged the tools by size, avoiding her father's eyes.

"Why don't you change groups and stop wasting your time with women who think war is a garden party?"

"Miss Cecelia won't allow it. She can't mix with the other groups, as they're full of shopkeepers' wives and schoolgirls, but she refuses to be alone with the old dragons. That's what she calls them." Gwyn looked up from the tools. "Besides, those ladies have a lot to learn, and maybe I'm the one to help them."

"That's my girl." He grinned and smoothed down the lock of hair winging over his ears. Nearing fifty, he was still handsome with the gray streaks through his brown hair lending an air of wisdom. He stood, grabbing his knee as his face contorted.

Gwyn caught his elbow. "Are you all right, Papa?"

He straightened, favoring his right knee. "Fine, fine. Old wound flaring again. Must be rain coming."

"You should rest." She tried to lead him to the stool, but he pulled away.

"No time." He waved her off. "Cars will be coming soon for the party."

"Ruthers? Ruthers, are you in here?" Neville, the first footman, popped his head around the corner. "Ah, there you are. Hello, Gwyn. It seems the florist has forgotten the centerpiece for the grand hall. There's no time to unload his lorry and rush back to retrieve it. Mr. Whiteson has asked that you pick it up."

Papa hesitated. "Of course."

"Very good. I shall tell Mr. Whiteson not to worry about it. And to stop berating the florist, who brought enough flowers to fill the king's garden. Oh! I nearly forgot. This came in the post for you, Gwyn." Reaching into his breast pocket, Neville extracted a cream envelope and handed it to her before leaving.

Gwyn glimpsed at the neatly printed address from San Antonio, Texas, and tore open the paper. With heart pounding, she scanned the contents. Her heart sank. Waitlisted. "Stinson has had a record amount of applications for this year. My name has been added to a list, and, should an opening arise, I'll be informed directly."

"That's good, isn't it?" Papa asked. "You haven't been turned down."

She'd waited so long. Disappointment sank in her stomach like a thick batch of motor oil. "I suppose."

"Chin up, girl. It's not a refusal, and it means I'll get to keep you here with me a while longer."

Gwyn tucked the letter back inside the envelope. Disheartening as it was, she did her best to shake off the frustration. "You're right. A minor setback, but nothing I can't wait for. Besides, I couldn't soar around over there happy as a lark knowing all the bad things happening in my own country."

"That's my girl. Now, this flower pickle. What bad timing." Papa sighed and jammed his grease rag into his back pocket. "I was hoping to fix that sticking gearshift before I drive His Lordship to the train station tomorrow."

"I'll go," Gwyn said, eager to take her mind off the letter. "I'll get the flowers and be back in no time."

He eyed her with suspicion. "Sure this isn't an excuse to take a drive on a lovely autumn day?"

"Oh, Papa." She rested her hands on his thick shoulders. "Whatever gave you that idea?"

"Because you're every bit your mum, God rest her. Any reason to dash about and you'll take it." He grinned and pinched her chin. "Take Lizzie and hurry on."

Gwyn turned to the rust bucket that was Lizzie. A second-hand donation from the Earl of Cranstem, Lord Somerset hoped her father could return the Model-T back to her former glory. Gwyn doubted even her talented father's hands could complete such a feat. "If I'm not back before nightfall, assume she's driven me into a ditch and send out a search party." Not bothering to reclaim her hat, Gwyn climbed behind the wheel.

Papa turned the crank until the engine sputtered to life. Grabbing the hand brake, Gwyn eased her foot onto the clutch.

Lizzie coughed. And died.

"One more time." He spun the crank again. This time Lizzie roared. "She should be good now. I've been tampering with the accelerator. Perfect time to see how far she'll push."

"She'll fly, I know she will." Gwyn saluted before easing onto the clutch again. Lizzie lurched forward and chugged down the gravel drive.

Passing the entrance to Clarendon, Gwyn pulled on the throttle. Her leg cramped from pressing on the clutch, but just a few more yards and she'd be free from suspicious eyes and tattletales on the house grounds.

At the end of Clarendon Downs, open road rose before Gwyn. She let the clutch out and pushed down on the throttle. Lizzie jerked and rushed, finding freedom beneath her tires. Gwyn's eyes watered from the stinging wind as they flew down the road. Hairpins dislodged with each bump, freeing dark curls to whip in front of her face. She pushed them back with a laugh, the headache from the day slipping away with each mile.

"That-a-girl." She patted the wooden steering wheel. "Let's see what you can really do."

Pulling the lever forward, she carefully released the left pedal and the speed gauge inched its way closer to thirty miles per hour. Practically flying! The wind whipped around her face and coaxed out a grin of pure contentment.

If only she could drive forever. If Lizzie could sprout wings, they could travel around the world in the extraordinary manner of Phileas Fogg, seeing new lands, meeting exotic natives, and defying the odds of a girl like Gwyn ever succeeding.

The English countryside would have to suffice for now. At least until she could convince her father to let her join one of the voluntary groups going to France or Belgium, now that she wasn't going to flight school.

Turning down the wooded road leading to the village, a white puff of smoke erupted from under the hood. Groaning, Gwyn pressed the gear pedal into neutral, then eased off as she pulled the brake and steered into the grass. Lizzie came to a twitching halt.

"Of all the times you choose to give out on me." With an annoyed shake of her head, Gwyn climbed out and rolled the bonnet back to peer inside. "Pardon the intrusion, Lizzie. Let's see what's going on in here." Shreds of fading light danced over the black and gray parts. "Please don't be a blown gasket."

Lizzie coughed another white plume into Gwyn's face. She fanned the choking steam away and groaned. Even better. The radiator.

"Sorry, Mr. Whiteson." She sighed, rolling her sleeves up. "Looks like her ladyship must hostess on without her floral arrangement."

Another party. Another daughter on parade. Slowing his horse under a canopy of oaks, William tugged at the top button on his dress uniform to ease the suffocating stiffness against his throat. He should be at the hospital visiting his wounded men and ascertaining who to send back to the Front. He found few things more heart-wrenching than telling a man on his hospital bed that his duty to king and country was not yet complete. As their commanding officer, William allowed no one else to shoulder the burden.

Of course, that wasn't the real reason he was called home on emergency leave. His father needed his help recruiting other young lads, and what better way than to use a uniform straight from the Front. Heaven knew the boys needed all the help they could get. And those Jerries needed a fresh taste of the Oxfordshire and Buckinghamshire lads.

Excitement trilled in William's veins. New men could make up for the decimation at Festubert and bring back a little enthusiasm to the fight, until they became as disillusioned with the killing and filth as those who had come before. Even he had fallen prey to the despair. Someday, when this war-to-end-all-wars was finally over, and if he managed to survive, he could settle down to a life of peace and leisure.

"Cheer up, Titan." William patted the sleek black neck of his thoroughbred. "I know you'd rather be at the barracks, but I hear Lord Somerset has stables filled to the loft with hay and oats. Maybe even a pretty filly in the next stall. Just don't let her turn your head right before battle. We have to keep our focus, old chap."

Rounding a bend in the road, he spotted an automobile parked in the grass. Its bonnet was rolled back, but there was no one in sight. Urging Titan into a trot, he came around the front of the auto and promptly yanked on the reins as his mouth slacked open. Sticking out from underneath the contraption were two of the longest and most shapely legs he'd ever seen, complete with bunched skirt, stockings, and silver buckle heeled shoes.

"Oh, golly molly, Lizzie. You have such horrid timing." A highly-irritated, muffled voice came from under the metal contraption. "You pick the one time I don't have my toolbox to spring a leak."

William cleared his throat. "May I be of assistance?"

The disembodied feet kicked at the dirt as the legs wiggled down to reveal a slender waist, arms, shoulders, and a dirt-smudged face with two wide green eyes.

"Forgive me for startling you." William dismounted as the girl jumped to her feet. Tall for a woman, she nearly met his eye line. "I thought you may have been in distress."

"Well, yes—I mean, my motorcar is." The red splotches on her cheeks disappeared behind the dirt spots. Glancing down, she wiped her black hands against her skirt. "Radiator hose has a leak, and the clamp is loosening against the return line."

He had no clue what she was talking about, but he nodded anyway and focused on the one word he understood. "The clamp cannot be tightened again?"

She shook her head, sending the lopsided knot of dark brown curls further to the side. "It's too rusted, but even if it wasn't, there's still a hole to contend with."

"And you don't have your toolbox."

"No, I … how did you know?"

"It was on your list of complaints to Lizzie, who I surmise is this lovely tin box."

"Don't call her that." The girl scowled at the auto. "She's been anything but lovely today."

"I can see that." William laughed. The corners of the girl's mouth twitched, drawing heat up his neck. He cleared his throat before it could reach his face. "Where is your driver, miss? Surely he did not leave you here to fend for yourself."

"I have no driver."

He reared back. "You drove this and now intend to fix it yourself?"

A thin line puckered between her eyebrows. "Who else would fix it?"

"Forgive me. I merely assumed …" She frowned. He squeezed his hands into fists and looked to the auto for a distraction. "Would you mind if I take a look?"

The corners of her mouth eased, but the skeptical pucker on her brow remained. "Be my guest."

He peered into the cavity holding the engine, other various parts, and a web of tubes. All covered with grease and rust, and he without an inkling of what was what. Why did he never take the time to learn the basics about these new-fangled contraptions? His wandering eye latched onto a clamp. "Is this the one giving you problems?"

She leaned in next to him, and he caught a whiff of oil, roses, and—tincture of iodine? An odd mixture for a lady, to be sure. Then again, this particular lady didn't seem the kind to sit quaintly in a parlor all day.

"Yes," she said. "See how it's warped back and flaking at the juncture?"

William pinched the two ends between his fingers and squeezed. The clamp groaned but didn't budge. He squeezed harder. Nothing.

"I'm afraid too much more force, and it'll break." He dusted the rust bits from his hands. "What about the hose hole?"

"It needs to be patched or replaced, neither of which I can do here."

"May I look?" Without waiting for a reply, he sat on the ground, but she quickly stepped between him and the car.

"Please don't." She held out her dirty hands. "I won't allow Lizzie to ruin your fine clothes, not like she has mine." She glanced down at her stained skirt and frowned. "Not that I would call these fine."

"I would see it as a favor if my uniform developed a few undesirable spots on it. It would be unacceptable for presentation." He dropped his voice. "Particularly for boring parties."

Her eyes widened. "The party! Oh, golly molly. I forgot all about those flowers." Spinning around, she grabbed a jacket from the driver's bench and shoved her arms into it. "I must go. Thank you for your assistance."

"I hardly think I assisted in—wait! Where are you going?"

"To town." She started walking down the road. "I need to retrieve an important flower basket and cannot return without every last stem."

"On foot? It'll be too dark to see the road before you arrive, and much too dangerous for a lady alone." He jogged ahead to close the distance between them. "Please allow me to escort you on my horse. It'll be much faster."

She shook her head, sending an errant curl into her eyes. Her hand flew up to bat it away, leaving a grease streak across her cheek. "And impossible to carry a floral arrangement."

He glanced at Titan, then back to her. "Quite right. Then I'll take you home where you can acquire a more suitable contraption to transport flowers, though I could never understand the need for centerpieces. They only block the way when you're trying to converse with someone across the table."

"Unless it's someone who likes to talk about the rate of grass growth, in which case the arrangement is quite effective." She laughed, pulling a smile from him. He couldn't recall the last time a woman had made him do that.

He swept his hand towards Titan. "Shall we?"

"You're very kind to offer, but I hardly think it appropriate."

"I assure you, miss, that there is nothing inappropriate about escorting a stranded lady back home." He didn't bother mentioning the inappropriateness of finding said lady under the belly of a motorcar. Somehow such custom impropriety didn't fit her.

Staring at Titan's saddle, she shifted from foot to foot. "Are you sure there's enough room?"

William swung onto the saddle and patted the space behind him. "Right back here. My sister used to ride with me like this."

She shook her head, not budging. "I haven't had the best experiences with horses."

"And yet you'll ride around in that?" He pointed at the auto.

"They don't bite and kick."

"I promise you will be completely safe. Titan is a perfect gentleman."

She considered a moment, then finally nodded, walking back to her auto. "Can you come closer to Lizzie so I can step on the running board? I don't think I'm quite tall enough to leap up like you did."

Maneuvering Titan, William offered his hand as she stepped up. She grasped his hand, took a deep breath, and jumped. It took a few seconds of grappling, swinging legs, and panicked cries, but she finally settled in behind him.

"You'll need to hold on," he said.

"I am."

Glancing over his shoulder, he saw her white fingers latched to the back of the saddle. "Unless you have glue on your fingers, that won't keep you on. Put your arms around me."

Horror flashed across her face. "I don't even know you!"

"Captain William Crawford, at your service. Now, please put

your arms around me."

She shook her head. "Your uniform will be ruined."

"A price I'm willing to pay so I won't have to take you to hospital after you've fallen off and bumped your head."

Hesitating a moment, she finally sighed and scrubbed her hands over her skirts. Wrapping her arms around his waist in a death grip, she blew out a breath. "I'm ready."

"Are you sure you're all right back there, miss ... I'm afraid I don't know your name."

"Gwyn, and yes, I'm all right." William didn't bother pointing out that her voice was strung tighter than a pack of grenades. "And thank you for doing this, Captain Crawford."

"You're most welcome." He tapped Titan's flanks, setting the horse into motion. "May I ask where we're headed?"

"Just head north for about three and a half miles."

"Three and a half miles! I'm surprised Lizzie made it that far."

"So am I, but part of the way is downhill, so I was able to coast."

"Coast?"

"Allow her to ride with the momentum. It's the best way to feel the wind on your face." She sighed, tickling the hairs on the back of his neck. "The only way to feel freedom."

Spoken so low, he almost missed her words. Freedom in a reckless deathtrap? "Lizzie is hardly the only way to feel the blowing wind."

"Yes, but driving certainly is faster than running."

Running and driving. Who was this woman with her arms wrapped around him? The evening was going from dread to delight. William urged Titan into a trot. "I'll take your word on the driving, but I prefer a good old-fashioned horse. There's nothing like the power of a horse's legs as he kicks up the ground beneath him."

"And I'll take *your* word on that." Her fists bunched into his stomach as she clung to him. "Oh, please don't make him do that."

William pulled back on the reins, trying his best not to concentrate on the curving warmth pressed behind him. "Not the time for a gallop?"

"Not unless you wish me to spoil your lovely uniform, and I would hate to do that because it looks like you spent a great deal of time polishing those buttons."

"Longer than I care to admit, but most of my uniforms lost their shine and polish long ago in the deep ends of the trenches."

"Have you seen the fighting, Captain?"

His fingers tightened around the reins. The past year he'd seen enough fighting and killing to last him a lifetime. Too many men blown apart, too many faces buried in the frozen ground, too many times leading his men into slaughter. "Yes. I've seen it."

The clopping of Titan's hooves filled his ears. Steady and strong, the rhythm echoed off the towering alder trees. Thank God his favorite horse was not drafted into the army like most other animals in the country. *I'm sure Father had some sway in that.*

"Have you always wanted to be a soldier?"

The question took him off guard. No one had ever asked his preference before. "I've always known I would serve. Do I think this is the life for me?" He shrugged. "For now it is. Just like every other able-bodied man in the country."

"You haven't been wounded?"

"Not that I'm aware of."

"Then why are you here? Oh, golly molly, I didn't mean that the way it sounded. It's just that you said able-bodied, but most capable men are across the Channel. Not that you're incapable—"

"You think I'm shirking my duties."

"No! Of course not."

"Fear not, Miss Gwyn. I'm no truant." He couldn't stop the smile as she sagged against him with a sigh. "I'm here on orders to inspect my men on convalescence."

"That's very kind of you."

"Some of them won't think so when they're deemed well

enough to return to the Front."

"Are conditions so bad that our wounded are forced to fight again?"

"It never hurts to have a bigger army than the enemy. We can use all the help we can get."

"What kind of help?" Her voice pitched with excitement.

He bit back a groan. Not another do-good rich girl creating problems. "The men always enjoy care baskets from home."

"Yes, I've tried those." Her tone fell flat. "Sister said my mittens served better as pot holders and that I'd better stick to rolling bandages."

Hospital work. He hadn't imagined the tincture of iodine. "I'm sure whatever volunteer work you do is valuable. Even rolling bandages."

"I wish it were more. You can stop here."

William pulled Titan to a halt and stared down the sweeping drive lined with poplars. Hundreds of lights twinkled from the house. "Clarendon Downs? This is where you live?"

"Yes, but I can walk from here." She squirmed behind him. "I've taken so much of your time already."

"Nonsense." He grabbed her hands, lest she try to leap and break her neck. "How fortunate that this is my destination as well."

"It is?" Panic leaped in her voice. "Oh, dear."

William spurred Titan on. Why would a girl of Clarendon Downs's society be trapped under a motorcar without a chaperone or chauffeur in sight? Proper young ladies did not spend their valuable time in garages. Or perhaps he'd been away for too long.

"Please stop here, Captain." Gwyn's fists clenched against his stomach as Titan trotted to the wide front door.

Jumping down, William reached back and grasped her waist. Alarm twisted her face as he pulled her towards him. Her hands latched onto his shoulders like hooks. She slid off Titan's back and into his arms, close enough for him to see the thickness of her eyelashes.

The anxiety faded from her face. Her fingers relaxed, and a wobbly smile spread over her full lips. "Thank you, Captain Crawford. You certainly saved me a long walk—"

"Gwyn?"

Her entire body stiffened. "Mr. W-Whiteson."

A tall man with silvered hair marched through the front door, puffed-out chest first. "Gwyn. What are you doing here with the captain?"

Gwyn leaped away from William as the older man bore down on her like a man-o-war. "The auto broke down on the way to town, and Captain Crawford was kind enough to see me back. I was to get the flowers."

The man's bushy eyebrows shot straight up into his hairline. "The flowers? But I told … never mind all that. Off with you now. I'm sure your father will want to know about the motorcar." He sucked in a deep breath and turned his eye to William. "Captain Crawford, I apologize for the inconvenience. Please come in."

"There was no inconvenience," William said. "I was more than happy to help the lady, though I think it's only fair to blame Lizzie for this one."

Whiteson scowled.

Gwyn groaned. "Thank you again, Captain Crawford. Good luck with your men."

"Yes, I—"

She hurried away without a glance, leaving him feeling the fool. What in the world was that all about? And why was she running toward the garage?

CHAPTER 2

Running her finger down the checklist, Gwyn stopped at the next unchecked box. She turned her brightest smile on the man lying in the bed. "Ready for your exercise, Corporal Brown?"

Brown's chest rose and fell, expelling deep breaths. His non-bandaged eyelid twitched. Gwyn crossed her arms. "I know you're not asleep, Corporal."

A soft snore fluttered from his bruised lips.

Gwyn walked to the side of the bed and leaned in to whisper. "You can do better than that."

A snort erupted from his throat.

"Oh, that's much better. All the practice has paid off, but you still need to exercise."

Brown's intact eye fluttered open. "Why, Nurse Ruthers. I didn't realize you were here. How nice to awaken to such a lovely face."

"Flattery, flattery." She clucked her tongue to fight the rising grin. "You thought Nurse Shearing was on duty again, didn't you?"

"She sponges off my feet with ice water instead of warming it like you do." He struggled into a half-sitting position and glanced around the room. "And she wears too much perfume. Gives all the men headaches."

"Then you shall be glad to know there is a freshly mowed path in the back garden so your afternoon exercise will be filled with the sweet smell of grass and falling leaves." Gwyn pulled back the covers and angled his crutches into position. "If you're able to do more than one lap, Mrs. Hower will add an extra dollop of cream to the pie slices tonight."

Brown hefted his legs over the bed and grabbed the crutches.

Gwyn held her arms in a large circle around him as he stood, ready to catch him should he stumble. "Careful now."

Once he was stable, he hobbled away. Sadness pinged her heart. Though more fortunate than both of his brothers buried in Saint Grace's kirkyard, he'd never work at the newspaper office again with one remaining eye and a shattered hip.

She shook off the pity. He was alive, and that was all that mattered.

"Gwyn." Sister glided down the center aisle, clad in her pristine white uniform and cap, with a stack of laundered linens. "I need you to strip the beds of the men gone to the exercise yard."

"Yes, Sister." Gwyn bit back a groan. She hated stripping the beds, especially alone. Hospitals taught nurses to tuck and yank the sheets so firmly into place that—come hurricanes or the Kaiser's army—those linens wouldn't budge.

Thirty minutes and a thin line of perspiration later, Gwyn gathered three beds' worth of dirty sheets and arched her back. Careful to breathe through her mouth, she trudged down the aisle, trying not to knock over any trays with her tower of spoils.

"After you drop those off, I need you to help change Sergeant Montine's bandages," Sister called as she walked past holding her ever-present clipboard.

"Yes, ma'am." Gwyn turned the corner and smacked into a mountain in a uniform. Pillowcases and blankets toppled from the precarious stack and scattered around the floor like dirty snow. "Excuse me, sir." She grabbed at items as they slipped across the freshly waxed floors. "I wasn't paying attention."

"My fault for standing as a roadblock," said a deep voice.

Dropping to her knees, Gwyn gathered the linens. Highly polished boots creaked as the man squatted next to her, a sweat-stained top sheet in his hands.

"Oh, thank you ever so—" Gwyn rocked back and landed on her bottom. Her pulse lurched. "Captain Crawford." After thinking of almost nothing but him for the past two days, he was there. Surrounded by soiled bedsheets. And she sprawled right in the middle of them.

"Allow me." Holding her elbow, he helped her to her feet.

"Thank you." She had to tilt her head back to meet his gaze. One of the few men to make her feel delicate in his presence instead of like a lumbering giraffe. She smoothed a shaking hand over her skirt. "I don't know if it's luck or bad timing, but you do find me in the most ridiculous situations."

Dressed in a khaki uniform and Sam Browne belt, his wavy blond hair parted and slicked to the side, his smile readied itself more easily than it had the night of the Clarendon party.

The skin around his dark blue eyes crinkled. "At least this time Lizzie wasn't involved."

"She could cause quite a commotion in here, no doubt."

Cecelia rounded the corner and stopped with her mouth forming a perfect pink O. Shimmering in soft green and navy ribbons, she looked as if she'd just stepped from the fashionable streets of London. "What's happened here?"

"I was carrying these to the laundry." Gwyn scooped the scattered sheets into her arms. "I dropped them."

Cecelia wrinkled her nose. "I can see that." Looping a gloved hand under the captain's arm, she flashed a smile. "I've brought William, I mean Captain Crawford, to see how our facilities run. He showed the greatest interest in them the other night."

Gwyn shifted her load to better see his face over the top. "Are any of your men here, Captain?"

"Four." A slight V furrowed between his eyebrows. "Most of the others were too severe to send across country and will remain in London for the time being."

For the time being. Did he mean they would be sent home or back to the Front? "I hope you find our simple facilities to your standards. We take great care and pride in our men."

"I'm glad to hear that. These men deserve the best after what they've been through."

"And that's what I'm so eager to show you, William." Cecelia flashed him a dazzling smile. "With top-notch nurses like G, the Ox and Bucks receive more personal care than in some overcrowded London hospital short on staff."

William raised an eyebrow. "Top notch, eh?"

Heat fluttered up Gwyn's neck. "I wouldn't say that."

"I would," Cecelia said. "She spent three hours trying to teach me how to properly roll bandages, though I could never understand why they need to be rolled when they are only going to be unrolled later."

The linens weighed heavily in Gwyn's arms. "If you'll excuse me, I have a laundress to see."

"May I carry those for you?" William held out his arms.

Gwyn clutched her load as a barrier. Men in shining uniforms didn't carry dirty laundry. They rode mighty horses and escorted elegant women to parties. "I can manage. You enjoy your tour."

She scurried away, depositing her load in the steaming bleach-filled laundry room, then hurried back to redress Sergeant Montine's bandages. Not to see William, or to see if the ward met his standards.

"Is that too tight?" She watched Montine's face, searching for a wince of pain.

"No, it's just fine, miss." He gave her a gentle smile. The glass that had shattered in his face had done little to mar its sweetness. "A big day for us to have a captain touring our beds."

Gwyn tried to keep her eyes on the task instead of watching William examine the perfectly lined bottles in the medicine cabinet. "Have you met him yet?"

Montine shook his head. "He's examined every bottle in the cabinet so far. Sister watches like a hawk from her office door."

Gwyn giggled. "I doubt he'll find the slightest thing to correct under her management."

"No, but I think she'll want to have the entire place scrubbed free of fingerprints as soon as he leaves." Glancing around, he turned back to her and dropped his voice. "Is it true they're sending some of the men back?"

She'd heard the whispers between the concerned hospital matrons, but none thought it possible. At least until last month when a lorry arrived to take three of the recovered men to the docks for transport back to France. Two of them were killed almost immediately. "I believe the conditions on the Front continue to cry for help, and there aren't enough men to fill the duties."

"Will they send me back? It broke me mum's heart the first time I left. Can't imagine what this'll do to her."

Gwyn desperately wanted to soothe the panic flaring in his eyes, but lying only made the truth that more excruciating when it came out. She couldn't bear to see him in any more pain than he already was. "It's not up to the medics to decide such things, and right now your only duty is to get well so you can return to that plow on your farm."

Nodding, Montine lowered himself back onto his pillows. His chest pumped in quick breaths. "He won't tell my officers that I'm well enough to walk, will he?"

"No, Sergeant." She tucked the blanket over him. "I'm sure he won't."

Gwyn carried her tray of unused bandages back to the supply cabinet. Why was this job like a double-edged sword? One minute rewarding, the next heartbreaking.

Cecelia flitted over and leaned against the cabinet door like a wilted dove. "Is he not the most delectable man?" she cooed. "Who could ever resist a man in uniform?"

"You weren't too eager to meet him the other night." Gwyn pushed the row of bandages over to make a new one.

"That's before I saw him. Lush hair, and without an ounce of fat ringing his middle like all the others." Cecelia poked her in the ribs. "You didn't say one thing about his blue eyes."

"I was more concerned with Mr. Whiteson stomping around

the garage like a dragon because I failed to retrieve those flowers. He seemed to think the entire night balanced on the edge of failure because of it."

"Oh, bother with him." Cecelia flipped an unconcerned hand in the air. "Mother could not have cared less about them after she saw Captain Crawford."

The morning after the party, Cecelia had regaled Gwyn with stories of the good captain's dashing arrival, his attentiveness during supper, his easy laugh at Lord Somerset's jokes, the brilliant red of his tunic turning his blue eyes to deep sapphire. He was everything Cecelia had dreamed of but never imagined would actually appear on her doorstep. Lady Somerset had outdone herself in manhunting this time.

"He's escorting me to Lady Donovan's charity benefit on Saturday. I don't think parties are his cup of tea, at least not until I mentioned they are auctioning off a pair of eighteenth-century Spanish guns. Men." Cecelia cast a furtive glance at William as he examined the bulletin's daily list of exercises. "Of course, Saturday is too far off, and I need to keep his attention as much as possible. I suggested that tomorrow would be perfect for a picnic, but he's only interested in touring more facilities and wards. Did you know his father is a colonel? That's how he got leave to come here."

"I'm sure his orders will leave him little time for picnics or frolicking." Gwyn's lips twisted. What other hospitals were on his list to visit?

Cecelia huffed. "That's exactly what he said. You would think after months in the filth with hairy men, he might appreciate an afternoon strolling about with a girl."

"Don't be so put out with him. Military men take their duties very seriously, and I'm sure he doesn't mean to slight you." Gwyn grabbed her clipboard and pencil, checking off the boxes. Franklin needed his legs stretched.

"He didn't slight you in your hour of need."

"I was stuck under a car. It's hardly the same thing."

Cecelia's chin dropped. "Of course, you're right. I should not say something so tactless."

Gwyn squeezed Cecelia's arm. "Will you help me for a moment with Franklin? It's much easier if you distract him while I ready his legs."

Cecelia followed Gwyn across the ward. With a brilliant smile, she recited lyrics to his favorite song while Gwyn pulled the sheet back and gingerly wrapped her arm around one of his footless legs. As she slowly bent the knee, he jerked away.

"No!"

"It's all right Mr. Franklin." Cecelia patted his shoulder. "She's just trying to—"

"You're hurting my foot!"

Gwyn clamped onto his leg. "Private Franklin, please calm down."

Franklin twisted and dug his fingers into the bed. "You're hurting me. My foot. You're cutting off the blood. I can't feel it."

"It's not there, soldier." William's words cut through the air. Standing on the opposite side of the bed, he gazed down at Franklin with unblinking honesty. "You lost them both. Do you remember what happened?"

Gwyn shook her head, trying to catch William's attention. Was he really so thick-headed to ask such a horrible question? The doctors and sisters always told the nurses not to ask questions that might drum up painful memories. To Gwyn's astonishment, the panic faded from Franklin's eyes.

His body stilled, and his leg fell limp in her arm. "It was near Vimy Ridge. Orders came to flatten a small artillery near the south wall. Jerries destroyed most of the wall while taking aim at us." He swallowed and grazed a finger across his lap. "Mum always said I had feet like tree trunks. Guess that's why they got caught when the wall blasted down."

"Your own mum said that?" William laughed with a shake of his head. Gently, he took Franklin's other footless leg in his hand

and began to bend it back and forth at the knee. "I shouldn't mock too much. Mine always complained that my head was too large for a proper hat."

Back and forth the men went, as easy as school chums. Gwyn kept her silence as she and William worked each leg in an alternating push-pull rhythm.

"Let's see, I started off in Normandy," William said, "then on to Paris, and from there Brussels."

Franklin swung his gaze to Gwyn. "Last week, you said that's where you would like to go, isn't that right, Miss Gwyn?"

Gwyn stopped, suspending his leg in the air. "I believe so, but you know how I ramble."

"I'm afraid the Continent is hardly the place for a relaxing retreat right now," William said. "Unless you think bunkers are first-class accommodations."

"I don't." She lowered Franklin's leg to the bed. "But I would still like to see the Continent. And Africa, and the Far East, just like Jules Verne described."

"I'm afraid the world right now is hardly as exciting and adventurous as he described. Why else would it be called a novel?"

"Do you not care for novels, Captain?"

"I do, but not so much when I know they are fantasies. To me, you cannot beat a biography and a well-cushioned chair in the late afternoon light."

Predictable. Straightforward biographies and war journals always appealed to his kind. And Sister. There wasn't a biography on great women she had yet to tackle.

"My father has a well-stocked library of every biography you can imagine." Unaccustomed to being left out, Cecelia swerved the attention back to where it belonged. "You must stop by soon to see it. He's always eager to discuss such things with other enthusiasts."

"If my schedule allows the time, that should be delightful." He tucked Franklin's leg back under the cover and turned his blue eyes across the bed. "And you, Miss Gwyn? Does your schedule allow for reading?"

"My work at the hospital and in my father's garage keep me occupied most days."

"That's a lie." Cecelia pointed a finger at her. "Your nose is usually so far stuck in a book or a pamphlet on war efforts that I have to keep you from falling into ditches and mud pits."

Gwyn fluffed the blanket over Franklin's legs and grabbed her clipboard. "That's a tad exaggerated."

Cecelia crossed her arms. "Hardly. The other day you shoved a flyer under my nose about the rising need for ambulance drivers."

"Someone needs to carry those poor boys off the field. The Red Cross is training people to drive. Why not take volunteers who can already drive?"

William's eyebrows raised. "Such as you?"

"Such as me."

"As much as I hate to expose our womenfolk to the horrors over there, we are in desperate need of transportation. Not just for medics and the wounded, but for supplies." He took in a deep breath. The belt creaked around his trim waist. "A unit formed not too many years ago—all female—to administer first aid on the field and transport the wounded back to the dressing stations. The First Aid Nursing ... something."

"Yeomanry."

His lips twisted. "I see you've heard of them."

"I have an appointment with them at ten a.m. this Thursday in London."

"You sly minx!" A nearby patient startled at Cecelia's cry. "You never told me."

"I only received the confirmation yesterday."

"Have you told your father?"

"He doesn't like it, but he didn't refuse to allow me to go." Tears had filled Papa's eyes, which he'd dashed away with the oily rag from his back pocket. He'd gently pinched her chin and said how she was like her mum. And mum would never have said no to such an adventure.

William clamped his arms behind his back. The skin around his mouth pinched white.

"Is everything all right, Captain?" she asked

"Quite." He didn't look at her, though.

"You don't approve?"

"As I said before, I do not wish to subject ladies to the carnage of war." His gaze hooked back to pierce her. "And that is exactly what will happen if you go there. You cannot imagine the horrors that await you. I would spare you, and the souls of every man or woman, from such a black fate."

"But you also said how badly our troops need supplies and support. Someone must do this. I may not lift a gun to aid, but I can use what limited skills I do have."

His gaze softened as one corner of his mouth flickered up. "With courage like that, you won't need a gun."

Heat rushed all the way from her toes to the tips of her ears. Other than her father, no man had ever given her such credit. And no man had ever tripped her heart over like a spinning crankshaft the way William did.

Gwyn ground that spinning crank to a halt. Fine men with three-star captain's insignia lining their shoulders didn't bother with insignificant girls like her. They needed socialites like Cecelia on their arms for officer balls and bidding them farewell from the train station while waving lacy handkerchiefs. William would only get grease marks on his trousers standing next to a chauffeur's daughter.

"If you'll excuse me, I need to check on the bed linens," Gwyn said, making for the door. "I hope you enjoy the rest of your tour, Captain."

Needing to find a moment's peace from the heart-tripping presence of Captain William Crawford, she pushed through the double doors and burst into the side garden thick with the scent of warm green grass.

"Get a hold of yourself." She pressed her hands to her warm cheeks. Allowing a man to have such an effect could only derail her plans.

"Did I say something wrong?"

Gwyn nearly jumped out of her shoes at William's voice.

"I'm terribly sorry to startle you," he said.

She pressed a hand to her chest to calm her battering heart. "I needed a little fresh air. Sometimes the tincture and bleach mix together for a ferocious headache."

He fiddled with the buckle of the belt slanting across his chest. "I didn't wish to sound high handed in there. It's just that some lads touch foot in a war zone with grand ideals and heroic aspirations, seeing through rose-colored glasses painted with propaganda, if you will."

"Did roses ever tint your glasses, Captain?"

"Hardly. My father is a retired colonel from the South African War, my grandfather the War of 1812, and so forth back to the dawn of time. There hasn't been a generation of Crawfords not born for marching orders." Resignation clipped his words. "No roses for me, I'm afraid."

"At all?"

"Nothing but hard facts and expectations."

Gwyn sighed, the statement weighing her down like a sinking rock. "How dreary."

"You must have facts to navigate this life. Otherwise, you are lost with nothing solid to cling to."

"But they give you nothing to soar toward. What is life without a dream to strive for?"

His lips quirked. Heat rushed back to her face as she caught herself staring at their broad fullness. "Forgive me. Sometimes my mouth runs without permission from my brain."

"Miss Ruthers, you are by far the most interesting girl I have ever met."

"Captain Crawford, you have no idea."

CHAPTER 3

Gwyn smothered a yawn behind her gloved hand. Shifting on the uncomfortable chair, she focused on the posters lining the taupe halls of the First Aid Nursing Yeomanry's headquarters.

SACRIFICE LUXURY FOR VICTORY

A NEW HAT	FOUR STEEL HELMETS
A NEW DRESS	FOUR SERVICE RIFLES
A NEW FUR COAT	ONE MACHINE GUN

Somehow, she doubted a fur coat could cover the cost of a machine gun. According to the men back home, the cold was more likely to do them in than the Kaiser's guns. A large mink stole or rabbit coat would smother winter's bite. Add the Russian *ushanka* hat, once so popular, and the men would be toasty warm during those long cold nights. She giggled at the image.

The clacking typewriter stopped as the secretary glanced up with a frown. Gwyn covered her laughter with a cough. The bespectacled woman gave her one last glare before turning back to her work.

If these women didn't know how to laugh at themselves, being crammed together in tents and ambulances on foreign soil would be more of a challenge than Gwyn first thought.

She ran a hand over the soft wool and crepe burgundy dress Cecelia had loaned her for the interview. It was supposed to make her feel confident and look professional, but it did nothing to calm her jittering nerves. Neither did Captain Crawford's comment from the other day. Gwyn shook her head to clear the memory of his words and his persistent blue eyes.

They have to like me. Who is better qualified to drive an ambulance than a chauffeur's daughter?

The telephone on the secretary's desk jingled, startling Gwyn from her chair. Someday she might grow accustomed to those noisy oddities.

A voice crackled from the other end of the line. The secretary nodded and returned the receiver to its cradle. "She'll see you now."

"Thank you." Gwyn stood and passed a hand over her skirt and hair, ensuring they were wrinkle and flyaway-free.

"She won't care." The secretary watched her over the rim of her glasses.

"I do." Gathering her folder of papers, Gwyn swept down the long hallway lined with pictures of uniformed women atop horses and behind steering wheels. The thumping of her heart echoed louder and louder in her ears until she stopped at the last door. Taking a deep breath, she knocked.

"Enter."

Grace Ashley-Smith, Commandant of the FANY, sat hunched over a stack of papers behind a heavy, dark wood desk. "Close the door and take a seat. I'll be right with you."

Gwyn shut the door and perched on the edge of the chair squared in front of the desk. It creaked as she maneuvered her feet to keep from hitting them against the desk's solid front panel.

Bookshelves filled with worn leather volumes lined the office. A large window stood behind the desk, bathing the room in grayness from the drizzle outside. In the corner next to the door stood a wilting plant in desperate need of water and a floor lamp that glowed soft yellow.

Ashley-Smith scratched a note on the top paper, slipped it in a folder, and pushed it to the side. Folding her hands, her dark eyes locked on Gwyn's.

"You're here to apply to the FANY?" she asked in a soft Scottish burr.

"Yes, ma'am."

"No ma'am. Lieutenant. Do you have a resume?"

"Yes, m—Lieutenant." Gwyn drew the crisp copy from her folder and slid it across the desk. Relief rippled through her that Cecelia had forced her to wear gloves. If not, Lieutenant Ashley-Smith would be reading a sweat-smeared resume.

A clock on the bookshelves ticked the ten o'clock hour. *Tick, tick, tick.* The seconds passed as Ashley-Smith scanned the paper. Gwyn leaned forward, eager to see a flicker of hope, but the woman's face was unreadable.

Finally, she looked up and folded her hands over the resume. "I'm sorry, Miss Ruthers, but you simply do not qualify."

Shock poured over Gwyn like a bucket of icy water. *Not qualify?* "I'm not sure I understand." She swallowed hard to keep her voice under control. "Did you see that my father is a chauffeur? I have been driving longer than I could walk."

"Yes, your qualifications for driving are unquestionable and quite impressive, but as a chauffeur's daughter ... how may I phrase this?" She spread her hands wide. "As the daughter of a professional, could you afford the expenses? A FANY is responsible for the cost of her own uniform, beginning supplies, haversack, training, and, of course, travel."

"I didn't realize." Desperation bolted through Gwyn's mind. "What if I found a sponsor?"

Ashley-Smith shook her head. "I'm sorry, but even if you did manage the funds, you do not meet our age specifications."

"But I thought with the war and the desperate need for drivers—"

"That we would relax our requirements? Our standards of excellence are what set the FANY apart from any other rag-tag group." Ashley-Smith's serious, dark eyes softened around the corners. "I am very sorry, Miss Ruthers. We need good women like you."

Gwyn crushed the folds of her skirt as grief rattled through her.

She sucked in a deep breath to numb its effects. Self-pity would get her nowhere. Standing, she turned for the door. "Thank you for seeing me."

Ashley-Smith came around her desk and offered her hand. "Should your situation change, come back in three years, war or not. As I said, we need more good women in our ranks."

No matter which way William tilted the umbrella, raindrops drizzled their way down his neck. He checked his watch. Ten forty. Surely he hadn't missed her.

He glanced up and down Earl's Court. Black brollies dotted the footpaths as people hurried about their business with shoulders hunched forward to ward off the wet splatters of awnings and drain pipes. Taxis didn't bother dodging potholes as their thin wheels slipped over the cobblestones, spraying unsuspecting walkers with muddy water.

Ten forty-one. Gwyn did say her appointment was at ten, did she not? Or was it ten thirty? Served him right. A proper fool waiting in the rain unannounced like a common stalker.

The brick and white trim building across the street stood silently against the falling wetness, its stern façade daring the elements to do their worst as it refused to bow. He imagined the women inside as much the same. What new breed were these women who forfeited the safety and comfort of home to slug in the trenches with bullets racing overhead? They cut their hair, wore uniforms much like his, used military rank, and, most insulting of all, considered themselves capable of performing the same duties as men.

Why did he find himself fascinated by a woman who climbed under automobiles with wrench in hand, and who now sat in the office across the street signing away her life to drive ambulances in a war zone? A woman whom he had jogged through the soggy streets of London to see before she hopped on the next train back to Great Malvern.

Ten forty-four. What if she'd canceled the appointment?

He yanked up the collar of his coat, wishing he'd brought his sketchbook to keep busy. The clean lines of the buildings would flow smoothly beneath his pencil. Smooth and orderly, that's what he needed. Not a woman spun with complications. He had enough responsibilities without worrying about someone else's grand expectations of him.

Ten forty-five.

The white door opened and out stepped a tall woman dressed in deep red. A matching hat shielded her face as she looked up and down the street. She shot a look over her shoulder to the closed door, squared her slim shoulders, and marched away into the rain. One glimpse of those lopsided brown curls sent William's heart clipping. He hadn't missed her after all.

He dashed across the street. "Miss Ruthers!"

She kept walking, the drizzle leaving dark spots on her shoulders. "Miss Ruthers!"

He jogged behind her and grasped her elbow. She spun around, her handbag poised midair. "Unhand—oh. Captain Crawford." The shock on her face faded into bewilderment. She dropped her swinging arm to her side.

William tilted his brolly over her head, though it was too late to save her wilted hat feathers. "My commander's office summoned me to London, and I remembered you would be in town. I thought it would be nice to see a friendly face after reporting to old craggy war dogs for two days."

Concern flickered in her wide eyes. Today they were the color of forest leaves. "I hope everything is all right."

"Yes, they just needed an update."

"Of men to send back?"

He clamped his teeth together before the groan could escape. By themselves, the words were accusatory, but, meeting her gaze, he found only sympathy. "I'm afraid so."

"What an ugly business this war is." Her shoulders sagged as she glanced back to the building she'd exited. "Some cannot escape what they have been called to do, while others sit and wait."

Before he could comment on her cryptic words, a loaded bus swerved by and splashed water over the back of his trousers and boots. So much for his pressing and polishing until the wee hours of the morning. "Might I suggest we get off the footpath before we drown? I know a small teashop around the corner."

She twisted the handle of her handbag.

"They serve the sweetest biscuits you can imagine."

Her lips eased into a smile. "I'd love to."

Finding the shop, they settled at a small table beside the front window and sipped their tea over a plate stuffed with chocolate biscuits, raspberry cream puffs, and lemon sugar rolls. The smell of warm coffee lingered in the air as the soft hum of other patrons drifted from surrounding tables.

Prisms from the overhead chandelier danced across Gwyn's hair, turning it a rich chestnut. William smiled, imagining it felt just as luxurious as it looked. The battle-hardened knot in his stomach eased for the first time in months.

"Verdict?" he asked as she bit into a cream puff.

Gwyn licked a drop of cream from her finger and smiled. "Delicious. I've always envied people who know of the great little hole-in-the-wall shops. Privy to secrets unknown to the rest of the world."

"Stick with me." He added a slice of lemon to his tea. "I'll show you all the spots worth knowing, though I can't take credit for discovering this one. My mother's friends rave about it every time they come to London. I normally don't frequent places with such spindly chairs, but the sweets call to me."

"Then I am ever more grateful that you forsook masculine comforts to eat pastries with me." She raised her cup. "To sweet eating."

He clinked his cup to hers, grateful the daintiness didn't chip.

The regiment boys would never stop their ribbing if they could see him now. But, then again, they never took tea with such a lovely companion.

"My goodness, this certainly was a welcomed distraction." Gwyn dabbed the corners of her mouth with her napkin before carefully folding it on the table. "I'm surprised Miss Hale didn't accompany you. She dearly loves a trip to town whenever the opportunity arises."

William shifted uncomfortably. Cecelia Hale, as lovely as she was, hadn't crossed his mind since dropping her off after the picnic she had planned two days ago. "Yes, she's mentioned shopping several times. Most of which I did not understand, so I kept my mouth shut."

"It's best to let her do most of the talking." Gwyn dropped her gaze and picked at the edge of her napkin. "You'll grow accustomed to it."

But chatter wasn't something he wanted to grow accustomed to. At least not chatter from Cecelia Hale. "I'm afraid my limited time left will not allow for such opportunities."

Gwyn's fingers stilled, but she didn't look up. "She'll be disappointed."

Would Gwyn? "One of many disappointments I'll bring her."

She finally looked up. Her mouth parted, but what words she was to say died as a waiter dressed in starched black and white brought a fresh pot of tea to their table. Gwyn poured herself a new cup and took a long sip. "Nothing like warm tea and a little sugar to pick one's spirits up."

"Were they trodden upon?" William added a drop of milk to his cup.

She leaned forward, circling her hands around her teacup. "The FANY rejected me."

Relief spiked through him. Safer rolling bandages in dear ol' Blighty than rumbling over shell-broken roads in France. "I'm sorry. I know it meant a great deal to you."

"Every day I read the paper. We're told that each of us must do what we can to help win this war." She twirled the cup between her hands. "They should include their specific requirements instead of being so coy."

"You think the army is selective in war duties?"

"Not when it comes to knitting mittens. No, I take that back. My attempts at knitting were rejected as well. I forgot to add thumbs."

"Thumbs are useful when loading shells."

"Yes, thumbs provide importance. So do one's age and socioeconomic background." Her cup clattered in its saucer. "Does age really matter when a man is dying?"

No. Bullets were the most indiscriminate objects he'd ever seen. Ripping through homes, animals, generals, and boys without a whisker to their soft cheeks. "Perhaps they wish to spare young minds. Once the horror is inflicted, it never goes away."

She gripped the edge of the table, searching his face with a direct honesty that caught him off guard. And he was never caught off guard. His fingers curled into his knee, unsure of what was to come.

"Do you believe you'll ever find peace from this chaos?"

The breath he didn't realize he'd been holding eased out. "I pray for that every day, but this is the life I've been given, and I'll accept the consequences. You have a choice I was never allowed."

"I was not born a chauffeur's daughter by accident. My skills, my knowledge, my grease-stained fingers have a purpose. I cannot sit on my hands and watch others take my place behind the wheel. If one opportunity doesn't want me, then I shall find one that will."

A silent groan filled his throat. She'd read too much propaganda, and, like the rest of the country, she didn't see the death sentence behind it. "Why are you so eager for this fight?"

"I am eager to make a difference by using what humble skills I have to offer."

"I sense this is more than simply rolling bandages and nursing the wounded."

She turned to the window and traced a raindrop as it slithered its way down the glass. An unpinned curl of rich mahogany dotted with mist slipped over her ear. Most girls would have tucked it away or had it properly pinned in the first place. He liked that she didn't.

"If I told you the unabashed truth, you would despise my selfishness."

"Try me."

Dropping her hand to her lap, she turned back to him. Green steel glinted in her eyes. "I long to see the world beyond a garage. If I can help our boys at the same time, then why not go now?"

"Your work at the hospital is just as valuable." *With no one shooting at you.*

"Of course it is, and the volunteers there are doing a wonderful job, but I can do more."

The battle was turning against him. He shifted in his seat, bracing his elbows on either side of the china dessert plate. "What would dear Mrs. Shearing say if she heard your plans?"

"I'm sure it would be along the lines of 'good riddance.'" She grinned. "She's considered me a hindrance from the first day. If not for Cecelia, she'd have me booted to scrubbing bedpans."

"Scrubbing bedpans is an honest day's work that someone as devoted as Mrs. Shearing should not twitch her nose at."

"I don't think one could help it."

William burst into laughter, startling several of the customers around them. A stitch pricked his side, reminding him of how long it had been since finding something to smile about.

The lady sitting at the table behind Gwyn eased from her chair and glided to their table. Tall and thin with elegant black hair sprinkled with gray and a sharp nose protruding from a long face, she looked like a flightless crane.

William surged to his feet. "I do apologize for disturbing you, madam."

The woman raised a hand. "Not a word of that, young man. It's good to hear a man laugh again, especially one in uniform. It gives me hope in such dreary times. I came over because of your conversation. Yes, I know how rude it is to eavesdrop, but I could not help myself. It's not every day you meet a woman driver." Dragging the chair from her table, she plopped down between them. "Lady Dowling, at your service. And you are, my dear?"

Gwyn's jaw sagged, but she snapped it up. "Gwyn Ruthers, your ladyship. And this is Captain Crawford of the Oxfordshire and Buckinghamshire."

William bowed at the waist. "Your ladyship."

Lady Dowling flapped her hand at him. "Sit, sit, Captain. This is your table that I've barged upon."

William maneuvered his way into his chair, knocking the thin legs with his knees.

"As I said, I overheard you say you've been rejected from the FANYs." Despite the wrinkles at each corner, Lady Dowling's eyes glinted like sharpened razors. "A lot of pretentious go-getters for turning away such an eager volunteer. Their loss, I say."

"They do have their rules." Gwyn's mouth twisted.

"Rules, bah." Lady Dowling turned unflinching brown eyes to William. "Captain, have you ever known the Huns to obey the rules? Does the Kaiser ask for permission before he lobs shells over our trenches?"

"Not that I'm aware of, your ladyship." William bit back the urge to grin.

"There you have it." Lady Dowling smacked a wrinkled palm against the table. "As you said, Miss Ruthers, or may I call you Gwyn? What does age matter when men are dying? We need help now from those willing and able."

Gwyn's eyes flicked to William's before turning back to Lady Dowling. "I completely agree."

"I know you do, that's why I'm sitting here." A smile creased the papery skin around Lady Dowling's thin mouth as she leaned forward. "We need courageous hearts like yours. More specifically, *I* need them. I'm starting my own private hospital and ambulance brigade in France, and I'd like to recruit you."

CHAPTER 4

Excitement buzzed in Gwyn's ears as Lady Dowling's mouth continued to move, but she heard not a word. A chance to serve on the front line as a private recruit? To travel to France? She pinched herself to keep from leaping up and clicking her heels.

"I've managed to acquire a few motorcars for my fleet," her ladyship said. "Not that I count three as a fleet, but it's better than none. As a chauffeur's daughter, I trust you know your way under the hood."

Gwyn nodded as her eagerness threatened to jump out in full force. "I do."

"Excellent, I shall leave repairs in your hands. What else?" Lady Dowling tapped a long finger against her chin. "I have ten nurses and two orderlies recently turned away from the army due to crooked spines, though you can't tell. I need one more driver and a few extra beds, and, of course, I'm waiting for the Red Cross supplies to come in, but we should be ready to sail within the month. Perhaps two depending on how the training goes."

"A-a month?"

"Yes, dear. We need to sail before the Channel turns icy or we wait until spring, and that is much too long."

William leaned forward with brow furrowed. "You say this is a private hospital? No funds or support from an organization?"

"Just a few donations from the Red Cross, but everything else is from my own pocket, or my late husband's, I should say. As the Marquis of Dowling, he left me a sizeable sum upon his death, and, with no sons, I may do as I please with it. While I wait for grandsons from my daughters, I shall use my fortune to help those less fortunate by opening my chateau in France." She reached over and patted Gwyn's hand. "Don't worry, dear. I shall pay for all expenses, including salaries for those who come to work for me."

"I … that's very kind." Gwyn's heart thumped like a gasket ready to blow. It sounded too good to be true.

William sat on the edge of his chair, one palm flat on the tabletop. "With no organization affiliation, you will have no protection, no demanding rights upon the government, and no voice in how the wounded are collected and distributed."

A smug smile stretched across Lady Dowling's face. "My dear Captain. I know you are accustomed to rules and regulations, that everything must run through at least twenty people before it is approved. That is the military. In the real world, money talks. And I have more than King Midas."

"But this is war, m'lady." He glanced across the table at Gwyn. A frown puckered his brow. "If anything should happen …"

"If anything should happen, my workers and I will not be left to the enemy's hands," Lady Dowling said. "I introduced Lord Haig to his lovely wife, Doris, and they are frequent guests at my table along with General French and the Churchills."

"With all due respect, France is hardly the place to worry about dinner guests. Their prestige may not reach that far in the field."

"Then it's a good thing I have written authorities from each of them, signed and sealed, should I need a leverage."

A waiter brought new tea and a plate high with biscuits. Gwyn refilled her cup, but her stomach was too topsy-turvy for more sweets. "Where is your home in France, your ladyship?"

"South of Amiens, in a green valley dotted with poppy fields. *Maison du Jardins*, we call it."

"It sounds lovely."

If possible, William sat even straighter in his chair. "That's near the Somme River."

Lady Dowling nodded. "My husband and I used to take picnics there all the time. Quite the enchanting view."

"I doubt the views are so enchanting now." William tapped a finger on the table. "There's been heavy fighting in that area."

"What better place for my hospital?"

An electric current rippled through Gwyn, sparking and charging until she felt it ready to burst into light. "I think it sounds wonderful. Close to the action allows us better access and quicker service to the men. The greatest complaint amongst the medical staff and wounded is always the dangerous routes from the battlefield to the clearing stations. If we can cut that in half, they'll have a fighting chance."

The same current fired in Lady Dowling's eyes. "Precisely."

William, however, doused it all with his waiting bucket of practical water. "Ladies, as stalwart and courageous as this plan sounds, having anything more than a dressing station so close to the field is folly. The wounded need rest and clean bandages, not bombs exploding overhead and Germans marching down the poplar-lined drive."

Gwyn wished she had a real bucket of water. She'd dump it straight over his head. "The wounded need some place to go. More places mean more care."

"That's not a guarantee. It's a dangerous situation for all involved, the wounded and staff. A staff that may or may not be trained to deal with battlefield conditions."

"Before being allowed to work in hospital, all volunteers are put through extensive training," Gwyn said. "I lived in a tent for a week, cooking, washing, and drilling before they allowed us to touch a bandage."

"But your feet remained on English soil far from shrieking shells and muddy trenches."

Gwyn flattened her feet on the floor to keep them from kicking him under the table. "Everyone must start somewhere. I'm fairly sure Florence Nightingale and Clara Barton were not experts their first day in the field."

"If I may interject before the guns continue to blaze." Lady

Dowling clinked the side of her cup with a spoon. "Each person on my staff has been nurse-trained, and the drivers will each need to complete a competency course. The hills around my country estate in Lanchester should provide the perfect test. Miss Ruthers, I believe you could help design a course to weed through the inexperienced drivers. Nothing too long, of course, and all the rain should provide plenty of mud which I understand is a large predicament in France." She cupped a hand around her mouth and whispered, "Captain Crawford should appreciate that."

"Does that mean you'll hire me?"

"If everything I overheard is true, then I would be a fool not to." Lady Dowling's eyes shifted to William. "Unless your young man has any further objections."

Heat flamed across Gwyn's neck and cheeks. She didn't dare look across the table. "He's not mine. I mean, we don't ... we are only acquaintances."

The thin skin around Lady Dowling's mouth puckered. "Pity." She dabbed the corners of her mouth, pulled a small white card from her handbag, and stood. "Here is my card. If we have an agreement, I'll expect your arrival in two weeks."

Gwyn cradled the card with reverence. She could almost feel the wind of France blowing across the embossed letters. "Don't you want to test me first? Make sure I know how to steer my way around a cow?"

"Certainly. You must pass the driving test along with all of my other recruits. I'll only take the best. Once all of my troops have passed muster, we will sail from England at the same time, as a unified front. I hope you approve of that, Captain."

Standing, William grasped his hands behind his back and bowed slightly. "I pray all of our troops will be as unified as yours, m'lady."

"Amen to that. Good day to you both."

The room shrank in the wake of Lady Dowling's departure. The chatter of nearby tables droned like faraway bees, oblivious to

Gwyn's world spinning like a top. So many things to do. Gathering her gloves and string purse, she pushed her chair back. "I really should be going. Lots to prepare."

"I'll walk with you."

Gwyn considered an objection but changed her mind. No matter his stilted views, he didn't deserve rudeness.

Outside, the rain stifled itself behind thick gray clouds, allowing them to walk without a brolly. Cecelia's feathered hat, on the other hand, had seen too much drizzle to revive under the small break.

They walked for two blocks before William cleared his throat. "I apologize for my forwardness back there. I didn't mean to play devil's advocate."

Gwyn kicked a pebble, sending it flying into a puddle on the footpath. "You may have discovered a new interrogation tactic. Lull one's enemies in with promises of warm tea and sweets. They'll fall unguarded into your hands."

He grimaced. "My time in the trenches with foul men has robbed me of simple manners, particularly with the ladies. I can be rather boorish."

"Not boorish. Straightforward. An admirable trait."

"It didn't seem so admirable back there. I was ready to dig a foxhole for incoming fire."

"We're on the same side, Captain. We just have different ways of approaching it. You rely on caution while I throw it to the wind."

They stopped in front of a window display. A poster with a little girl standing outside of a demolished building read MEN OF BRITAIN! WILL YOU STAND FOR THIS? Tears filled the girl's eyes as she clung to her burned doll.

Without asking, William tucked Gwyn's hand into the crook of his arm. His warm fingers closed over her hand, brushing the underside of her wrist. Her pulse skipped, and she turned to him.

"I would do you a disservice if I did not bring to your attention all the dangers before you fall head first into them." Worry feathered the lines around his mouth. "It's a fate I wish to spare you from, even if you hate me for saying it."

The tightness that had built in her chest eased. "I truly appreciate that, Captain, though I know you're not entirely keen on the idea."

A muscle in his jaw twitched. "Perhaps not, but a pretty face on the battlefield will be a welcomed change. Are you sure this is what you want to do?"

"Yes," she said without hesitation. Her list of long-awaited adventures practically burned a hole in the pocket where she'd tucked it safely away. It was like taking a piece of Mum with her wherever she went. "I've been waiting my whole life to live beyond the confines of England, even if it means going to war."

Smiling, he squeezed her fingers and started down the footpath again. "Then God help the Jerries because they don't stand a chance against Lady Dowling's brigade."

CHAPTER 5

"But where will you get the autos?" Papa shut the valve on his oil can and spun around with eyebrows drawn. "Even as a duchess, the purchase price of five would set her back years in debt. Not batty, is she?"

"No." Gwyn screwed the new headlight into place and arched her aching back. After her week-long training camp at Lady Dowling's sprawling country estate, the jolts of potholes and hairpin turns still rattled in the memory of her bones. "You know how rich people are with their money. They don't have to worry about stashing it under the mattress for a rainy day like we do."

Papa shook a wrench at her. "I won't have my daughter scampering off with a woman who can't manage her own money, duchess or not. Wars aren't fought with money. If she thinks she can just throw a fistful in the Kaiser's face and all will be well, then she better think again."

"She's a marchioness." Gwyn snatched the wrench from him before it went flying then tapped the headlight wires into place. "She owns two of the autos, the other three are donated from her friends. She's turned them all into first-class ambulances." She stepped back and admired her work. "You'd be proud to sit behind any one of those wheels."

He harrumphed. "Not me sitting there, it's you. In France. During battle. And no daughter of mine will trust her life to some rust bucket that shimmies apart under the first pothole."

"Lady Dowling's chauffeur took me on a private tour of each auto. We checked them from fender to exhaust whistle, and each one received the Ruthers' stamp of approval."

"I wasn't there to give it." Papa mumbled, turning back to his oil can.

Gwyn slipped her hand over his shoulder and squeezed. "But you taught me everything you know."

"Aye, I know it."

"Everything will be all right. I promise."

He wrinkled his reddening nose to the side and sniffed. Hunching his shoulders, he poured fresh oil into his can. "What about these other drivers? Qualified, or rich girls who think because they've ridden in the back of a Rolls Royce, they can drive one?"

Gwyn pulled out a low stool and eased onto it. "Every girl there knew her radiator hose from her gasket. Of course, most of them only knew one or two models, the ones they drove at home, so I had to explain the differences and locations of things in the models they hadn't seen. They're a bright group, though, eager to learn and quick to not repeat mistakes."

"And you'd take charge?"

She nodded, digging out a dried sliver of grease from under a nail. "Only because I have the most experience. I may have to give them a rundown on more in-depth repairs once we get there." Her hand stilled as a terrifying thought popped into her mind. "I wonder if Lady Dowling has spare parts at the ready."

"Make sure you get them." Papa topped off his can and slid it back into its place on the shelf. "War-blown roads are bound to cause bent axles, slipping clutches, and worn bearings. It could take weeks or months to get them shipped across the Channel."

"I'll send her a note first thing in the morning."

Gwyn sighed and leaned her head against the wall, inhaling the pungency of oil and rubber. Lady Dowling's home smelled of fresh lavender and beeswax, beautiful scents to awaken to, but—in the darkness of her private bedroom—Gwyn had longed for the familiar scents of grease and metal.

"Still think she's too mad to take a bunch of naïve girls over there." Papa slapped a glob of wax onto the Renault's fender and worked it into dull circles.

"Is that your only concern? You think Lady Dowling belongs in an asylum?"

"Wouldn't be a proper father if that was my only objection. There's a little thing called a war exploding across the Channel."

"Papa, we've gone over and over that."

"Only because I don't think it's sunk into your thick skull yet."

A smirk pulled at her lips. "Hmm, wonder where I got that from?"

"And then there're the men."

Her smirk disappeared. "They need help. There are too many of them for us to take care of here. Imagine how bad it is over there."

"That's not what I'm talking about." He paused mid-stroke to fix her with a stare. "I'm talking about the lonely ones, the ones with wandering hands, the ones who haven't seen a respectable girl in months."

Heat flamed up her cheeks. "I know how to handle those. The Red Cross Sisters taught us how before we started at hospital."

"Darling girl of mine, this is war. In a foreign country. Lonely men can be desperate."

"Then they can keep their desperation, and I'll keep a crank under my seat."

"Unless it's that captain coming to call. And don't act like I don't know about him."

Her hand curled around her wrist as if the touch of William's fingers still lingered there. "He did not follow me to London. I told you."

Her father's stare drilled her to the bone. "I know you're occupied with things other than men, but someday that will change. You can't run on this wild streak forever, and I won't leave you alone."

Gwyn rolled her eyes. "Oh, Papa."

"Yes, Papa. And as your papa, it is my duty to see you taken care of after I'm gone."

"You shouldn't worry so much. Maybe after the war, with my driving experience, they'll hire me permanently for city transport with proper pay. I can drive one of those mass transit buses around Buckingham Palace and wave to the king as he stands on the front stoop with his morning paper. If I'm not racing through the skies doing barrel loops to my next port of call, that is."

"For now, you worry about potholes in France, and we'll trust the rest to God."

Gwyn shot off her stool. "You're really letting me go?"

His strokes slowed over the bonnet, the cloth bunching between his stained fingers. "You've inherited your mum's spirit. We didn't have the means to go far, but I couldn't clip her wings any more than I can yours. They've always spread far beyond these old garage doors. This is your chance."

"So that's it? Our little bird is flying the nest?" Cecelia stood in the doorway, fists on her hips and eyes narrowed. "You'll just leave with some stuffy old dowager?"

Lady Dowling was the last person Gwyn would consider stuffy, but there was little use to mincing words now. "This is my chance to finally go somewhere, at least until it's safe to travel again after the war, and my father has agreed."

"Of course he agreed. He never tells you no." Cecelia clamped a hand over her mouth and shook her head. "I'm sorry, Ruthers. I overstepped my bounds."

Papa didn't flinch. "Did you need something, Miss Cecelia?"

"I need to go into town tomorrow, but ..." Cecelia stared at Gwyn for a long moment, her thin blonde eyebrows drawing together. "But I believe my plans have changed."

Gwyn knew that tone. Nothing but hare-brained scheming ever came of it. "What do you mean, changed?"

A smug smile crossed Cecelia's angelic face. "If you think you're getting into the excitement all by yourself, then you better think again. You're not the only one who gets what she wants."

Disbelief crashed over Gwyn like an avalanche. "Miss Cecelia, you don't belong in France."

Cecelia batted an unconcerned hand in the air. "I know, I know. Dodge the shells, rescue the wounded. Do we not work side-by-side at hospital? Why should we not work together over there?"

"Because you don't have an interest in going over there."

"Well, I do now."

Gwyn hiked an eyebrow. "And what's prompted this change?"

"I told you. I won't be left behind."

"That's hardly the right reason to—"

"I've decided. Now I need to make up my father's mind, which shouldn't be too difficult considering his nose is so far stuck behind a newspaper he doesn't notice anything beyond the racing tickets."

"You'll need Lady Dowling's permission before you start anything."

"A quick note with a generous donation of tires and medical supplies should remedy that." Cecelia looked straight past Gwyn. "And Ruthers, I do require the car tomorrow. I'll need to find new outfits proper for the trenches. Ten o'clock, shall we say?"

Gwyn's mouth flopped open. "Cecelia!"

Cecelia waved over her shoulder as she marched down the drive. "I'll pick you up something too, G."

Cecelia Hale under shell-filled skies. The girl couldn't go a day without a scented bath and three-course meal. What was to become of them?

"She thinks this is some kind of garden party." The worried pits around her father's mouth deepened. "Talk her out of it. Baron's daughter or not, I won't have her endangering you."

"Have you ever tried talking her out of anything? It's pointless. Threats and tears don't work either." Gwyn sighed, rubbing her fingers into her temples. At least she'd have a fine dress should the Jerries take them. "Papa, you might want to start praying a little sooner. The angels will have their workload in heaps."

CHAPTER 6

England's ragged gray coast melded into the choppy water, leaving nothing more than a line on the imagination. Nearly three months behind schedule due to training and supply gathering, it was a miracle the entire Channel wasn't iced over. The daily passing of hospital ships and destroyers had helped keep the frozen chunks at bay.

Seawater sprayed over the rail, dousing Gwyn with flecks of ice as she strained to see the last glimpses of home. When it disappeared, she stared ahead as the ship plowed forward to the unknown. Wind and water crashed against her ears, loud and terrible and thrilling. Somewhere through the mist, a new land awaited her. She pulled out Mum's paper and read down the long list of neatly scripted places, the ink more brown than black in the twenty-five years since Mum had penned it. Gwyn lightly traced the third place listed. France. As soon as her foot struck ground, she'd cross it off. One down. Forty-nine to go.

"Too late to turn back now, girlie."

A man with a bleached beard and a piece of wood rolling between his chapped lips watched her.

"I have no intention of turning back," she said, tucking away her list.

He spat into the whirling gray below. "Ain't you afraid? Men's getting killed over there."

"I would be a fool not to be afraid, but I cannot do nothing."

"What do you think you and your frilly skirted friends are going to do? Bake them pies and knit socks?"

Gwyn cocked an eyebrow, daring him. "Drive ambulances."

"Desperate, are they?" He cackled. "Ain't got any gimp men left to take the task?"

"They can't handle a steering wheel the way we can."

He snorted, picking the slender wood around his teeth. "You're addled if you're thinking you can do this. You'll prove nothing 'cept you should've kept your skirts in the kitchen. Bah."

He stomped off, muttering and shaking his head. Lecherous old sea codger. Gwyn took a deep breath, willing his words to roll off her back. He didn't know anything about her—and certainly not about women—to think they all wanted a lifetime in the kitchen, baking and knitting.

The ship surged over a white-foamed wave and plunged down nose first. Water tumbled over the deck, soaking her new leather shoes and emerald skirt.

"So much for arriving in style," she muttered, lifting her foot from the frothing bubbles. Not that it mattered how she looked, but Cecelia had insisted on making a fine first impression for *their boys*. Poor CeCe. She hadn't anticipated seasickness ten minutes out of port.

Gwyn needed to check on her cabin mate. But first, a quick glimpse in storage to ensure the autos remained lashed properly. The dock workers had no clue what they were doing, much less what knots to use to keep the autos locked down.

Twenty minutes and several rope burns later, Gwyn pushed into her tiny cabin. At first, she thought it ridiculous to worry about accommodations when France was less than twenty-five miles away, but the captain had explained that it could be hours or days before they arrived depending on their turn to dock. Red Cross ships got first priority.

"Cecelia?"

A long moan crept from the corner bunk. "Shut the door. Too much light."

Gwyn shut the door and wobbled across the cabin, pressing her hands to the wall as the ship rolled beneath her feet. "How are you feeling?"

Curled into a ball, Cecelia threw an arm over her face. "How does it look like I feel?"

From the gray light streaming in the porthole, Gwyn noted the perspiration dotting Cecelia's ashy-tinged forehead. "I went to the galley to find you some ginger snaps or lemon drops, but the cook's only store is for lard and dried biscuits."

"What about the provisions Lady Dowling's cook has? We've brought enough food and medicine to last the next ten years."

"Emergencies only, I'm afraid."

Cecelia peeked out from under her arm. "Aren't I an emergency?"

"I believe she means the troops."

"How am I supposed to help them if I'm left in this condition?"

Gwyn rolled her eyes. "I've never heard of anyone dying from seasickness."

"Maybe I'll be the first."

"Perhaps you shouldn't have eaten that entire box of chocolates before we left."

Cecelia bolted upright, bopping her head against the top bunk. "Forgive me if I don't have an iron constitution like you. You're probably flitting aboveboard while imagining your ten fathoms adventure under the water, or whatever nonsense it is that you stuffed into your trunk. As if a person needs two trunks full of books."

"It's called *Twenty Thousand Leagues Under the Sea*, and I enjoy my books. Perhaps they'll come of use to the men while they recover." Gwyn balled her hands on her hips. "Much more so than those new hats and gloves you brought."

"We are staying with a marchioness. One must be prepared." Cecelia rubbed her head with one palm, dislodging a perfectly pinned blonde curl. Her gaze drifted down Gwyn's dress, her eyes widening the further down they went. "What happened to your new shoes? Water stains will never come out of that ribbon."

Gwyn stared at her ruined attire. She should have taken better care of them, even if she didn't think them necessary. "I was standing near the rail. I'm sorry. I'll pay you back, I promise."

Waving a disinterested hand, Cecelia flopped back down on the stiff mattress. "What does it matter now? I was silly to think new trimmed frocks served a purpose where we're going."

"It was a nice idea," Gwyn said, hoping to ease the tension. "And they truly are lovely."

"But they don't belong, just like you think I don't." She cracked open an eye and smiled. "Admit it."

Gwyn pulled up a chair and balanced herself on its warped seat. She tucked her ruined shoes under her skirt. "I do wonder about your eagerness to join when you've never mentioned it before. You seemed quite happy to work in Malvern's hospital until the end."

Cecelia's eyes glimmered in her pale face. "I need a new pool to select a man from. The one at home went stale a long time ago."

"If not for that impish look, I might think you're serious. You aren't, are you?"

"I doubt this is the appropriate place to find a husband, or at least that's what Mother told me before we left. One could easily lie about their breeding over here." She fluffed the lace on her cuff and hummed an off-beat tune. "Besides, I've already found the perfect catch, and he just so happens to be here. How convenient to have his regiment so very near Lady Dowling's estate."

Gwyn's stomach quivered. "Anyone I know?"

Cecelia tilted her head, a smile spreading across her face. "Captain William Crawford, who else?"

Gwyn pressed her hands into her lap. Why should she care who Cecelia set her cap for? Or who set their cap for Cecelia? The quiver turned to a tremor. "Please tell me you are not crossing the Channel for a man."

"No. His presence is merely a perk, and I only know where he is because he made mention of it while asking me to talk *you* out of coming. As if that would do any good." She blanched as the ship lurched to the side. "Will this boat never stop trying to kill me?"

A knock sounded, and, without waiting for a reply, the door opened. "Ruthers, you in here?"

"I'm here, Eugenie," Gwyn said.

Eugenie, a short, stout girl with cropped black hair and broad hands, filled the doorway. "Captain says we're sixth in line to dock. Lady Dowling wants us all on deck to watch the process."

"What for? It's not as if we've never seen boats disembarking before." Cecelia moaned from her bunk.

"Lady Hale." Eugenie squatted into a wobbly curtsy. She ran a hand down the brown and black fur coat draping her body. A soft blush bloomed across her chapped cheeks. "Thank you ever so for the coats, all lovely and warm. All the girls say so."

"I was glad to put them to good use. Every woman deserves to look beautiful, even if they are last season. The Jerries will never know such dictates of fashion, of course." Cecelia propped herself back on one elbow, a frown puckering her brow. "Are you sure Lady Dowling meant all of us?"

"It's just what she said, ma'am. Ten minutes, Ruthers."

Cecelia swung her legs off the bunk and pressed a hand over her eyes as the door clicked shut. "Have I suddenly earned a new noble title that I'm unaware of?"

"I don't think she's had much opportunity to learn forms of address in Liverpool, so she overcompensates by using the only title she knows. You should feel honored."

"I suppose it's better than undercompensating. Why must she call you Ruthers? Every time she says it, I look for your father."

Gwyn shrugged. "She tried joining the FANY but discovered the same trouble I did. I believe she thinks all units over here are militarized."

"If she thinks I'm getting up to the sound of a bugle every morning, she'd better not be within throwing distance when she blasts it."

Gwyn grinned at the idea of Cecelia cramming her new corset down Eugenie's bugle, but the laughter died in her throat. Most likely they would awaken to the blasting of shells.

Precisely ten minutes later, Lady Dowling's entire crew assembled on deck and hung over the rails, pointing at the whale-sized Red Cross ships and whispering amongst each other. Gwyn clutched the rail as doubt, fear, and excitement mixed in her stomach like a bubbling stew.

They waited quietly in a snaking line of ships as a bloated Red Cross ship and two smaller ships glided past them to make the narrow crossing home. Their decks were full with men swathed in bandages, most stained through with dried blood. Mud caked the tattered clothing and haunted faces, but their eyes searched heavenward as if for a glimpse of pure beauty and relief from the misery behind them.

Moving her gaze inland, Gwyn's breath caught as she counted the rows of men stretched out along the docks. At least seven deep with barely space between them for the white-aproned nurses to carry supplies and buckets of water. Red trickled between the wharf's wooden boards and spread into the chopping water like feathered fingers. Even from a distance, she could hear the moans as more ambulances rumbled over the roads to deposit new loads of wounded.

"Have you ever seen anything like it?" Cecelia breathed next to her.

Gwyn's fingers curled around the rail as plumes of dark gray and black billowed into the sky far back over the hills. The immensity of it all pierced her heart. "God help us."

"Do you think we're nearly there?" Cecelia shouted over the rumbling engine.

Gwyn shrugged, though it was doubtful Cecelia could see it. Nothing could be seen on the pitch-black road, if that's what one could call it. Lady Dowling had told them repeatedly that headlights were not used because it attracted the enemy. Same with the windscreens which were removed to avoid reflecting light, but now the drivers sat bared to flying rocks and chafing windburn.

Hunching over the steering wheel, Gwyn tried to follow the pale moon's glint off the bumper in front of her, but it was near useless. Lady Dowling's French chauffeur had no respect for driving in a straight line or warning his following motorcade of potholes. A welcome present for the English, no doubt.

"We've been crawling for nearly three hours." Gwyn dodged a rut. "Surely it's close." The car behind her squealed in the rut and bounced back. First thing tomorrow, she'd have the drivers check their axles.

"Do you think they'll have lovely soft beds and a warm fire waiting for us?"

"Lady Dowling sent a telegram informing her staff that we would arrive today, so I hope the house is somewhat ready. As for me, I'll be happy with any bed that doesn't bounce."

"And preferably one that doesn't smell."

"It's not that bad. Just a little paint and oil." Gwyn sniffed carefully. "And maybe a bit of upholstery left in the rain too long, but that's probably how she got the autos at such a bargain."

Cecelia scoffed. "A bargain? Two bits is overpriced for this rust bucket."

"She's not a rust bucket, she's just not what you're used to. What's the point in sending a newly minted Rolls Royce into war?"

The tires rumbled over a stretch of ruts like claw marks in the frozen ground. Gwyn's bottom teeth bit into her upper lip as the tires jumped and slammed into each cut of earth. Gripping the lever for dear life, she shifted into low gear. The cylinders whined, but she kept the wheel straight until they finally rolled free.

She patted the dashboard. "Good girl."

"Good, my hatpin." Cecelia scooted back to her corner of the seat from where she'd been jostled. "She's certainly the most cantankerous one in the lot."

Smugness curved Gwyn's lips. "None of the other girls could handle her."

"Ah, yes. And so the Great Gwynevere rushed to the rescue, proving her motor skills and abilities far superior to mere mortals."

"Take care who you mock, *Lady* Cecelia. One turn of my steering wheel, and you'll fly right out that door and into a pile of mud."

"Ugh, the mud. It's everywhere. I thought the French countryside was filled with green hills and red poppy fields. Did you see those porters drop my trunks in that bog when we disembarked? I doubt it'll ever scrub free."

Gwyn veered and dropped the right front tire into a hole. Cecelia flew up and hit her head. "Sorry." Gwyn flattened her lips to keep from smiling. "Soon you'll see many things more disturbing than dirt, so I suggest you stop complaining now."

"I wasn't complaining. Much." Cecelia huffed and settled into her corner. "Do you think it will be horrible?"

"It won't be pleasant."

"But it won't be like hospital at Malvern. The men there are always bandaged before we get them. And Sister always takes the difficult cases." Long minutes passed. "I've never seen a man die before." Her voice was eerily quiet.

Gwyn's numb fingers slipped over the wheel. She'd never seen a man die before either. Never seen one with his insides hanging out, or burned beyond recognition. All this time she'd focused on driving, on saving lives, and going to a foreign country. She never stopped to realize what her work truly meant. Her work was to save dying men. How short-sighted she'd been. "We won't think of that," Gwyn said. "We'll think of them each as another life pulled from the brink."

"Do you think it's as easy as that?"

"No, but we can't dwell on the negative. It'll claim us faster than a bullet if we allow it to."

"G, you're the only person I know who can find a pinprick of light in the dead of night."

"Speaking of light, do you see that?" Gwyn pointed straight ahead. Tiny yellow dots flickered through the trees.

"Troops?" Cecelia clawed Gwyn's arm. "Do you think they're ours or theirs?"

The lead car turned onto a private drive bordered by a low stone wall. A three-story house sat regally at the end of the circular drive. Gwyn smiled with relief. "Neither. I think we're here."

Cecelia's nails remained entrenched. "Are you sure? I've heard the Germans are quite tricky."

"Then they've learned how to disguise themselves as a house." Gwyn pried off her captor's hand. "Those are lights coming from the windows."

Two maids hurried through the double front doors as the motorcade rambled in. Hopping back and forth on their feet, the maids dashed to Lady Dowling's car before the engine even turned off. Mr. Whiteson would never approve of such a lack of decorum.

Lady Dowling bounced out of her car, spry as a rabbit, and began talking in rapid French as her maids rattled on while gesturing wildly.

Gwyn leaned over to Cecelia. "What are they saying?"

Cecelia scrunched her nose. "Something about wounded soldiers and open doors. Their accents are too thick to understand completely."

The maids ran back inside as Lady Dowling marched to their car. With her gray hat and cape, she looked like a general. "They've started arriving. One of the gardeners told a medic in town that we're ready for patients. He forgot to mention we had yet to arrive. Come on, girls. This is why we're here. Gwyn, tell the drivers to park on the other side of the house while the nurses get to work."

Cecelia didn't budge.

Gwyn nudged her in the ribs. "That means you."

Turning with wide eyes, Cecelia shook her head. "I can't. What if I don't know what to do?"

"Just take a deep breath and remember your training." Gwyn patted her hand. "You can do this."

Cecelia eased out the door and joined the nurses rushing inside. The drivers pulled their cars around, parking them in a perfect row for an organized exit when the time came. Gwyn had the drivers unload all the personal trunks and suitcases and pile them against the house.

In a nearby building filled with oil cans, spare tires, and all manner of tools, Gwyn found several lanterns that she dragged outside and set around the cars. For the next four hours, the drivers checked each ambulance from top to bottom and back to front. Two broken wheel spokes, one loose axle, and three stretchers not properly mounted were the only casualties.

"How are we supposed to fix this?" Eugenie clambered out from under a Model T's chassis. "It's three in the morning, freezing, and the lanterns aren't enough to do repairs by."

Gwyn toed the front tire. She hated to admit it, but the truth was unavoidable. "We'll wait until morning when I can do a complete inventory of what's in the garage. If something happens between now and daybreak, we have three good ambulances to take. Pray it doesn't come to that."

"Keep your prayers." Eugenie spat on the ground. "God ain't in war."

Uneasiness pricked Gwyn's heart. She never considered God picked and chose what He was a part of.

"Well, we are. And the more power on our side, the better." She turned to the other drivers huddled together in front of the lanterns. Her mental checklist hosted a hundred things to do, but none of it could be done with frozen fingers and muddled heads. "I think we've done all we can for now. Let's get this luggage inside and see if the nurses need any help."

Eugenie groaned, shivering in her coat. "We're not their mules. Let them get their own bags. We need sleep."

"Don't you think they're tired, too? They're binding up men in there, so the least we can do is carry in their bags." Gwyn took a deep breath before she climbed on a soapbox. "We're a team now."

The grumbling turned into grunts as they moved trunk after trunk into the main hall. Long after sunrise, Gwyn stumbled into an upstairs room set aside for staff. She shuffled across the floor until the tips of her boots bumped into a metal bed frame. With one last blink of exhaustion, she crashed onto the thick mattress, asleep before her head hit the pillow.

CHAPTER 7

William squinted through his field glasses and scanned the horizon from his position in the trench. Nothing but blasted earth, charred tree stumps, and gaping holes as far as the eye could see. Good. Maybe the Jerries would stay in their pits today and give them a respite from last week's bombardment.

Intelligence reports said otherwise.

While General Allenby stretched the Third Army from Ransart to Curlu, the German army buried themselves further into secure defenses. They'd be snug as bugs in their dugouts come winter.

"Like rats, they are. Building little nests to wait us out." Captain Roland Morrison dropped his field glasses into the case hanging from his belt and tugged his gloves on. "I hope they rot with frost during the night."

"They'll give one last push before winter hits," William said. "According to our sources, that is."

"And you believe that?"

William's lips twitched. "I believe whatever the Army tells me."

"Go on with you now, Will." Roland laughed and slapped him on the back. "That kind of thinking is what got us here in the first place."

"I thought the call to honor and glory for Britain is what got us here."

"That's what they tell me, but then I wasn't about to be labeled a coward for not signing up. Have you seen the white feathers they're giving chaps who refuse to put on the uniform? My best mate from university, first man in his class to enlist, was walking down the Mall without his uniform on and those madwomen threw a fistful of feathers into his face. Can you imagine?" Roland shook his head, his tin hat wobbling back and forth over his sandy blond hair. "He was killed last month. Jerries shot him off the top of his horse."

William lowered his field glasses. Numb and cold, he flexed his fingers from their stiffened grip. Another man gone. How many would they lose before this hell was over? "I'm sorry."

"He was never a good rider." Roland stomped his feet, clearing his throat loudly. "Speaking of things to see. Have you taken an eyeful of the new tenants over the hill? Bunch of nurses setting up shop in that chateau. Dowling's Darlings, the boys are calling them."

"They have female ambulance drivers as well. That should come in handy. Extra drivers, I mean."

"Who cares about them? Dog-faced girls who belong under a bonnet."

"I know one of them." The memory of shapely legs protruding from under a car curled through William's thoughts. "And she's anything but dog-faced."

"You can keep your wrench monkeys. I'll take me a nurse. One with pretty blonde hair to shine in the candlelight as she nurses me back to health."

"I don't care for blondes." Biting his tongue for the slip in control, William shoved gloves on his hands.

"Well, I do. Especially if she's got a title to go with it, which I hear a few of them do." Roland's boyish face scrunched up. "Or at least their fathers do."

"Titles aren't everything. It gives you a lot to aspire to and not much room for failure."

"You're thinking much too hard about this one, old chap. Not everything is about success and failure, though in my case, success will be snagging the right woman to adore me night and day. You've already managed that."

Poised to jump down from the fire step, William froze. "I what?"

"Come off it, Will. No need to play shy." Dimples pierced Roland's smooth cheeks as he grinned. "All the chaps know. Cecelia Hale, daughter of Lord Somerset. Convenient she's so near, eh?"

Roland jabbed him in the ribs, but William shoved him off. "You're hearing false reports. I've met Miss Hale several times, and she was kind enough to escort me around the hospital wing in Malvern. Nothing more."

"Letters rubbed with rose oil are a little more than nothing. Why don't you ever reply to them?"

William groaned. "Because they make my hands smell when I open them, and she's the daughter of a baron who deserves better than a soldier."

"She doesn't seem to think so."

"War makes for lonely people. Once back on home soil, surrounded by properly titled gentlemen, she will realize there are more suitable matches to make." William stepped down from the fire step. "I'm not one of them. At least not for her."

He stomped off, his heavy boots thudding down the dirty duckboards lining the bottom of the trench. Each step squished mud over the edges of the planks. Two months back in country, and already the rumors buzzed as rampant as flies on stale meat.

Roland's steps echoed behind his. "Then you won't mind if I have a go?"

"If you can get past Lady Dowling, then Miss Hale is ripe for the picking."

"I'm not worried about the old battle-axe. I'll just wait until the girls have a day off and go into town."

"Glad to hear you have a tactical plan."

"Have to with the competition."

Green eyes rimmed with dirt danced in William's mind. There was no competition.

Rounding a curve to a new bay, his toe caught the edge of a warped plank. Blast it all. This was war, not some garden party where he could chase skirts. If he didn't keep his wits about him, he'd end up with a face full of mud, or worse—a bullet to the head.

"Sir." Dormer, his company's sergeant major, popped out of a dugout like a gopher and offered a full salute. "Morning report is available at your convenience."

William ducked into the tiny shelter and angled himself around the stack of crates that served as an impromptu table. In practiced routine, his eyes fell down the list of occurrences, upcoming drills, and the incoming units to relieve the frontline troops. A week at the front on constant alert, and his men could finally fall back to the reserve line for a breather.

"Everything appears in order, Sergeant."

"Yes, sir." Dormer didn't budge.

William flipped his gaze up. Trouble brewed on his sergeant's face. "Is there something else?"

"Sattler is low on canteens and field socks, sir. He sent a request in last month, but the stores are stretched too thin."

William frowned. Men without water and dry feet were as good as dead in this festering hole. "Why isn't this in the report?"

"Because he knows where he can get some."

A groan rumbled in William's throat. His quartermaster was as clever as they came. The man could find a speck of bread in a snowstorm, though sometimes his greatest restocks came after a battle when the ground was littered with fallen articles. "We haven't had a confrontation in this area in over a week."

"No, sir. It's not one of those sources."

Realization dawned. "Ah. One of his *other* means."

"Yes, sir."

William crossed his arms, tucking his hands underneath for warmth. He didn't like restocking from unknown and possibly questionable sources, but Sattler had yet to fail at acquiring the goods.

"See if he can scrounge for something better than this sludge they're calling coffee while he's at it."

Roland leaned smugly against the wood brace supporting the

roof as Dormer tromped off. "Thought you forbade anything not army supplied."

"I'm against my men getting trench foot and going without water."

"But using Sattler's methods? He's got a market from here all the way back to Liverpool black enough to color the sky like coal."

"I also notice those are rather new-looking gloves covering your delicate fingers. Lined with fleece, are they? Funny enough, I don't remember any like that in the gift baskets sent by the sweet little ladies of Oxfordshire."

"As sweet as they are, those little ladies can't darn a properly warm mitten." Roland held out a hand and examined his well-ensconced fingers. "Besides, I don't have Sir Philip Crawford sitting on my shoulder and poking my conscience at every turn."

William creased sharp folds into the morning report. No, his father would wait until the army supplied his men because that's what a good soldier did. He would expect no less from his commanding-officer son. In the meantime, the entire unit's feet could rot and fall off.

Duty and honor. Two words drilled into William from the day he first took a breath. The words had always presented a black-and-white world to him, but war had introduced him to shades of gray. He was honor-bound to serve, and that service directed his duties to his men. How could he serve them without providing for them?

He slid a final crease into the paper and tossed it into the pile to be burned. "Have the men gather their items. The reserves should come in next—" A whistle trilled the air. "Did you hear that?"

"I hear only the rejoicing of my heart that we'll leave this bog soon."

Every muscle in William's body went rigid as he strained to hear the warning again. *Tweeet!* He knocked Roland out of the way and barreled down the bay. "At the ready!"

Men scrambled to their feet, throwing rifles to their shoulders. "At the ready! Keep your heads down!"

A shell screamed overhead, exploding in the ground behind them. Metal fragments covered in mud shattered everywhere, pinging off helmets. Screams stabbed the air as men crumpled to the ground.

A boy, no more than nineteen, sagged into a wall of sandbags.

William caught him before he collapsed. "Stretcher!"

The storage door creaked open. A chilling breeze ruffled the pages of Gwyn's book.

"Who there's letting in that cold?" Eugenie bellowed from the workbench. "Don't you know—oh, it's you, your ladyship, I mean Miss Hale."

Cecelia stomped in and closed the door behind her. Her red face was barely visible beneath the green silk scarf wrapped around her head. "Cecelia, please. No use for formalities over here." She unwound the scarf and stuffed it into a pocket of her cream-colored fur coat. "What on earth are you two doing out here? You'll freeze to death."

"Hence the reason we're sitting next to a stove." Gwyn turned a page. *Huckleberry Finn.* A childhood favorite.

Perching on the edge of a stool, Cecelia held her hands in front of the potbelly stove. Red embers glowed as bright as her nose. "There are plenty of fires inside where the wind doesn't howl through cracks, and it doesn't smell like … whatever this smell is."

"Grease and rubber," Eugenie said, using a wire brush to scrub a pile of screws. "Her ladyship's staff don't reckon how to keep a garage in proper working condition.

Cecelia wrinkled her nose. "So I see."

"Smell or not, someone must always be on duty should the call come." Gwyn turned another page. Huck and Jim needed to row for their lives on the flooding Mississippi if they had a hope of surviving. "And the cranks freeze if they're not turned often. How are the patients doing?"

"Better," Cecelia said. "We almost lost Private Collier last night, but Lucille managed to get the bleeding under control. She always seems to know what to do."

Gwyn looked up at the quiver in her friend's voice. She dog-eared her page and closed the book. "It takes time to learn these things. Lucille's mother was a nurse, was she not?"

Cecelia turned her hands over in front of the stove and nodded.

"Maybe you can stand beside her the next time and observe, or ask to be on the same shift."

"We are on the same shift. She took over for me when I fumbled the dressing."

"Everyone blunders from time to time, CeCe." Gwyn leaned forward and dropped her voice. "This morning I was giving the cranks a turn, and I sneezed. Wound up tighter than a spring, the crank flew out of my hand and nearly took off Eugenie's head. Can you imagine? Where would I find a replacement driver this late?"

A small smile perked the corners of Cecelia's mouth. "That's horribly twisted."

"I only mean—" A ring rattled the air. Gwyn jumped up, knocking her stool back and lunging for the telephone.

A dispatcher's voice crackled on the other end. "Attack ten miles northeast. Several wounded and three critical. Ambulances requested."

"Got it." Gwyn hung up the phone and scanned the map tacked to the wall. "We're up. Attack at Longueval."

"Good luck to you," Cecelia said as she dashed back to the house. "Back safe!"

Gwyn yanked her wool knit cap on top of her head and ran outside, tugging on her gloves as Eugenie sounded the siren. The girls sprinted out of the house and to their cars, cranking away until the engines choked to life. Gwyn shouted instructions and jumped behind the wheel. Blood raced through her veins, but she kept steady lest her eagerness kill the old Royce before they got out of the gate.

Wind burned her cheeks as she turned onto the open road. First in the convoy, she had the advantage of seeing every rut and turn, but it also meant she had nothing to block the wind sweeping through the valley and down the hills. She yanked the driving goggles over her dry eyes before they froze and tucked her chin down into her thick fur coat.

Gwyn turned off the main road that led to the small town and onto a makeshift lane of frozen dirt and mud pits. "Leave it to the army to make things more difficult than need be." She gripped the wheel as the uneven terrain threatened to rip it from her grasp and send her careening into a tree trunk. The wheels squealed in protest against the sucking mud.

"Come on, Rosie girl. We're not going to let a little mud stop us now, are we?"

Punching the throttle as far as Gwyn could, Rosie jerked ahead and chugged on. More squealing sounded behind her, but Gwyn didn't stop to see who it was. The wounded needed her. The drivers knew what to do in an emergency.

Wind billowed in the treetops, clacking branches together and snapping twigs that tumbled to the ground. Soon low rumbles punctuated the wind. Louder and louder they grew, like approaching thunder, as Gwyn drove on.

Her pulse pounded. This was it. The moment she'd prepared for. Her chance to prove herself.

The trees gave way to a barren field bisected with trenches like a horrific quilt. Shell holes large enough to drive a lorry through gaped black in the ground. Gray smoke floated around as bullets fired between the opposing front lines. Gwyn's breath stuttered in her lungs at the stench of sulfur, burnt metal, and something she did not want to identify. The khaki lumps scattered across the ground left little doubt as to its origin.

Dear God in heaven. She pulled her gaze away and focused on the path in front of her. Those men may be gone, but some with a chance waited for her.

To the rear of the trenches and out of shell range, three tents stood surrounded by sandbags and piles of earth. A crude sign with a faded red cross stood in front. Pulling to a stop near the first tent, a private with a medic badge around his arm scowled at her. "You ain't the RAMC."

"No, we're a private unit." Gwyn jumped down. She didn't have time to deal with this nonsense. "The nearest Royal Army Medical Corps is too far from here to respond. Where are your wounded?"

Eugenie and two other drivers popped up next to her, red-faced and goggles fogged over.

"What's a bunch of females going to do, eh?" The private sneered.

Gwyn took a step forward, ready to knock him aside if necessary. "Get your soldiers out of here and to a hospital unless you'd rather them bleed to death while you run your mouth."

His pimpled face twisted. "You three over there. You, girly, follow me."

Gwyn ducked into the first tent. A concoction of blood and chloroform smacked her in the face.

A major with a blood-smeared apron came around the side of an operating table. "You the ambulance?"

"Yes, sir."

Brown eyes looked her up and down. "Not what I was expecting, but I'll not split hairs if you have a transport."

"I have four. Two stretchers each or six men sitting."

He waved her further into the tent and pointed at the two tables that occupied most of the room. "I've got three stretcher cases and seven that can manage upright. Sergeant Boller here"—he pointed to the man with a bright red bandage wrapped around his thigh—"is my most critical. He needs an amputation, I'm afraid."

Boller rocked up from the table, sweat pouring down his face. "No! I won't let you take it."

Two medical assistants pushed him back down and restrained him as the major dribbled chloroform onto a cloth and pressed it gently over the thrashing man's thick nose. Boller twitched, then relaxed.

"It's not much, but it'll take the edge off." The major sagged. He ran a hand over his face, pressing the edges of his trim black mustache down. "If he rouses on the way, hit him in the head with a rock. It'll be less painful than that shrapnel in his bone."

Movement rustled outside the tent. Loud voices clashed as heavy objects hit the ground. The tent flap yanked back.

"Major Bennett, I have four more men for you to look at, one with a broken leg, and I'd like a report on my men that have already been brought in. Why are they still here, sir?"

Surprise charged down Gwyn's spine. Of all the medical tents in the field. "We're loading the men as quickly as we can, Captain Crawford."

"Gwyn? I mean, Miss Ruthers. You're the medical detail?" Splattered in mud and reeking of sweat, William was a far cry from the starched uniform and polished boots of London. He turned to the doctor with a furrowed brow. "I thought the RAMC was covering us."

"They have their hands full with that little skirmish north." Bennett's eyes narrowed at Gwyn. "Is there an issue with Lady Dowling's services?"

"Of course not." Gwyn curled her fingers tight against the fur pockets of her coat. "We have every available resource that a base hospital has."

"Except that you're not a hospital. Not a military one at least, and once my men are taken into private care, it will make it that much more difficult for me to keep track of them outside the system." William took off his tin helmet and ran a hand through his dirty hair. Without the use of brilliantine, it flopped across his forehead. "I'm sure Lady Dowling has the best services she can offer, but what if the patients need a clearing station, or more, a train or boat to a port embarkation? Has that system been set up?"

Gwyn wanted to defend their capabilities but could not because they had never discussed taking the men further than *Maison du Jardins*. She uncurled her fingers to release the building pressure. "If the men require additional transport, then we will see to it without delay. Whatever it takes."

William's jaw worked back and forth. Gwyn needed to cut him off before the brewing argument spewed out. "Captain, I'm afraid that our talking is hindering my assignment to get these men to care, and one is in immediate need of an amputation."

"An amputation. Who?"

"Sergeant Boller," the doctor announced without looking up from his examination of a new man. "Entire left leg. Shrapnel."

The skin around William's mouth pinched white. "Get him out of here as quickly as you can."

Without wasting another second, Gwyn had the wounded loaded into the ambulances. Tags hung from their buttonholes so the new doctors would know their conditions and what precautions the field medics had taken. Her transfers tucked safely inside, she shut the door.

William caught her arm as she climbed onto the driver's bench. Dark circles rimmed his eyes, bright blue against the dirt smeared across his face. "My intentions were not to discredit you in there."

The weight of his hand settled through the thickness of her coat. The bluster from earlier disappeared. "You're only looking after your men, Captain. I expect no less."

"You looked ready to go toe-to-toe with me."

"If that's what it took."

The corner of his mouth lifted, reminding her of the man she'd clinked teacups with a hundred lifetimes ago. The man who had waited for her in the rain. She pulled her arm from his grasp and grabbed the throttle. Rosie roared into action.

William stepped back. "I'll be on the reserve line in a few days. I'd like to come by and see my men if possible."

Gwyn nodded, tamping down her eagerness to see him again. Only there was someone else anxious to see him as well. "We'll give you a full tour of the facility. Cecelia will be glad to see you."

The corner of his mouth fell. "I—yes, of course."

"Until then, Captain. God be with you." She eased onto the clutch and pulled away. Away from the blood-stained tents, the bullet-strewn field, the helmets being collected, the man standing motionless where she left him.

Gwyn yanked the goggles over her eyes. Enough of that. She had plenty of men to deal with at the moment.

Gwyn sagged onto her cot. The single candle on the nightstand flickered dimly against the damask wallpaper and heavy silk drapes pulled across the windows. Silence enveloped her as if the room desired to match the trudging of her heart.

Sergeant Boller never made it off the operating table. The shrapnel had worked its way into his femoral artery. Though the doctor had assured her it was inevitable, she knew each tire bounce—every mud-slicked rut—had caused it.

A hot tear burned down her cheek. Then another. They rolled off her chin and landed with soft plops in her lap. Crying wouldn't help. It never did.

Crying hadn't brought her mother back. Buckets of tears, and Gwyn's mother remained as lost to her as the moment she took her last breath. She swiped the tears with the back of her hand. Never a handkerchief handy when she needed one.

With exhaustion pulling at her, Gwyn turned to the only thing that ever brought her comfort. Books.

She glanced at the trunk at the end of her bed. Tales of adventure, mystery, brotherhood, far off places, kings and queens. For the first time, none of it stirred the ache from her heart. Nor the dread of knowing William was out there. It could have been him bleeding in the back of her ambulance. Bloodless lips, cold fingers, vacant eyes.

She shook off the chill clawing at her, but the uneasy pounding of her heart wasn't so easily shunned.

The candle flickered again, drawing her attention to the nightstand and the worn book lying under her pocket toolkit. Scooting to the edge of the cot, she picked up the book and ran her fingers over its worn cover. Not even the coolness drifting in from the window cracks could rob the old leather of its warmth. She flipped open the cover and ran a fingertip over the beautifully scratched words in the top left corner.

To my darling wife, Amelia, on the birth of our daughter.
I may not be able to shower you in the riches you deserve, but
I hope to shower you in the riches of our Father's love.
May His words never leave your heart.

Forever,
Bernard

A new tear slipped down Gwyn's cheek as she smiled. Dear Papa. He had made sure this eternal book was packed on top of all the others. And tonight, it called to her.

CHAPTER 8

Giggles floated down the hallway from the salon-turned-patient quarters. Gwyn paused before turning the corner and checked her reflection in a full-length gilded mirror. Rumpled clothes, hair flattened on top and sticking out on the sides, heavy eyelids, and a smudge of oil along her jaw. Not having seen a hot bath and warm bed in over twenty-four hours, this was as good as it would get.

Licking the tips of her fingers, she tried to tame the worst offending hairs, but back out they sprang. She dropped her hand in frustration, more at herself than the hairs. Why should she be expected to look ballroom-ready? Was there not pride in coming off an all-night shift? Of course, coming off a shift normally meant she met the next crew. But today ... she pinned a strand behind her ear, willing it in place. A smile crept over her face.

Rounding the corner, she nearly ran into a handful of tittering off-duty drivers and nurses crowded around the door to the patients' quarters. "Don't you girls have anything better to do?"

They jumped at the sound of her voice, their faces burning bright red.

"Not today we don't." One of the drivers turned back to the open door.

"It's not every day we have an able-bodied one come in." One of the nurses, with spectacles perched on the edge of her nose, sighed. "I almost forgot what they look like walking around."

Eugenie wrinkled her nose. "I like mine a little more solid built and low to the ground. Like a dock worker used to hard labor."

The nurse stared at her as if she'd sprouted a third head. "*He* stands before us, and all you can think about is some stevedore from Liverpool?"

"All I'm saying is I like my man on the square side. If he were tall like that one in there, I'd be sick worried because he makes the perfect target." Eugenie's eyes slid to Gwyn. "G is tall, so I'm sure she don't mind the height much."

A pulse sprinted in Gwyn's neck. She prayed it wouldn't rush the blood to her face. "You bunch are about as sly as a sprung engine in May. Captain Crawford is here on official business. Nothing more."

"Then why's he been asking for you since he got here?"

As if on cue, William's voice drifted out the door. Deep and calm, and rich as dark panels of wood. She raked a hand through her hair. "Possibly because I drove several of his men here."

Cocky grins and wiggling eyebrows angled her way. They wouldn't stop until they had a few answers. Gwyn sighed. "His father is a friend of Lord Somerset. That's all."

"I'm sure it's not all, but we'll wait to prick you another time. You best get in there." Eugenie jerked a thumb over her shoulder. "Your competition is thick as flies on a banger covered in gravy."

"There is no competition." Why did she feel so adamant in announcing that? And why did it contradict the excitement of seeing him? No sense in giving into that now. She couldn't afford distractions, even if they came in the guise of a handsome face with startling blue eyes.

Taking a deep breath, Gwyn marched into the ward and down the center aisle between rows of metal-frame beds. A sumptuous room, blue watered silk curtains covered the windows, and a massive marble fireplace filled the center wall, now flanked by glass cabinets lined with a variety of medical supplies. Once filled with the heady scent of ladies' perfume and champagne, the smells of fresh linens and tincture of iodine now swirled about the grand room.

William leaned over a man's bed, brow furrowed. Lady Dowling stood on one side of him while Cecelia stood on the other, but her eyes didn't stay on the patient.

"How often are the compresses applied?" he asked.

"Every four hours or as needed," Lady Dowling said. "These patients will be due for another round in two more hours."

"And each nurse is trained in the application?"

"Every nurse is trained in all procedures, from cleaning bedpans to attending the doctor in surgery." The old woman's chest puffed out as she narrowed an eye at him. "Each nurse is assigned a position but is required to know the position above and below hers as well."

"Very efficient."

"We could show your generals a thing or two," Gwyn added. "The trenches wouldn't know what hit them."

He looked up, one corner of his mouth lifting. "I believe they wouldn't."

Butterflies swarmed her stomach as she met his gaze.

"Ah, Gwyn there you are." Lady Dowling's mouth puckered as her gaze swept a full examination over Gwyn. "I'm sorry to call you in right after your shift, but Captain Crawford has been quite insistent on seeing the garages with no other guide than you."

"You make me sound quite demanding, Lady Dowling," William said.

"Nonsense. You don't fluff words, and I appreciate that. This is war. Where but in war can you find an all-female staff?" Lady Dowling smugly smiled. "And I happen to have the best, despite what the Duchess of Westminster thinks. Formal dressing to welcome the wounded. Have you ever heard of such bad time management?"

"I should think it would lift the men's spirits after being surrounded by mud and other dirty men." Cecelia wrinkled her nose, then fluttered her lashes to William. Her slender white hand reached to touch the pink ribbon trim of her blouse. "A beautiful dress can do wonders, can it not, Captain?"

"Indeed it can, Miss Hale." A shorter man who looked too

young to wear an officer's rank piped up. With dimples curling into his soft cheeks and large brown eyes, he could pose for a cherub. "What heart would not beat faster at such a pretty sight?"

A heart that's shot through. Poor boy. He'd yet to realize he was out of his league. At least Cecelia was gentle, offering an accommodating smile as her disappointed gaze trailed to William.

"I don't know much about fancy dresses, but I would like to continue the tour," William said. "If you don't mind trudging back into the cold, I should very much like to see the garage, Miss Ruthers."

Gwyn's toes grew warm under his smile. She stopped it cold before it reached her ankles. She had a pilot license to get, not a man. "I should be happy to escort you and your—" she squinted to see the other man's rank— "em, other captain."

"Roland Morrison, at your service. Just not in the cold." He puckered his lips. "This is the first time I've been warm in over five months. I'm not going back out there until absolutely necessary. Sorry, ma'am."

"That's quite all right," Gwyn said. "I'd want to stay next to the fire as long as possible in this cold. Perhaps you would enjoy seeing the kitchen prepare for the noon meal, if Lady Dowling agrees."

Morrison eagerly nodded as he inched closer to Cecelia. "Yes, of course. If Miss Hale will point me in the right direction."

"But I—" Cecelia's eyes darted between the two men, oblivious to how one man stared at her like a starving man stared at a ham sandwich while the other busily counted gauze rolls on a nearby stand. Just when her composure looked ready to slip, breeding surged in. "I shall be delighted. If you'll just follow me."

Gwyn offered her friend a small wave, but Cecelia's eyes clouded with disappointment as she slipped from the ward with Captain Morrison tagging behind her. At least one of them would enjoy the trip.

"Now, Gwyn. Be sure to keep him away from Gutless Gert." Lady Dowling shoved Gwyn and William out the door. "I have enough fingerless patients to deal with without adding one unnecessarily to the lot. Be sure to come back to the kitchen for a bite to eat before you leave, Captain."

"Who is Gutless Gert, and why does she want my fingers?" William asked as they stopped at the back door.

"She's our jack." Gwyn slipped on her fur coat. "To prop up the cars for maintenance. If you're not paying attention, she'll gladly take off an appendage."

Outside, snow fell in tiny puffs of lace that covered the barren ground and surrounding fields in a wintery blanket. Gwyn lifted her face to collect the swirling flakes on her lashes before they melted on her skin. "I've always loved the snow. It makes everything so beautiful."

"It also turns to slush."

Of course. He'd been buried in snow and mud for months, and she wanted to lie down and make snow angels. How stupid she was to make such a remark. "We can return to the house if you like. Find a hot cup of tea."

"Ah, tea." A peaceful smile tilted his firm lips. "The drink of kings. A luxury these days when all we have is black coffee filtered with dirt, though my quartermaster did manage to smuggle in a bottle of brandy once. Had it confiscated two hours later when General Fowler made a surprise inspection."

"We often use brandy when the morphine runs out. Lady Dowling likes to add drops of champagne to make it fizz."

"I'm not a drinking man, but I know many who would start a war over such sacrilege."

"Tell them we have enough on our hands with the current one."

"I'll do that, or maybe not. If they get wind of spirits in the vicinity, they'll beat down your door, wounded or not."

"I would rather have them all storm the castle able-bodied, and I'm sure most of the men here would as well." Hopelessness flitted in her chest as it did every time she thought of those filling beds inside. She brushed it off and looked down the row of motorcars.

The only life-saving mode she could provide. "Until that time, we shall keep our fleet ready for them."

William's eyebrows lifted as he followed the sweep of her hand. "Impressive. Most units have only one ambulance assigned to them, if they're lucky."

"They should enlist Lady Dowling. She'd give them an entire fleet of Stellas." Gwyn patted the hood of the Sunbeam she stood next to.

"Is Stella yours?"

"Oh, no." Gwyn's chest filled with pride as she pointed to the car at the opposite end of the row. "I have Rosie, the most elegant—and dare I say—most fussy lady on the block."

"You have a knack for procuring the fussy ones. I remember dear ol' Lizzie far too well."

Gwyn guided him down the line. Their boots crunched in unison over the frozen earth. "I have a soft spot for things that don't run like they're supposed to." *Like me.* "But, unlike Lizzie, Rosie isn't covered in rust and has yet to choke on me."

Reaching the end, she patted Rosie's bonnet and swept off the snowy blanket to reveal her deep green color. "Beautiful, isn't she?"

"Yes, she is, and a shade of green I've never seen before." Gwyn looked down at Rosie's bonnet and frowned. Rosie's green was standard issue. She looked up and caught William watching her. He quickly looked away. "I've never understood why cars, or wagons, or any*thing* is referred to as 'she'." He dusted snow off the front fender with sharp flicks of his hand.

"Because they're temperamental, and yet society cannot do without them."

His head rocked back with a laugh, a deep sound that softened among the falling snowflakes. "You are absolutely right. You tell me how disagreeable Rosie is, yet here I am dusting off her cold arms and head."

Gwyn leaned her forearms on the bonnet, her fur coat impenetrable to the cold metal. Flakes landed on his shoulders, glistening atop the buttons. A pistol at his side and soft golden hair cropped his under cap, he looked oddly out of place standing next to the Rolls Royce. "You don't know anything about autos, do you?"

His eyebrows shifted. "And what gave me away?"

"I knew the minute you poked your head under Lizzie's bonnet. At least then you didn't call her fender an arm."

He grinned sheepishly, a slight dimple pulsing in his cheek. "You've called me out. I'm afraid I'm better with horses. I can recite a horse's lineage from the greatest stud and dam lines, but I couldn't tell you the difference between a spark plug and a radiator cap. All in what you're accustomed to."

He with his high-born horses and she with her rusted-out parts. Two worlds forever pulling apart. If she kept her wits about her, she'd let them keep pulling until she no longer thought of him when the din of the day quieted down. But how could she keep her wits about her when he kept showing up?

"Growing accustomed to one thing can leave you in a rut." She pushed her pesky thoughts aside. "Why stay in a rut when new experiences await just around the bend?"

"Like moving to a new country?"

"Under ordinary circumstances, I would wholeheartedly agree, but this trip is nothing so carefree as packing one's bags for a grand adventure. The challenges are never-ending."

"And you like them?"

"I like putting my hands to useful tasks, no matter what others may say about it." She edged her toe into the ground.

"The explosions, the horror, the pain. It hasn't frightened your resolve to stay?"

She grinned. "Did you hope it would send us all scurrying back across the Channel to the safety of rolling bandages and darning socks from our front parlors?"

"Yes."

Her smile dropped. "Still, after all this time, you don't think we belong here."

"I prefer not to see you here, nor anyone for that matter." He looked down, scraping a handful of snow together into a tiny pile on the bonnet. With one hand, he flattened it. "I've written too many letters to families who will never see their sons or husbands or fathers again. I could not imagine the sheer despair of writing one about a daughter."

Gwyn clamped her fingers together to keep her frustration down. "We're not asking to stand next to you in the trenches, merely the opportunity to do our part when and where we can. And my part was no longer in England."

Shadows haunted his eyes like distant memories marching along a foggy pit. "Would you be happy there again?"

"I should like to, though my feet are much too restless to gather dust for Blighty at the moment. Too many fascinating places in the world to see."

A tired smile flitted across his face. "I've never been afflicted with restless feet. They don't mix well with a soldier's life. Hurry up and wait, and all that rot."

"Yours will happily settle after the war."

"God willing. But not until the mission is done."

Gwyn suspected the man would hold his feet to the fire until they burned off if that's what the mission called for. The thought of such dedication cinched her lungs. Did he not feel suffocated knowing his decisions were not his own but commanded from someone higher?

She shrugged off the cinching bands. For one day they deserved a chance to think of the possibilities beyond the war. "Once the mission is over, where will you settle? A seaside resort? An Alpine lodge? A country farm, perhaps?"

"Perhaps." William's shoulders drew taut, his jaw a line of granite. "I came to see my men, Miss Ruthers. All of them. Would you take me to see the rest?"

Sadness wrapped around Gwyn's heart as she nodded. They

trudged up the small hill behind the house, their footsteps crunching in the snow. A waist-high fence squared off the top of the hill. Small wooden crosses dotted the ground within.

Silence enveloped them in its wintery cloak as they stood outside the gate. William's lips moved as he read each marker. Gwyn didn't need to. She knew them each by heart.

"We held a small service and sang a hymn," she said, tugging her coat closer against the wind. She was never sure how to approach people in their moment of mourning. All words seemed inadequate. "This will be a beautiful spot in the spring, with the poppies blooming all around."

"Thank you for burying them here," he said quietly. "With so many wounded, it's often difficult to transport all the soldiers home."

A freshly hewn cross stood dark brown among its faded comrades. It belonged to an eighteen-year-old Irish boy who had never spent one night away from his mother before enlisting. He never made it off the ambulance. "I'm sorry, Captain Crawford. Sorry we could not do more."

"There is only so much one can do. The rest is in God's hands. Or so the thought helps me to sleep at night amongst the grenades exploding over my head."

"Sometimes I think God is much too mighty to involve Himself directly in our squabbles."

William pulled his eyes from the crosses to look down at her. "Then why do we pray for Him to guide our swords and smite our enemies?"

Gwyn shrugged. "Because they're doing the same thing. Should we not benefit from more fervent invoking of His name?"

"Day after day, breath after breath, I hear men invoking the holy name to intervene, yet this war continues. Will it continue on? I assume so. Will we all survive it?" He took a deep breath, pushing out the brass buttons down his coat. The straight line of his shoulders sagged a tiny bit. "Many more crosses will dot the countryside before this atrocity is over."

Gwyn gripped the fence, smashing the snow to ice beneath her gloved palms. And how many crosses would be added because she did not drive fast enough, long enough, or careful enough? How much more blood would she clean from the back of her ambulance before dropping onto her cot with her mud-caked boots still on? "I never realized how difficult it would truly be," she whispered. "I wasn't so naïve to not know what happens, but to see it … it turns the world into a very different place."

He reached out, fingering a loose lock of hair that had slipped out from under her wool cap. A soft tug tingled her scalp as he rolled the hair over his finger and tucked it gently behind her ear. "I'm sorry you had to see it this way."

At the simplest brush of his fingertips against the sensitive skin behind her ear, Gwyn was sure he heard her heart pound its way into her throat. "Captain Crawford—"

"William."

"William." His name rolled over her lips smoother than expected. "I'd like to—"

"What in heaven's name are you doing all the way out here?" Cecelia's voice trilled over the rush of blood in Gwyn's ears. "This hill is much too windy to stand on."

"I wanted to see my men." William tucked his hands into his pockets.

Shivering, Gwyn pulled her collar higher to warm the skin his hand had abandoned to the chill.

Cecelia floated along the path wrapped securely in her white fur coat, her dainty heels perfect picks in the ice. "A lovely spot once the flowers are in bloom. I hope it brings the families some small amount of comfort." Questions flooded her eyes as she glanced at Gwyn then back to William. "If you're done with the motors, I can show you my plans for a vegetable garden come spring."

William shook his head. "Another time. We've stayed long past what we should unless Captain Morrison has deserted me, in which case I am the one who has overstayed his welcome."

"You could never overstay. The men are delighted to see you, and Captain Morrison is more than happy to stay in the kitchen next to the warm stove."

"You mean the warm food."

Cecelia laughed, lighter than the falling snowflakes. "Yes, that too, but I think he's left enough. Gwyn, have you eaten since coming off shift? You should head back to the kitchen before your tummy rumbles away."

Gwyn started to argue with Cecelia's attempt to get rid of her, but what good would come of it? She was a chauffeur's daughter who had spent a few moments with a courageous soldier. Dreams came and went. And her dreams should not include Captain William Crawford, no matter how warm his fingertips felt against her skin.

A wail split the gray afternoon air. Adrenaline spiking, Gwyn raced down the path to the garage, booted feet pounding behind her.

"Is it a gas attack?" William shouted.

"It's the call to cars!" The other drivers sprinted to the waiting autos. *Please, please don't be a gas attack.* They had yet to encounter one, but all reports told them they were some of the most gruesome wounds to behold. A pale blonde scrambled out of the garage tugging mittens over her hands. "What is it, Roz? All hands n—"

Gwyn's foot hit a patch of ice, pitching her forward. William's hand clamped around her arm, pulling her upright without losing his stride. "Steady on. The war isn't going anywhere."

"All hands needed," Roz called as girls jumped in front of their motors, cranking the engines to life. "Sorry, Gwyn. I know you just came off."

Gwyn waved her off. "Don't worry about me. Where are we going?"

"They've got an overflow in Reims from Verdun. Fritz has been blasting the French for over a month now, and the hospitals can't keep up. They're leaving the wounded on the side of the road."

"They're abandoning their own men?"

William's hand uncurled from her arm. "When there are too many, the commanders and medics have no choice but to leave those still able to walk and those who won't make it."

"If there are too many for the Red Cross to carry, how can we fit them—" Gwyn gestured to the cars roaring to life in front of her, a sickness thudding into her stomach. "How do we choose?"

"We're to take the first we see and transport them to a depot." Roz hopped into her Model T. "Keep going back for as many as we can."

But not all. Most of those men would be left to the mercy of the German army if mercy was what they gave. Rosie's crank moaned in the cold air, but Gwyn spun it faster and faster until the car choked to life. She couldn't think about the decisions to come, only saving as many lives as possible.

"They won't all make it." Solid and calm, William stood like a mountain against the storm crashing around them. "If you have to decide, you'll know by their eyes."

Gwyn jumped behind the wheel, gripping it tight as his words rang like a death bell in her head. "I'm glad you're not there. You or your men."

Sadness haunted his eyes as they swept over her face. Each feature in slow turn. "Be safe, Gwyn. And Godspeed."

CHAPTER 9

"I never thought we'd see warm weather again." Gwyn swooped down, plucking a bright green blade of grass from the side of the road and holding it to her nose. "One more cold snap, and I thought my toes would freeze off."

Cecelia inched up the hem of her cornflower-blue skirt and stepped around a mud hole. "Tell me again why we couldn't take the motor?"

"Because it's just over a mile to the village, and the fresh air will do us good."

"You can obtain fresh air riding in a motor. And keep your shoes clean."

"A good stretch of the legs then."

"I'm on my feet all day."

Gwyn rolled her eyes and tossed the grass into a field where fat green buds burst at the seams with the frills of red poppy petals. "All the motors are needed at hospital in case there's an emergency. A baron's daughter with tired feet is hardly an emergency."

"When you put it like that, I suppose I can enjoy the sunshine on foot."

"That-a-girl."

"Matilda said the beignets in Vache Colline are some of the best she's had." Cecelia linked her arm through Gwyn's. "Even better than her family's French chef can make."

Gwyn's mouth watered at the thought of the pillowy softness melting in her mouth, the golden flakes and white icing sugar sticking to her fingers. The closest thing she'd come to a beignet was the rubbery donuts they offered in the local pub back home.

"Alice said they serve real lemons with their tea and have Belgian lace curtains. Is there something special about Belgian lace?"

"Oh, yes. It's some of the most exquisite handiwork." Cecelia smiled with a far-off look. "I'm hoping to purchase a few yards for my trousseau. It'll make the most beautiful wedding veil. The girls started a sewing circle at the orphanage last year, and creating a bridal headpiece would be the perfect opportunity to showcase their skills. I'm considering using part of my allowance to open a shop for them when we return. Don't tell Mother. She doesn't mind giving them our money but abhors getting her hands anywhere near them."

Gwyn's foot skidded into a puddle as the weight of a rock slammed into her heart.

"Careful or you'll ruin your dress. Or my dress, I should say. It never did a thing for my pale complexion, but this shade of green has the most tantalizing effect on your eyes."

Gwyn unstuck her tongue from the roof of her dry mouth. "Are you planning a wedding?"

Cecelia's smile curved wider. "No, but it's nice to have the material on hand. The question may pop up any day, and a girl must be prepared."

"You're certain a question is coming?"

"Perhaps not today or even next week, but a girl must have hope. To have your own house, your own servants, your own way of doing things. Never under anyone's controlling thumb. To live with a man who chooses you, who will want to listen to everything you have to say because he loves you." Cecelia's smile widened as she hugged against Gwyn's arm. "Oh, G. Won't it be wonderful to be married?"

"Marriage isn't really in the cards for me right now. Stinson only accepts unmarried women."

"So many rules. I don't understand why you're willing to torture yourself with them."

"Marriage has quite a few rules of its own. Or at least

expectations."

"Mine won't. My husband will love me no matter what." Her smile faded. "Even if I give him twelve daughters instead of the son he always wanted."

Gwyn squeezed Cecelia's hand, hoping the touch would draw away the pain in her friend's words. Lord Somerset never let his daughter forget she wasn't born the son he longed for.

The quiet village of Vache Colline perched on top of a low hill surrounded by a patchwork of farms once known for their fatted cows. The plump cows now served their duty to the armies. As they entered the village, little shops with matching blue doors and scalloped windows lined the main street like boxes of confectionary sweets. Shutters were thrown open wide to let in the fresh air. Pale pink hyacinths and buttery daffodils dotted windowsills, adding an intoxicating burst of color and sweetness.

"My, it's quiet around here," Cecelia whispered as they passed a group of women who gave them the barest of smiles before hurrying off with their baskets. "I always imagined quaint French villages with laughing children and women gossiping over fresh fruits at the grocer."

Gwyn smiled at a man who tipped his hat in her direction before going back to sweeping his doorway. "If the Germans marched up your driveway, would you have reason to smile?"

The teashop spread over an entire corner at the far end of the main square. A slanted tile roof, bright red shutters, and candy-colored birdhouses hanging from the eaves welcomed visitors to the open doors and cozy tables within.

"Looks like we found where they're keeping the charm." Cecelia peeled off her white-netted gloves and tucked them into her silver-beaded purse. Even in wartime, she was perfectly attired for tea. "*Bonjour*."

French and British soldiers of all ranks occupied several of the small round tables, lingering over steaming cups of coffee and golden pastries. All eyes turned to them, the tiredness lining their thin faces turning to interest.

Gwyn looked over the tops of their heads and spotted a table near the large bay window. She tugged on Cecelia's arm. "Back this way."

"How can you see seats past all these dashing uniforms?"

"Because I see enough of them every day."

"Not sitting upright."

Dodging between two sergeants grinning ear-to-ear, Gwyn fell back as a tall man jumped up to block her path.

"Miss Ruthers, how delighted I am to see you," said Major Bennett. With slicked black hair, cheeks free of whiskers, and intelligent brown eyes, he was easily the most handsome man in the room. "I didn't see Rosie in the square. Is it your day off?"

"My first in over a month," Gwyn said. "And Rosie more than deserves the day off."

"She deserves a medal if I have anything to say about it. That girl has saved my men more times than I care to count." His head cocked to the side, eyes widening at something just beyond her shoulder.

"Forgive me." Gwyn stepped aside. "My friend, Cecelia Hale. She's a nurse at Lady Dowling's hospital."

Major Bennett inclined his head, an entranced smile curving his lips. "For the men to be treated by such an angel, lucky devils."

"We do the best we can," Cecelia said. "Are you stationed nearby, Major Bennett?"

"Right now, I'm treating the men near Bray-sur-Somme, but I go where they need me. Medics move more freely than the average soldier, and thankfully I work with drivers as capable as Miss Ruthers. I can tell you that most ambulances are hardly so swift."

"A medic. How we need more wonderful men like you. I don't suppose the Front can spare you? The nurses at hospital could use a handsome doctor ordering them about."

Cecelia's teasing smile sent a shock of red straight up Bennett's neck and into his hair. Gwyn fought the urge to roll her eyes as

Cecelia added another lovesick token to her collection. The delicious scent of sweet bread wafted by on a tray fresh from the kitchen, sending Gwyn's stomach rumbling. "We don't want to take up any more of your time, and I've been dreaming of these beignets for weeks." She inched towards the table near the window. "Unless you care to join us?"

Major Bennett shook his head, the corners of his mouth turning down. "Thank you, but I was just on my way out. I only have half of the morning off and promised to count the bandage supply with a rather surly quartermaster upon my return."

"You have my sympathies, Major," Cecelia said. "Bandages and I do not get along well."

Bennett gathered his hat from the table and tucked it under his arm. "Miss Hale, a delight to meet you. I hope it's not too long before we met again. And Miss Ruthers, take no offense when I say I hope it is a very long time before I see you again."

Gwyn gave him a mock salute. "As do I, Major."

Bidding the doctor goodbye, Gwyn weaved her way to a table beside the window and took a chair facing the door.

"He seems nice." Cecelia plunked her purse next to a vase filled with white crocuses. Her fair eyebrows lifted. "Handsome too."

"He's a good man. Why, just the other day—oh no. Not interested."

"Why not? You said yourself how good he is, and clearly you get along well. If not him, then who?"

Gwyn ran her hand over the wooden table, smoothed down from years of patrons. "I'm not interested in husband-hunting in the middle of a war. They're so desperate for a glimpse of a girl, they might propose to a hat rack if it had a skirt draped over it."

"Don't be vulgar." Grabbing the sides of her chair, Cecelia hopped closer. "Come on, G. Somewhere in this wide blue world there must be a man for you. And don't tell me he needs motor oil under his nails and the sand of some far-off land dusted in his hair."

Tracing a burn mark from where a steaming cup of coffee must have sat, Gwyn thought of William staring under Lizzie's bonnet without a clue of what he was looking at. Yet he hadn't given a care to smudging his perfectly polished uniform. For her.

"No, I wouldn't mind a little dirt." She turned in her seat to catch the waitress's eye. "Now, on to those beignets before they're all gone."

An hour later, they headed back to *Jardins*, their gait much slower.

"Ooh. I shouldn't have eaten that last one." Cecelia rubbed her stomach and moaned. "I'm sure I won't eat again until next week."

Gwyn grinned, her stomach gurgling happily. "But well worth a belly ache. The hostess said they're usually served with icing sugar. I'd like to come back after the war when rationing has stopped and try them."

"You do that. Meanwhile, I'll stay in good ol' Blighty with a nice cup of English tea and a plate of scones, thank you."

"What's this I hear about scones?" said a voice behind them.

If the sun weren't shining at its peak in the crystal blue sky, Gwyn would have sworn she had conjured him straight from her nightly dreams. Turning, she prayed she didn't have pastry flakes stuck to her face. "Captain Crawford. Captain Morrison. You've escaped the lines."

The men tipped their peaked caps. Gold buttons gleamed on their freshly washed and pressed khaki uniforms.

"Apologies for the winded appearance." William swiped a dot of perspiration trickling by his ear. "We had to sprint to catch up. Not what I wanted to do on my day off."

Cecelia beamed as if just handed the crown jewels. "How lovely and most fortunate that you spotted us. Did you come from the village?"

William nodded. "We hoped for a few pastries, but they had just run out.

"That may be our fault," Gwyn said sheepishly. "We had more than one helping."

"Then I can't be too upset. You ladies deserve a relaxing day out." The warm blue of his eyes locked onto Gwyn as if they stood alone on that dusty road. "The late-night runs have been exhausting."

"I couldn't agree with you more, Captain Crawford," Cecelia said. "And what could be more relaxing than to enjoy a leisurely stroll with two handsome soldiers? Are you game?"

"Of course we are," said Captain Morrison with dimples flashing.

"Excellent." With a smile, Cecelia linked her arm through William's and gently pulled him forward. "You can fill me in on all that's happened since we last saw one another. Snow was on the ground then, can you believe? Are you coming, G?"

William looked over his shoulder, the corners of his mouth pulling down before Cecelia said something to draw his attention back. Gwyn fought the flicker of disappointment that threatened to burn away the pleasantness of her day off.

"Miss Ruthers, shall we?" Captain Morrison offered his arm. The polite smile on his boyish face did little to diminish the disappointment in his eyes as they trailed after William and Cecelia. Cecelia chattered away, pointing to the budding poppies and brown rowed fields that once grew corn. William nodded, answering her questions with a simple yes or no.

"How are you enjoying this warm weather?" Captain Morrison asked.

"Much better than the icy rain and frozen fingers. Though the sun can bring out new difficulties."

"Such as strolling down a dappled lane all the while pining for someone who does not pine for you?"

Her arm slipped from his. "Pardon?"

Without missing a step, he snatched it back to the crook of his arm. "Miss Hale. I see her preference runs elsewhere, but do you think that has me discouraged? Of course not. It proves I must work harder to steal her affection."

The man's persistence was a marvel. Gwyn leaned toward him. "Do you have a plan of attack?"

"Chocolates and flowers."

"Impossible with sugar rationing."

Roland's mouth screwed up. "Poems of declaration."

"I'm afraid she's never cared for the poets."

His eyes squinted in deep thought, fingers tapping against her hand. "These tactics usually work, but perhaps I'm rusty with lack of practice. What solicits your affection, Miss Ruthers?"

"Elbow grease and an engine that purrs like a kitten."

Roland threw his head back with a roar of laughter. William's head snapped around, but Roland waved him off. "About face and mind your own business, Will."

William shot him a withering look before facing front again.

"I tell you, Miss Ruthers," Roland whispered, jabbing a finger in William's direction, "the only thing to rev his engine, as you might say, is pedigreed horseflesh and polished parade boots."

Gwyn laughed, startling several birds from their perch in the nearby trees. Several feet in front of them, the back of William's neck blotched pink. "Shh. He might hear us."

William dropped Cecelia's arm and turned on them. "You two are louder than a set of Jack Johnsons. Of course I hear you."

"Then what say you? Horseflesh or engines?" Roland tapped Gwyn's hand and whispered loudly in her ear. "Shall we take a bet? Ten francs says he chooses the horse."

Gwyn shook her head. "That's not much of a bet when we're well aware of his less-than-favorable attitude towards motor cars. I know army pay is inadequate, but you need to find a VAD nurse if you plan to supplement your income by hustling gullible women."

Laughing, Roland rocked forward and clutched his knees. He swiped at the tears gathering under his pale lashes. Giggles bubbled up Gwyn's throat at the sight.

William balled his fists on his hips. "You two keep on like this, and we'll have the Jerries bearing down on us to see what the ruckus is all about. For precaution, I'm splitting you up."

Smoothing the front of his khaki tunic for composure, Roland turned to Gwyn and lowered his voice. "It has been a delight, but I cannot turn down this opportunity."

Gwyn winked. "Go get her, tiger."

"You two are having a jolly time back here," William said as he and Gwyn continued their walk. Cecelia cast a reluctant look over her shoulder as she took Roland's arm. Gwyn was sure she'd get an earful as soon as they were alone at hospital.

"He's a jolly fellow."

An unpleasant noise rumbled deep in William's throat. He swooped down and plucked an unopened poppy, twirling the stem between his fingers. "Is that what you look for in a fellow, I mean besides the elbow grease? Jolliness?"

"Pleasantness and laughter are important to any relationship."

"And a sense of adventure?"

The teasing note in his voice plucked a quiver along her heartstrings. "Doesn't hurt."

"Anything else?"

Her palms grew slick despite the intermittent shade of towering oaks lining their dirt path. Why had she agreed to this snug bolero Cecelia had insisted on? Pulling the pin from her straw hat, she snatched it off her head and let it trail at her side by the pale green ribbons. A sweet breeze bursting with the scent of grass and cool earth ruffled through her hair, freeing the heat trapped beneath the twisted waves. But the breeze did little to lift the heat of William's gaze.

She flapped her hat over her cheeks. "Golly molly, you're inquisitive today."

It was his turn to remove his hat and run a hand through his hair. Stippled sunlight danced in its shades of wheat and gold. "Sorry. Army life has left me with little tact."

Seeing the pink bloom across his face, Gwyn's confidence sprang. "In that case, what are you looking for?"

"Someone to polish my boots and feed my horse carrots. All with a smile, of course."

"And what woman wouldn't smile over such a prospect?"

He leaned down close, his warm breath tickling the sensitive skin behind her ear. "And, on special occasions, I'll let her muck out the stalls."

Gwyn clasped her hands to her chest. "Oh, rapture."

"Swooning yet?"

"Like a gothic romance novel."

Their laughter pealed through the air, rustling the leaves overhead as squirrels darted down the branches. William grinned broadly, flashing white teeth and the smallest of dimples in his tanned cheek. The careworn lines etched around his eyes lifted, leaving only the clear deep blue reflection. For a moment, brief as it was, he shrugged off the cares of a war and gave her a glimpse of the real man beneath the soldier. It was better than opening a Christmas gift and twice as beautiful.

A flock of brown and white birds soared over the field, dipping down and arcing through the sky as one. Gwyn shielded her eyes against the sun as they fluttered high over the trees and dropped down onto the top branches. It was difficult to imagine battles raged not far away with such joyful chirping and tweeting in front of them.

"Most think those things are true about me."

Gwyn swung her hat by the ribbons in agitated circles. "People have a way of being wrong about others. Especially when they're supposed to fit a certain mold."

"Especially when they didn't choose that mold." He sighed and tucked his hands behind his back, the flower clutched tight. "My uniform is shiny and demands perfection, but my tastes run much simpler than that."

"You don't want shiny?" His arm brushed hers. Zinging currents rushed through her body, summoning every sensation of awareness to the spot he'd touched. Ahead, Cecelia's polite laughter tinkled in the air like a crystal bell.

His walk slowed to a stop. Head down, he examined the dirt-covered toes of his boots. Finally, his eyes tilted up. "No. I don't." Cradling the closed bud in his palm, he offered it to her.

She took it and ran her finger down a cracking seam. "A shame it hasn't blossomed yet."

"It will. When its time has come."

The air stopped in Gwyn's lungs, building pressure until it was ready to burst free from all sides. "When might that be?"

"I'm not certain, but I gladly look forward to it."

"Look forward to what, Will?" Cecelia's strained voice burst the aching pressure. Cool air soared down Gwyn's throat and into her lungs, banking the warmth that had settled there.

"A cold cup of water after this walk." William straightened. Gone was the man. The soldier had returned. "I can't remember the last time I had something more than tepid wetness from a canteen."

"We have more than enough cups full of fresh well water back at *Jardins* if you're spared the rest of the day from returning to duties." Though her smile was carefully placed, Gwyn saw Cecelia's fingers curl white over her purse strings. "I'd love to have your opinion on the rehabilitation room we've established in the east wing."

"You have a rehabilitation center? Precisely what I've been telling Red Cross for months, that hospitals need places where the men can strengthen their muscles after surgery."

"I remember you commenting just that to Lady Dowling. She took it to heart, and now I hear the Duchess of Westminster is thinking of installing one." Cecelia swept her arm to the left fork in the road. The way back to *Jardins*.

"As much as I'd like to see it, we need to head back for rifle drill. Another time." William tipped his hat and turned to Gwyn with a bow. "Miss Ruthers."

"Godspeed, Captain." Disappointment flared. How long would it be before she saw him again? Days like today were rarer than gold filigree steering wheels, and seeing him on the battlefield … she never wanted to see him there.

"By the way, Will. You never answered the question." Roland examined his nails, picking something from the corner of his thumb. The corners of his mouth quirked with mischief. "Horseflesh or engines?"

"I've always preferred horses," William said. "Graceful, impressive, and favorable, because I've been with them my whole life. When people see me, they expect to see a horse." He paused and slid his gaze to Gwyn. The air stopped in her lungs once more. "But there's something to be said of these new motored contraptions. Exhilarating and like nothing I've experienced before. I'd say they're getting into my blood."

Roland frowned. "Well, that doesn't really answer my question."

William grabbed Roland's arm and hauled him to the right turn in the road. "It does for now. Ladies."

Back straight and shoulders firm, his long legs ate up the ground as Roland scrambled to keep up, his rapid-fire questions muffled by the distance.

Cecelia crossed her arms and tapped her purse against her side. "What do you think he meant by that?"

"Haven't the foggiest." Gwyn turned down their path, her feet light as air as she pressed the delicate blossom-in-waiting to her cheek. "But it sounds like he's ready to go for a ride."

CHAPTER 10

"You cannot wear those."

Gwyn twirled in front of the mirror, blocking the reflection of Cecelia's scowling face from the doorway. "And just why not?"

"Only those radicals marching in front of Parliament and riding bicycles wear them." Cecelia huffed and plopped on the bed. "And with all the men around here. What are they to think of you?"

"That I'm practical." Gwyn propped one leg out, admiring the fit and comfort of her new jodhpurs. They were once part of Lord Dowling's riding attire, but a few quick stitches with a needle, and they worked for a woman.

"Indecent is what you are. Do you know how much ungainly attention you'll attract strutting around in those … those … things?"

"Will it matter when I can move wounded in and out of the ambulances without tripping over cumbersome skirts? Not to mention how much easier they allow me to get under the cars for repairs. Men wear them for a reason."

"You're not a man."

"I'm doing a man's job."

"After this war, the men will want their jobs back, and there will be no need or want for your pant-clad legs among them."

Gwyn turned away from the mirror, all excitement for her new trousers doused. "You are truly mean sometimes."

Cecelia dropped her head and fingered the flowers on the quilt at the end of her bed. "I didn't mean it like that. I'm sorry. I just don't want you to be a scandal. Others don't know you the way I do, and they might think you're not a lady."

"People are trite and should learn to keep their tongues from wagging about things they don't understand."

"Perhaps, but it is how the world spins. Men have their place, and we ours. War won't change that."

An ache welled inside Gwyn's chest as she turned back to the mirror. For all her privileges and standings in the world, Cecelia couldn't see the whirl of changes right before her eyes. The war was creating a new world full of new people and ideas. Only time would tell who was strong enough to stand after it was over.

Cecelia picked at a loose thread along the quilt's border, tugging it until the edge slowly separated into two pieces. She twirled the free string around her finger.

"What's truly bothering you, CeCe?" Gwyn sat on the bed beside her friend, tucking her peeling leather boots out of sight. "It's not just the trousers and my scandalous legs."

"It's nothing. I'm just tired and irritable after last night's shift. This summer heat makes everyone cranky."

Gwyn braced her palms along the edge of the bed and bumped Cecelia's shoulder. "That's not all. Tell me, or I'll slide down the banister while whistling *Ta-ra-ra Boom-de-ay*."

Cecelia pursed her lips. "You wouldn't dare."

Sucking in a deep breath, Gwyn puckered her mouth and blew. Cecelia's hand clamped over Gwyn's mouth before she could get a note out. "Don't. I believe you."

"What happened last night?"

Shrugging, Cecelia moved her finger along a faded green vine connecting two roses. She traced each of the petals before flattening her hand over them. "Another night to prove I don't know what I'm doing here." She looked up, unpolished longing twisting her face. "Sometimes I wish I had your assurance in the job at hand, without the trousers, of course."

"I've known my niche for a long time. Living above a garage your entire life only makes you talented in a few things."

"But you like motoring around and tinkering under bonnets."

"Yes and no. I don't care for smelling like oil all day, but the motors give me a chance at what I truly desire. Unrestrained freedom. What are you good at that you actually enjoy?"

"Fashionable dressing." Cecelia snorted, fingering the pinstripe trim of her navy skirt. "They don't need that particular skill here."

"No, but you gave all your lovely new clothes to the women in town when they had only rags to keep them warm. They even had enough left over to make dresses for their little girls' dolls."

A delicate pink blossomed across Cecelia's cheeks. "Every woman, no matter her age, deserves a new dress to feel pretty."

Gwyn smiled. Despite her shortcomings, Cecelia would never stop trying to make the world a more lovely place. "What else?"

"Dancing. Another strike."

"What about the music? You love the piano, and don't tell me you don't enjoy having all eyes on you when singing those beautiful arias."

Cecelia's winged eyebrow arched. "This isn't the place for a nightly concert."

"Why not? The men need healing, not only in body but in mind and spirit as well. How many times have you heard them cry for Elsie Janis to bring her tour this way?" Gwyn sprang off the bed, wobbling Cecelia as the mattress shifted. "Lady Dowling has a piano in the front parlor. You can play for the men each evening after dinner. Let's go tell her."

"Wait, wait, wait." Cecelia grabbed Gwyn's arm before she made it to the door. "She has it pushed into a corner for a reason."

"Only because no one has put it to use. You can put it to good use, for the men. Imagine how excited they'll be to listen to something other than their vital stats." Gwyn hooked her arm through Cecelia's, guiding her through the door. "You could wear a few of those frilly outfits to top off the performance."

Excitement lit Cecelia's face like a rainbow. "I'll even cut the fingertips off those hideous lace gloves for playing. Mother will be furious."

"Then we won't tell her."

Laughing, they skipped down the stairs and outside to find Lady Dowling standing on the front steps.

"No, not there!" She cupped her hands around her mouth as two maids carried a wobbling table across the sprawling grass. "That's where the sack race is run. Do you want to see my crystal punch bowl trampled to the ground?"

From the dark looks of the huffing maids hauling the massive wooden table to another spot on the lawn, they couldn't care less about a punch bowl.

"Yes, right there. Careful now, and make sure the legs aren't stuck in a hole." Deep lines wrinkled Lady Dowling's mouth as she turned to the new invaders on her porch perch. "You're not here to tell me the ice cream has melted already, are you?"

"No, m'lady."

"That's one blessing." Lady Dowling flapped a wrinkled hand in front of her face. "It's only past seven, and today is already shaping up to pour on the heat."

Gwyn swiped at the beads of perspiration gathering along the nape of her neck. "But what a lovely July day it will be for the first ever Dowling Day Celebration."

"The cars are bannered and polished? Driver uniforms ironed and clean?"

"Yes, m'lady. Each girl is ready to show her stuff in the big race this afternoon. Eugenie and I smoothed over the holes in the drive yesterday, so there's nothing to slow us down."

"Good. I've heard the men already making bets on which motor will win. I don't advocate betting, but they need a spot of entertainment to keep the morale up."

Gwyn grinned. "Then why should the entertainment stop there? Let's keep it rolling with a little singing."

Lady Dowling raised a sparse eyebrow. "I didn't realize you sang."

"I don't, but Cecelia does." Gwyn nudged Cecelia forward.

"Like a songbird."

To Cecelia's credit, she didn't shrink back under the marchioness's hawk stare. "I'm no Emma Calvé, but I'm told I can hold a note with the piano. I noticed you have one in the front parlor."

"It's been gathering dust ever since my husband passed. He was the musician. It's time we put that old thing to use again. You'll play for afternoon tea, after the motor race." Brushing past them, Lady Dowling marched across the lawn pointing and shouting new instructions about the chairs and tables.

Back inside, Cecelia clapped a hand to her cheek and shook her head. "I can't believe she agreed."

"Why wouldn't she? That woman would bend over backward in her corset and pantaloons if it would help her boys."

Cecelia giggled. "True, but I don't think they'd appreciate the spectacle."

"All the more reason for *you* to provide the entertainment." Rummaging in a maid's closet, Gwyn found an unused cloth to wipe off the top of the piano and its ivory keys. "I wish I knew how to play. There's nothing lovelier than a piano."

"It's easy." Rousing from her stupor, Cecelia found a stack of sheet music in a cabinet and rifled through the yellowing pages. "If you don't mind the hours of practice with a griffin of a music teacher who works you until your fingers bleed."

"If that's the price, then I'm content to enjoy the performance from the audience."

"I can play a few that the orphanage girls always enjoyed hearing." Pages rustled back and forth through Cecelia's fingers. "Hmm, I wonder which of these William would like."

The cloth slipped from Gwyn's hand. Grabbing it, she clutched it tight to distract the rush of excitement racing towards her heart. "Is Captain Crawford coming?"

"No, I only remember him remarking on a few songs during Mother's charity benefit. Perhaps this one." Cecelia spread the music on top of the piano and tapped a finger across the black dots and lines. "If only he would return my letters."

"He's busy fighting a war. I doubt salutations are the first priority on his list."

"That Captain Morrison has plenty of time to write." She sighed noisily. "Almost twice a week."

"Quite an admirer you have."

"Not the one I want."

A painful breath caught in Gwyn's throat. Her mind zinged to the poppy petals pressed between the pages of her Bible. "Why do you have all your hopes pinned on William? Has he given you any indication to hope?"

"Not exactly." A thin line puckered Cecelia's fair brow. With a dainty shrug, the line smoothed. "Men don't always know what's best for them. It's our duty to point them in the right direction."

Gwyn rolled her eyes. "There are plenty of good men out there who don't need their arm twisted by a would-be-bride."

"Those good men are already taken or don't qualify. William is available—outside of this war, that is—handsome, in good social standing to satisfy Mother and Father and is loyal to the bone. The perfect qualities for a husband."

And almost the same for a dog. What about mutual affection? What about dreaming of the color of his eyes, or aching to hear him laugh? Or realizing you couldn't breathe until he came into the room? Golly molly. Where was Gwyn's head going? Those feelings were fine for fairytale damsels who happily traded their lives to ride off into the sunset with their princes. Stinson didn't allow princes, and without a pilot license, she could never hope to cross off all those places on her mother's dream list. A dream that had become Gwyn's own.

Gwyn yanked the velvet cushion off the piano bench and smacked the dust off with her hand. Damsels indeed. The blue depths of William's eyes over the rim of a teacup called back to her.

"Does he ever ask about me?"

Gwyn's head snapped up. "Ask? Who?"

Cecelia rolled her eyes. "William, of course. Who else do you think I've been talking about this whole time?"

"When would he ask me?"

"When you go to pick up the wounded. Surely you see him."

"Each pickup is different. I haven't seen him since that day in Vache Colline." And not an hour went by when she didn't wonder if he was safe.

Cecelia leaned her forearms on the piano top and narrowed her eyes. "You would tell me, wouldn't you? If you'd seen him?"

Gwyn shoved the cushion back into place. "Your Marianne Dashwood tone frightens me a bit."

"Dashwood? Have I met her? During the season perhaps. One attends so many balls that it's impossible to remember every introduction."

"A literary character. She was in love with a man named Willoughby and wrote him incessantly to … never mind."

"I don't care for reading." Cecelia scanned her music again. "It squints the eyes."

Gwyn went back to her dusting, relieved Cecelia hadn't continued with her interrogation. If the questions kept coming, Gwyn might accidentally give away how much she truly enjoyed William's company, and she'd rather not experience Cecelia's reaction to that admission.

Gwyn tapped the top of the piano. "Does she expect us to haul this outside?"

Cecelia looked up from her papers and frowned. "My goodness, I hope not."

"Knowing her I wouldn't be surprised if she—" The floor rumbled beneath Gwyn's feet. Dangling crystals from the chandelier tinkled against each other. "What was that?"

"An earthquake? What a horrible day for one. You don't think it upset the punch bowl?"

The ground trembled, knocking two green china vases from a side table. Tidbits shattered over Gwyn's toes. Her gaze flew to the windows and the brilliant blue skies beyond. "I'm not certain that was an earthquake. We're not but fifteen miles from the Front. A few of those artillery shells are known to cover quite the distance."

"Don't scare me like that. We may hear the cannons echoing on a clear night, but nothing that big to shake the ground beneath our feet." Cecelia raised her foot and shook off the broken fragments of porcelain. "We're perfectly safe where we are."

"No one is entirely safe. Not during a war."

The warning bell rang. Gwyn's gut churned at the terrifying clang. *Please, God. Let me be wrong.*

Feet pounded down the hall. Their communications operator raced by the parlor and through the open front door, sprinting across the grass to where Lady Dowling directed party decorations. A few agonizing seconds later, they dashed back inside.

"Stations! Stations!" The marchioness screamed. "Our boys are coming in! Slaughter on the Somme! Stations everyone!"

Bodies heaped on the ground, leaving not a patch of mud uncovered. The smell of blood, singed flesh, and smoke choked the air as bullets and short-range shells screamed overhead. The Germans' firestorm charged across No Man's Land, ripping into wave after wave of troops going over the top.

William backed off the fire step and grabbed his knees as fear and bile roiled in his stomach. Yanking the canteen from his belt, he raised it shakily to his lips and forced the sickness down with sheer will. He wouldn't give in to it.

He marched down the line, determined to rally his men. Mud and human disgust squished under his boots with each step. Boys too young for their first whiskers clung to their rifles as tears streaked down their dirty faces. The seasoned troops pulled on their rolled cigarettes and cursed with each drag.

"Keep that muzzle out of the dirt, son." William pointed at the forgotten weapon. "Check your ammo pouches and chin straps. I don't want a loose helmet flopping around if they call us over."

"You mean when they call us, Captain." A sergeant with callous brown eyes stared up from where he squatted. "It's a slaughter when we hit the dirt. Ain't gonna be anyone left to fight those Jerries."

"It's our job to be ready, Sergeant," William said.

The man spat. "For king and country. Bah."

"For the man next to you. For your brothers."

He spat again. William continued on. Some men were so hardened that no amount of brave words could pierce their armor. Those weren't the ones he worried about.

William stopped next to a private who was trying to load his Lee-Enfield rifle. "Rub a little dirt on your hands."

The cartridge slipped from the boy's sweaty hands. He caught it before it landed in the sludge. "I-I'm sorry, s-sir."

"Take your time. You want to make sure it's loaded correctly and not jammed."

"That would be bad."

William smiled grimly. "Yes, it would. Have you been rubbing whale oil on your feet?"

The boy's chin dipped down. "Yes, sir."

"How often?"

"If it's not raining. And Sundays after chapel."

A sure path to trench foot. A nasty disease spread by cold and closed conditions that rotted the feet. "Every day. That's an order."

"Yes, sir." The boy wiped a hand across his grimy face, knocking his tin hat to the side. "They really gonna call us up, Captain? Surely our boys can get across those craters and wires to Fritz before they need the reserves."

William's heart clenched. The very same thought had kept him awake night after night. How do you send men straight into fire while praying they never call for you? "Anything can happen, and we must be ready for it. Including keeping a ready weapon. Let me see you load it."

"Will! Will!"

William turned to see Roland barreling down the trench, red-faced and eyes wild. "Calm yourself, man, or you'll give the Germans a new target!"

"That's exactly what I'm talking about." Roland skidded to a halt. He tilted his helmet back and wiped the black grime from his forehead. "Almost the entire Newfoundland regiment has been wiped out. The reserve line is coming out six hundred yards from the front. What are these commanders thinking?"

"They're following the objectives given them."

"They keep following them for much longer, and we'll be the ones tangled in the barbs."

Despite the earth shaking with explosions, silence surrounded William as every man within earshot leaned in. The private's rifle dropped to the mud. Grabbing Roland by the collar, William hauled him around the bend. "You *cannot* speak like that in front of the men." He hissed. "We must keep them calm even with our minutes counted."

Roland yanked away from his grasp. "Keeping them in the dark will do no one any good."

"There's a way to do it. Screeching like a madman will only set them on edge."

"Fine, fine." Roland scowled and adjusted his belt. "You should still know how close we are to going over."

Stones plunked in the pit of William's stomach. A familiar feeling when the truth hit him in the face. "I'm all too aware of the chaos around us, though exact communication has been … limited."

Metal hissed, sharp and terrifying like a banshee.

William grabbed his helmet and hunched over. "Get down!"

Dirt, mud, and shrapnel blasted over the trench, dousing its occupants. *Ting ting ting*. Metal bits pinged off William's helmet and scattered into the mud sucking at his boots.

Roland uncurled from his ball and grinned. "Close one, eh?"

"They must have a few Jack Johnsons of their own." William wiped the mud from his eyes with the back of his equally filthy hand. No screams of agony. Good, good.

"Captain Crawford. Is there a Captain Crawford here?"

Looking over the heads of his hunched-over men, William spotted a lieutenant picking his way down the duckboards. The man eyed the rank of each man he passed and stopped at William. "Are you Captain Crawford?"

William frowned, taking in the boy's scared eyes and shiny buckles. Lieutenants like this never bore good news. "I am."

"You're to come with me, sir. General Haig has requested your presence immediately at HQ."

The stones in William's stomach crashed together. No. Never good news.

CHAPTER 11

Chaos.

Horns bleated and drivers cursed as they jostled for position in the long string of ambulances trolling their way to and from the battlefield. The makeshift road wasn't wide enough to drive two abreast, so motors veered into the ditch. Wheels squealed and spun in the mud, splattering the unfortunate driver behind. But no matter how loudly they rumbled, the scream of battle would not be drowned out.

Gwyn swerved her way into the pickup area and ground to a halt. Uncramping her legs from riding the throttle the entire way, she swung them over the side and down. Straight into a puddle of red and brown. She bit down on her back teeth to keep calm.

A horn blasted behind her. "Get out of the way, girl!"

Gwyn jumped back as an ambulance careened past, his back axles sagging low to the ground. A rut threw the back doors open, and two poorly bandaged hands scrambled to slam them shut.

"Think he'd realize he's got dying men in the back," Eugenie growled next to her. Her dark hair stuck out in every direction and mud covered her cheeks.

Gwyn nodded but said nothing. Tensions ran high enough.

They picked their way between the motors. It didn't take long to find the field hospital. Bleeding men and bodies covered the ground, their cries and sobbing like the lowing of cattle. Some begged for death.

A hand clawed at Gwyn's foot. Dirty fingernails gouged into her boot.

Anguish punched in her gut as she eyed the hole torn across

the man's neck. "We'll get you." Reaching down, she squeezed his hand and placed it back on his chest. "We'll take care of you all."

Ducking into a large dugout, her feet slid on discarded bandages. She caught the edge of a crude table.

"Unless you know how to amputate, go twitch your nose someplace else." A surly voice came from the back corner. "I don't need weak women fainting on me."

"We're ambulance drivers." Gwyn stepped over the pile. "Fresh reserves from Lady Dowling."

"Reserves? From that old battle-axe? Where are the trains Maxwell promised us? Three out of eighteen, explain that to me."

Gwyn tamped down her anger. "I'm afraid I can't."

"Then what can you do? Stand there and stare while I saw this man's leg off, or do you have actual help to offer me?"

"Now look here, sir—" A hand gripped Gwyn's shoulder and pulled her to the other side of the hole.

Major Bennett shook his head and dropped his hand. "Don't. Colonel Lang has been awake for over seventy-two hours, and we don't have enough hands to deal with the wounded."

"Well, we've come to help in the best way we can," she said.

"They promised eighteen ambulance trains, but only three have shown up. The wounded are being left in the open at the depot with only their original field dressings. No nurses, no orderlies or doctors on sight." Bennett pointed at the bleeding men piling up as far as the eye could see. "We're not prepared."

"Then we'll get them off the field as fast as we can and come back for more. At least a depot is safer than having shells exploding overhead."

A tired smile flitted across his face. For just a moment, Gwyn saw how handsome he really was. "I'm glad you have determination, Miss Ruthers, because we need all we can get."

Gwyn picked her way back to her ambulance and found Rosie sagging to one side. With a cry of panic, Gwyn ran around the back of the auto. A piece of shrapnel stuck out of the back tire.

Perfect. Why had she ever let Eugenie talk her into removing the spares for the race? Much good extra speed did them now. She kicked the offending tire with all the anger she could muster.

"Ow!" She doubled over and grabbed her throbbing toe.

"What's going on back here?" Eugenie came around the front of the motor and took in the situation with one glance. "Oh."

"Oh." Gwyn dropped her foot. "And we have no spares."

Eugenie's mouth screwed up, flattening her thick nose. "You're stuck here."

"So it would seem."

"I'll bring a spare my next round."

"That'll take hours, maybe days from the looks of things."

"What other choice do we have?"

Gwyn slumped against Rosie. She'd come all this way for nothing. No, not for nothing. Jerking up, she threw open the back doors and counted the first aid supplies. *Thank you, Lord.* At least the kits had stayed in place. She slammed the door shut. "I'll stay and help the medics as much as I can until someone can bring back a spare. When you see the girls, tell each one of them to get those spares back on board. We can't afford another disaster like this."

Eugenie saluted. "Yes, ma'am. Is that all?"

"Be careful around the potholes."

"Oh, good." Eugenie scratched a hand behind her neck and into her dark hair, ruffling it like a scared chicken's feathers. "Thought I had a yelling headed my way. You know, because it was my idea to take the spares out for the race."

"We didn't think."

"You the driver of that rig up here?" A man wearing a Red Cross band on his arm shouted between the cars. "We're ready to load you up."

Sadness and guilt tangled over Gwyn's heart as she watched her friends drive away with their ambulances loaded, their mission underway. Left behind, covered in dust, and the one thing she was good at taken away.

Her father's voice rattled in her head. *"God gave you hands and a mind. If your hands are taken away, use your mind and get back to work."*

If she couldn't drive, then by golly, she was going to wrap bandages. Even if they were into ridiculous little bows. Gathering what supplies she could carry from the ambulance, she marched back to the medical tent. "How can I help?"

"Have you ever assisted in an amputation?" Major Bennett cracked his knuckles as he stared at her with uncertainty. "No? Quite all right. I have the chaplain in here to help. Take these extra field kits and patch as many men as you can before daylight fails us."

Gwyn slung the packs over her shoulder, adjusting the belt so they didn't bang against the back of her legs. "I have more supplies in my ambulance, in case I need to refill."

"I can't thank you enough, Miss Ruthers." The shadows around his eyes lifted. "I know your desire is to transport, but I believe your auto breaking down has a greater purpose. Now, more than ever, we should see God's hand in the small things."

The straps across her chest cut into Gwyn's lungs. For One so lofty, the Almighty had a way of presenting Himself rather frequently in conversations of late. A shame He remained absent on the battlefield. How many more would suffer?

William. Her heart squeezed. "Have you treated anyone from the Ox and Bucks? Second division."

Bennett's lips scrunched, bristling his thin black mustache. "With all the casualties and filth covering their uniforms, it's difficult to properly identify each regiment. You know someone?"

Heart anchored with fear, she nodded. "I'm afraid so."

Bursts of yellow lit the night sky as the guns pounded a short distance away. Gwyn sagged against a tree stump, her ears ringing.

After hours of making her way among the wounded, only the loudest explosions caused her to jump.

Slipping off her field kit, she stretched her aching back. After fieldwork, she was sure to become a permanent hunchback. A blessing compared to what her eyes had witnessed. Pushing the images of writhing figures away before her mind caved in, she yanked open the medical bag and counted her precious few remaining supplies. No possible way to stretch out what she had if those supply lines didn't start moving again, and soon.

"Nurse! Nurse!"

Gwyn rubbed her head. Night and day she heard that call, but no nurses set foot so close to the Front. Only her. She sprang to her feet. *She* was the nurse now.

"Here!" Grabbing the kit, she lurched into the darkness towards the frantic voice.

A sergeant popped over the ridge as an explosion ripped into the air, highlighting him from behind. "You the nurse? You gotta come with me, ma'am."

Staring at the ground, Gwyn picked her way over the craters. The booming flashes of gunpowder lit the way. The footsteps in front of her went silent. Panic crept up her chest. "Sergeant?"

"Here, ma'am. There's a ladder down to the trench, just swing your leg over."

Fumbling in the darkness, her hands brushed against wooden handles. Swiveling around, she put one foot on the rung. Her foot slipped. Backward she flew. Strong arms caught her before she hit the ground.

The sergeant steadied her on her feet. "All right there, ma'am?"

"Yes." Her voice shook. If she couldn't pull herself together, she would be of no use to anyone. "Where is the man?"

"This way."

Walls of earth towered on either side of the trench, narrow enough that she could almost stretch fingertips across to touch. Soft lantern light glowed from dugouts along the way. Filthy men huddled together. Gwyn's lungs burned as she tried to breathe, but the air was thick with the stench of unwashed bodies, dirt, sour blood, and human waste.

Eyes forward, she tried not to pay attention to the open mouths and disbelieving stares greeting her. Heat fanned up her neck as the crude whispers grew louder.

"Are we near the Front?" she asked.

The sergeant glanced over his shoulder. "These are the reserve lines. Paradise, we call it."

More twisting and turning passages. Finally, Gwyn spotted a dugout with several men clustered around the entrance.

"Make a hole," the sergeant barked, shoving Gwyn into the fray. "Medic here."

"*Gwyn*? What in blazes are you doing here?" William shot to his feet, banging his head on the roof. He glared at the sergeant. "What is she doing here? I told you to find the medic."

"They're all busy, Captain. She's who they told me to find."

Relief pumped in Gwyn's heart. William was safe and whole.

"Couldn't stop until you landed right in the heat of things, could you?" Shifting in front of her, William lowered his head until his face was inches from hers. "Satisfied? Or maybe you'd like a rifle to march straight to the Kaiser's door."

His anger cut her to the quick. "Every medical person's hands are busy with more than they can handle. My presence is merely an oddity of fate." She took a step back, releasing the pressure between them. "I'm here to help, William. Let me."

His brows bunched together, but he didn't argue. Good man. Her patience drained, she swept a critical eye down his body to ensure he was still in one piece before turning her complete attention to the motionless boy on a makeshift cot of crates. Pale as a sheet, stained bandages swathed his neck.

Kneeling beside him, Gwyn slipped off her field kit. "What happened?"

"Shot in the neck." William knelt close to the boy's head.

"Name is Truman. Walter Truman."

"Mr. Truman? Walter, can you hear me?" Gwyn motioned for the lantern as she pried open each of his eyelids and checked for dilation. From the dulled reaction, he'd lost a lot of blood. "How did it happen?"

"Trying to give himself a Blighty, he did." One of the men gaggling around snarled. "Did it work for you, eh Truman? Can't even shoot yourself in the foot proper without dropping the gun first and nicking a neck vein."

"That's enough. Back to your posts," William said. "And if I hear one word of gossip about this, I'll have your stripes."

Gwyn dug through her bag and pulled out the small length of precious linen. It wasn't nearly enough. "Do you have spare bandages?"

William shook his head, the lantern swinging in his hand. "I had to scrounge for these."

Looking around the tiny space, she tried to locate something, anything applicable. *Think, think, think.* Reaching back into her bag, she found the scissors and thrust them at William. "Cut my cuffs."

She almost smiled as he took them and carefully snipped around her wrist. He trusted her enough not to ask questions.

"As soon as I remove this old bandage, lift his head and put the cuff over the wound." She knotted her other cuff to the end of the linen. "Ready?"

Hands at the ready, he nodded. Pale and motionless, every rational verdict screamed that the boy should be dead, but still the warm stickiness flowed between Gwyn's fingers. She whipped off the old bandage, and William covered it with the makeshift one. With quick movements, she wrapped a strip of linen around the boy's neck to hold the bandage in place.

"We need to get him to hospital." She tied off the strip's ends into a knot. "Why was he not brought to the dressing station before?"

"Men have been waiting hours, days even, for a medic to come by. At least here someone could look after him." William's usually light-blue eyes looked more like dark pools rimmed with black and red. Exhaustion sagged every line in his body.

Gwyn touched his arm, noting her hand was as filthy as his sleeve. "I'm relieved you're not at the front line. I searched the faces every day …" Her words caught in her throat. "I didn't know if God would hear me, but He answered my prayers."

Something flared deep in William's eyes, startling her. An intensity that she had never seen before, yet understood at once. He leaned close, close enough for his deep breaths to stir the loose hairs across her temple. Heat slashed across her cheeks.

Blinking, he vanquished the moment. "I'll find stretcher bearers to take him up."

William cursed himself. What was he thinking? And with a man dying in front of him. Shame pierced him like a hail of bullets. His duty was to protect his men, and that protection failed when he was busy wondering how Gwyn managed to smell of flowers when surrounded by squalor.

"Find me a stretcher." He barked at two men lingering outside the shelter.

"They're all at the Front, Captain. Too busy scurrying up and down the COMMS line to pay us any mind."

Sweat trickled under William's tin cap. He rubbed the spot in irritation. "Then tie two jackets together and bring them in here."

Two hours later the sun broke over the blackened ridge. Truman was added to the line awaiting transport to a clearing station. If he made it to hospital by afternoon, he might have a chance.

Gwyn had said no more than six words to him since he'd almost forgotten himself in the dugout. He'd seen his intensity reflected in her eyes. But it was no good, not here and not now. He was accountable to the men and his task which did not include her burnished hair in lantern light, skin that looked like it was carved from cream, and lips that begged for his touch.

Distractions.

Giving into them only spelled misery and disillusion. What if she saw the flaws? The imperfections he struggled against daily? Without the uniform to hide them, she might not like what she found.

But Gwyn wasn't like anyone he had ever come across. Since the first day he'd met her, she'd made her distinct way of doing things quite clear. She hadn't needed him on the side of the road, or waiting for her in the rain, or appearing at hospital with hopes of spending time with her.

Steeling himself once more for rejection, he marched to Gwyn's disabled ambulance. An assortment of tools spread next to her as she hunkered by the flat tire.

At his approach, she sighed heavily. "I appreciate your earlier offer, Captain, but I'm managing quite well on my own. I'm sure your duties have more pressing issues for you."

"The guns are rather quiet this morning, so I find myself with a minute's respite. Roland has the command back in the line." Swooping down, he picked up a tire iron and flipped it over in his hand, measuring its smooth surface against the manageable weight. "Should we run out of bullets and resort to hand-to-hand combat, these should come in quite handy."

"Exactly what we need." Gwyn grunted, yanking the inner tube from the damaged tire and inserting it into the new tire another driver had dropped off. "Closeness to look our enemies directly in the eyes." She worked the tire over the exposed rim as easily as most women worked dough on a counter.

He didn't want to interrupt her, but the manners deeply ingrained in him refused to let him stand by quietly. "Allow me." His fingers brushed hers as he reached for the tire. "Your hands need to be saved for more life-saving work."

She didn't let go. "I'm an ambulance driver, Captain Crawford. This is my work."

"And here I thought it was stubbornness."

Her head turned up, eyebrows drawn together. In the morning light, her eyes glowed like emeralds. "You may call it that, but I call it getting the job done. When was the last time you changed a tire?"

"I've shoed my fair share of horses over the years. A tire can't be that much more complicated."

"It's entirely different."

"And you know this how? Shoe any horses lately?" He tugged the tire. She was stronger than he expected.

She smirked. "Common sense."

A long shadow loomed over them. "Has anyone ever told you the futility of arguing with a woman, Captain Crawford? You'll lose every time."

William leaped to his feet and saluted. The tire plopped to the ground. "General."

General Ivor Maxse waved him off with an uninterested salute and turned his full attention to Gwyn. "You the field angel I've been hearing about?"

Gwyn rose to her feet, wiping her hands on the sides of her trousers. "I'm not sure what you mean."

His small, deep-set eyes bored into her. "The driver who's been forced to make herself useful in my fields until her equipment gets fixed. Are you or are you not she?"

"I am."

"Good. I'm recruiting you. You no longer drive for that duchess, but for me."

Gwyn shook her head. "Sir, I'm afraid that's impossible. Lady Dowling—"

"Was not happy when I informed her, but she'll survive. Pack your bags. You're moving out with the troops to Trônes Wood."

CHAPTER 12

Steam seeped from the ground as if the afternoon's rain had dislodged a pipe under the earth's surface. Gwyn tugged at her damp collar, releasing the heat trapped behind her neck. Every inch of clothing and strand of hair stuck to her skin, and any part that couldn't adhere itself like a soggy bandage was caked in muck. Long ago she'd stopped caring what the black and brown mixture consisted of.

Adjusting her position on Rosie's running board, Gwyn leaned her head back and closed her eyes. They watered in relief. Over a week since she'd slept in a proper bed or eaten a proper meal, and—most disgusting of all—properly cleaned herself. Not that the men noticed. She could dress in a skinned cowhide, and they'd still manage a whistle through their cracked lips. No matter that they marched closer to the danger waiting for them in the woods.

A fly circled her head. She waved it away, but it dived in closer until the rapid wing beats droned in her ear. Pulling a folded envelope from her pocket, she whacked the insect with a solid *thunk*. It landed in a puddle several feet away.

"Good riddance," she muttered. "As if there wasn't enough buzzing in my head."

She creased the envelope between her fingers, its inner words searing her thoughts more profoundly than the heat.

How very upsetting it is to lose you, Lady Dowling had written, followed by a rant against General Ivor Maxse, the army, the war, the Kaiser, and where they could all march straight to. A postscript instructed Gwyn to return to *Maison du Jardins* as soon as possible, or the marchioness would see to it personally that General Haig's sterling military career was reduced to nothing but peeling potatoes.

Gwyn turned the letter over in her hand, tracing the scripted address. Lady Dowling had lifted her spirits, but Cecelia's tear-stained note haunted her.

My dearest Gwyn, how can they demand such a thing of you? A lady in battle amongst all those men. Can they really expect you to attend them all? And you will be there with my brave William, day and night. It is wholly unfair that you spend so much time with him while I am here. Come back to me safe and sound, for I do not know what to do without you prodding me, and, of course, look after dear William for me.

Heaviness pulled on Gwyn's heart as she tucked the letters safely back in her pocket. Dear William was arguing for the umpteenth time with his commanding officer a few feet away. His angry voice and sharp gestures did nothing to dissuade the stone-faced man. She was moving out with the troops, and that was final. No tactical arguments or maneuvers were going to change Ivor Maxse's decision. If she wasn't so miserable, she could almost appreciate William's dogged determination to get her kicked off the line.

"Never in all my life have I encountered such stubbornness." William marched over to her.

Gwyn quirked an eyebrow. "Never?"

William yanked off his Tommy hat and plowed a hand through his hair. It spiked in all directions. "Pardon?"

"I was trying to be ironic. Never mind."

A mad pulse throbbed in his red splotched neck. "Whoever in all of civilized society thought it a grand idea to bring a female to the heart of battle? And give her no choice about it to boot. The British army never ceases to amaze me with its lack of common sense."

"Common sense tells me that medics, even third-rate ones, are needed on a battlefield. Seeing how I'm the one with the ambulance, I guess that elects me to the position."

"The army isn't a democracy ruled by elections."

Gwyn rolled her eyes. "Then I gave into my moral obligation and conscience to help those in need without a thought to my personal safety."

"Precisely. Personal safety. When was the last time you had rifle training?"

"Around the same time they allowed me to vote."

William's eyebrows clashed together like culminating thunderclouds. "You're making a mockery of this grave situation."

"Do you see me laughing about it?" Gwyn sighed and dug the toe of her boot into the dirt. Thank goodness she'd rebuffed Cecelia's insistence on packing the dainty heeled ones with silver buckles. "I've always longed for a new adventure. Somewhere no one else has ever been. In future, I'll be careful what I ask for."

The spots of undiluted anger faded from his skin. Squatting in front of her, his gaze pierced her with unfathomable sadness. "You never asked for a press gang into the army."

"No, but it's too late to send me back now. I'd be a sitting duck, and you'd be without an ambulance. So, here we are. Together for the time being."

"Aye, here we are, and here most of my men will stay." He gouged his fingers into the ground, splaying them wide. "Many of them will be dead in a few hours."

"You can't think that way."

He pulled his fingers from the dirt and pointed to the earthen banks on either side of the road leading to Trônes Wood. Craters dotted the surrounding blackened fields. "This place bears the scars from mere weeks ago. I cannot afford to lie to myself. And neither should you."

"You think I'm just another silly girl with romantic notions floating in my head of bravery and mending wounded soldiers. Maybe that's partly true." She picked at a tear on her knee. Jagged fingernails caught the loosening threads. Filthy and unkempt, she must look a sorry mess. Not that William had said a word about her appearance, but she couldn't imagine he didn't wish for her to run a comb through her hair like any normal girl would. A girl like Cecelia.

"I've never once thought you silly. Headstrong and idealistic, perhaps."

"When I was very young, I found several newspaper clippings from Nellie Bly's trip around the world. Thinking I could do the same, I built myself a hot air balloon from my mother's pantaloons. I didn't accept defeat then, and I won't cave to it now."

"Between you and me, I'd be disappointed if you did."

His words pricked her calmness as they continued their march closer to the edge of Trônes Woods. Why did he always say the most unexpected things when she needed to keep him at arm's length? Her eagerness to not disappoint him hit her like a loaded-down lorry. Since touching foot on war-torn soil, her eyes had opened wide. Then he came along and upended everything she thought she knew about herself.

As the deep blue of twilight settled in the sky, columns of men stretched before her like restless snakes as they stopped for a brief repose. William passed between the lines, pressing a hand to a shoulder here, giving a nod there. The men straightened a bit after he passed them, summoning one final ounce of strength from somewhere deep within. He had found the secret to pulling the impossible from them.

"Get in a spat, did you?" Rosie shifted her weight as Captain Morrison plopped on the seat next to Gwyn. "With Will, I mean. He's as prickly as a cat pushed in the river. I've known him since university, and only two kinds of people make him that way. Seeing how his old man ain't here, my guess is it's you."

Gwyn shifted her gaze to his muddy boot prints all over her floor. "Do you not have troops to inspire?"

"Nope." He propped one ankle atop the opposite knee. "That's Will's calling. See how well he does it? Why would I want to disturb that?"

So you're not disturbing me. She turned away from staring at the boot prints.

"It's a shame Miss Cecelia couldn't join you. Not that you're unpleasant to gaze upon. Far from it, but I prefer blondes. The dark hair, that's more for Will."

Gwyn smoothed back the hair over her ear. Her finger snagged a knot. Frowning, she tugged, but it refused to yield. What she wouldn't give for a mirror. She'd zealously ripped them from each auto as a precaution against reflections at night. William may prefer dark hair, but surely he didn't want it resembling a sheep's coat caught in the briars. Given his penchant for impeccable uniforms, he'd want it perfectly pinned back. She sighed and dropped her hand from the snarls. Smooth hair was overvalued.

"Does she ever ask about me?"

Captain Morrison's voice pulled her back to the grit before them. "Other than how could you possibly consume a week's worth of rations in one sitting?"

"I did no such thing. The cook said she liked to see a man eat, so I ate." His face scrunched. "Have you heard her compliment my Oxford vocabulary, or my charming demeanor, my stylish good looks, or that I can tango better than any Argentinian?"

"Sadly, she omitted your tango abilities."

He slapped the seat. "That's it. As soon as we return from the woods, I'm organizing a party with punch, canapés, and a full orchestra that will allow me to sweep her off her pretty little feet once and for all."

"Cecelia is very busy with her nursing duties, so I doubt she has much time to be swept off her feet, wonderful party or not."

He rubbed a hand along his smooth chin. Somehow, he was the only man without a smudge on his face. "Are you sure it's not because she has an eye for Will? Or is it because we're nearly the same height? I can add a bit to my heels if that's her only qualm."

"I hardly feel at liberty to discuss the matters of another woman's heart, particularly her preferred heel height."

"You're dodging my question."

"Yes, I am."

"You're also dodging all my mentions of Will, though why I'm speaking of such a strapping man to the only girl in miles is beyond me."

A smile pulled at Gwyn's lips. "Perhaps the miles slack your standards, even for dark hair."

"You are hardly a slack in standards, Miss Ruthers. Quite the opposite." Grabbing her hand with a flourish, he raised it to his lips for a loud kiss.

"Hard at work, I see." William leaned against her open door, his lips pressed into a thin line.

Heat burned its way across Gwyn's face as she pulled her hand back.

"Morale is important, old chap," Captain Morrison said, not the least bit ruffled. "Every troop deserves a moment of the commander's time. And that includes our lovely driver."

"Captain Morrison was just practicing his charm until he can put it to good use on the fluttering hearts back home," Gwyn said. "He seems to think I'm an adequate substitute, which is hardly the case."

William's face didn't budge. "Perhaps he could go work his charms on the cook. The man needs a little encouragement."

"Encouragement and three crocks of butter sprinkled with sugar wouldn't help that man, but I'll do my best." Morrison eased himself off the seat. "Farewell, beautiful lady. I leave you in the hands of a surlier companion."

"Is he always like that?" Gwyn asked as Morrison walked away. From his gait, one would think him strolling in Hyde Park and not the perimeter of a battlefield.

"The heat's made him worse." William picked at a dried mud flake along the doorjamb. The dried brown curled under his nail and flitted to the ground. "What were you talking about?"

You, and how I can't properly think anymore. "Disappointments and avoidance."

"Oh." He scratched a ding where the windscreen was normally attached. "I've been meaning to come back here and check on you, but we've been having a few problems with the supply cart getting stuck in the ruts."

"Rosie can help pull it out."

"If it gets stuck again, I'll take you up on that offer."

In the fading light, she could barely discern his features from the shifting shades behind him, but she was vividly aware of his every breath, each twitch of his fingers, each shift of his shoulders. With the flickering gun lights shooting just below the clouds in the distance, she knew the rapids were not long off.

"You never told me if you made it."

Gwyn jumped at his voice. "Pardon?"

"Your trip around the world. With Nellie Bly."

He did listen. "The last I heard, Miss Bly is covering the war from Austria. She may have traded her traveling for a reporter's notepad, but I'm not giving up. I'm still trying."

"Not with pantaloons I hope."

"No, next time I'll have a different mode of transportation and a pilot's license to make it official."

"Are they allowing women to fly? That came out wrong. I mean to say, it's rare to hear of a female pilot."

"A few daring ladies have made names for themselves up in the big blue sky. They hop around the world visiting exciting locations. The Stinson school is one of the few offering to teach women, on the condition that they be healthy and unmarried. Hopefully, once the war ends, they'll move me from the waitlist to the attendance roster." She grinned and patted Rosie affectionately on the dash. "For now, this trusty old girl gets the job done."

"She's soldiering on quite well. Much better than my supply carts."

A thrill of pride shot through Gwyn. "It's all in how you talk to her. She likes to know she's doing a good job."

"She is doing a good job. Much better than I gave her credit for."

"You didn't think she could do it?"

His fingers tapped a steady beat against the roof. "I had my reservations, very hefty ones I might add, but she's proven me wrong at a number of turns."

Gwyn's palms prickled at the pause in his voice. "In future, you shouldn't judge a book before you've read it. Or in this case, a car you've never driven."

"A car … yes." He kicked his foot against the front tire. "Are you doing well, Gwyn? I need to know you're all right."

She clasped the steering wheel, fighting the urge to calm his agitated fingers. "I'm managing. Once you get past the bottled chicken and beef tea, things aren't quite so bad. They could do with a spot of milk, though."

He snorted. "And lose the boiled leather taste? Never. I've been eating it for so long that I've learned to swallow without much chewing."

"Did your father teach you that trick?" As soon as the words left her mouth, she regretted them. "I mean … I'm sure it was the army that forced you into such a habit."

"No, you were right the first time." He drew a deep breath and exhaled it. "My father prepared me from birth for my calling. Right down to eating hardtack and sleeping in the rain. It's what's expected of me."

"What's expected of us isn't always what we want." The disparaging voices tapped her memory, eager to break in and tear apart the stronghold she'd struggled to build since coming to France. "If you could do something else—anything in the world—what would it be?"

Oh, how she wished she could see his face. The deep V between his brows, the strong lips pressed into a line, the light blue eyes deepened in thought. She wondered if anyone had asked him before.

She prodded when he remained silent. "I bet it has something to do with horses. Starting a ladies' riding school, perhaps?"

"You could be my first pupil. That is if you could forgo your horseless carriages long enough."

"You must admit they've been rather handy lately."

"I'll give you that, but even if they sprout wings, they will never equal the thrill of riding on the back of a horse with hooves pounding like thunder."

"Until they throw you."

He chuckled. "It wouldn't be my first time flat on the ground."

"Then why would you choose such a temperamental beast?"

"I might ask you the same question about ol' tin Lizzie, who you left on the side of the road."

"Lizzie doesn't bite. She merely belches black smoke in my face when in second gear."

Their laughter mingled together on the warm night air. For the first time in the blurred stretch of days she'd been stranded at the Front, the tension ebbed from her weary bones. For just that moment, she wanted to imagine that all was right with the world and with the man next to her. Tomorrow's tragedies could wait.

"Will!"

Morrison's voice rang out in the dark. The soldiers' shuffling and murmurs grew still as he pushed past them, almost ramming into Rosie's bonnet.

"Calm down, man, before you alert the entire countryside of our position," William said.

"They need us," Morrison huffed. "They need us now. The Scots Fusiliers are getting pushed back into the southeastern corner. High command wants the woods taken at all costs. They're giving us two days to get ready."

CHAPTER 13

German artillery screamed from their firing positions on the high ground near Longueval, drowning William's voice as he and Gwyn stood at the edge of Trônes Woods. He leaned forward and shouted. "No! You'll stay here as instructed."

"I'm here to do a job. I can't do that stuck in the back."

"You're in the back for safety. The wounded will be brought to you."

"And you think the men can find me through all that jungle?" Gwyn pointed at the tangle of deep green stretching before them. Gunfire crackled like lightning between the leaves. "They'll be dead before they can clear the underbrush."

"And if I allow you to tramp around in that underbrush, you'll be dead." William didn't budge. After a night of arguing, she'd stood her ground, but he could see the strain starting to crack her. "How do you propose to carry men loaded down with fifty-pound packs all by yourself over such wooded terrain with enemy fire overhead?"

"I'd find a way."

"Illogical stubbornness. If you want to do your job and do it properly, you'll stay where they know to find you."

Where I know to find you.

Expecting another assault, he stood with feet braced apart and fists planted on his hips. Most women would have cried themselves into a ball by now, but not this one. She'd subjected herself to the same torture as seasoned soldiers without one uttered word of complaint. At least not a complaint of discomfort. She had more than enough complaints about him and his so-called high-handed ways.

Shells shrieked, splintering a copse of ancient trees to sticks a mere fifteen yards to their left. Grabbing Gwyn, William tucked her head under his arm and pulled her around to the back of the ambulance. He'd marched his men into a death trap, but their orders were to take the woods at all cost.

William's heart hammered in his chest, each beat determined to keep the woman in front of him from adding to the bloody count. At all cost.

Uncurling from under his arm, she pushed a long, dark strand of hair behind her ear and nodded. "Very well. But if those men can't find me, then you better believe I'm not going to sit on my hands while they die out there."

If he tied her to the hood now, she'd be of no use to anyone. "If the worst happens, you need to find General Haig or General Ivor Maxse. Don't hide, don't wait. Run. Do you understand?"

"Yes, yes." She flipped her hand through the air.

He grabbed it. "That's an order, Gwyn."

The defiance slipped from her eyes, softening the lines around her lips. For just a moment, a soldier's parting indulgence, he allowed himself to imagine what they tasted like.

"Be safe, William. Please." Her fingers curled around his. With a light squeeze, her hand fell back to her side.

Snatching his revolver from its leather holder, William turned from her and dove into the woods exploding with bullets. Each step erased Gwyn further and further from his mind. If he was going to survive this, and with her in tow, he needed all focus straight ahead.

"Sir! Sir! Captain!" A second lieutenant nearly bowled him over. "They've got snipers in the brush. Picking our men off like chatts on a dog."

"How many men so far?"

"Ten I've seen, sir. At least a dozen others bleeding out."

Curse it all. With impenetrable clumps of trees, roots, and rocks bulging under every fallen leaf—and now snipers—there was no way the wounded stood a chance. How were they supposed to make it back through this hornet's nest?

Grenades blasted feet away. William dove to the ground as dirt and tree bark splattered across his back. Warm stickiness ran down his cheek. He rubbed a hand over the trail before it could drain into his mouth. Red.

No one stood a chance against this.

Men scrambled from the woods like frenzied ants, their mouths opened wide and moving, but Gwyn had long ago stopped hearing their shouts amidst the pounding of artillery. The earth shook as she stumbled around the car in search of the first aid kit. Her feet struck something solid. A man, face down. Another one. Gone before she even had time to notice him, or the blond streak of hair poking out from under his helmet.

Her heart stuttered. *Oh, God. Oh, God, please no.*

Dropping to her knees, she rolled him over and gasped with relief. Lifeless brown eyes in an unfamiliar face stared up at the bright blue sky. Shame engulfed her. Though he wasn't the man who clouded her mind, he didn't deserve this fate.

Gently, she closed his eyes and folded his hands over his chest, then checked his haversack for supplies. Half a roll of linen and two aspirin tablets. She tucked the precious finds in her pocket before resuming her search for the missing kit.

The ground quaked, tilting the world sideways. Gwyn grabbed hold of Rosie to steady herself. Those Germans got better and better with each aim. Soon they could—no, she wouldn't think about that. One second, one man at a time. Her fingers dug into the hot metal, Rosie's paint chipping beneath her fingernails. William was still out there.

A bear of a man in a Highland kilt emerged from the blasted tree line. His barrel chest puffed in and out as he hefted a rifle in his gashed hands. His frantic eyes scanned the area and stopped on her. His bloodied lips moved, but no sound came from them.

Running forward, he skidded to a halt in front of her. Again his mouth moved, but she heard nothing. A blast several feet away shot dirt flying into the air. Gwyn ducked, covering her head from the filthy rain.

"Medic!" The man grabbed her shoulders and stuck his face inches from hers. "Medic!"

The man's thick brogue flooded in Gwyn's ears in one mighty crash. "Yes, that's me!"

"I've got lads wounded bad in the brush, ma'am. They're bleeding out all over."

"Can you get them here, into the clearing?"

"No, ma'am. I canna drag them by myself. Please, ma'am. You've got to come."

Gwyn's heart twisted. If she left now, the incoming wounded would have no one waiting for them, but all the wounded needed her. No matter what William demanded, she couldn't ignore the cries of desperation. "I don't have many supplies left. We'll have to get creative."

A bulky Adam's apple bobbed under the Scot's red scruff. "Follow me, ma'am. And keep your head down."

Streaks of blood smeared nearly every twig and leaf as Gwyn followed him into the woods. British and German bodies littered the brown floor, their dying wails piercing the gunfire. Gwyn pressed a hand to her mouth. Her eyes watered against the thick smoke as it choked her lungs, but they pushed further into the heart of raging battle. Mighty oaks whittled down to toothpicks by charging bullets. Scorched earth sagged beneath each footstep.

"Here, ma'am," the man said, ducking under a snarl of tree limbs. "Watch your head, now."

Gwyn lowered her head, but not enough. Gnarled twigs snagged her hair, yanking it at the scalp. She jerked at the tangled strands, desperate to free herself before a sniper spotted her. Why hadn't she followed Eugenie's lead and cropped the curls?

"Where are the men?" She pulled the last few hairs free.

The soldier hunkered down and brushed away handfuls of fallen leaves. Three men lay still as death beneath them. Pulling out what limited supplies she had left in her kit, Gwyn went to work.

Sweat poured down her face, stinging her eyes and leaving them blurry as she tried to wipe away their excess blood. Practiced memory guided her hands as she worked, bullets zinging all around like angry bees punching into the trees and dirt.

"The Lord is my shepherd ..." One of the boys whispered as his hands clenched tight over his gaping middle. "He makes me lie down in green fields."

Gwyn tried to move his hands away, but he held fast.

"I walk through the valley of death." His eyes turned bright and glassy. "Can you see it, miss? The table He's prepared for me?"

"I need to look at your wound. You must move your hands. Please," Gwyn said.

He smiled crookedly. It must have warmed his mother's heart many a time. "I go to dwell in my Father's house. Do you know it?"

Gwyn bit the inside of her lip. She nodded.

Red bubbles frothed at the corner of his mouth. "Sure will be nice to rest after this."

Tears burned her eyes. "Rest is good."

"Tell my mum ... tell her ..." Air hissed from the wound, deflating his chest. He moved no more.

Gwyn swiped her ragged sleeve at her streaming eyes and nose. She turned to the remaining men with determination. "We'll have to use their jackets and belts for makeshift stretchers. Keep the leaves over the wounds."

Binding up the men as best they could, Gwyn and the Scottish sergeant loaded them onto the makeshift litters and began the slow retreat back through the woods. A tree, upright when they entered the woods, now blocked their path.

"We canna get around it," the sergeant said. "We'll have to go over."

Blessed thing she hadn't worn some cumbersome skirt. Gwyn stepped over the log and lifted the first wounded man's head over. Her arms spasmed under the weight. "Help me get his legs over. And watch that jagged bark."

"Halt! Wo sie sind!"

Gwyn's heart lodged in her throat. Two Germans with rifles pointed at them stepped from behind a tree.

"Setzte ihn ab." One of them made a lowering motion with the tip of his rifle.

Carefully, Gwyn and the Scot lowered the wounded man to the ground.

"Gun." The German pointed to the rifle on the sergeant's back. "Drop."

The soldier slipped the rifle strap off his shoulder, but he didn't let it go. The Germans yelled, pointing to the ground. The soldier shook his head.

One of the Germans marched to Gwyn. He pulled a pistol from his belt and pressed it against the side of her head. The cold metal sent fear slicing down her shaking body. She choked back a sob.

The Highlander's eyes swerved to hers. Tears streamed down her face in a silent plea. Pressing his lips into a white line, he dropped the rifle.

Without blinking, the other German raised his rifle and shot both wounded men. The sob clamored from Gwyn's throat.

Ripping the belts from the makeshift litters, the soldier jerked Gwyn's arms behind her back and wrapped the leather around her hands, yanking it tight. He poked his rifle tip into the tender spot of her spine, prompting a cry of pain. Her feet stumbled over the torn earth and broken bodies as they trudged back through the decimated forest. To the German line.

CHAPTER 14

Tiny feet scurried in the corner. Another rat coming to inspect its new chamber mates. Gwyn leaned her head against the basement wall and closed her eyes. She didn't need to see it. After the last ten, they all started to look alike.

"Bloody rocks. Digging into me back." MacDonald, the soldier she had been captured with, sat next to her and rubbed his spine. "Canna sleep either, lass?"

Her first hours after the Germans threw her in the cellar, she'd barely been able to breathe, what with fear squeezing her lungs. Exhaustion soon numbed the despair that had become her reality in a matter of hours. "Can anyone really?"

The Scot hooked a thumb at the snoring men next to him. "Two years of artillery firing over your head and hunkering down in bog holes, this is pure heaven to some."

"I'd hate to see the other places."

"My old platoon," he chuckled. "Drillmaster had eyes blacker than coal and carried Auld Hornie's pitchfork to be sure. Dinna worry, he got blown back to the hole he crawled from first day on the Somme."

"Oh, my."

Scratching a thick hand through the red whiskers on his cheek, he sucked in a lungful of air. "Least it smells better in here."

"Mr. MacDonald, I believe you've been in the trenches far too long if you enjoy the smell of moldy stone and unwashed men."

"And I say you dinna know stench or appreciate the sweet release from it until you've spent muddy months dug in with over two hundred Highlanders. You've never hated the smell of wet sheep so much."

"Keep the blithering down," a man growled from where he tossed and turned in the corner. "Give a man some peace."

"Watch your tongue, you boggin' mule. 'Tis a lady present."

"She don't belong down here."

The Scot curled his massive fists and turned to the man. "Well, she is here, and I'll give you this one time to not say another word about it."

Panicked about the damage his one hand could cause, Gwyn touched MacDonald's shoulder. "Please. Everyone's temper is short down here. It's best not to exacerbate it."

"I'll beat down every last one of them who dares to blink at you wrong." With a mighty huff, he settled back. "Been at war so long men forget how to act around a woman, but I tell you true, it sure is nice to see one again."

"I don't know what kind of women you're accustomed to seeing, but I highly doubt I qualify as something pleasant-looking at the moment."

"Lass, I'm not picky these days. A mule smiled at me last week, and it was the happiest moment since my da bought me my first wee dram." He slapped his bare knee. "Listen to me. Going on about pubs in front of a lady. Me mam would box my ears if she found out. Apologies, lass. This war—"

"That's the first time someone's accused me of being a lady." She scoffed, folding her knees in front of her. "I was born in a tiny room above a garage. A chauffeur's daughter, nothing more."

"A garage is nothing to snub your nose at. Good honest job, driving, even if it is for the highborns."

"Oh, I'm not ashamed of it by any means. I'm quite proud my father can stand on his own feet."

"Something he's taught you to do, eh? Not many girls jump at the chance to go to war."

A dry laugh crackled between Gwyn's lips. "Yes, and look where it's got me."

"I heard about you, you know. Word spreads fast when there's a skirt near the Front. Trench Angel they call you. Bet that's an interesting story."

Gwyn picked at the threadbare material covering her knees. "It's not so interesting. Just a simple girl wanting more from her simple life. Seems curiosity got the better of me, and I fell down a rabbit hole thanks to a flat tire."

"Like Alice. Minus the tire."

More tiny feet scuttled in the corner. Whoever the new visitor was, he'd brought friends this time. "Are you a great reader, Mr. MacDonald?"

He waved a dismissive paw in the air. "Never had the patience to learn all those squiggly lines, too many things to fish in the village loch. But my sister always had her nose in a book, and I'd beg her to read to me every night about giants and trolls, knights and dragons."

Where was their knight now, to come and rescue them from the pit? What would William say when he discovered she'd been captured? Maybe he'd been right all along. Maybe she should have stayed home where it was safe. The fear she'd battled so hard to keep down tremored through her chest. She took a deep breath to keep it at bay, but the action awoke her stomach. It growled like a dog fighting for its bone.

She pressed a hand against her middle to stop the rumbles. "If they want to kill us, they certainly picked the slowest method possible."

MacDonald scratched the shaggy hair around the back of his neck. Chatts. Another slow method of torture. "If they'd wanted us dead, then they would've done it by now. If we're lucky, we'll be in for a prisoner exchange. Until then, get comfortable."

"You seem calm about the prospect. Have you been a prisoner before?"

"Aye. Near Spion Kop in South Africa. You can't imagine the heat. Then my da was captured the first time we fought in that desert land, and his da before him somewhere in Persia. We're a long line of survivors, we Highland MacDonalds."

Tall and thick-shouldered, with bulky arms, matted red hair, and a gashed nose, Gwyn had no trouble imaging the lineage of his wild race clamoring from the high crags with their battle axes raised. "Your line of tenacity serves you well. Sometimes I wonder if any of us will survive this war."

His chest swelled on a heavy sigh. "Most of the lads had a target painted on them afore they even left home. Like young Grovers. Thank you for trying to help him, though in the end, it did him nay good."

Grovers. Gwyn couldn't forget his boyish face turned hopefully to heaven. Peace on his dying lips. Would she have such peace at her last moment? Would she fall into the Almighty's embrace or pitch into darkness?

"Did you no good either," MacDonald continued. "Look how low I've brought you. In a stinking pit with stinking men. I should never have asked you to come with me."

"You sought medical help. There's no shame in that."

"From a woman, I sought help. And a braw job you did. A braw job. But you don't deserve to be here, and I'll never live the shame down."

"If I recall, you didn't twist my arm."

"But you hesitated. You knew it wasn't right."

Guilt flashed in her chest as William's last words thundered in her head. "I only knew it wasn't right to leave a man in need. What's done is done."

He sighed wearily. "Aye, done."

Footsteps pounded across the floor above them, shaking dust from the rafters. A key turned in a rusty lock at the top of the stairs leading down into their pit. More cellmates? Gwyn's pulse quickened. Her stomach roared. Perhaps some bread and water?

Boots thumped down the stairs and paused on the last one. A head peered over the rail. "Medic!" he barked in heavily accented

English.

Gwyn's pulse skipped an unsteady beat. MacDonald laid a heavy hand on her arm.

"Medic." The guard stepped down to the floor. He peered around at the sleeping men until his gaze stopped on her. He motioned her forward with one hand. "Come."

She started to rise, but MacDonald's grip tightened. The guard took a step forward, reaching for the holster at his side. "Come," he said. "You help now."

"It's all right, Mr. MacDonald," she whispered, unlatching his fingers. "I don't think they want to hurt me. His commander probably has a scraped finger."

"If that's true, make sure it festers," MacDonald whispered, cracking his knuckles in the guard's direction.

The guard led her up the stairs, then down a series of long halls on the first floor, up a short flight of stairs, another hall lined with oil paintings of finely dressed gentlemen, and finally to a door tucked in the back corner of the building. Yellow light gleamed under the door crack. Pushing it open, she was greeted by a soldier's back. Her guard said something and stepped aside.

Gwyn blinked several times to adjust to the garish lantern light. As the dancing spots faded in her eyes, she scanned the tiny bare room and focused on the chairs positioned in the middle with two bedraggled men tied to them.

She gasped.

"William!"

No. If he closed his eyes and opened them again, she would be gone. A figment of his exhausted imagination. William squeezed his eyes shut—wishing he had the use of his hands to rub the grit away—and opened them. There she stood.

Eyes wide and jaw hanging down, Gwyn hadn't expected to see

him either. She took a step inside, body poised to rush forward. To him. A move that the Germans would gladly intercept.

"Nurse." William stopped her before she could give away their connection. "What a shame to see you here."

Her brow dipped in confusion. "And you, Captain," she said with the same formality. "I can only assume I've been brought in for medical reasons."

William nodded his head to the left. "Captain Morrison was razed by a slug. Lost a bit of blood."

Roland's head lolled towards him. "I'm fine."

William frowned. "Is that why you're slurring worse than a sailor on leave?"

"I'm shot, Will. See how well you talk after that."

Gwyn spun to the soldier behind her. "This man is wounded. Why is he bound?"

The German guard shouted a garble of words and shoved Gwyn on the shoulder. With a look that could curdle milk, she stepped away from him and knelt in front of Roland. Without a word, she ripped open his trouser leg to expose the wound. And sniffed it.

"What are you doing?" Roland jerked away from her, but the ties held him tight.

"Smelling is the best way to test for an infection," Gwyn said. "Thankfully, you don't smell like cheese."

"Well, that's a relief." Roland sighed. "Never was a cheese man myself. Upsets the digestion."

"It needs to be cleaned, wrapped tight, and changed every few hours." She turned back to the guard. "I need supplies. Bandages."

The guard replied in German, but Gwyn shook her head and repeated her order. Again the guard spoke in German.

"He doesn't understand you," William said. Why hadn't he paid better attention during his language classes instead of drawing pictures of horses in the back of his lesson books?

"Surely he's not completely daft. It's obvious what I need." She pointed at Roland and made a wrapping motion around his leg.

The guard yelled to someone in the hall. Minutes ticked by before a brown sack was thrown into the room.

Gwyn rummaged to the bottom of the bag. "Seems they're not much better off than we are with supplies, but at least they have Lysol swabs."

Her fingers tugged at the leather straps around Roland's wrists. Face scrunching in concentration, she dug her thumb under a knot and wiggled it to make an opening. "I'll have you a tad more comfortable in a jiffy."

The guard leaped forward and snatched her hands away. *"Ihn nicht berühren!"*

William strained against his bindings as angry red finger marks bruised her wrist. "Touch her again like that, and it'll be the last thing you ever do, *Gefreiter*."

The guard mottled purple as his hand flew to his rifle. Contempt flashed in his eyes.

"Go ahead." William dropped his gaze to the rifle. "We'll see what your commanding officer thinks when you've bloodied two prisoner captains without his order."

"Enough. Taunting him won't help our cause." Gwyn rubbed her wrist. "The issue at hand is Captain Morrison. I can still clean the wound with him bound."

She bent her head to the task, swabbing, wiping, and dabbing while Roland made pathetic noises through clenched teeth.

Black and purple ringed her eyes, dulling their green brilliance. Somewhere she'd found a string to tie back her dark hair, but thick pieces had wriggled loose to flop over her brow and ears. How long had she been here? And how had the Germans found her? William cursed himself. He should have tied her to the hood of her ambulance when he'd had the chance.

"Done." She wiped her hands on a small swath of unused bandage and turned to him. "Now let's see about that gash on your cheek."

William turned away from her reaching hand. "It's nothing. A scratch." A scratch from landing on a pile of rocks when he was shoved in the back of the head with a Mauser rifle.

"A scratch with dried blood," she said. "I'll clean it before it gets infected and heals with a nasty scar."

Heat rushed in his veins at her soft touch. Gentle as the kiss of the wind, she cleaned the area, never once meeting his eyes. Probably for the best. One glance and she'd see how the astringent stung like bees on fire.

He dropped his voice. "Have they mistreated you?"

"I'm a prisoner of war, Captain. Not a guest at the Savoy. But no, I've not been mistreated." Her gaze flitted to meet his. Desperation leaped from her eyes. "The men below need food and better care. Some of their wounds are festering."

"Men? And they've kept you below with them?" The ropes cut into his wrists as he clenched his fists to stay under control. "How many of them are there?"

"Eight."

"Ranks?"

Her hands stalled for the first time. "Mostly enlisted, and two lieutenants, I believe. I have trouble remembering what all those stripes and stars amount to."

Rocking back on her heels, she took quick inventory from his face to his feet. Discomfort wriggled down his spine at her inspection of his pathetic appearance.

Boots scuffled outside before the door sprang open. Major Trommler sauntered into the room, a twist to his thin lips. The spotless uniform hung limp on his skinny bones, and his straight black hair was slicked back into a high shine. William doubted the man had seen one day of combat.

"Ah, the nurse has arrived. *Wunderbar*." Trommler circled his prisoners, each footstep creaking the floorboards. "How convenient to have such an angel patch you up. Is it not, Captain Morrison?"

Roland blinked hard as his head rolled to the side. "I'd take a hairy-armed monkey if he knew what he was doing, but a girl is nice too."

Trommler clapped a hand on William's shoulder. "And you, Captain Crawford? What do you think of our angel?"

"Nurse Ruthers has done a fine job." William resisted the urge to sink his teeth into the man's pale knuckles.

"You've met the *fraulein* before?"

William didn't dare glance down at Gwyn as his mind raced. "Nurse Ruthers was assigned to my unit, but she is not military affiliated. She is a civilian, and therefore, I ask that she be released without—"

"She was found aiding British soldiers. Civilian or not, I cannot allow her to roam free."

"With all respect, Major, she doesn't deserve to be here. Especially not kept alone in some hole with a group of soldiers."

Trommler's thin eyebrows rose. "Are you saying your men lack honor?"

"My men are trained with the highest degree of loyalty and service, but men are men. It is for Miss Ruthers' sensibilities that I request she be moved to private quarters."

Stopping behind Gwyn, Trommler's small eyes bored into the back of her head. William sensed the battle in the man's head. If he granted the request, he'd be giving into a prisoner's demands, but if he sent her back to the slums, then this honor he talked about would be turned to mud.

"*Fraulein* Ruthers, do you find your quarters unbearable, as the good Captain has pointed out?"

Gwyn's hands knotted the knees of her trousers. "I would not keep my worst enemy in such conditions."

"You would like to be removed from them."

Standing to a height that forced the major's chin up, she leveled him with a gaze that could cripple most brass in their boots. "I wish to remain with the men because when our troops smash through your lines and march into Longueval, I want to make it easy for them to find all of us in one place."

Trommler's head reared back. His mouth opened and closed like a fish. With trembling fingers, he smoothed the gold buttons down his tunic until they calmed. "Brave words, *mein lieber*. Perhaps you should have been in uniform after all." Snapping his fingers, he brought one of the guards to his side. "*Feldwebel*, our lovely guest wishes to return to her holding cell."

The guard grabbed Gwyn by the shoulder and shoved her to the door.

"Oh, and *Fraulein*," Trommler said. "If you should need anything, don't hesitate to keep it to yourself."

It took every ounce of willpower for William to not tear through his bindings and run after her. A boot in a Jerry's face would win him no grace with the commander, so he sat with blood pounding in his ears louder than a battery of guns.

Trommler grabbed a chair from the corner and dragged it to sit in front of his captives. With excruciating slowness, he propped one booted foot atop the opposite knee and brushed away all wrinkles from his jacket before turning a half sneer to William.

"And now that I've had my cigarette and coffee, and you've been nicely cleaned up, we can continue with our questions."

CHAPTER 15

An odorous wall of soiled clothes, unwashed men, and mold hit William in the face as soon as the basement door swung open. His stomach churned, the back of his throat longing to gag. And this was where they kept her.

"Next time keep your mouth shut, Will." Roland grumbled behind him as they eased their way down the rotting stairs. "As officers, they may have kept us upstairs. With fresh air."

"They've already got one lieutenant and a woman down here. We're nothing special."

Wet coughing sounded in the dim space below. Shuffling and hushed voices. And scampering clawed feet.

"Captain Crawford?"

Gwyn.

His foot touched the stone ground. Dim morning rays peered in from a window cut high in the wall, highlighting the lounging figures on the floor. All eyes fixed on him, but he sought only one pair. A small shape moved from the corner, dwarfed by a hulking shadow.

"Welcome to our quarters, Captain," Gwyn said.

William checked himself before rushing forward to gather her in his arms and assure himself that she was well. Only with his arms around her would the fear of the past few hours be put to rest, and once he'd felt her warm and safe against his chest, he would shake the ever living daylights out of her for not staying by the ambulance as ordered. But all that would have to wait until the dozen pairs of eyes weren't trained on him.

Gwyn turned her attention to Roland. "Captain Morrison, I

see your leg is well enough to stand on."

"Hurts like the dickens," Roland muttered.

A snicker came from the shadow hovering behind Gwyn.

Roland's lips pinched. "Is there something funny, *Sergeant*?"

The shadow stepped forward, revealing a bear of a man with shaggy red hair dressed in a filthy Highlander's kilt and tunic. "I was just thinking you should swap injury stories with Duncan over there. He gets lonely with the only leg wound."

"Why don't you take a load off next to Duncan, Roland?" William gave his attention to the Scotsman. "What's your name, soldier?"

"Lieutenant MacDonald of the Second Battalion Royal Scots Fusiliers." He shrugged at the lack of stars on his shoulder. "I got a wee promotion when all my officers were killed the first day."

"And you're the man in charge now."

"No, sir. That's you."

"Oh. Oh, yes." Tension wrapped around William's neck. The cold, musty floor looked as inviting as a feathered quilt and pillows. Perhaps someday he could take that rest and let someone else hold the reins.

"William, come and sit down." Gwyn curled a hand around his arm. "Let me take a look at the scrape. It's been hours since I bandaged it."

William shook his head despite the pull of her warm touch. "I'd like to meet the men first. Take stock of the wounds and—"

"And wake them all when they haven't had a proper night's sleep? I'll make introductions for you later."

He allowed her to lead him to an unoccupied spot along the wall and sank wearily to the floor. As Gwyn prodded his cheek, he plied MacDonald with questions about his capture and their captors.

William forced his attention to remain on the report, but Gwyn's soft fingers dashed every intelligible word from his head. As they trailed down his jaw, he longed to lean into their touch and let them whisk him away to a far off place filled with the sweet scent of roses from when he first met her.

"Do you think the major will give us medical supplies?" Gwyn's voice jolted him back to the rank cell. "I can hardly see that he would. We're barely given enough food to keep the grumbling from our stomachs."

"I've eaten better during the Highland famines," MacDonald said.

William sighed and leaned his head back against the wall. The absence of her fingers left his skin cold. "He gave no formal reply, but I reminded him that if he wanted a prisoner exchange, then keeping us alive is in the best interest of his own captured."

"Bet he didna like hearing that."

William grimaced. "No, he didn't."

A moaning broke the quiet murmuring as a man struggled to sit up. Gwyn started to rise, but MacDonald waved her down.

"You've been awake the whole night. I'll see what he needs." He ambled away, leaving them alone.

Though she remained seated, her gaze followed the hulky man. Bands of tension twisted to the back of William's skull. "You follow his orders, but not mine."

"He looks more menacing than you."

"Perhaps I should grow a beard."

"You already are, though menacing isn't the word I'd use to describe it."

"How would you?"

A gleam sparked in her tired eyes. "Never you mind."

Something squeaked in the corner. William turned to find a scrawny brown mouse licking his tiny feet.

"We call him Fredrick," Gwyn said. "Wilhelm only comes out at night."

"You've named the vermin?"

She shrugged. "It took two days of voting before we all agreed. Gave us something to think about instead of no food and the awful smell."

"How did you get here in the first place? The Germans could not have pushed in so far to reach you at the ambulance." Dropping her gaze, she picked at the worn patches on her knees. Of course. "You didn't stay at the ambulance," he stated flatly.

"Men needed me." She lifted her face back up. "MacDonald said they—"

"MacDonald? He's responsible for you leaving your post and getting caught?" With more anger than he'd felt in months, William grabbed the wall to lever himself up.

Gwyn yanked him right back down. "In case you've forgotten, *Captain*, I am not one of your soldiers. I never swore an oath to obey your or any other military orders."

"While in the field, you are under my protection and supervision. I told you to stay by the ambulance."

"Men needed me."

"*I* needed you to stay put." He gripped his hands together to keep from reaching out and shaking sense into her. Did she not care for the worry she put him through? "They could have found you—not captured—by the ambulance."

"Well, I didn't stay there."

"Clearly."

"They would have died, William." Her jaw worked, tightening the muscles in her delicate neck. "They did die. The Germans … they found us."

The coughing, scratching, and whispering of the basement had stopped as the surrounding men leaned closer to William and Gwyn's conversation. William shifted his back to them for a small bit of privacy.

Gwyn blinked rapidly as tears crowded the corners of her eyes. The anger beating in William's veins dulled to a throb. He'd tried so hard to shield her from the harshness exploding around them, but she didn't like shields. She overthrew them at every turn.

He pressed the heels of his hands against his eyes, relieving the burning tiredness. He knew what was best and yet she refused to—his hands fell woodenly to his lap. He sounded exactly like his father. "You should never have had to see something like that."

She crossed her arms over her chest, turning her nose away from him. "Because I should never have left England in the first place, you mean to say."

Like an arrow to the bull's-eye. "There is that."

"Our country is at war. All hands needed at the wheel to win this, and my abilities can be of great use here. I could stay no more than you."

William grimaced as his father's parting words at the train depot came to him. "*Show them what you were made for, son. Don't blemish the Crawford name.*"

"I doubt that very much," he said.

"Back home, I'm forever being told what I should be, what I should do, and where I should go without the chance to change it. In my best interests for feminine comfort, it's said."

"Comfort doesn't sound so bad."

She snorted. "Try walking a day in my skirts."

He tugged the fabric encasing her leg. "Impossible these days."

She slapped his hand away. "Nothing is impossible, though you would look ridiculous."

"Tell that to the Highland regiments. They think they look quite ferocious, but don't call them skirts. My mother's uncle is from Inverness, and he took it rather personally when he was offered a pair of trousers to cover his bare knees." He hooked a thumb over his shoulder to where MacDonald hovered near a man with a makeshift sling. "I'd wager your bulldog bares a shiny shin from time to time."

"Don't you dare say a bad thing about Mr. MacDonald. He's been a true godsend keeping the men calm and comfortable."

"A godsend wouldn't have led you into capture," William muttered.

A drumroll of cannon fire shook the overhead rafters. The lads were taking a beating. Or what was left of them.

Gwyn picked up a pebble and rolled it between her fingers. "How long do you think we'll be down here?"

"Have somewhere else to be?"

"I don't like this new sour side of you. If you plan to keep it up, go find a new corner to sulk in." She threw the rock, bouncing it off the opposite wall.

"Apologies. Lack of sleep and food. To answer your question, I don't know. And I don't think Fritz knows either. General Haig is determined to take the woods at all costs, and the Germans are determined to hold it at all costs. And so, our stay. We're more valuable alive."

"The Germans may not feel that way." She raised a hand to stop his protest. "I may not have seen the sun for several days, but my eyes aren't so bad that I can't see the worry on every man's face here. Including yours. How strangely it's changed since the beginning."

"Changed? Granted it's been a while since I've seen a mirror."

"All of your faces. Mine too, I suppose. In the beginning, everyone said we would win and be home before Christmas. That was almost two years ago, and time has marched its heavy footsteps across each one of us."

"You should have been a writer with words like that."

She smiled, tired lines crinkling the corners of her eyes. "No. That requires sitting in one place for far too long."

"Not such a bad thing. Especially after this."

"Is that your plan?"

"My plan is escaping this place. The rest will happen in due course."

"But surely there's something you want to—"

The door at the top of the stairs squealed open, shooting each of William's nerves to the edge. Heavy boots stalked down the stairs. William threw his arm out, blocking Gwyn from the intruder.

"It's breakfast." Touching his hand, Gwyn pointed to the dark corner where Fred or Harry, or whatever that mouse's name was, scurried from his hole and sniffed the air.

Two large plates slid to the floor. The heavy boots stomped back upstairs.

William eyed the torn and half-eaten food bits on the tray. "This is all?"

"We get whatever they don't finish upstairs." She picked at a crust of toast. "I guess they weren't very hungry this morning."

Fury poured through William as he watched the men choose which crumbs to take. They couldn't all survive on this. They needed to get out of there. The sooner, the better.

CHAPTER 16

"Whoever has that hammer better knock it off." Gwyn threw her arm over her head, trying to block out the noise. "Ow!"

Struggling into a half-sitting position, she realized she'd elbowed William's knee. Her sleepiness vanished faster than an engine erupting in smoke. She'd been using him as a pillow.

"Those aren't hammers." He rubbed his knee.

Gwyn sat up. Pins and needles stung down the arm she'd been laying on. She tried stretching it but succeeded only in hitting William again. "Not hammers? Oh, the guns."

"Yes, guns. Do you mind stretching in the other direction? This entire side of my body is a bit sore."

She stopped mid-stretch. "You have more injuries you didn't tell me about?"

"I only got them last night."

"Last night? What were you doing last—oh." Numbness paralyzed her arm, dragging it down like dead weight. Yet the shame from her nighttime behavior flared with vitality. She'd snuggled up to him like a common trollop. And had the best night's sleep in close to a year. "You should have shaken me off."

"You're rather persistent when tired. I had no choice."

She smacked her forearm for a prickle of feeling to return. "Please stop. I don't need to hear any more about my ill-mannered sleeping habits."

Taking her arm, he massaged the sleepiness away. "Not even the dream where you ordered the entire battalion to dive off the coast of Africa in search of Atlantis?"

Warmth tingled beneath her skin, but not from the awakening blood. His thumb circled her elbow. "And did they?"

His brow scrunched. "I'm not sure. You found a rock digging in your side and flopped over."

"I never can find out the ending to a good dream." She stifled a yawn. "What time is it?"

"If I had to guess, near four in the morning."

Copper sparked in the several days' growth of the blond beard along his jaw. The irrepressible desire to run a finger over the stubble lifted her hand of its own accord. He flinched, then leaned into her touch.

His whiskers scratched the sensitive skin on her palm, the soft intake of breaths whispering between her fingers. Her heart pounded at what the small movement meant. The possibilities behind it. Possibilities she wasn't ready to meet or settle into.

Yet, William was far from settling. He was a man worth striving for.

"You'd look fine with a beard." She traced her fingers along his jaw. "A short one to lend a roguish air."

"I've never gone rogue a day in my life."

"I believe it." She brushed the stubble under his lip. He shivered. "All the more reason to do it. Live a little before you're an old man and these handsome blond whiskers have turned gray."

An easy smile stole over his face, erasing the deep worry lines. "Handsome, eh? Next, you'll have me in a dinner jacket with a rose clamped between my teeth."

"I prefer daisies, and for once I'd like to see you out of uniform without the weight of duty on your shoulders. Something not buttoned to your chin or gleaming with buckles."

"Afraid you'll be waiting a while for that pretty picture." A deep V creased his forehead as he glanced down at his rumpled jacket. The top three buttons gaped open, revealing a stained white shirt beneath. "Barring current circumstances."

"I'm patient."

He grinned. "All evidence to the contrary."

Gwyn's heart flopped over. Was it possible for him to be more devastatingly charming in a German prison than regally sitting atop a horse? "In this case, I'm willing to wait. Fair?"

The laughter in his eyes faded to smoky blue. He pulled a curl from behind her ear and wrapped it around his finger. "More than fair."

His husky tone stopped the air in her throat.

She panicked and moved her hand to the wound on his cheek. "This is looking better."

"I told you. Nothing more than a scratch." The hazy blue in his eyes disappeared. "Those guns are getting louder."

Gwyn dropped her hand back to her lap. Why did her fingers suddenly feel cold and useless? "Maybe they've brought in reinforcements."

William cocked his ear to the window. "They're not solely German, and the shots are in opposing directions."

"How can you possibly tell that?"

"Practice."

Of course. His father probably had a back garden full of artillery.

"Bleed my ears dry." Roland moaned on the other side of William. He sat up, rubbing his hands over his head. "Can't they call a truce for one night so a fellow can get a decent night's sleep?"

"We've brought in reinforcements," William said.

"The Scots? No, we'd hear those caterwauling pipes. The South Africans then. About time they put their noses in the fight."

Feet ran across the floor above them. Angry voices drifted down between the cracks.

"Whoever they are, they certainly have our keepers on edge." Gwyn shielded her eyes against the falling dust. "We might bust free of here before long."

William moved to stand below the window like a jungle cat sensing his surroundings. "Maybe. Maybe not. Something's not right."

"Of course something's not right." Roland smacked the ground next to him, waking several other men. "We're stuck down here in this festering hole while the world falls apart around our ears."

Spinning around, William leveled him with a narrow gaze. "I'd like a word with you in private, Captain."

"Private? Look around you, Will. There's nowhere to go."

William's shoulders tensed, his back ramrod straight. His mouth opened, but an explosion cut off any words. Screams ripped the outside air.

Another blast. And another. As quick as raindrops splatting to the earth. Gwyn covered her ears against the terror.

"Get down! Cover your heads!" William sprinted around the room, shoving men to the floor as splinters rained down from the beams overhead.

The men huddled together, those more able covering the severely wounded. Any second now the final blow could strike. Well, Gwyn wasn't ready to die like this.

She sprinted up the stairs and pounded on the door. "Let us out! You can't leave us here!"

William grabbed her arm and tried to haul her back down the stairs. "Get away from there."

She twisted in his grip. "I'm not staying here like a rat in a cage."

"Step outside that door, and you're guaranteed to have a mortar land right on you."

"Better that than crushed to death in a basement."

BOOM!

Rocks and shards cracked off the walls. A ceiling beam broke with an earsplitting crack and slammed into the bottom step, knocking Gwyn backward. Strong arms grabbed her and clutched her to a solid wall. William tucked her head into his chest, covering her with his arms. His heart beat wildly against her cheek, drowning out her own panic. If there was a good way to die, this was it.

The door banged open, and two Germans rushed down the

stairs, flattening William and Gwyn against the wall.

"*Aufzustehen! An den füßen!*"

Gwyn dug her fingers into William's jacket. "What are they saying?"

"I think they want us out."

Hope flared. "They're turning us loose?"

The guards grabbed the men's arms and shoved them to the stairs. The slower ones got rifles shoved in their backs. "*Aufstehen die treppe!*"

William took her elbow. "Just do what they want."

The hope of freedom died as more armed guards awaited them on the other side of the door. "*Außerhalb!*"

They grabbed her arms, yanking her away from William and dragging her down a long hall. Broken glass crunched under her feet, and thick smoke clogged her throat. Through the busted windows, she saw soldiers running, their faces streaked with terror.

"What's going on? Are those men retreating?"

Outside, the air choked with exploding gunpowder and screaming shells. Buildings crumbled, streets gaped with black holes, and trees had been blasted to stumps. All around them men ran as officers screeched their commands.

Her captor shoved her face-first against the building, pulling a long string of rope from his pocket and knotting it around her hands.

"No, don't." She tugged against the rope that cut into her skin. "Please, let me go. I'm of no use to you."

She twisted her head to see him. Cold steeliness darkened his gaze. Double-knotting her ties, he yanked the end to cinch it tight. Gwyn's teeth cut into her tongue as she bit back a cry of pain.

William, Roland, MacDonald, and four other prisoners were shoved against the wall next to her. Her captor made quick work of tying their hands to her leash.

She glanced down the line, counting each of them. Twice. "Where are the other men?"

William didn't look at her. Her stomach churned.

"William. Where are the other men?"

"Left behind."

The churning in her stomach turned sour. "We can't leave them."

"They're dead weight to the Germans."

"William—"

His fierce gaze pierced her. "Wherever they're taking us, the journey alone would kill them. Left here, they might stand a chance if our troops find them."

An argument tumbled over her tongue, but the hardness of his gaze stopped her cold. She swallowed against the tightness in her throat. Giving into the overwhelming sense of helplessness would do her no good now. Not with shells rupturing overhead.

"*Aufhören zu redden!*" The guard shouted in William's face, sending spittle everywhere. Grabbing the rope, he jerked them forward. "*In schritt. Marsch!*"

Sunlight cracked over the dim horizon as they marched with the retreating soldiers. Gwyn's feet dragged like lead as each step took them further away from the British line. Would anyone notice their absence? Would she see home again? During all her begging and planning to leave, she'd never told her father how much she loved passing the days with him in the garage. He often lamented that he never gave her the opportunity to grow up as a lady, but she told him that ladies never had any fun. He laughed so hard over that.

God, I know You're a little busy with both sides of opposition calling Your name at every turn, but if You could spare a moment for my small plight, I'd be grateful. Just a chance to see my father one last time. He deserves a better daughter than me, but he loves me anyway.

By late afternoon, she was almost rethinking her plea. Gray clouds heavy with rain did little to cut the stifling heat. Her aching body longed to drop alongside the road and never move again, but William's solid presence and steady footsteps behind her kept her spirit upright.

Her wrists were torn and bleeding as the weight and movement of the prisoners behind her pulled against their connected bindings. Glancing down at her stained and crusted clothes gave her no hope of wrapping her wounds in clean strips once they stopped. If they ever stopped.

"We should be close to their reserve line," William whispered. Despite the dragging miles, he sounded as fresh as a newly minted engine. "See those trees ahead?"

Throat ready to crack from lack of water, Gwyn merely nodded.

"It's where we should stop for a rest. Are you able to make it?"

"Of course I can. If there's a goal, I'll make it." Her feet screamed in protest, but she wasn't about to admit that to him or anyone else.

Heading so far north, they had to be close to the conquered Belgium border. The countryside bore the heavy marks of assault. Miles of fortified trenches crisscrossed the blackened fields. Deep tunnels dug in the earth like moles. The Germans had the clear advantage of time and position.

The trees grew into a thick line that extended well down a back ridge. Metal flashed between the green leaves and dense underbrush. William was right about the waiting troops, but all she could think about was sweet relief from the sweat pouring down her back.

Led over flimsy boards connecting the trenches, Gwyn tried to ignore the whispers from the German soldiers hunkered down in the pit. Hatred contorted their lean faces. The mumbling grew louder as they elbowed their comrades, pointing and spitting as Gwyn and her fellow prisoners trudged by. Curses stung her ears. She didn't understand the words, but their meaning was perfectly clear.

Crossing a shallow trench, a grimy hand snaked out and tugged on her trouser leg. Gwyn jumped. Her mouth opened to shriek, but her tongue seized in terror. She yanked her leg away, biting back the fear clawing at her throat. She kept her eyes forward, determined to not let them see her fear.

"*Hier. Hinsetzen.*" At the back of the maze of trenches, the guard pointed to a wide pit carved under a tree. "*Sitzen.*"

Gwyn peered down. It was large enough to hold several men and deep enough for them not to see out. Dried earthworms clung to blackened tree roots that rippled through the ground like bones. The rotting flesh and bark fouled the air. The fear clogging her throat rippled down her legs. She shuffled back. William's solid chest stopped her.

"It's all right," he whispered.

She shook her head.

"I'm right behind you." His calm voice stroked her nerves. "Go, or the guards will be more than happy to oblige us."

Taking a deep breath through her mouth, Gwyn edged into the pit. The ropes pulled as each man slipped down behind her. Once in the hole, the three men at the end of their chain plopped down, jerking the rope hard. Gwyn cried out as she toppled backward onto William's feet. Tangy blood sprang from where she bit her lower lip.

William dropped next to her and pulled her into a sitting position. Alarm etched his face as he cupped her chin in his hand. "Are you all right?"

"I'm fine."

He brushed his thumb over her cut. "You're bleeding."

"I've had worse when Lizzie slipped a gear on a corner."

"I've not a clue what that means, but I know it didn't involve trained men losing their nerve in front of a lady." He turned a withering glare to the culprits. "You men. Has all sense of training left you completely, or did the sun soften your heads? Apologize to the lady at once."

With heads down, the men mumbled their apologies.

"It's all right," Gwyn said. "Everyone is exhausted."

"Exhaustion is no excuse to lose one's bearing, prisoner or not."

Gwyn rolled her eyes and patted the ground next to her. "Let's rest before you decide on the courts-martial." Shifting his weight back and forth, William finally settled next to her. "Better?"

He grunted, casting another dark look to the end of the line. "Slightly. The bottom of my feet rubbed off about three miles back. I need to do a foot check."

"A foot check?"

"Every day, if conditions allow, I have my men remove their boots and socks to check for infection, blisters, and rot. Trench foot is more crippling to a force than bullets."

Gwyn glanced around their dirt-packed hovel and touched the stinging flesh of her wrists. "If there is an infection, we don't have a clean area or supplies to care for it."

Capturing her hands, he held them up for inspection. She tried pulling away, but he held fast. "You're so concerned about the welfare of others that you didn't tell me about your own injuries."

"No use discussing what can't be helped."

His fingers brushed over her sensitive skin. Warmth tingled down her arms, spreading into every aching hole she'd tried to bury under the need to prove herself. Except now, under his steady touch, she forgot exactly what she needed to prove.

"You haven't read about some ancient Celtic herb to heal rope burns, have you?"

Gwyn pulled away from her distracting thoughts and tried to focus. "If I did, the Celts could hardly help us from here."

"Maybe your trusty MacDonald has some stashed in a sporran." William cast an eye over his shoulder to where the hulking Scot squatted in front of the last man, doling out his own colorful reprimands. The longer he talked, the thicker his brogue rolled out. "Though if he's anything like my great-uncle, he'll only carry a flask and an extra round of shot."

"I'd like to meet your uncle."

"You won't be meeting him anytime soon. He's a notorious womanizer and older than the Wars of Independence."

Gwyn stretched her cramped legs, rolling her ankles back and forth. "And now I want to meet him even more. For the long life of history, not the trifling."

"Doesn't matter your intentions, his are completely dishonorable."

"Dishonor in your family? I don't believe it."

"My mother's side is a long line of miscreants and cattle rustlers. Perhaps I shall prove it to you one day, but for now, I'm taking care of your wrists."

Frowning, he scanned the entire pit before turning his attention to the two guards lounging on the upper rim.

"Medical supplies," he called, pointing to Gwyn's wrist. "The lady is hurt."

"*Mund halten, Englisch!*"

A pulse ticked up his neck. "Medic."

The soldiers leaned together, conferring in low voices and pointing into the hole. Finally, one of them shoved to his feet and stomped away. A few minutes later, he came back with Major Trommler in tow. Gwyn's heart crashed. Whatever that little man was doing there did not bode well.

Standing on the rim of the hole, Trommler clasped his hands behind his back and smiled. Like a vulture seeing his prey struggling in a field. "Settling in comfortably?"

"Could use a few chairs," Roland called. It earned him a quick jerk on the rope from William.

"Miss Ruthers needs medical attention," William said. "Her wrists are torn and bleeding. Infection could set in."

Trommler's thin eyebrows rose. "Is that so? *Fraulein* Ruthers, your injury, *bitte?*"

Gwyn pushed to her feet and stepped forward. The rope stopped her short, and the men at the end pretended not to notice.

"Never mind." Trommler held his hand up. The gleam in his eye gave no doubt how much he enjoyed the spectacle. "Hold up your hands from there."

Gwyn raised her hands, waiting while he pursed his lips and

tilted his head back and forth. Heat slashed Gwyn's neck and cheeks as the seconds ticked by.

"*Ja, ja.* I can see that they are a little red." Grabbing one of the guard's arms, he started down the embankment with unsure steps and fingers clutched white around the other man's arm.

Securely at the bottom, he straightened his jacket. Reaching behind his back, he pulled out a black handled dagger and pointed it at Gwyn. "Let us take care of this problem for good."

"No!" Jumping back, Gwyn's feet twisted in the soft ground, and down she went. Pain shot up her tailbone.

Trommler waved the knife in front of him. "Wait. And before the rest of you men think of leaping in front of her, take a look at the guns trained on you." With one quick stroke, he sliced the rope from her hands. "Much better, *ja?*"

Relief engulfed her stinging wrists as she clutched them to her chest. "Thank you."

"Behave yourself, or I'll regret taking them off." Trommler climbed back to the top. Taking a canteen and small bundle of cotton strips from the waiting guard, he tossed them at her feet. "You don't want me to regret something, I promise you that."

Gwyn blinked in surprise as her heart returned to a normal beat. Her hands were still attached to her body, and, hopefully, she could keep them that way.

"Must the rest of the men remain tied?" she asked before the major could disappear.

"Do not push your luck, *fraulein*. That pretty face will only allow you so many favors, and you've already used most of them."

"You shouldn't test the Jerries." William squatted next to her. Unscrewing the canteen cap, he poured water onto one of the strips. "They've got the weapons."

Gwyn took the strips from him and swabbed her wrists. The water was much too warm to refresh her pulse, but it was wonderful to clean the skin all the same. She took a sip from the canteen and passed it around to the other men. "We're in a hole. Where do they think we'd run?"

"Have you heard the phrase 'give a man an inch'?"

"Of course." She rolled one of the strips around her wrist. It refused to stay put.

William leaned close and held the end in place while she wrapped. He rubbed a finger gently over her palm. "Well, in the army we say 'give a man an inch, and he'll take your life'."

The military and their practical bleakness. Trained for war and taking other men's lives in the name of duty. Gwyn breathed a prayer of thanksgiving that she didn't have to live with that survival mindset. At least until recently, her life was blessedly comfortable.

Weariness stretched up her bones as she glanced around the dirt pit. Of course, blessings were all in the eye of the beholder.

Hours later, another mixed blessing blew in. The looming gray clouds opened, releasing the heavens. Gwyn lifted her face to the first precious drops. *Plop ... plop ... plop*. Her parched skin soaked in the sweetness like an overheated engine run too many hours. She rubbed the backs of her hands, neck, and cheeks, feeling the layers of grime wash away under her fingertips.

Plop, plop, plop. The steady drops saturated the hair on top of her head, cooling her scalp. She didn't worry about the untamable mass to come once the mugginess set in. Nothing could take away the beauty of that moment.

Splat. Splat. Splat. Mud splattered across the tops of Gwyn's boots. The drops fell fat and heavy all around, digging into the earth as thunder rolled. The drips ran together, creating rivers that collected in a shallow basin at the center of the pit. Faster and faster the rain came.

"William, I think we may have a problem."

"Just a little rain. Nothing we haven't dealt with in the trenches." He didn't bother lifting a hand to wipe the rain dribbling down his face.

"Only this time no one's shooting at us," Roland added with a half laugh. The other men joined in.

Gwyn shielded her eyes and glanced up. Rain smacked her in the face. "It's turning into more than just a little. And in the trenches, you at least had a way out."

"Captain, the lass is right." MacDonald sniffed the air. "It's more than a wee shower, no doubt. And she's moving fast on a south wind."

Shouts echoed from the trenches. Metal scraped against metal as the Germans undoubtedly hurried to cover their guns and powder storage. Their guards huddled together, stuffing the ends of their rifles beneath their jackets and lowering the brims of their hats as the rain slanted sideways.

"Chaos all around. No one paying any mind to us now." Roland pointed to the guards. "This could be our chance, Will."

"We have to get them down here first." William squinted. "Or at least to the edge."

Gwyn eyed the guards, the pit rim turning to sludge, and her fellow captives. Hope tingled in her veins. Escape.

"How do you plan to get them there?" she asked. "They'd be mad to risk their footing so near the edge."

"Mad … no, I'll settle for uncertainty." With eyes set like a trained hawk, William examined every inch of the rim and pit before turning to Roland. "Get face down in the mud."

Roland balked. "Are you insane?"

"We need a distraction to get them down here."

"You expect me to put my face in this cesspool? How am I supposed to breathe?"

"Turn your head to the side. Make it believable that you've been struck faint."

"I've never fainted a day in my life. How am I to make that believable?"

"Like this." MacDonald smacked him in the back of the head. Roland fell face down in the muck.

"Not what I had in mind, but it'll have to do." William turned to Gwyn. "Scream."

"But I ..." Gwyn shook her head. "What if they don't believe us?"

"You want out of here? Scream."

Opening her mouth, Gwyn let forth the worst sound she could conjure. The guards shouted at her, but she kept going, hopping around and pointing at the downed Roland. Her fellow captives joined in the ruckus.

"Was ist da los? Ist dass der mensch tot?"

Gwyn fell to her knees beside Roland and shook his shoulders. "Help! He needs help!"

More German shouting as the guards pointed down to the pit. They couldn't leave a prisoner dead, especially not a valuable officer. Gwyn waved her hands in the air, motioning them down.

The shorter of the two ventured over the edge, sliding his way to the bottom. As he bent over Roland's prostrate body, MacDonald punched him in the back of the head. Bone cracked, and the man landed face down.

His companion fumbled for the rifle caught under his jacket, his slippery hands unable to grip the butt.

"Get the knife!" William pointed to the fallen guard.

Gwyn flipped back the edge of the jacket and ran her hands around his waist. Yanking the knife from its sheath, she sawed through the men's ropes.

William scrambled up the embankment and grabbed the soldier's foot, dragging him into the pit. Fingers clutched around the rifle, the man tried to fire off a shot, but MacDonald ripped it from him and butted him on the side of the temple. Red blood streaked down his face as he crumpled into the mud.

"We don't have much time." William climbed up the slope and peered over the rim. He turned back and held his hand down to Gwyn. "Come on, now."

Gwyn clawed at the earth as her feet slipped in the rivers of mud. She stretched her fingers towards William, but the sludge slid her back down into the pit.

MacDonald hooked an arm around her and boosted her up. "Up you go, lass."

Sprawled at the top with William crouched next to her, Gwyn's heart beat in her throat as the other prisoners crawled their way out. Roland flopped next to her like a spineless fish.

"Watch it, will you? Bleeding Scot." He moaned, gripping his head. "I'll have a headache for a week thanks to you."

MacDonald tucked his newly acquired rifle close to his side and swiped the mud from his mouth. "Better than drowning in a stinking hole."

"Keep close, heads down, and make for that copse to the west," William said.

Gwyn squinted through the sheet of rain at the fuzzy outline of trees just beyond an open field. Her heart thrummed in her ears as she calculated the distance. They were sitting ducks if the Germans spotted them.

"Ready." William's voice rose above the rain. "Go."

He shot forward. Gwyn kept right behind him, running as fast as her legs could pump. The bogged earth squished beneath her feet, throwing her off balance. Her muscles screamed against the pain, but she wasn't going down. Not this time. Wind tore at her hair, lashing it across her face like whips.

Halfway there. Halfway. Keep going.

POP! POP! POP! POP!

Gwyn shook her head, dislodging the water from her ears. Gunshots.

William turned his head. "Keep going!"

POP! POP! POP!

Gwyn pushed harder. Her lungs burned. The tree line loomed closer and closer. *Stay alive. Stay alive.* Leaves slapped her face and branches tore at her clothes, but she kept going. An arm snaked around her waist and hauled her behind a tree. William's breath was hot in her ear as he crushed her against the tree, covering her body with his. The dank mustiness of wet bark penetrated her nose as she drew in ragged breaths.

William's heart battered her back. "Are you hit?"

She shook her head, incapable of drawing a simple breath to speak.

"Anyone else hit?"

"Farrow." MacDonald huffed from two trees away.

"Where is he?"

MacDonald pointed back to the field. "Gone."

"How do you know?" One of the prisoners shouted. "Did you even see? We have to go back."

"Hole in the head. He's gone."

"We can't leave him. Me and him signed up together. I can't tell his mum I left him rotting in a field while I ran for my life."

"You won't be telling his mother anything if you leave these trees. It's too dangerous. We press on," William said.

"I'm sick and tired of all you officers thinking you know what's best. Your kind is what got me here in the first place." The man sneered. "I decide from now on."

William pushed away from the tree and curled his fingers into fists. "You'll stand down now, soldier."

"Let it go, Tindall." The second prisoner held Tindall's arm. "The Germans won't let you step foot on that field."

Tindall yanked his arm away. "Some friend you are. Siding with the brass. I'll do it myself."

William jumped to block him, but Tindall darted to the field with his friend hot on his heels.

POP! POP!

They crumpled to the ground three feet from where Farrow stared unseeing to the sky.

MacDonald spat and cursed, but William's face was stone, the straight lines of his shoulders harsh against the shivering branches around him. His eyes shifted to where Gwyn still clung to the tree. His hands unclenched. Only then did she see the dagger poised between his fingers.

"Press on." Slipping the knife into his belt, he grabbed Gwyn's hand and pulled her further into the dense growth of trees.

Hours seemed to pass as they slogged through the woods. Every rock and bush turned to a blur. They could be in Belgium or Timbuctoo for all she knew.

"William." He didn't stop. "William." She pulled on his hand. He turned his head. "We can't stop."

Her toe caught a tree root. The same root she'd tripped over not long ago. "Why are we going in circles?"

"To throw off the Germans if they try to follow us." He held back a branch to keep it from snapping her face. "It's too dark for them to start now, and the rain will have washed away our tracks, but come morning, they may try."

"Aye, but let's hope they dinna turn loose the dogs," MacDonald said, bringing up the rear. "Hate to get a nasty set of teeth in my a—em, coming from behind me."

On they trudged as darkness enveloped them. Gwyn gave up anticipating their path as she clutched William's hand in her waterlogged one, letting him lead wherever his instinct took them. Soft drops of rain splatted against the canopy high above, dribbling to the leaves far below and adding to the muck wrapped around her boots. Every few steps, a drop splattered her cheek, but she didn't bother wiping them away. Soaked to the bone, it was a useless waste of her rapidly depleting energy.

Wet earth mingled with acrid powder as gunfire rumbled low in the distance. The battles continued their rage. On and on it went, never an end in sight. But it would have to come to an end. Who would be left standing? And if—God forbid—it wasn't the British, then how would they ever get home? She'd have to learn French. It wasn't a bad language, but her tongue did have trouble curling to the perfect—

She smacked into William's still back. "Ow! Oh, I'm sorry." Gwyn rubbed her nose and peered around him.

They'd reached the edge of the wood.

CHAPTER 17

"Where are we?"

William moved closer to Gwyn, curling his fingers around hers. He pointed south to the sunken road cutting down the western border of the field. "Amiens is just over that hill. With luck on our side, we can skirt Albert and make the British lines in a day."

Her green eyes turned to him. Tiredness smudged under her lower lashes. "And if luck isn't on our side?"

"Then you'll have a hurried lesson in low crawling." He wrapped his other hand around their joined ones and squeezed. "For now, we'll take advantage of this stream to refill the canteen."

"I might dunk my whole head in and wash off this filth."

"As long as you do it after we've filled the canteen. Can't risk getting chatts in the drinking water."

"If I have chatts, I shudder to think what the rest of you have."

"We should keep pushing under this cover," Roland said. Clouds blanketed the night sky, allowing only slivers of the moon and stars to peek through. "The further we can get away from what's coming, the better."

"Fifteen minutes. We can all use it." William rubbed the kinks from his hand with his thumb. Hours of holding Gwyn's had left it feeling useless now that she'd let go. He glanced over to where she knelt on the grassy bank and splashed water over her face. "Anything to eat in that haversack you managed to snag, MacDonald?"

Handing his rifle to Roland, MacDonald plopped down on the soggy ground and dug around in the bag. He pulled out a small tin of sausage and a few biscuits that looked like hardtack.

"Guess they're as bad off as we are, though we haven't come to eating rocks." MacDonald divided the shares and attempted to break off a piece of the biscuit with his teeth. "Need goat's teeth to chomp through one of these bannocks."

William took his and Gwyn's share and squatted next to her. "Here, you need to eat something."

Passing him the filled canteen, she pushed a strand of limp hair from her eyes and frowned at the dubious biscuit. "My stomach is so full of rainwater I'm sure that would sink straight to the bottom."

He handed her a sausage. "Give this a try first."

She chewed slowly and nodded. "This may be the best thing I've ever tasted. Sure beats the bowls of bully beef, but right now, I'd tuck into one with glee."

"A good chase will have you doing all sorts of odd things." He gave half a laugh. A strange feeling considering the day they'd just escaped.

She smiled, and the feeling no longer felt strange. It was right, sitting with her, longing to brush the damp tendrils from her cheek and kiss its smoothness. His thumb burned with the memory of caressing her lip. Warm and soft fullness, begging him to linger.

"We shouldn't linger," she said.

William's thoughts reared. "I wasn't."

"Captain Morrison is right. We should push on while we still have darkness." Her smile faded. "I know you only stopped because of me."

"You can't walk until your feet bleed."

"If there's a goal, then I'm not stopping until we get there. I'll deal with bleeding feet afterward. And don't tell me you want to do a foot check."

William shoved the hardtack in his mouth and chewed as carefully as possible to keep his teeth in place. It'd been days since he'd last taken off his boots. Blistered and hot, his feet cried for release, but if he took off the covers now, there was no chance of getting those swollen, watered logs back in. "Not much point. We have no dry socks or whale's paste to secure them."

"You certainly know how to turn a girl's head, Captain. Whale's paste on a moonless night."

The hardtack stuck in his throat. Turn her head? With whale's paste? Even he had to admit that was as unromantic as discussing rotting feet. Not that there was anything appalling about the paste—it had numerous benefits in the field—but if he *did* want to turn her head, what would he say? Moonlight and flowers sent the biscuit roiling in his stomach. Women expected those things, but Gwyn was unlike any woman he'd ever met. What would she expect?

The biscuit turned sour. More expectations. More possibilities to disappoint. All he'd been good for—been trained for—was giving orders and carrying soldiers through them. Despite all his planning and mapping every decision, failure still flared. Like today. Three men lay dead in a field under his watch. He couldn't even spare the honor of bringing their bodies back home.

Surging to his feet, William stalked several feet away to two towering elm trees that had managed to avoid destruction. Faces of the dead boys—English, Irish, Welsh, French, and German—paraded across the field before him. Their ghostly march keeping time to the guilt pounding in his heart.

"Have I said something?"

Gwyn's gentle voice pierced like nails as she stood behind him. He couldn't even stop the failures from touching her. "Go back and rest. We'll leave soon."

"Because we were laughing one minute, and the next ... as if you'd thrown a bucket of freezing water on yourself."

He dug his fingers into a wet elm. Bark chipped beneath his nails. "This isn't the time for laughter."

"If we can't find something to smile about in the worst patch, then we're doomed."

"You still feel like smiling after today?"

Fallen leaves rustled as she shifted her footing. "Reason tells me no. This is one of the worst days of my life, but it's become one of the best because I'm still alive."

"Not all of us lucked out, or has the war numbed you to the sight of death?"

"No, but I try not to vent my frustration on those around me. What happened today was not your fault."

"It's my duty to get my men—all of my men—to safety."

"Those bullets could have hit any one of us. It could be me in that field, or you. You led us from that pit, and that's what matters. With even one life saved, today was not a failure."

He hooked his thumb beneath a chunk of bark and ripped it off. "Failure is in the eye of the beholder."

She stepped in front of him, close enough to search his face. "Why do you give yourself so little credit? The war is not yours to bear alone."

"And you think you should have a share in its weight? Think you can bear it?" He shook his head. The conviction in her eyes burned him to the core, but not in the way she intended. "Naivety does not become you, Gwyn."

"Nor does shortsightedness flatter you." She plunked her hands on her hips. "I may have been stuck above a garage my whole life, but it hasn't left me immune to hardship."

"Women's rights and petticoats hardly compare to this."

"We each have our own battles to fight, but you know what I think, Captain Crawford? I think you're upset that I've infiltrated your precious ranks of brotherhood."

"So you have. Is it the adventure you hoped for?"

"At least I'm not too scared to venture from safety and try something new instead of staying where everyone expects me to."

Her words hit him like a two-ton mortar, imploding his sturdy defense. Quiet anger seethed in the debris. "I wasn't given the carefree path you trod. My duties led me elsewhere, and I intend to see them through."

"Straight into misery."

"And how would you know?"

"Because I see the same desire to break free that I have inside of you." Flinging the heavy drape of hair back over her shoulder, she turned away from him and stared across the field. He heard the sharp intakes of breath and slow hiss of release.

Crickets chirped their song in a nearby bush, their cadence a lonely sound that penetrated the heavy mugginess drowning the air. The call was answered by another chirping of restless legs, and another, and another until the night filled with the crickets' mournful tune.

Finally, Gwyn spoke. "If you could do one thing, anything in the whole world, what would it be?" Her voice was low and thick like smoke curling around him.

She didn't understand. Could never understand. But the more she pushed, the harder it was for him to keep her locked out. Determined thing, she was. What happened when she pushed so far that there was no going back? Would she laugh at his longing to live a simple life raising horses, not for military usage, but for the simple pleasure the beautiful creatures brought? Or worse, would she find him lacking and turn away?

He shook his head. "It doesn't matter. This is my world."

"There's nothing wrong with dreaming, William. If I didn't dream, I wouldn't be here." She whipped around, a glare pulling her delicate eyebrows together. "And don't give me cheek about how I shouldn't be here in the first place."

He snorted. "You haven't listened to me yet. It'd be a waste of my breath."

She stepped to him. Slivers of moonlight bathed her skin. "What are you so afraid of?"

His pulse throbbed. Less than an arm's length away, if he just reached out … "I hardly know myself."

"The man who plans every detail? I doubt that."

"Then prove to me how wrong I am." He moved forward, leaving a hairsbreadth between them. "Tell me what it is that I'm afraid of."

Lips parted, her shallow breaths gripped him with longing. "You wear those captain's bars like armor. One day, they will fail to protect you."

She spun on her heel, but he caught her elbow and pulled her back. Her frantic heart beat against his chest. His eyes fell to her mouth. "Why not now?"

He claimed her lips with an urgency that sent waves of heat through him. Restraint fled as he wrapped his arms around her. He caressed her back, pulling her closer until her warmth melted into him. Her lips parted on a gasp, and he couldn't stop from tasting the sweetness that had long tempted him. His hand moved to the back of her neck, angling her head. She shivered as he brushed his fingers through her dark hair. Heavy and wet, water droplets slipped between his fingers.

Her fingers curled into him, her mouth molding under his in sweet release. Her frantic heartbeat pounded against his chest, coaxing his pulse to match hers. Her hands roamed over his shoulders to curl around his neck, scorching the sensitive skin beneath her smooth palms.

He traced the gentle curve of her mouth, brushing his lips along her jaw and ear. She sighed softly. Desire trilled in his blood as he swept back to meet her lips once more. It seared him like a white-hot poker, sharp and true to his core until he felt nothing beyond the woman in his arms.

And then she was gone.

Pressing a shaking hand to her mouth, Gwyn whirled away, leaving him cold and confused.

"Nice going, Romeo." Roland leaned against a tree, shaking his head. "In all my experience, I've learned there are two people in the ranks that you do not want to rile. The cook and the medic. Thankfully, MacDonald is a Scot and doesn't offend easily, but her, well, just pray you don't get a splinter."

William gouged a hand through his hair. Curses leaped over his tongue. "Glad you caught the show."

"Only the finale." Hands in his pockets, Roland pushed off the tree with a grin. "About time you got on with it. You wanted to. She's wanted you to."

"Get all that by the way she stormed off, did you?"

"The pangs of yearning and blossoming affection are obvious to even those with a blind eye. You two hit everyone between the eyes."

More like she was gearing up to punch him between the eyes. And not with blossoms. Still, the sigh from her soft lips hinted at the desire spiraling deep within her. A desire he had stirred. "Is there a reason you're prowling in the bushes, other than looking for cheap thrills at my expense?"

"Our fifteen minutes are up. In case you hadn't noticed." With a wink, Roland strolled away whistling "Any Time's Kissing Time."

CHAPTER 18

Goodbye, life. Goodbye, flight school. Goodbye, traveling the world. Gwyn kicked a rock into a dried mud patch on the side of the road and continued with her list. Goodbye, breeches. Goodbye, autos. Hello, horses. She stopped to snap a twig under her heel. William paused and glanced over his shoulder before continuing on their march.

And what of the things she'd gain by giving into him? Into his kiss? It certainly wasn't a promise of any kind. A flare of passion from a man long at war perhaps. And yet ... the way he held her, tilting her mouth to meet his, tracing the curves of her lips with exquisite tenderness and hunger.

She stumbled as heat trembled down her legs at the memory. She'd read about stolen kisses and their power from Guinevere and Lancelot, Heathcliff and Cathy, but to find herself in a man's arms for the first time was like floating in the most incredible dream. And the most confusing.

"All right there, lass?"

Gwyn jumped at the sound of MacDonald's voice. He loomed over her, reddish eyebrows drawn together.

"Fine, yes," she said. "Pebble underfoot."

"Keep moving," William called over his shoulder.

"The lass had a bumble."

William stopped and turned. A warm breeze flowed over the brown fields and ruffled through his hair. "Is she ... are you all right?"

Gwyn tilted her chin up, embarrassment rushing to her cheeks. It was the first time he'd spoken directly to her in over a day. "Just a rock in the road. Press on."

"Do you need to rest?"

The embarrassment heated to annoyance. "Certainly not."

His mouth opened, but he shut it and resumed the trek. Broad shoulders taut, back straight as a board, and arms stiff at his sides, he was a soldier on a mission.

A heavy sigh rumbled in Gwyn's chest. Two days ago he hadn't been a soldier. He'd been a man who found her desirable. And she'd pushed him away.

"Captain's got a bee in his bonnet, nay doubt." MacDonald matched his long strides to hers. His sporran bounced in perfect rhythm. "Been sour since the woods. O' course those lads running into the guns like they did would put any man off, but they had their own minds about it. Canna change that. The captain takes everything on himself though, doesn't he? Shouldn't. Not like he hasn't lost a man before. Wonder why this one's got him so vexed."

Her inability to surrender was due to some ridiculous notion that love was the ruination of freedom. Love offered a girl a limited view from her kitchen window. Love kept a girl from chasing adventure around the world. Dreams abandoned for another person's in the name of love. To live in a tiny flat above a garage. Yet somehow Mum found such happiness there, even while yearning for exploration.

Love.

Gwyn kicked another rock. It disappeared into a tangle of dried wheat. Who was talking about love after one kiss under a moonless sky?

"Lassie, you keep stopping like that, and I'll just have a wee sit."

"Oh, sorry." Gwyn quickened her pace before William could turn around again. "Lack of sleep has my mind wandering."

"Feel free to talk it out loud. Helps me sometimes."

Gwyn smiled. "Not this time."

"Ah. Personal problem. Have me three sisters, so I know all the advice if you want to give it a go."

"Thank you, no. I think I'll stew on it for a bit."

"Like the Captain. Ruthers, if you keep stopping—"

"This has nothing to do with Will, the captain."

A frown pulled at his wide mouth. "Didn't say it did. Just that you both got the same brewing expression. And got it around the same time. If I were an observant man, I might say—"

"Well, don't."

"Just saying, with two of the three sisters married, I can help."

Gwyn jumped as if he'd zapped her with a lightning rod. "Who's talking about marriage?"

"No one. Unless you want to."

"I most certainly do not."

"Quiet!" William had stopped, motionless as a deer in a clearing. Mouth pressed into a grim line, he stared at the eastern sky. Wisps of smoke curled over a crop of trees. "MacDonald, you come with me. Roland, you stay here with Gwyn. Keep your heads down. We'll be back soon. That smoke looks to be nothing more than a campfire."

"As the more senior officer, I should be going, not MacDonald," Roland said, a defiant scrunch to his chin.

"He's not the one with a busted leg. You'll stay here and keep a lookout."

"Lookout, bah." Roland crossed his arms and huffed. "More like a babysitter."

"I don't need a babysitter, nor am I going to sit here as an unarmed target." Gwyn brushed past Roland to plant herself in front of William. The memory of last night's kiss burned in her chest. She squelched it before it had time to spread. "I'm going too."

"No."

"Yes."

A muscle ticked in his neck. "You'll stay here as commanded."

Gwyn rolled her eyes. "I'm fed up with commands. You want me to stay put, then you'll have to tie me to a tree. But first you'll need a rope, and I doubt you have any of that stuffed in your boot."

His neck muscle clenched, a vein pulsed wildly beneath the tanned skin. The crystal blue eyes glittered like ice. If she wasn't so hot, hungry, and exhausted, she might have summoned the sense to heed the warning.

"Captain Morrison and I are vulnerable near the road. It's safer for the group to stick together." She eyed the trees. "You said it looked nothing more than a campfire. Doubting yourself?"

"The only doubt I have is your ability to stay clear of foolish predicaments." He inhaled deeply, straining the buttons down his chest. "But I know for a fact you won't stay put, and, unfortunately I'm all out of rope."

He pulled the German knife from his belt and handed it to her. Heavy and cool in her palm, Gwyn wrapped her fingers around the handle.

William's hot hand clamped down on top of hers. "If there's trouble, don't try to use this. Just run." She nodded and tried to pull her hand back, but he held tight. "I'll have your word on it, Gwyn. No heroics."

The same intensity burned in his eyes as the last time he'd stood so close to her. His hand had been warm then too, his gaze intent on her mouth. Her palm grew slick against the handle. "You have my word."

His gaze flickered down to her lips so briefly that Gwyn thought she'd imagined it. And then his hand was gone.

Easing off the dusty road, they stalked through the tall grass. Gwyn batted the dried weeds from her face as she trudged behind Roland. Poor man was getting the worst of it as the slender stalks snapped back in place behind MacDonald's broad back and smacked the captain on the ears.

Gwyn clutched the knife tighter, grateful for her thick boots and long trousers despite the sweat they trapped inside. She didn't want to imagine what kind of rodents and slithering creatures watched her with their beady little eyes.

Her head bumped into something hard. William. He glared back at her. In front of him towered the edge of the woods.

"Sorry," she mouthed.

He grabbed her wrist and flipped it so the knife pointed down. Leaning down, his warm breath hissed in her ear. "Try not stabbing me."

"Sorry. I didn't get much weapon training on the driving course."

The side of his mouth twitched, fluttering butterflies through her stomach. Butterflies. Golly molly. They were approaching the enemy, not an ice cream social.

"Keep your head down, and remember your promise." Signaling to the other men, they crept into the woods.

Moving as one, they ducked and stalked between the towering trees. Their heavy boots making nary a sound on the grass and twigs while Gwyn's heels managed to crunch every leaf on the ground. Oh, to have their training. She'd never seen soldiers in head-on confrontation before, but their confidence was enough to bolster hers, weak as it was.

Smoke purled through the air, tickling her nose with burning pine sap. A relief against the onslaught of gunpowder usually singeing the winds. Until she caught a whiff of blackened meat.

The men stopped. Low voices rumbled from the other side of a fallen log. William pointed down, then forward. MacDonald and Roland hunched over and scurried behind the log. Heart in her throat, Gwyn followed and landed with a soft thud on the grass beside them.

"Two. Infantry," William whispered, peering through the leaves. "A small wagon and farm horse. They're not in a hurry."

MacDonald angled up on his elbow and looked. "Deserters. No more than lads."

Gwyn edged herself to the top of the log and thumbed back a few leaves. Two soldiers not old enough to be in university hunkered over a tiny fire where a skinned rat blackened on a stick.

Filthy uniforms hung on their skinny bodies, their lean faces intent on the meal before them.

"How do you know they're deserters?" she asked.

"Food is scarce, but no soldier in the German ranks is that skeletal and ragged." Sadness tinged William's voice. "And there's no reason for them to be this far from their lines with an empty wagon and horse."

Deserters. The slime of the military. No one was more hated than a coward fleeing his duty. If caught, the penalty was death. As much as Gwyn despised disloyalty, her heart heaved with sadness for the poor boys. They must have been terrified to risk a firing squad.

William turned and leaned his head against the log. Squeezing his eyes shut, he pinched the bridge of his nose and sighed. Gwyn longed to smooth the deep wrinkles from his forehead, to tell him he need not put himself in this difficult situation. But her words would fall on deaf ears. He was here, and there was no backing down now.

"We've got a clean shot," MacDonald said.

William's eyes flew open. "No."

Roland shifted uncomfortably. "They're deserters, Will. German cowards."

"They're boys on the run."

"And they might be sitting on a stash of pistols. Better them than us, or some other detail on patrol."

"We'll take them alive." William's tone cut the argument like steel. "MacDonald, you ease around the other side, Roland behind, and Gwyn stay with me. Wait for my signal."

The men moved into position as Gwyn tried to keep her frantic heart from beating clean through her chest. The dagger slipped from her sweaty fingers. Picking it up, she laid it across her knees and swiped her palms against her thighs.

"Do you remember what I told you?" William's low voice whirred in her ears. She nodded, gripping the knife again.

"Don't hold it like that." Prying her fingers from the handle, he rearranged them to firmly enfold the grip. "You don't want to hammer or slash down at your attacker because they can easily block it. You want to slice in and out, like filleting a fish."

"Filleting a fish." Her stomach twisted. "But fish are fish, with tails and fins, and humans are … are …" Her hand shook, threatening to drop the knife again. She'd seen men with bayonet wounds, their insides out and cut like fine ribbons. But it had been the enemy's handiwork, not her own. "Why are you telling me this when you want me to run?"

"Because I can't leave you helpless. You're better off knowing and not needing it than finding yourself a victim." He scouted through the bushes again. "They're in place. You stay right here. Understand?"

She nodded as the tension knotted her insides. William checked his rounds one last time and started to rise from his crouch. Gwyn caught his arm. "Please be careful, William."

His eyes softened for the briefest of seconds before snapping back to soldier steel. Springing to his feet, he pulled the rifle against his shoulder.

Click.

The German boys froze and stared at the man who had mysteriously risen from the ground.

"Slow and easy, lads," William said as MacDonald and Roland came into the clearing. "Keep your hands where I can see them. *Englisch?*"

Terror collided with confusion on the boys' faces. "*Nein.*"

William stepped further into the small area, the pointed rifle steady in his hands. "Check them, Roland."

As Roland approached, the younger-looking boy began to tremble, his eyes darting all around like a spooked horse. He backed away.

William's aim followed him. "Don't do it, boy."

The boy broke into a run.

CRACK!

The boy hit the ground. William cursed and sprinted to his side, joined by MacDonald and his smoking rifle.

"I told you not to shoot." William growled, holding the squirming boy down as he tried to clutch his bloody knee. "What am I supposed to do with him now?"

"Bandage him up." Gwyn knelt beside him. Without hesitation, her feet had carried her to the sight of blood.

William grabbed her arm as she reached for the boy's knee. "I told you to stay put."

She jerked away from of his grasp. "Only if there was trouble. The only trouble here is this boy squirming in agony. Search the wagon for anything I can wrap this shattered knee in. And some kind of brace. Sticks if need be."

Warmth pulsed over her fingers as she examined the open hole. Thankfully, the bullet had gone straight through. "Mr. MacDonald, I am in no way condoning this, but that was quite a shot."

"Best way to stop a cattle reiver," he said, puffing his thick chest out. "Enough to stop 'em cold and keep 'em alive."

She ignored the pride in his voice and took the canteen William had found. She washed the wound before wrapping it in torn strips of tarp. The boy winced, biting hard down on his lip. Hatred burned in his eyes as he watched every move she made.

Rocking back on her heels, Gwyn pushed a damp bit of hair from her forehead and examined her work. Sister would have a seizure if she saw such an unsanitary and crude dressing. But Saint Matthew's was a long way away. "That'll have to do."

"Better than what he deserves," Roland said from where he perched atop the other captive. "I'd say your shot was about three feet too low, MacDonald."

William's face set to stone. "I wanted no shooting."

"They're deserters, Will. Keeping them alive is not what the cowards deserve," Roland said. "You know the law."

The muscles in William's neck seized, and for the first time,

Gwyn clearly saw the burden he carried. Did he obey the orders of man or the orders of honor? "They're not British citizens."

"So you want to set them free? Or maybe you plan to bind them hand and foot and carry them all the way back to headquarters if we can ever find it. I'll tell you this, I have no intention of marching any mile with a Kraut at my back."

"They don't want to be here any more than we do." William pointed at the burning rodent. "They're starving to death. I doubt they could overtake you on a march."

"It may have been a tasty meal to start, but it's burned to the bone now. Stinking up the air." MacDonald grumbled and kicked the makeshift spit onto the grass. "Filthy rat."

Too much sun and heat. The men wavered on the edge of going for each other's throats. And Gwyn was ready to push them all into the nearest river. At least when the women turned foul, they only used scathing words as weapons. Her current companions carried guns.

Plopping down, she plucked a dried blade of grass and rolled it between her fingers. How lovely a river sounded. Cool and fresh to wash away weeks—months of grime. She wiggled her cramped toes, eager to feel the watery flow between them. Perhaps, for just a minute, she could slip off the confining boots and—

Her scalp split with fire as the wounded German grabbed a fistful of her hair and yanked her head back, exposing her neck to the blade he'd slipped from her belt. She clawed at his arm, but he held tight.

"*Nicht kämpfen oder ich werde dich aufschlitzen.*" His voice shook.

"William." She gasped, throwing her arm back at the boy's face.

His hand trembled, scraping the knife against her skin. Wet drops trickled down her neck. "*Ruhig sein!*"

Terror blazed in William's eyes for an instant before fury rolled across his face. He threw the rifle against his shoulder and aimed. "Let her go, or I'll put a bullet straight into your skull."

"Don't. You'll hit her." MacDonald readied his gun.

William swung his gun and pressed the muzzle to the other German's head. "Then his *freund* goes first."

The boy under William's gun sobbed and pleaded with his friend, garbled words muffled as Roland pressed his elbow against the back of his neck, pressing the boy's face into the dirt.

Gwyn's head throbbed as her captor dug his fingers in and twisted. But it was the stifled sob that gave him away. He'd gotten himself into something he had no way out of.

"Please, please let me go," she whispered.

The blade pressed harder. Her pulse pounded out more trickles of blood. Red exploded across William's face.

"Lassen sie mich und meine freundin gehn!" Her captor yanked her head further back until she cried out. *"Und ich werde nicht verletzt das mädchen."*

Tears pricked Gwyn's eyes from the pain shooting to the roots of her hair. And then—like the snap of a twig—the pain vanished, along with her patience for pushy Germans. Balling her fist, she smacked his blown knee as hard as she could.

Howling with pain, the boy fell back clutching his knee. Gwyn leaped to her feet and grabbed the knife. "I saved your life!"

William was at her side, attempting to wrest the knife from her, but she refused to let go. She needed it. Needed it to keep her safe. Safe from all the Germans desperate to snuff her out. Well, she wasn't ready to be snuffed out.

A rough hand caressed her cheek. "Let go, Gwyn."

Tears stung her eyes. Her fingers opened, surrendering the knife to William.

Grabbing the boy by his collar, William dragged him to where his friend lay prostrate under Roland. "On your knees. Hands behind your heads."

Tears streaming down their faces, the boys shook their heads in confusion and offered their bare hands as a plea. Impassive as stone, William watched in silence as MacDonald shoved the boys into position. Gwyn's failed captor buckled and stuck his busted leg out, unable to bend it. The tarp around his wound seeped deep red.

"I would ask for last words, but you can't understand me." William's lips barely moved as he shrugged his rifle into position. "I'll trust the sobbing is making peace with God."

The boys cried harder.

Gwyn's heart sagged. "No, William. Please no."

"They're deserters." William's voice was cold as stone. "He tried to slit your throat, or can you not feel the blood running down your neck?"

Gwyn touched the side of her neck. "He was scared. This is wrong. We're not murderers."

William's shoulders strained the fabric across his back. Minutes passed without a twitch of the fingers. Gwyn's lungs constricted with each pulse of the vein in his neck. Finally, he threw his gun down.

And punched the boy in the jaw.

"Get their boots off and strip them down to their underwear. They'll be too humiliated to assault a cat on the return trip to the Fatherland."

A minute later, with barely a shred of clothing to hold their dignity in place, the boys knelt trembling in front of William. With a low growl, he waved them off. "Get out of my sight. Go!"

Scrambling to his feet, the abled-bodied boy hauled the other to his good foot and slung an arm around him for support. Crying together, they limped off into the woods.

Exhausted, Gwyn shuffled back to the log she'd hidden behind and slumped down. Her arms and legs felt as if a stack of tires weighed atop them, and her brain was as oozy as motor oil. Her eyelids fluttered shut to a relief of darkness. The days seemed never to end. They were doomed to wander in circles until their feet turned into bloody nubs or another German patrol overtook them. Would they be as lucky to escape the next time? A tear squeezed from the corner of her eye. How much longer?

A finger gently wiped away the tear. Suddenly, there were too many to control. She fell into William's arms and let the dam break free. His arms wrapped around her, stroking her back and hair.

"It's over." He pressed kisses to her forehead. "It's all over."

"It's not all over." She sobbed. "We're stuck here in the middle of nowhere. Probably forever."

She felt his mouth tilt into a smile. "Probably not that long."

"How do you know?"

"Because I have the German's map that tells me salvation is not far from here." He rubbed a finger under her chin, trying to nudge it up.

She wiggled her head away. The rough material of his jacket scratched against her cheek. "I don't want you to look at me."

"Why not?"

"I don't want you to see me like this. Ugly and puffy-eyed." A hiccup wriggled its way up her throat. "You'll hold it against me later."

"How could I hold the impossible against you? Never use that word ugly again." Cupping a hand under her chin, he forced her to look up. "I see nothing but beauty and strength."

It was too much. The wave of golden hair blown across his forehead, the crystal blue eyes, the soft lines around his generous mouth, the heat pulsing from his skin to her fingertips. She pressed her lips to his, only meant as a light brush, but the touch ignited a desperation she could no longer ignore. Raking her fingers through his hair, she pulled him close, melting her mouth to his. He moaned and wrapped his arms around her, caressing the curves of her neck and waist. Ecstasy shimmered down her spine. How did this man make her feel so alive in a way that no speeding motor ever had?

"Will, we need to—oh, for crying out loud!"

Gwyn fell back at Roland's exclamation. Fire burned across her face.

"Honestly, you two need to put bells around your necks so I

know where you are at all times," Roland said.

William shot to his feet and glared at his friend. "You're the one who needs a bell. Hiding in the bushes all the time."

"If you look closely, you'll see that I'm still standing in the open, while you are the one ensconced." He peered around William's shoulder and winked slyly at Gwyn. "And what a lovely entrapment."

"Is there a reason you're here?"

Roland tapped a finger to his lips in mock thought. "Hmm, I forget. Though I'm sure it has something to do with cracking on." Laughing, he strolled back to where MacDonald pilfered through empty boxes and tins in the German wagon.

"I'm sorry about him." William turned back to her. "The sun's addled his thick head more than usual."

"No, he's right. This is hardly the place or time. You should know I'm not in the habit of throwing myself at unsuspecting men."

"Do you usually give warning?"

"No. Oh, golly molly. I mean, I don't know what I mean." She buried her face in her hands and prayed for the earth to open and swallow her whole. "This has been a very long day."

Gently, he uncovered her face and squatted in front of her. The brilliance of a star dazzled in his smile. "You should get in the habit. But not with any old bloke. One in particular, and he promises not to mind. Suspecting or not."

Gwyn tingled as he tucked a loose hair behind her ear, allowing his fingers to linger on the sensitive skin just behind the curve. Gazing into his eager face, she shooed her hesitation away. William felt so right, so comfortable, how could he possibly carry those invisible shackles she'd run from her entire life? His kisses, his touch was not of a man wishing to crush her.

"Do we have an agreement?"

"Is this some sort of contract, Captain Crawford?"

"Yes, and here's how to seal the deal." He kissed her, full and possessive on the lips, and tweaked her on the chin. "Let's go before Roland comes back with MacDonald in tow."

Gwyn took his hand, lacing her fingers between his. Why ever had she held back from him for so long?

CHAPTER 19

Bloated carcasses lined the roads. Black craters gaped like wide, toothless mouths in the surrounding fields. Explosions had destroyed the gentle countryside, turning it into a pit of decay.

Gwyn pressed a hand over her nose to block the stench. It would take an entire tub of turpentine to rid her nostrils of the burn.

"Poor blighters." MacDonald lifted his hairy leg to step over a foot. "They deserve better than to rot away like this on foreign soil."

"There aren't enough hands to collect them all." William frowned as he stopped at a crossroad's sign. "That's their target."

Gwyn looked where he pointed. A small village with brown rooftops nestled at the end of a long stretch of scorched wheat fields. "How do we know who's taken it?"

William examined the ground. "There aren't eastern tracks leading in."

Gwyn looked at the boot prints, horse tracks, shredded bushes and weed stalks. "How can you tell in this mess?"

"See these here." He pointed at two long, wide lines. "They're directed west, but stop and retreat. Nothing continues west. You might say they threw it in reverse."

She grinned at his attempt at motor vernacular. "If I didn't know any better, I'd say you're part Indian, trained by an Apache tracker. I once read they could stay on your trail until your horse eventually gave out."

"No, no Indian. Just trained. Though my father did give me a tactic book once, based on one of their leaders, Geronimo, and a cavalryman named Custer."

"Crazy Horse was with Custer."

"None of your barmy clusters holds a candle to a Scot in the dark," MacDonald said, puffing his chest out. "Highland men are the best trackers, and everyone knows it. How else do you think we slipped past the lobsterbacks and smuggled Bonnie Prince Charlie right out from under their noses?"

Roland snorted. "You lost that war, my friend, or were you too busy tracking to notice?"

Doubt tickled Gwyn's thoughts as she stared at the jumble of tracks around them. "Shouldn't we make sure before waltzing in? What if the Germans did this and doubled back to throw us off?"

"On the off chance four escaped prisoners would come behind them looking for clues? Do you know how difficult it would be to double back an entire battalion? MacDonald and I will scout ahead." William's brow slanted, daring her to protest. "Unless you don't mind belly-crawling over that field to see for yourself."

Gwyn shuddered as she imagined crawling over scorched earth and creeping bugs. "I'll wait here."

She and Roland passed the next hour playing a rudimentary game of noughts and crosses with rocks and acorns until William and MacDonald sauntered back, smiling and covered in dirt.

"Not a Kraut to be found." Sweat streaked down MacDonald's grimy face. "Lots of rubble, but there's life."

And where there was life, there was bound to be food. Gwyn's stomach gurgled at the thought. Beef bully or liver stew sounded like a king's feast after all these days of barely anything to stick to her ribs. And if they had fresh water for a sponge bath—oh, heaven!

Eerie quietness cloaked the town like a shroud. Skeletons of shops stood stark and devoid of their innards. Homes ripped in two, with black burns smudging the once pearly rails and eaves. Brown rooftops sagged like droopy eyelids over unhinged front doors. Rocks, stone, timber, demolished furniture, and shell fragments lined the street creating a winding path between heaps of rubble.

An old man with a broom paused while sweeping debris from his front walk. Stooped and white-haired, his gnarled fingers clutched the splintered handle for support. His front wall was missing, revealing a richly carved dining table with three chairs. The fourth rested in broken pieces under the man's broom.

Tears clogged Gwyn's throat as she offered him a small wave. How could she complain about a bath when this poor man swept his belongings into a rubbish pile in front of his destroyed home?

Shaking, the man straightened his curved spine and doffed his hat to his heart. Gwyn's lips lifted to a watery smile. The place was not completely destroyed.

"Let's try there." William pointed to a tall stack of bricks high above the other buildings. A church bell hung dangerously from a split rope. "If there's any kind of organization, it'll come from the center of town."

As they approached the building, British and French soldiers lounged on the church steps, smoking. Swathed in bandages with makeshift crutches scattered at their feet, they stared blankly at the ground as they waited their turn for the roaming liquor flasks. Nurses dressed in dingy white aprons with scarlet crosses on the front weaved between them, checking a head wrap here and readjusting an arm sling there.

Hot tears scorched the backs of Gwyn's eyelids. They had made it. Perhaps God wasn't too busy to look out for them after all.

William squatted in front of a lieutenant with a stump leg. "What unit are you from, son?"

"Manchester Regiment, sir. Apologies for not standing." The lieutenant gestured to his missing leg. "Having a spot of trouble with that lately."

"No need to apologize for bravery." William clapped him on the shoulder. "Are all of these men Manchester?"

"No, sir. We're a mangled lot from all over. French, Irish,

Scots, even a South African bloke managed to crawl his way from Delville." He took a long drag of his cigarette. "Died yesterday from infection."

"Where is headquarters?"

"I've seen a few brass walking into that building over there. Should be headquarters if there's one set up." Gray smoke curled from his chapped lips. "Sorry I'm not much help, Captain, but this place has been pure confusion for the past three days."

"Is that when it was bombarded?"

"That's when it stopped. After four days of back and forth, we finally bruised those Jerries hard enough to send them scurrying away. Not long after, the sisters came rolling in, and here we are."

"Did they bring plenty of supplies, bandages, food?" Gwyn asked.

The lieutenant's eyebrows lifted as he looked her up and down. "Some, ma'am. And the locals have been helping to fill in where they can."

Gwyn started for the stairs, but William caught her elbow. Deep lines pulled his mouth down. "Where are you going?"

"To scrounge around for something. We haven't had proper food in weeks. It's a miracle any of us are still standing." She dropped her voice. "And Roland's bandage needs to be changed. It's been much too long, and he's limping, though he tries to cover it."

His worried lines turned white. "If you're not back in half an hour, I'm coming in to get you."

She patted his hand with a smile she hoped was encouraging despite her apprehension at what lay inside the church doors. "Fine, fine. Go find headquarters while I enlist Captain Morrison to help sniff around for a kitchen."

Gwyn pushed open the church doors. The stench of war hit her like a hammer. She resisted the urge to empty her stomach into the nearest corner.

"Eh gads! That's awful!" Roland's nostrils flared as he waved a hand in front of his face. "Poor devils."

Gwyn gave him a quelling look. "Let's just find the kitchen."

"You can still think of food?"

"Would you prefer I leave you here and go in search of it myself?"

"And leave you to boast of finding the last crumbs to be had? I think not."

Weaving through the rows of wounded, they ducked into a side hall and glanced around. Steaming heat poured from the right. At the far end of the hall, a large wooden door was propped open. The smell of broth and potatoes leaked out. Inside the room, a thick-shouldered woman with short black hair stood at a long workbench pouring hot tea into cups.

Gwyn stepped behind her and cleared her throat. "Excuse me, ma'am. Could you tell us where we might find a few scraps to eat?"

"Well, I ain't no ma'am—holy smokestacks! Gwyn!" Eugenie's haggard face lit up. Throwing her arms around Gwyn she thumped her on the back, crushing the air from Gwyn's lungs. "We found Rosie, or what was left of her." Eugenie picked up the teapot. "There was so much mess in those woods that no one could tell sideways from thataways. We thought the Germans got you for sure."

Sadness crushed Gwyn's heart. Rosie, her pride and joy, her wheels of freedom, the survival of the wounded. Mangled and abandoned. Tonight the old girl deserved a proper toast.

"Lady Dowling was furious." Eugenie pulled more cups down from the shelf and filled them with the steaming brew. "When she heard they didn't find you, she marched straight to General Haig and gave him two earfuls. She's been snippier than a fish on a hook lately, but I think it's just a show to cover what's really wriggling in her gut. Of course, I'd be the same if I'd just lost my home."

Gwyn jerked out of her inward gloom. "*Maison du Jardins*? It's gone?"

"Germans leveled it about two weeks ago. That's why we're

here."

"Oh, Eugenie. I'm so sorry. Was anyone hurt?"

Eugenie shook her head. "We managed to get the men outside in time, but there's nothing left." She slapped a hand to her forehead. "Here I am jabbering on. You must want to see Hale."

Cecelia. Excitement zipped through Gwyn. "Is she all right? Where is she?"

"Right as rain. Out back. Tent number seventeen."

"Did she just come off a late night shift? You must have a lot of help here to allow a rest from nurse rotation."

"Sure." Eugenie's face pinched as she turned back to her cups. "Just stay to the left, and you'll see them behind the gardens."

Gwyn turned to leave and noticed Roland still standing in the doorway, his eyes fixated on a basket of sliced bread. She'd completely forgotten her reason for coming in in the first place. "Captain Morrison, I'm terribly sorry for abandoning you."

His eyes didn't leave the basket. "Not to worry. I can handle myself. Go find Miss Hale. I'd rather she not see me in this state anyways."

"Yes, but your leg." Growling stomach or not, she couldn't leave that festering bandage on his leg. "Eugenie, where can I find supplies for a leg wound?"

"You just leave him to me." Eugenie grinned and fluffed her cropped hair. "I always liked assisting a good-looking officer in need."

"Don't worry," Gwyn whispered, squeezing his arm. "You're in good hands."

"That's what I'm worried about." Roland dragged wary eyes from the bread to Eugenie. "With a busted leg, I can't outrun those 'good hands.'"

Feeling lighter than she had in weeks, Gwyn skipped down the back steps and beelined for the cluster of tents tucked behind a shriveled garden. At number seventeen, she paused and patted her hair. It felt sticky and stringy, just like the rest of her.

"Cecelia?" No answer. "Cecelia, are you there?" Peeling back the flap, Gwyn ducked and stepped into the tent. Soft light trickled in through the vent at the top, highlighting a tiny desk and stool, a chamber pot, and two rickety cots with a body covering one of them.

"Cecelia?" The body rose and fell in the steady rhythm of sleep. Gwyn gently shook her shoulder. "Cecelia, wake up."

Cecelia leaped off the bed, eyes wide with alarm. "I'm sorry I'm late! I just laid down for a minute—who are you? What are you doing in here?" Jumping away, she banged into the desk. She grabbed a brush and brandished it like a sword.

Gwyn held her hands out. "Calm down! It's me."

The brush went slack in Cecelia's fingers. "Gwyn?"

"Yes, who else would I be?"

"From the looks of you ... some kind of deranged animal." She dropped the brush and threw her arms around Gwyn's neck. "I thought you were dead. They told me they couldn't find you. And Rosie, I'm so sorry about her. Eugenie has taken to fixing her every chance she gets."

Her friend's hot tears streamed down Gwyn's neck, soaking her shirt and back. Gwyn held Cecelia tight as her own lungs constricted with joy.

"Come, come, and sit down." Cecelia swiped the tears from her cheeks and pushed Gwyn onto the cot. "Tell me everything."

Gwyn started slowly, the tension building until the entire story poured forth like a raging river. Exhaustion claimed her by the end, and she fell back against the lumpy pillow, her eyelids heavy.

"My, my, my." Cecelia shook her head as she sagged on the edge of the opposite cot. "A prisoner, wandering in the woods, a knife at your throat. I think I would have slunked under a rock and cried."

Gwyn ran a hand over the scratchy blanket bunched next to her, tracing each curve like the ripples in sand. Nearly threadbare with pilled knots dotting the length of it, she imagined a lamb's ear never felt softer. "You wouldn't have, not with the Germans breathing down your neck. Survival is a strange beast."

Restless at the memories of what she'd done, what she'd had to do to outrun that beast, Gwyn stood and crossed to the desk. Somehow, it hadn't devoured her. Sitting in that filthy basement, she had prayed for deliverance, and it came from the sky as if the Almighty Himself had thrown the shells. And then racing across that field. Not one of those wild bullets had hit her. Shielded again. Could it be so simple? To call on the holy name, and He was there?

She fingered a stack of stationary emblazoned with the Somerset crest, a silver filigree pen, and matching tortoiseshell brush, comb, and hand mirror set. The perfect accessories for a lady's desk. In a war zone. Only CeCe—or more accurately, her mother. No war would stop Lady Somerset's spending. Gwyn smiled to herself, picking up the mirror.

Cecelia's hand flew out, horror sparking across her face. "Oh, G. You may not want to do that."

Too late. The reflection blinked in unison, bursting the hope that the nightmare staring back at Gwyn was a horrible trick of her sleep-deprived mind. Dull hair hung around her face and shoulders in dirty clumps. Her skin was mottled red with freckles across her nose. She blinked again, not wanting to see the purple bags under listless eyes.

Ignorance had been bliss.

She placed the mirror face down on the desk. Tears pricked.

"Oh, G, don't cry." Cecelia pulled a semi-clean handkerchief from her sleeve and dabbed around Gwyn's face. "It's not so bad."

Gwyn stood limp and uncaring as the tears fell faster. "You can't even stand near me with your crisp skirt and pristine nails, all scrubbed fresh and shiny. I'll bet the pigs don't even smell as bad as I do."

"The troops took all the pigs long ago, so there's nothing to compare." Cecelia caught a stray tear off Gwyn's chin. "And you have every right to look … downtrodden after your ordeal."

"Downtrodden?" Gwyn sniffed and rubbed her nose on the

back of her sleeve. "You sound like a vicar during a Sunday sermon."

"Blame the doctor." Cecelia sighed and slumped on the cot again, chin in her hand. "He hounds everyone into service once a week. The other day, I was awake long enough to hear the lesson on rejoicing when you're down on your luck."

Gwyn smoothed the handkerchief between her palms to dry the blotches creeping closer to the delicate C embroidered in the corner. "Doctor who?"

"Bennett. He's much nicer looking than I originally gave him credit for, with a smooth voice, and he's excellent with the patients."

"How has he come to be here?"

"That whole area was shelled, as far back as *de Jardins*. The army herded us here in desperate need of medical help." She attempted a smile that didn't reach her eyes. "We call ourselves the nomads."

Gwyn's self-pity dried up. "What happened?"

Cecelia picked at her gray cotton skirt, bunching the fabric between her nails. "It was night. We heard the guns, but something was different. The shots more determined. I'm sure I don't have to tell you how scary it was the closer they came."

Gwyn nodded. She knew all too well that terrible sound.

"The windows began to shake, then shattered over the men." She paused, her knuckles white in her lap. "I started grabbing mattresses to shield them. It worked for a time, but we needed to evacuate."

"That was quick thinking with the mattresses."

A smile flitted across Cecelia's face. "It took all night to get the men to safety, and in the morning there was nothing left standing except a chimney and part of the staircase. All those beautiful things smashed to rubble."

"Things can be replaced. The important thing is the lives you saved."

"I nearly forgot!" Hopping up, Cecelia dug into the small storage box at the foot of her cot and pulled out a carefully wrapped book. "I had just enough time to grab this and those pearl earrings my grandmother gave me."

Gwyn peeled back the cotton wrap and gasped. Her mother's Bible. Tears clogged her throat as she flipped straight to Proverbs. There, nestled right next to chapter three, was her and mum's dream list and William's petals. Safe and sound.

"Not all things can be replaced," Cecelia said.

"Thank you, thank you." Throwing her arms around her friend, Gwyn hugged Cecelia tight. She could lose every possession in the world, but to lose this—her mother's final gift—would have broken her soul.

"It's kept me entertained while I wait for the soap cakes to finish forming."

Gwyn sniffed, determined not to let the emotions get to her once again. "Why are you forming soap cakes? Do you have that much time between nursing shifts?"

Cecelia's cheeks flushed pink. "I'm in charge of hygiene since I dropped a glass bottle on a colonel's broken foot. Doctor Bennett said the colonel probably deserved it after complaining that officers should receive care before enlisted no matter the injury, but Lady Dowling had no choice but to put me somewhere else. Now I'm in charge of all things bath, and let me tell you, these men need it." Her delicate nose wrinkled. "Speaking of which—"

"Gwyn?" The roar came from outside. Heavy boots pounded the dirt. "Gwyn!"

William. She'd nearly forgotten about him. He was the last person she wanted to see at that moment. "I'm here."

The tent flap rustled, and William's head poked in. Relief washed over the grim line of his mouth as he zeroed in on Gwyn. "Thirty minutes. I've been looking for you everywhere."

"William!" Cecelia squealed and launched herself at him. He caught her before she toppled them both backward. "Oh, Will. I'm so glad you're safe." Cecelia wrapped her arms around his neck. "Gwyn told me the whole story. How horrible for you all."

William looked at Gwyn over the top of Cecelia's head. "Yes, but we're back now. A little worse for the wear."

Cecelia's mouth curved like a cat's anticipating its cream. Her long eyelashes blinked as she took in every part of his face. "You look just fine to me."

The happiness warming in Gwyn's chest turned cold. Cecelia still wanted him, and by all rules of society, he should choose her and not some greased-up chauffeur's daughter. If Gwyn had a wise bone in her body, she'd stick to her plans of adventure and travel far outside the length of a man's arms. The coldness turned into a writhing knot.

Cecelia slipped her arm down to hook around William's elbow. "You both look just fine, except you could use a good cleaning. And I know just the place."

Linking her other arm with Gwyn's, Cecelia dragged them from the tent jabbering on about the latest shipment of rose and mint leaf soap cakes from her mother and how they would rid them of every last remnant of their harrowing journey.

But there was one part of the journey Gwyn had no desire to rid herself of. And he was firmly attached to her best friend's arm.

CHAPTER 20

It was no use. No matter how many times he plowed the comb through his hair, it wouldn't lay down without a splash of styling oil. William stared at the hanging mirror, willing the blond hair to lay flat behind his ears. It ignored him and curled.

"Just use spit. Work it into a paste." Roland rubbed a fresh towel over his head. He'd stepped out of the makeshift washroom, which consisted of two copper hip baths and buckets full of lukewarm water set behind the church, half an hour ago and couldn't get over the thrill of running a clean cloth through his neatly scrubbed hair.

"Disgusting." William flung the comb down and snatched a cup with shaving cream. Whipping the cream into a froth, he slathered it on his whiskered cheeks, chin, and throat. Then, taking the stropped razor, he eased it down the sides of his face in long, even strokes. Foamy clouds flecked with grizzly hairs fell to the ground.

At least Gwyn wouldn't think him some madman of the woods any longer. No wonder she hadn't wanted to kiss him last night. His mouth pulled up at the corner. Perhaps a clean cheek would give him the advantage next time.

If there was a next time. The hurt in her eyes when Cecelia had hurled herself at him had hit like a fist to the stomach. Did Gwyn really believe he preferred any other woman to her? As beautiful and well-connected as Cecelia was, she could never hold a candle to Gwyn's spirit and courage. Her enthusiasm to tackle every obstacle with the tenacity of a thoroughbred had rankled him to the core when he first met her. The woman needed to learn her place, but he soon saw that her place was not among the other women. She was ahead of them, forging her own path.

The razor paused mid-stroke. How had he let such an independent woman wriggle her way into his disciplined life? And now that she was there, what was he going to do about it?

Women didn't belong in his life, at least not now. The war didn't allow for such distractions, and distracting those females were. They played by their own irrational rules, gave into emotions at the drop of a hat, and expected the perfect husband complete with slippers and pipe. And yet Gwyn expected him to have his own dreams and plans, to seek his own happiness outside of what others dictated to him.

"Daydreaming again?" Roland peeked around the wooden pole that hung the shaving mirrors. "Let me guess, it involves a pair of bright green eyes and long dark hair."

William frowned and turned his razor back to his chin. "You're distracting me. Don't you have a few nurses to chase?"

"Only nurse worth chasing is after you. The rest of them have thick ankles and chapped hands. What do you plan to do about that?"

"They can always try lotion."

"Not the crones. The lovely Miss Hale."

"Nothing. Her affections are one-sided, and I have done nothing to encourage them."

"Seems the lady is blind to your lack of feelings." Roland ran a hand over his boyishly smooth cheek. "So blind, in fact, that she's outside ironing your holey shirt and threadbare trousers with the gusto of a newlywed. Can't say she's had much practice since there's a burn mark on the cuff."

"Blast it all!" William swiped at the trickle of blood under his jaw. "Doesn't she realize that—"

"That you're in love with her dear friend? No, I don't think she does."

William's fingers went slack, dropping the blade on the ground. "Love? Who said anything about that?"

The teasing light faded from Roland's eyes. Flipping an empty water bucket upside down, he eased himself onto it. "I've never seen you so agitated."

"I've never felt so agitated." William retrieved his razor. He pulled the blade across his trouser leg to wipe off the grass bits. If only his problems swiped away so cleanly. "At least with the Jerries you can sense the battle coming, you can prepare for the tactics and counter. War is predictable like that."

Roland snorted. "Women are far from your comfort zone. A fact you need to overcome because their qualities far outweigh Wilhelm's. And let me tell you something else"—he leaned forward, hands on his knees—"those guns you polish every day aren't going to keep you warm at night."

"She's not interested in staying warm, not when there's a motor engine around. Did you not see her glowing when Eugenie mentioned changing the spark plugs on Rosie?"

"You light her up more than ol' Rosie, mate."

William grabbed the leather strop and flicked the blade up and down its length, his mind whirling faster than a dervish. Gwyn's response to his kiss had left his blood hotter than a July day under full gear, but that didn't mean she wanted a ring on her finger. How could he cage such a rare bird within the strict rules his military life dictated? "Whoever you think does the lighting up, she has no intention of settling down. And I certainly don't need the shackles of one more person's scrutiny on me."

"We're not talking about your father, Will."

"And what about you? You're fine to follow around behind me, giving me lessons on life and love, but is this where you want to be? Do you have a devoted girl waiting for you at home?"

"No, I don't, but at least if I had one worth fighting for, I wouldn't keep her at arm's length." The bucket fell back as Roland surged to his feet and jabbed a finger at William's chest. "If you're too pig-headed to see it, then you deserve those cold guns. Happy cuddling."

Yanking the curtain back, Roland stormed off. William caught Cecelia's voice before the divider fell back into place. Perfect. After weeks of being shot at, imprisoned, and finally escaping, he'd railed at his friend and sent the only woman who meant anything to him straight into the arms of a busted-up Rolls Royce.

Grabbing a towel, William wiped away the remaining bits of foam from his face. His skin itched, but he would gladly endure it over those sweating bristles. With the tip of his toe, he flipped Roland's bucket back over and sat down. William stretched his legs, running his bare feet over the cool grass and wriggling his toes. Confined to scratchy socks, boots that rubbed a permanent scar into the back of his heels, and puttees that constricted blood flow to his legs for far too long, the simple touch of green blades against skin was heaven.

Closing his eyes, he pictured the hills outside Hereford, rolling and gentle as twilight turned the sprawling grass to blue-green. Horses galloped on the late spring breeze, their powerful muscles flexing and stretching beneath their shiny coats, their hooves devouring ground beneath them.

Gwyn would love their sheer speed. Barefooted and dark curls streaming behind her, he could see her chasing them, trying to catch up.

He smiled. That was the life she deserved. That was the life he wanted to give her.

"William?"

His eyes popped open at Cecelia's voice. Standing, he pulled back the curtain and met two anxious brown eyes.

"I was wondering what was taking you so long." Her thick eyelashes fluttered against pink cheeks. "I thought Captain Morrison was the one to pamper himself."

"His boyish good looks don't require as much attention as my grizzled face does," William said. Did she check on all the men like this? "I just need to pull on my boots, then I'll be out of the way for the next man."

"Oh, there's no line." Her cheeks flushed. "What I mean is, take all the time you need. You deserve it. Here, I hope you don't mind the liberty I took in ironing it for you. I thought you could use something crisp like your former uniform, which Gwyn said you lost along the way. It's so nice to see men in full-buttoned uniform. Very dashing."

Ignoring the off-center creases and brown burn marks, he slipped the shirt over his undershirt. His wrists protruded four inches longer than the cuffs. "Thank you for the trouble."

"No trouble, especially now that I've had lots of practice. My first few days on the job were horrendous. One of the other nurses had to show me how to boil water for scrubbing. Can you imagine? And now I'm the best fire-stoker in the unit."

"You should be proud of yourself. Most ladies shun such honest labor."

She beamed. "Nursing is not my calling, but I'm trying. Tonight I've volunteered to do something a little more in-line with my upbringing and play for the gathering."

William fumbled with the buttons on his cuff, but they refused to meet around the bulge of his forearm. Giving up, he rolled them. "What gathering?"

"A few of the men are putting on skits, and I've been asked to play a piano they found in the mayor's home. With things quiet, the men need a release, and the townsfolk need an excuse to smile again."

"We can all use an excuse to smile again."

"You'll be there?" Expectancy flared in her eyes.

"I have a few people to talk to over at headquarters, but yes, I'll try to be there."

She stepped closer, the scent of rose water floating around her like a halo. Her eyelashes fluttered like butterfly wings. How did women perfect that move? And why did they think it necessary? "Maybe afterward we can talk? Just the two of us."

A rock lodged in his chest. He didn't want to hurt her, but

she couldn't pin her hopes on him when his heart belonged to someone else. "Yes, there's something I'd like to talk to you about."

She smiled brighter than an angel, and the rock plummeted to his stomach. He'd rather face the Jerries in only his underwear than tell her his feelings could never match hers.

"Nurse Hale." Lady Dowling bore down on them like a U-boat, eyes narrowed, mouth pulled tight, and long skirt snapping around her thin ankles. "I trust you've finished the rest of the wash and have started on the bed linens? We'd hate to be down a pianist due to scrubbing duties."

Cecelia ducked her head. "Yes, m'lady." Giving William a sideways smile, she hurried back to her boiling pot.

Lady Dowling turned to him. "I heard you brought my girl back safe and sound. Thank you for that. We made ourselves sick with worry when she was reported missing. She wasn't the general's to command in the first place."

"No, m'lady. She wasn't, but Miss Ruthers performed admirably. Many of the men would have died without her talents."

Lady Dowling harrumphed. "She's a brave girl, a fine girl."

"Yes, m'lady. The finest I know."

Her eyes pierced him like a hawk. "And Miss Hale?"

Heat crept up the back of William's neck. "Very admirable."

"But not the one you want." William's mouth opened. The old woman grinned. "Welcome back, Captain." Pivoting on her heel, she marched back inside the church.

CHAPTER 21

William shifted against the low stone wall as the warm summer night filled with home-sickening melodies of old Blighty. Tears glistened on the troop's cheeks. Burly mustaches twitched. Those brave enough under the marchioness's watchful eye passed around flasks of comfort.

That morning, William had awoken as a man on the run, and he now found himself sitting behind a shelled city hall at a sing-a-long, not that he had any intention of singing. Sensitive ears didn't deserve his horrendous vocals. Tonight's serenade belonged to Cecelia.

Her fingers flitted over the piano keys with easy precision, keeping tune to the melody in a crystal-clear voice. She fairly glowed as all eyes rested on her, transfixed by the magic she created with each song. Nursing may not have been her calling, but entertaining others certainly was.

"And now, Major Bennett has graciously agreed to accompany me on a few duets." Cecelia tinkled the keys. "Are you sure you can step away from your patients long enough to give it a fair try, Doctor?"

Jumping up from his seat on the grass, Bennett joined her at the piano. "How could I say no to such a lovely partner?"

"You couldn't, of course." She flashed a smile that sent red spiraling across the doctor's face. Ducking his head, he ran a hand over the back of his neck.

William watched in disbelief as the always calm and collected doctor unraveled like a rug under Cecelia's fluttering lashes. With each gentle tease, she coaxed him closer until his arm brushed her shoulder.

"Why Doctor Bennett. How did you know this was a romantic song?"

The crowd roared with laughter. Bennett leaped back from Cecelia as she smiled and continued tapping out a melody. Tugging the front of his tunic, Bennett's red face faded to pink as he stepped back to her side. Poor man. He was smitten, and now the entire town and ragtag units of the British army knew it.

William crossed his arms over his chest and took a deep breath that did little to dislodge the knot in his stomach. He knew all too well the bumbling that came with falling for a girl.

Searching the crowd, he spotted the motley crew of ambulance drivers sitting on the far side of the piano. Gwyn caught his eye and looked away.

The knot in his stomach cinched tighter. Kissing her had blown apart his defenses, and there was no turning back, but Gwyn was going to make him fight every step of the way before she surrendered her heart. It was worth fighting for.

Light from the campfire flickered across her face in orange waves, dipping into the curve of her slender neck and the hollow at the base of her throat. With each small movement, red shimmered from the depths of the dark hair coiled loosely at the back of her head. Escaped tendrils brushed her cheek and neck. How silky those gentle curls would feel sliding between his fingers.

"*Sometimes when I feel bad and things look blue*
I wish a pal I had ... say one like you."

Cecelia's and Bennett's voices filled the air in perfect harmony. The crowd sniffed at the sugary words.

"*Someone within my heart to build a throne.*
Someone who'd never part, to call my own."

A longing pulled at William's gut, swelling the loneliness to aching clarity. Gwyn's lips moved with the song, but those were not the lyrics he longed to hear from them. The memory of her soft sigh as she leaned further into his kiss purled in his blood with desire. Never had he wanted anything so much, until now. He could think of nothing else but deepening the kiss and holding her tighter.

Gwyn turned to Eugenie and laughed. If he'd arrived ten minutes earlier, he might have managed a seat next to her and been the one to make her smile.

"Join in, boys. I want to hear how well you can serenade the ladies." Cecelia spoke over her piano keys. "Ladies, follow me. I want to hear everyone singing."

"If you were the only girl in the world and I were the only boy.
Nothing else would matter in the world today.
We could go on loving in the same old way."

Gwyn ribbed Eugenie. Frowning, Eugenie's lips moved to the words. Surrounded by war, Gwyn still found happiness in a simple song. A song that said nothing in the world mattered with the right woman at his side.

The melody started as a hum. The right woman at his side. A woman who expected things from him, but for his own happiness, not hers. A woman who made him feel more alive than he ever had. The hum vibrated to words on his lips.

Gwyn's gaze drifted over the crowd to his. Her mouth stopped moving but his didn't as he watched her lips form a soft O. Shadowed flames danced across her face, mesmerizing him with their hypnotic sway over her full mouth, cheeks, and eyes now hooded by night.

"If you were the only girl in the world and I were the only boy."

The corners of her mouth tilted up. No one existed beyond her. The flame in her eyes wrapped around his heart and tugged at him until there was not a space between them.

Clapping erupted. Gwyn's eyes dropped to her lap, her cheeks spotting red.

"Thank you, thank you." Cecelia rose from her seat and dropped into a perfect curtsey. "What beautiful voices you all have. If I had known, I would have made you serenade me sooner."

The men laughed and clapped louder. "Encore! Encore!"

Cecelia glowed. Sweeping her skirt aside like a queen in a ball gown, she perched back on the edge of her bench. "Well, if you insist. But only if the good doctor will join me. Isn't he splendid?"

Cecelia jingled a new tune, but William heard not a word of it as Gwyn's eyes turned to meet his again. His heart pounded faster than a machine gun. He couldn't wait any longer.

He motioned with his head. Her eyebrows pulled down. He motioned again. The eyebrows raised, and she nodded. Leaving his spot, he weaved through the crowd and made his way to the back. He couldn't wait to see her, to rake his fingers through the silky hair that had tempted him all night, to pull her close and feel the heat from her gaze sink into him. To show her the longing flowing in his heart.

Major Longmire, a squatty man with iron-gray hair and small eyes, blocked his path. "Crawford. There you are. Think of any more details you wish to add to your report? Why double-time wasn't made to get back in the fighting sooner? How you managed to lose three men while escaping?"

Anger clenched William's hands, demanding a fist to Longmire's fat nose. William gripped his hands behind his back until his knuckles popped. "My decisions were based on the resources and circumstances at hand. *Sir*."

Longmire's eyes gleamed like coal. "You are to report to Colonel Helms at once. He has a few more questions for you."

"I've told him everything I know, sir. I left nothing out of my earlier report."

"It seems he needs more."

"Yes, sir. I'll go straight to headquarters as soon as I—"

"As soon as now."

From the corner of his eye, William saw Gwyn slipping through the crowd. She didn't see him. "Yes, sir, but there's something—"

"Something as important as reporting to your commanding officer?" Longmire stretched up on his toes, putting himself eye-level with William's chin. "Get to it."

William searched again, but she was gone. He'd have plenty of explaining to do later, maybe find a wildflower not razed by shells to soften her up a bit.

Longmire prodded him in the shoulder. If William found a flower now, he'd ram it down the man's throat. If his night were ruined, then he'd make sure the frog man's was spent spitting out petals.

CHAPTER 22

The wrench spun like a dial, blurring faster and faster until it flew off the side of the engine and cartwheeled in the dirt.

Eugenie squawked. "Watch it, will you? You almost hit me in the face that time."

Gwyn swooped down and grabbed the wrench. "Sorry."

"What's with you today? Like a cat that slurped sour milk for breakfast, not to mention disappearing on me last night."

Leaning in under Rosie's bonnet, Gwyn tightened another loose bolt. "Just tired."

"Tired of thinking about that captain?"

The wrench slipped between Gwyn's fingers. She caught it before it disappeared into a tangle of hoses. "Whatever are you talking about?"

"I saw you two making eyes at each other last night." Eugenie pushed her greasy sleeve back up her arm before moving on to the next clamp.

"I'm sure he was watching Cecelia the whole time like everyone else."

"He surely was not, though I'm sure she was hoping he was. Don't know why she's so moon-eyed over him when that handsome doctor hangs on her pinkie."

"You find Major Bennett more of a catch than Captain Crawford?"

"It's all preference, ain't it? I like the ones who can do something besides shoot a gun. And if I got a cold, he could bring me beef tea." Leaning her forearms on the fender, Eugenie raised a thick eyebrow. Mischief twinkled in her eyes. "The captain's nice-looking too. You know that better than anyone after staring at him like a proper fish on a platter all night."

Gwyn's fingers balled around the wrench handle. "I was not."

"Then you both leave at the same time, and now you're sour today, dropping tools, and uninterested in the new clamps I borrowed from those Yankee chaps."

Gwyn looked over her shoulder to where the new American ambulance recruits laughed and smoked by their motors. "Do they know you borrowed them?"

"Course. Made a trade with that skinny one. Name's Walt, funny last name. Likes to draw cartoon rodents."

"If you borrowed, why the trade for smokes?"

Eugenie's mouth screwed into a frown. "These Yanks aren't very trusting with their things. Seems they like equal payment."

"Imagine that."

Eugenie cupped her hands around her mouth. "Hey, Walt! How you like those English cigarettes?"

Walt took a long drag and blew it out. "Good, but not great like an American. How you like those Yank clamps?"

"Better if they were English." Rolling her eyes, Eugenie turned back to Rosie's innards. "Americans wouldn't know quality if it were fish fins slapping them in the face. What do you think of ol' Rosie now?"

"Almost as good as new." Gwyn walked to the other side, patting Rosie on her front fender. "Let's crank her and see where that rattle is coming from."

But for one of the few times in Gwyn's life, the rattle couldn't hold her attention. She replayed every second of the night before. Why didn't William meet her? Was there a weapons emergency, or had he simply changed his mind and run the opposite direction? Or—worst of all—had she been so desperate for him that she'd imagined the desire in his eyes?

The engine sputtered, spewing white smoke.

"What did those Germans do to my girl?" Gwyn frowned and

poked under the radiator. "I'm starting her up again."

Eugenie finished patching a tire and stuck her head around the side of the bonnet. "She need water with all that smoke?"

"I think it's just a loose hose bolt, but let's make sure." Gwyn set to spinning the crank, but after a few turns, her arm began to ache. "Out of practice for a few weeks and I'm weaker than a two-legged cat."

"Don't let those cats fool you. They'll still get you if you rile them."

Rosie roared to life, belching white smoke. Finding the source, Gwyn hooked her wrench around the half-twisted bolt and tightened. It felt good to be in the grease again, to put her hands on things that made sense. A few quick turns here, and it was tightened, a few cranks there, and it started. If only she could take a hammer and bend life back to the way it had been.

"Why do I always find you under a smoking bonnet?" Gwyn jumped at William's voice, whacking her head on the bonnet. He grabbed her elbow as she teetered sideways. "Are you all right?"

"Fine." She leaned away from his touch. "You startled me."

His hand fell back to his side. "I need to talk to you."

"Oh? About what?"

He took a deep breath. "Last night. Today. What's coming."

"What's coming?" She took in his buffed boots, the reshaped hat, and the pistol strapped to his side. The seriousness on his face told her everything. "They're sending you back to your unit, aren't they?"

He nodded. "They need every available man, and since I have no injuries, there's no reason to stay."

But there was every reason. She swallowed the fear bobbing in her throat. "When do you leave?"

"Soon."

"And Captain Morrison?"

"He leaves too."

"But his leg. Surely he needs to rest before they put him in a trench again."

"The doctor said he can stand on it, so that's good enough."

Gwyn's fingers curled around her wrench, not wanting to believe the words ringing in her ears. "That's madness."

"That's desperation. We're running out of men and supplies faster than we can restock them. The army has started drafting the rejected."

"But you were a prisoner. They thought we were dead. Surely that ensures you a bit of time to recover."

"They've got men slugging in the lines with heart murmurs, crooked backs, and clubbed feet, not to mention the old men and boys still young enough to be in school. You think they care about me?" Yanking off his cap, he shoved a hand through his hair and down his neck. "Walk with me." She started, but he held her elbow. "Without this." He pried the wrench from her fist. "I feel like you're ready to club someone, and I'd rather it not be me."

"Eugenie, can you check the other hoses? I'll be back shortly, then we can take a look at that gasket," Gwyn said.

"Sure, sure. I think I can handle a few clamps on my own." All mischief disappeared from Eugenie's face as she looked at William. "If I don't see you before you leave, take care out there, and tell that Captain Morrison to keep that leg clean. I bandaged it nice and tight once. Don't want to see my handiwork go to pot."

William nodded. "Will do."

Gwyn and William walked along the long stretch of ambulances. The morning haze had burned away to reveal a bright blue sky streaked with thin white clouds that hovered motionless above them.

Chills tingled the hairs on the back of Gwyn's neck despite the early August heat. With her one pair of jodhpurs being scrubbed under Cecelia's careful eye, she'd been left to a long navy skirt and green blouse kindly donated by a local woman. The loose material felt odd floating around her legs, tangling between them when she moved too quickly.

Beside her, William tugged on his collar. "A few days without having to wear this scratchy thing and I've forgotten how bothersome it is in summer."

She much preferred his loose trousers and cotton shirt rolled up to his elbows. Just as he looked last night. Calm and relaxed, without the threat of marching off to battle. The chills sprang to her arms. "Why didn't you meet me last night?"

"I was ambushed and hauled off to headquarters." He stopped at the corner of a low-walled garden behind two abandoned houses. The smell of dead flowers and overgrown weeds mottled the air. "By the time they released me, it was well past midnight. I didn't think you'd appreciate me scratching on your tent at that hour."

"I was awake."

"If I had known, I would have—you do know I wanted to see you?"

She plucked a dried leaf from a curling vine and twirled it between her fingers. "I thought you'd changed your mind."

He stroked a finger down her cheek, igniting a trail of heat along her skin. The clear depths of his eyes darkened. "About you? No."

Low and rough, his voice raked over her with the intensity of a hundred glowing coals. She turned her face into his hand. "But with all these lovely nurses running around, I can't imagine holding you to a greasy mechanic."

"I imagine holding you. All the time." His mouth lowered to hers, claiming her lips with an intensity that jolted her down to her toes. She circled her arms around his neck and pressed into him, slanting her lips over every curve of his in a desperate attempt to satisfy her spiraling hunger for him.

He thrust his fingers into her hair, loosening the pins until the coiled braid unraveled down her back. A soft moan escaped as his lips swept along her jaw and back to her mouth, reclaiming her kiss.

Shivering, Gwyn dropped her head to his chest, clutching his lapels to keep upright as the world spun like a top. Safety, warmth, and belonging enveloped her within his embrace. How perfectly she fit there.

"Horses."

Gwyn stiffened. After a quaking kiss, horses were not the first thing he was supposed to think about. "Pardon?"

"You asked me if there was anything in the world I wanted to do. Horses. I want to raise them."

Her muscles relaxed. He was still thinking of her, in an odd manner. "Like a horse farm? I've read about places in America and Iceland where the wild ones still roam free. Maybe I'll add it to my list."

"What list is this?"

She'd never told anyone about her list. Certainly, Papa knew of its existence as it had been Mum's once, but Gwyn never told him how it inspired her to seek out adventures. It was a secret of sorts, one shared between mother and daughter, but now it was time to share it with someone else. Someone who carried her heart. "When my mother was a girl, she wrote a list of all the places in the world she wished to one day visit. She never got to see them, but I will. One day, I'll cross off every location on that list. For her and me." She squeezed him tight. "I think it could use a few new places."

"Would you like a travel companion?"

"I might need someone to help carry the luggage."

He pinched her shoulder playfully. "After all that traveling, it would be nice to end the day somewhere quiet, with wide land to run the horses and hills for the sun to set behind. The conclusion to a perfect day with no one shooting at me."

"Just animals to bite and kick you when you're not looking."

"Still wary of the beasts, are you?" He chuckled, the deep noise rumbling against her ear. "Titan was a perfect gentleman, as promised. I believe you may owe him an apology when we return home."

Home. So far away with no horizon in sight. Only heartache.

"Please don't go, William," she whispered.

His uneven breathing ruffled her hair. "I have to. They shoot deserters."

A harsh whimper strangled in her throat.

"Sorry. Bad humor."

"It's not humor because it's true, but it's something I never have to worry about for you. You'd stand guard over a pair of socks if they ordered it. Loyalty runs deep in those soldiering veins of yours."

"Family habit."

A whistle shrilled from the town center, ringing down the alley between the houses and cutting into Gwyn's heart. "Where are they sending you?"

"Back to the Front, east of here." The whistle sounded again. "It's time."

She nodded, the rough front of his jacket scratching her cheek, but she didn't care. It was real. During the long, frightful nights ahead, she could remember the realness of him, the wool of his coat, the clean scent of linen clinging to him, and the deep breaths expanding his lungs. "Be safe," she whispered.

Hooking a finger under her chin, he lifted her face and pressed a kiss to her cheek. "Stay out of trouble."

He marched down the alley towards the town's central square, each step leaving her colder and colder.

"William!" Feet flying, she threw herself into his arms. Into his kiss. Closer she pressed into him, desperate to savor the bittersweet moment. His hands twining in her hair, scoring her back, seizing the air from her lungs.

"No!"

The anguished cry pierced Gwyn's ears louder than a cannon. Spinning out of William's arms, Cecelia stood on the path behind them. Her entire body shook, her face white with betrayal.

Gwyn stepped towards her. "Cecelia, please—"

Cecelia whirled and disappeared around the corner.

Gwyn clasped her shaking hands to her stomach. Sickness roiled inside. She spun back to the alley. William was gone.

CHAPTER 23

"Please, let me in."

"Go away!"

Gwyn's shoulders sagged as she stared at the closed flap to Cecelia's tent. "We need to talk."

"I have nothing to say to you."

"You can't shut me out forever."

"If you say one more word, I'll scream." Cecelia's last words broke on a sob.

Turning, Gwyn trudged away, each footstep heavier than the last until they dragged in the dirt like weights. How surprising they did not crush to dust the broken pieces of her heart trailing behind.

Two days had passed since William left. His absence left a hole inside her she never knew could exist. Cecelia's tears ripped it further open. Gwyn had begged and pleaded outside Cecelia's tent for hours, drawing stares and whispers from the nurses and drivers walking by. Gwyn didn't care. Her friend was in pain, and she had caused it. Guilt wound around her heart like a vine of thorns, choking and pricking the life from her.

She never intended it to happen. William, a soldier dedicated to duty and a man striving for tradition, embodied everything in her life she didn't want. He ordered her around and would never find the underside of an engine as fascinating as she did. But he hadn't tried to shatter her dreams. He even had a few of his own.

Her selfish dream-building had shattered her friend's hope. Cecelia may never talk to Gwyn again, may never forgive her. But letting go of the one man who had burrowed into her heart would break it beyond repair. To choose one meant to lose the other.

She slumped against Rosie's bumper. Stars dotted the inky black sky, their brilliance dimmed by the haze of clouds. A cool breeze whispered by, warning of the changing weather on its way. A nice change until winter set in. Which was worse—melting into a sticky mess in summer or freezing to ice in winter?

"Why must life always be a choice?" She raised her face to the heavens, wishing she could see the reasoning beyond. "For once, could You not make the path split? Make one straight, unquestionable way filled with sunshine and daffodils?"

Was there a right or wrong choice? Choosing William betrayed her friendship with Cecelia, but for Gwyn to turn her back on him would be the greatest of betrayals to her heart. She touched a finger to her lips, where the memory of his kiss lingered. She could never part with him now.

Leaning forward, she braced her elbows on her knees and dropped her weary chin into her hands. "I know You're busy, God, and probably have more important people to talk to besides me, but if You could just end this war and let us all go home, I promise not to bother You with much else." She paused, debating her next words, but He was supposed to know her thoughts, so there was no point in trying to hide them. "I know I said I'd try not to bother You, but if You could keep William safe, I'd be so grateful."

"Talking to yourself?" Eugenie materialized from the dark with a lantern swinging from one hand and two cups balanced in the other. "Not shell-shocked are you? We'll have to send you to one of those French hospitals where they zap the men with electricity to scramble their brains back right."

"My mind is a bit muddled, but not that much. Lady Dowager will have a fit if she sees you with that light after curfew."

"She's patrolling the burn ward tonight, so there's no possibility of her seeing my little light."

"Quite defiant of you."

"Hardly." Eugenie snorted and plopped down on the ground,

handing one of the cups to Gwyn. Opening the lantern door, she blew out the tiny orange flame. "Them boys don't watch where they're flicking their cigarettes, and I'm tired of getting burned every time I walk by in the dark."

Gwyn wrapped her hands around the warm mug and breathed in the rich aroma of melted chocolate. A decadence in the middle of decay. "Maybe you should stop prowling around at night."

"And leave who to check on the cars?"

Gwyn winced. With her mind elsewhere lately, the ambulances had slipped somewhere to the back. "I'm sorry I've left you with all the duties. I promise to stop being dead weight."

"Don't give me that." Ripping off her worn cap and dropping it next to her, Eugenie fluffed a hand through her dark cropped hair. "You've had a rough turn. It's only fair you deserve a little time to get yourself back together. Hale still not talking to you?"

Everyone knew. Even Lady Dowling had questioned Gwyn about the sudden coldness between her and Cecelia. Gwyn took a long swallow of the chocolate drink. "She refuses to see me. Did you swipe this from Alice again? She was madder than a wet hen the last time you took her private stash."

"Not so private when she keeps it in a can at the foot of her bunk." Eugenie raised her cup and gulped. "Can't blame her. Hale, I mean. I'd do the same if I thought my good friend had stolen my man."

Gwyn jolted upright, sloshing hot chocolate on her leg. "What has Cecelia been saying?"

"Not a word, but silence lets the gossipers make their own mischief. No facts to contend with. And this is too good a rumor for them to pass up."

"Now there are rumors?"

Eugenie leaned back on her elbows and stretched out her stubby legs. "You and Hale been friends a long time, she gets her eye caught on a handsome captain and pines for him while he's gone. Meanwhile, you and he are camping together in the woods for weeks, she's here crying for both of you, and then on your return, you're the one found canoodling with him."

Gwyn groaned. "Those aren't rumors. It actually happened."

"Sure, but it's the added details that spice up the truth. You probably don't want to know about those." Eugenie's thick eyebrows wiggled like wooly caterpillars.

"Not really."

"Good, because I've seen your fingernails, and I know for a fact they're not long enough to scratch Hale's eyes despite what the other girls are saying."

Outrage shot Gwyn to her feet. The last precious drops of her chocolate flecked over the grass. "This is ridiculous. I'm going to rip Cecelia's tent open seam by seam if I have to and make things right again between us. Somehow. I refuse to be the topic of a bunch of giggling nurses' cruel gossip. Dragging Cecelia's name through the mud, who do they think they are?"

"Boxing the giggling nurses' ears sounds like more fun." Eugenie slurped back the rest of her drink and jumped up. "I'll go with you."

"I'm not lowering myself to their standards by going after them."

"It'll make you feel better. Besides, they preen around here like peacocks thinking they're so much better than us." She harrumphed. "Wouldn't have any patients if not for us."

A siren's wail scratched the air.

Gwyn froze. "What is that?"

"A warning," Eugenie said. "We only need to worry if it's followed by two short—"

Two short wails punctuated the warning.

"We're up. Let's get 'em cranked."

Running around to Rosie's front, Gwyn spun the crank until she charged with life. Adrenaline pumped through her veins.

A driver sprinted down the rows of ambulances. "Southwest, six miles! Boys got taken by surprise trying to detonate a bridge!

Let's go, let's go!"

Gwyn jumped behind Rosie's wheel, breathing a prayer of relief. William was east. The other engines roared and hummed. She tapped her fingers against the seat to keep her toes from launching to the pedal as she waited her turn to enter the column of motorcars. "Come on, come on."

Finally, the car in front of her jerked forward. They sped into the dark. The road bumped and twisted, jutting down and peaking over crater lips from cannon blasts. Gwyn's teeth jarred as she held onto the wheel with all her might. How would they manage this drive with men bleeding out in the back?

Mile after mile clicked by, each new bend twisting a knot in Gwyn's stomach. Surely they should be there by now? Dark villages slept beyond the barren fields to either side of the sunken road. Did their inhabitants lay in their beds counting the number of motors rumbling by, wondering if the next attack was coming for them?

Wind stung Gwyn's eyes. With her goggles blown to pieces somewhere near Delville Wood, she could merely blink to keep them from drying out. A blind driver, just what the wounded needed.

She pounded her fist against the steering wheel. "How much further?"

Dipping around another bend, the carnage spread before them like an anthill explosion. Blackened bodies lay motionless. Supplies and bridge remnants splintered the ground. Tangy metal, churned earth, and charred remains polluted the air.

Ten minutes later, Gwyn approached the front of the line. Slamming Rosie into park, she hopped down and raced to throw the doors open. "I can take two stretchers, three sitters in the back and one in the front," she told the stretcher bearers. "What have we got?"

"Shrapnel to the stomach." They loaded the first man. "And the other is missing a leg. Then we got a crushed hand, a knock upside the head, and possibly two feet that need to come off."

Two more times she made the trip, each drive longer than before. With the need for haste, she didn't have time between loads to rinse the bloodied floorboards or stretchers. Her thoughts barely lingered on the tossed-about fellows as she dodged ruts and holes with only a sliver of moonlight to guide her.

"This is the last of them," the field medic said on her third trip. Covered in dried blood and dirt, he pinched the bridge of his nose and squeezed his eyes shut for a second. "I bandaged them the best I could. Make sure to keep the boots on until you get to hospital, or the feet will swell and pool blood."

Gwyn nodded. He'd already told her that. Twice. Poor man.

"There's one more, there by that tree. Or what's left of it." The medic pointed to a leaning, leafless tree a few hundred feet away. "His mate had his legs blown off under that tree, and the private refused to leave him. The friend is long gone. The private won't make it to morning with his head gash. Your nurses can make him comfortable in the last hours, but that's all."

"We'll take care of him." Gwyn steeled herself for the battle to come. She'd dealt with her fair share of soldiers guarding their lost mates. It took every ounce of control she had to keep from socking them in the jaw and dragging them away for their own good.

"Good, then I can—" Something banged on the back of Rosie's door. The medic threw open the back door, and a corporal stumbled out spitting blood.

Grabbing his head with both of his hands, the corporal doubled over. "Don't put me in there! Don't leave me in the dark!"

"Calm down, soldier." The medic grasped the boy's shoulders and pushed him to the ground. "Tell me where it hurts."

Eugenie appeared, a roll of bandages stuffed under her arms. "Need some help?"

"I think we got it." Gwyn sat on top of the corporal's squirming legs so the medic could check his chest. "There's one up there by that tree that needs to get back, and quick."

"I'll take him," Eugenie said. "I'll just switch my front load into yours since you got an empty seat."

"Thanks, Eugenie. You're a lifesaver."

Eugenie tugged her lopsided cap back in place. "Don't I know it. Sure you don't need me here? Got plenty of experience wrestling my drunk da home from the pubs late at night."

"No, you take the tree case and get the rest of your load back. I won't be long behind, as soon as we get this one settled."

"He's in shock, and he bit his tongue." The medic rocked back on his heels. "He needs quiet and rest."

"Just like every other man here." Gwyn eased off the boy's legs. "Will he be all right to ride in the back?"

"Do you want him to have another episode riding beside you? Keep him in the back. There at least one of the other men can restrain him."

It took two men to pin the corporal under one of the stretcher shelves. Shivering, he curled into a ball and cried for his mother.

Sweat trickled down Gwyn's back as she climbed onto the driver's bench. She rubbed a hand over her aching eyes, working the collected grit back and forth under her eyelids. The end of this horrible night couldn't come fast enough.

"All right there, miss?"

The bandaged man next to her peered anxiously into her face. She smiled and patted his shoulder. "Yes, yes I'm all right. Bit of sand from the road, that's all."

"I've had sand in my face the past two years," he said. "Burns like the devil."

"That it does."

Up ahead, Eugenie's grill flashed in the moon as she turned the motor around and trundled her way back down the slope to the road. A ball of fire split the darkness, obliterating the tree and everything around it. The explosion cracked like thunder.

Eugenie.

Gwyn slammed on the brake and stumbled from her car, ears ringing and face burning from the bonfire of car parts. Her legs pumped, sprinting forward as smoke choked the air and knifed into her lungs.

"Eugenie!"

CHAPTER 24

"And so another soul is taken from us to fly to the bosom of Christ. May her passing remind us of the sacrifice required to lift the yokes of tyranny, and that each day on this earth is a blessing. She died doing what was right and what she loved with selfless devotion to those in need."

The priest motioned to the organ player. Off-key notes droned through the pipes to the tune of "Come Thou Fount of Every Blessing." Scratchy voices muffled by tears plodded through the chorus.

Gwyn picked at the fraying corner of the hymnal stored in the pew in front of her, not caring when her nail tore the corner of page ten. The mourners tripped over another verse.

"Sorrowing I shall be in spirit
Till released from flesh and sin."

And what if one wasn't ready for release from the flesh? What if it wasn't her time, and only by the thrust of a so-called friend did she find herself in the death angel's arms? The Bible spoke of God's perfect will, but what good came from taking Eugenie? Nothing—not a shoe, a hairpin, or a lug nut—left from the instant incineration of the half-buried shell. Nothing left but guilt.

"Come, my Lord, no longer tarry
Take my ransomed soul away."

The stone walls, slick with mold, stood unrelenting, not allowing the smallest bit of air into the stifling chapel. Gwyn tugged at her collar, the dash of lace at the throat determined to choke her. Her lungs puffed, but only a sliver of air skittered into them. Heat flashed up her chest.

Dressed immaculately in black, Lady Dowling stood before the group of devoted souls. Her eyes possessed a dull sheen against gray-lined cheeks. "We have lost a dear soul from our sisterhood. Surrounded by death every day, none is so tragic as when it is one of our own. So young and full of life, and always willing to lend a hand."

Gwyn hung her head. It wasn't supposed to be Eugenie's duty. She had been ready to go back to hospital. One simple request had changed everything. In front of Gwyn, nurses, drivers, and a few of the wounded Eugenie had taken that night huddled together, nodding and wiping at tears, at a grief so innocent. Little did they know a guilty intruder sat among them.

Gwyn's ears thundered with an erratic pulse that spiraled into her head before whooshing down to her feet. The walls loomed in. The room spun. She squeezed her eyes shut to stop the searing pain behind them.

Vaulting from her seat, she ran from the chapel. Ran from the mourners inside, from the words of solace that could do nothing for her heart and from the demons of guilt snapping at her heels. Her feet carried her all the way to a small cemetery. Rows of wooden crosses peeked out of the ground, each etched with a name and rank. She fell before a cross on the last row. The earth beneath it undisturbed, unlike the soft mounds rising from the others. There was no body to put to rest for this cross.

"I'm so sorry." Gwyn sobbed, digging her nails into the ground. "I'm so sorry, Eugenie."

Convulsions threatened to tear her apart. She rocked back and forth as the waves of guilt mounted to drown her. First her mother, and now Eugenie. Taken from her, taken much too soon. Where was God's perfect hand in that?

"Gwyn?" Cecelia knelt beside her and placed a soft hand on her shoulder. "I'm so very sorry, Gwyn."

Gwyn's throat tightened on another wretch of sobs. "Don't say you're sorry to me. I did this to her. I'm the reason she's gone."

"This isn't your fault. This is war."

"You don't know. You didn't see what happened."

"Did you drop that shell? Force her to drive over it?"

Gwyn covered her face, hot tears spilling between her fingers. Cecelia's arm circled around her, drawing her close. "There, there," she crooned. "Let it all out."

Burrowing her face into Cecelia's shoulders, Gwyn wept until her heart sagged empty. Cecelia stroked her back and hair, murmuring as the last of the tears dried on her lace blouse.

"It wasn't your fault, G." She smoothed the tangle of hair back from Gwyn's forehead. "It was an accident. A terrible accident that could happen to anyone. To Eugenie, to me, to you."

"It was supposed to be me." Gwyn swiped the fresh tear from her cheek. "I sent her in my place because I was doing something else."

"You helped a poor boy, out of his mind with fright. I met him last night, and he told me what happened. Stop blaming yourself."

"There's no one else *to* blame."

"Maybe blame is the wrong word. Maybe it's destiny." Cecelia curled her legs under her, spreading her black skirt over her ankles. "I read a bit of your Bible. I was so lonely without you, and it was just sitting there with its frayed pages. I had to see why someone would spend so much time reading it. Somewhere in there, I remember reading over and over that the Almighty has a plan far beyond our comprehension. Something about the seasons having a purpose."

"A time to every purpose under heaven," Gwyn whispered. Her mother had often repeated that verse when Gwyn's childish complaining got the better of her. "What was the purpose of this? Why Eugenie? Why my mother?"

"Maybe if your mother were still here, you would never have left home. You'd be changing tires next to your father instead of changing bandages and pulling men from the trenches. Lives are saved because you're here, and if you don't believe me, then walk back into that hospital and talk to those boys." Conviction flared in her brown eyes. "A fire sparked under you when your mother passed. You were never content to sit still after that, not that you ever did."

Dropping her gaze, Cecelia plucked a weed growing next to her and spun it between her fingers. "Truth be told, I've always been a little envious of that spark. I can see it's what William likes most about you."

What was left of Gwyn's heart broke. "I never meant to hurt you, Cecelia. Please believe me."

"Do you love him?"

There it was again. Love. Boldly demanding acknowledgment. "Yes," she whispered.

Cecelia's face pinched, the muscles in her throat working. She nodded and swiped at a tear. "I thought I could win him. My money, social position, charms, and pouting lips, but he didn't want it. He wants you."

"I thought you would hate me forever."

"I thought so too." She attempted a watery smile but sniffed instead. "It does hurt, and all the more painful because I'm not sure of which reason. Is it because of him or because I lost? I've never been thrown over, and certainly never saw myself in competition with a girl who has grease under her nails. It sounds so spoiled, doesn't it?"

"Yes." Gwyn cringed. Grief had left her dry of tact. "But it was never a competition, not for me. I did everything to avoid him."

"He's a hard man to avoid, especially if you're stuck with him, or any man, for two weeks in the woods." Cecelia shuddered.

"Not all of it was bad." Gwyn remembered the feel of William's arms around her. How she longed for them now. "Don't get me wrong, most of it was the worst experience I've ever had in my entire life, but we found moments to smile about."

Cecelia stared at Gwyn with a loneliness that penetrated her to her bones. Along with tact, Gwyn's tears left her devoid of thoughtfulness—bragging about what her friend didn't have.

"I didn't mean that the way it sounds, it's—"

"You did mean it. I can tell by your voice when you're thinking about him." Cecelia waved a dismissive hand despite the tear winking in her eye. "Not to worry. I'm never down for long. There's a handsome doctor here who smiles whenever he sees me. If I can get past the mustache, then he might be worth a go."

"Major Bennett? He's a good man. Kind to all the wounded, enlisted or officer. And obviously smitten with you."

She nodded, brushing bits of grass from her skirt. A tiny smile pulled at her lips. "He called me bright when I suggested all the linens be assigned to individual patients to cut down on unsanitary beds."

"That is a good idea. Those men are hunkered in the trenches so long they've forgotten what basic hygiene means, and the difference it makes."

Her smile brightened then faded as she looked at her silk shirt. Wet splotches setting into stains dotted her shoulder and front. "Adding clothes to the mix wouldn't hurt either."

Gwyn touched the crumpled lace embroidered with silver roses on Cecelia's blouse. "I'm sorry about your shirt. All my slobbering seems to have wilted the lace around the collar."

"I never liked this blouse. Mother bought it for my great-aunt's funeral two years ago. She'd burst into tears every time I suggested putting it in the mission barrel."

"And yet she sent it to you in a war zone. The perfect opportunity to lob it over to the Germans."

"Don't they hate us enough?"

"One more insult can't hurt." Gwyn's eyes wandered to the cross marker, freshly cut with the wood grains standing out like braille. She ran a hand over the flat grass blades. "Eugenie would've loved that assault."

Cecelia raked her fingers through the grass, gathering clumps of dead stalks and tossing them aside. "If we're still here in the spring, we should plant flowers. This place is much too bleak."

"Haven't you heard? The war will be over by Christmas."

"Oh, yes. How could I forget? Roses or daffodils? Maybe lilies. Mother could send a few from her garden."

Gwyn didn't bother to stop Cecelia's planning. With all the bleakness, it was nice to dream of a more beautiful world, where flower gardens could exist. Someday, God willing, Gwyn could plant her own garden in front of a small home, horses grazing in the pasture and William striding in after a long day of training them. When the war was over.

"Come on." Gwyn pushed to her feet and helped Cecelia up. Pins and needles prickled Gwyn's legs. "I need some help changing a tire, and you need help getting those wet spots out of your blouse. We can't let the Jerries think we're sloppy dressers."

"I don't know the first thing about tires."

"And I don't know the first thing about proper care of a blouse, but the world is changing, and we need to keep up with it."

The siren shrieked. The soap would have to wait.

Cecelia kissed Gwyn on the cheek and stepped back. "Be safe, G. I can't add your name to one of these rows."

Sprinting to the ambulance line, Gwyn pleaded for protection for all of her drivers. If they were lucky, orders would come from the south and west. Far away from William.

William folded the letter into precise thirds and tucked it into his jacket pocket. Reaching into his other pocket, he pulled out the leather journal and flipped open to a page near the back. Just that morning he had drawn Gwyn, a simple sketch of her face, with gray pencil smudged all around the flowing length of her hair. A small smile played on her lips as if she watched him with a secret. He'd agonized for over an hour about her eyes. How to portray their inquisitive glory while keeping the mystery of what she was thinking.

He stroked a shaky thumb over her cheek. He'd almost lost her. Her letter never stated it, but he read between each heavy word as she described the loss of her friend. And now she was poisoned with survivor's guilt.

The stabs of guilt, so painful one might think a knife was cutting your heart out. The difficulty breathing past the knot in your chest, the hollowness of your gut, and the pounding of your head. A lifetime of bearing and discipline had failed to teach him how to rid himself of it. Except to call it a sacrifice of duty and bury the crippling emotion deep down.

A fierceness to find her roared within him, to hold her close and shelter her from the storm raging all around. Her heart had broken enough over her mother. Now she carried the burden of thinking it should have been her and not Eugenie.

Slamming the book shut, he dug his fingers into the soft material, cutting gouges down the spine. Helplessness snagged him, pulling him down. She was out there every day, bumping over roads and retrieving men, knowing the next mile might be her last. And there was nothing he could do about it.

Blast this war. And blast the duty that strangled him at every turn.

"I see you're moody again." Roland loomed in the opening of the dugout shelter.

"I see you have nothing better to do with your time than bother me. Again."

"As a matter of fact, I just completed a rifle check." He entered without an invitation. Pulling around a short box, he plopped on top of it, his knees popping. "I can't wait to feel a real chair beneath me once more. What say you, Will? Or are you more interested in dreaming about soft lips and hair? I'd take that over a chair any day."

"Her friend was just blown to kingdom come, and that's what you have to say? Good God, man. Have some decency."

Roland's gaze dropped to his lap. "I only meant to cheer you. I'm sorry."

"You're doing a poor job of it."

"Aren't I?" He gave a nervous laugh. "I only meant to remind you that she's still here. Is it wrong to rejoice that Gwyn was spared?"

William shifted on his box, the rough corners digging into the undersides of his thighs. Shame picked at his conscience. As he had read the letter, his heart breathed a prayer of joy even as the next sentence of her letter recalled the death of another. "If I find a good answer, I'll let you know."

"She was a nice girl. Knew how to change a bandage proper, much better than Miss Hale." Slipping off his tin hat, Roland rubbed his elbow over the mounded top. "At least Miss Hale has found something better suited to her. I didn't want to be the one to hurt her feelings and tell her she had no future in nursing, even with that mustached doctor fawning over her."

Guilt sliced into William's shame at the mention of Cecelia. The horror on her face as she discovered Gwyn in his arms was nothing short of betrayal. And then he'd just left Gwyn standing there to plead with her friend.

William shook off the sour thoughts. What happened was done. Best to press on. "Don't set your bridle for one filly. There's more than one in the paddock."

Roland sighed, cupping his chin in his palm. "I adore it when you talk horses and women. Tell me, is that how you made Miss Ruthers swoon?"

"Hardly. The only time she wants to see a horse is as she speeds past on four wheels." William tucked his journal into his breast pocket, promising himself not to take it out again until he was alone. He'd go mad if he didn't stop thinking about her. "How are the rifle drills progressing?"

"Up to par." Roland sniffed, crossing his arms and staring out the door. "If I didn't know any better, one might think MacDonald had invented the idea."

"He *was* the one to suggest the men spar while they're on the reserve line. Keeps them in shape and lets off a little steam."

Roland huffed. "How, out of all the battalions in the field, did he end up right where we are? Shouldn't they send the Highlanders to the woods? Don't they like that kind of wilderness assault?"

"What have you got against MacDonald? Other than he tops you by at least eight inches."

"He's got a bad habit of throwing his weight around."

William doubted it had to do with the Scot's leadership capabilities and more with his imposing size. The men respected both, while Roland lacked both. A fact William was careful to tread around. "He has a way with the men because he fought in their ranks before they tacked brass on him."

"He's uncouth."

"Couth or not, compared to most of the generals I've seen strutting around on the parade grounds, I'd choose to fight alongside him any day. And so would you."

"I suppose." Roland's nose twitched. "Smell that?"

"Yes, you need to bathe." William pulled the pencil from his stationery box and hunched over the supply list he was supposed to complete by the end of the day. His quartermaster had annotated several notes by some of the items while crossing others out that he'd managed to acquire by trading packs of cigarettes and whiskey.

"I'm serious. It's similar to the stuff our groom uses to kill the rats in the stables."

"Easier to use a cat. Did Sattler get those extra bayonets he was eyeing from the French last week?"

"Get off the bayonets, Will, and smell."

William sniffed. Sulfur tickled his nose. Men scurried by the boxed shelter unclipping gas masks from their belts. Dread curled into his belly.

"Fritz has decided to throw us a poisonous tea party." William grabbed his hat and mask. Roland jumped to his feet, pawing the mask pouch strapped to his side. "Check the men. No one sits. The gas hangs low."

Hurrying down the trench, William turned into the nearest observation point and demanded the field glasses. Clouds of yellow-gray rolled over the ground as men leaped from their positions and ran back to the main line. A colonel raised his pistol high into the air and fired, shouting threats to the men abandoning their post.

"They're going to suffocate, sir." Next to William, the observer fumbled to tighten the straps on his mask. "Give me a bloomin' bullet over that stuff."

The Germans couldn't have designed a better way to torture their victims than through slow suffocation. The French gave the gases a go first, but it was the Jerries who proved to master its employ. Within seconds of inhaling, the vapors destroyed the lungs and sentenced the victim to a choking attack, crippling lines of men without ever wasting a single shot.

Masked black figures advanced forward, appearing behind the smoke.

William shoved the glasses back into the observer's hand and rushed to find Colonel Seymour. He found him in the COMMS trench blasting orders at his aides. "Sir, the Germans are advancing behind the screen of gas." William snapped a salute.

Seymour ignored him and continued his tirade on gun position to the shrinking lieutenant in front of him.

"Sir," William said. "We are losing ground. The front men can't hold the line without sufficient reinforcement."

Seymour turned cold eyes to him. "Then, Captain, take your men and provide them with sufficient reinforcement. I've got two blown cannons to deal with here."

William saluted and marched away. Fear galloped down his spine. His men had never charged into a gas explosion.

CHAPTER 25

Shrapnel flashed in the air, cutting down the mob of infantry streaming along the sunken road. Ashen-faced and frothing at the mouth, the retreaters knocked past the reinforcements in their desperate flight from the rolling gas and the Germans swooping in behind it.

"Hold steady and let them pass, men!" William dodged a dust-covered South African who raced past him clutching his throat.

Roland stumbled as a Zouave dressed in bright red baggy trousers knocked into his shoulder. "And you want to take us there? It's suicide."

William's jaw clenched. The worst kind of suicide, but he had no intention of being shot for cowardice. The obnoxious gas cloud clogged his nostrils, bringing tears to his eyes. They needed to gain the high ground for breathable air if they had any hope of taking on the Germans. "Keep your masks on, and check the man behind you. We push on."

William's lungs squeezed with his limited intake of oxygen. Hot, itchy, and filled with the musty smell of a storage chest, it was enough to make him gag before they even encountered the Jerries. So much for breathing easier.

The road bottle-necked with men too wounded for retreat. They stumbled, falling face-first into the dirt, leaving their mates to step around them. Bodies filled with shrapnel and laying with slack mouths were pushed to the side by those still able to walk. William's boots squished through rivers of blood and vomit.

A roar of thunder exploded overhead, followed by another and another. Men and packs flew into the air, spiraling to the ground like dead flies.

"Get down!" William grabbed the two men closest to him and threw them into the ditch. "Take cover!"

Dirt pounded the backs of his legs as he huddled in the ditch, sheltering a corporal beneath him. Shells dropped like rain, hailing destruction without distinction between the already dead and still living. William glanced over the hunched backs of his men. Gaping holes dotted his line. If they sat here any longer, the Germans would blow them to bits in less than an hour.

Keeping to the ditch, William moved his line forward until the shells thinned along the perimeter. He doubled back, his stomach dropping with each fallen soldier. The numbers shrank, but he kept his men moving until a jumbled regiment of dirt-covered Canadians blocked their path.

"Shore up the Mape's numbers, men." William pointed to the thin line of soldiers. Scanning the bars on their sleeves, he found the closest thing to their commanding officer. "Where are they?"

"Just over that ridge, sir." Hollow-eyed and green-cheeked, the sergeant major looked close to passing out. "We've been holding them back, but we're the last of the retreat defense."

"Where is the rest of your unit?"

"You probably met them on the road." He tilted his helmet back and wiped the grimy sweat from his forehead. A cough rattled in his throat. "Didn't have any protection. That gas came out of nowhere."

William ripped his mask off and forced it into the sergeant's hands. "Here. Take an easy breath." The man tried to hand it back, but William shook his head. "Then give it to that lad on the other side of you. I can't see with that thing on anyway."

Low crawling his way up the embankment, William peered through the tall grass. Yellow clouds wisped over the ground as the German line marched across the field. Further back, the glint of Stahlhelme-topped soldiers crested a small rise where the rest of the German army awaited the front attack.

William wriggled back down the slope to where Roland and the sergeant waited. "Pass the order to ready rifles and fix bayonets. We'll hold position here until I give the signal to charge." The idea of charging poured ice into his veins, but it was a last resort. No man of his was getting stabbed to death waiting in a ditch.

Anticipation flooded him, filling his bones until they shook with the effort to restrain it. He peered over the ridge. Just a few seconds more, and the enemy line would have to turn to volley. *Five. Four. Three. Two.*

"Fire!"

Muzzle tips exploded, spraying bullets at the unsuspecting German units. The heated fragments tore through packs and clothing, *pop pop popp*-ing as they ripped into flesh and bone. Shouts rippled down the line as the Germans turned to retaliate. The element of surprise gone, Brits and Canadians began to fall.

William aimed his pistol and squeezed the trigger. "Fire at will!"

Digging in and aiming across unprotected ground, his men picked off the Jerries faster than tin cans on a rail. Fear boiled in the Germans' eyes as they scrambled to reload.

"Bayonets at ready! Up! Charge!" William was first out, his men right behind him. He didn't think as he pushed down every ounce of crippling emotion. The trained soldier inside led the charge.

Men fell at his feet, gurgling their last words in a bloody froth. He kept running, tossing his spent pistol aside and drawing a fresh one from his holster. His pulse thundered in his ears louder than the cracking of rifles, the rush of adrenaline shaking all the way down to his fingertips. But his bullets never missed.

The Germans turned and fled. William raced to keep up. Thunder pounded in the distance. He tripped and crashed to his knees. Pain shot up his legs. His men had the Krauts on the run, but uncertainty coiled in his belly like a snake readying to strike. Then he heard the shrill whistling.

"Fall back!" He jumped to his feet. Pain ricocheted down his legs. "Incoming! Fall back!"

Shells burst overhead like deadly silver stars raining shrapnel. Red streamed between the dead grass patches, joining together and pooling in dried gaping cracks.

Up ahead, Roland weaved his way around the dead and retreating. The whites of his eyes flashed round beneath his helmet rim. "No! This way!" He waved his arm at the enemy line like a madman. "We've got them on the run, lads! Don't lose heart now. Forward!"

Cursing, William veered towards him. Men stumbled, heads swiveling between Roland and William and the conflicting orders. Of all the times the stupid man chose that moment to take charge. What idiotic scene of heroics was he playing at?

A shell blasted to William's left, throwing men and dirt sky high. His ears rang with the metallic blow and curdling screams. Dazed, his vision tilted as he rolled his head around. Roland stood in the middle of the field beating his revolver against his thigh to push open the cylinder. Jammed.

"You idiot! You trying to get yourself killed?"

Machine guns tattooed from the far side of the field, spitting into the ground. Roland went rigid, tiny pricks of red splattering across his chest. The pistol tumbled from his hand. He crashed to the ground.

The air seized in William's lungs as he sprinted to Roland's side. Taking in the exit wounds dotting his back, William rolled him over. Roland's face was chalky white. Blood oozed from the corner of his mouth. His eyes fluttered, staring at the sky.

"They got me, Will."

"Not yet they don't." William slung Roland over his shoulder and turned toward the British line. Hot wetness seeped through his jacket. Roland's arms and hands banged against the back of William's legs as each step jarred his entire body.

Sliding over the embankment and into the ditch, William eased Roland to the ground and ripped open his jacket. His once white shirt was muddied with blood and holes. Bile scored the back of William's throat.

"Sir, you're hit." A hand shook William's shoulder. "Sir, you're covered in blood."

William shoved him away. "It's not me. Find the medic."

Roland raised a shaking hand and grasped William's lapel. "Don't … don't waste his … time. I'm … gone."

William's hands hovered over the wounds. He needed to staunch them, but there were too many. "Keep your mouth shut and focus on breathing."

"Breathing isn't … isn't a problem when you've g-got a hundred holes in your l-lungs." Roland tried to smile, but a cough spewed out pink froth.

William swiped the edge of his sleeve over Roland's lips. "Quiet, Morrison, or so help me, I'll have you court-martialed for insubordination as soon as we get back to Blighty."

Roland wheezed as he tried to move his head. William lifted it and cradled it on his thigh. His fingers stuck together as he combed away the matted hair from his friend's forehead.

"Tell my m-mother I want to be b-buried with a large headstone with my full rank-k. C-can't have anyone thinking I was a n-nobody when they come to lay the wreath." He clawed his fingers into William's chest. "Tell her-r, tell her I was a good s-soldier. That I didn't run. T-tell her for me, Will? Please."

William nodded as the bile gave way to tears. He grasped Roland's hand. "You'll have a new uniform, too, I promise."

"G-good. Hate d-dirty clothes."

"I know you do." William tucked his nose against his shoulder and blotted the runaway tear. "I remember the first time in training they made us crawl through the mud. You were awake until o'three hundred scrubbing out the stains on your trouser knees."

"Should've had-d me a good woman t-to do the scrubbing. O-one like Miss Cecelia."

Blood trickled from Roland's nose. William wiped it with his thumb as his heart drowned in sorrow. "She'd have them clean in no time flat."

"My laundress a-angel." Roland's eyes glazed over as he looked from William's face to the sky. Roland's back arched. Sharp breaths hissed from the holes in his chest. He slumped back, his chest still and eyes unseeing.

Weight like a fifty-ton mortar pressed on William's lungs. He bit off the howl of rage spiraling in his chest and willed it into fighting anger. "I'll beat them back, Roland. I swear I will."

Gently lowering his mate's head onto the sand, he closed Roland's glassy eyes and tucked his hands safely across his chest so no errant boot could trample them. Jumping to his feet, William grabbed the man nearest him.

"Where's the medic?"

"Dead, sir. We ain't got no one else."

"Then I want you and you—"—he snagged a Canadian private by his collar—"—to start carrying off the wounded. We need a firing position, and these bodies are in the way. Get to it."

They grabbed Roland first, hauling him to the other side of the road. William turned away as his friend's head lolled back.

"Fall in and move forward. We're going to outflank them before they can take us all out." Motioning his men toward the protection of the embankment, William marched up and down to wave them on. Shells shrieked closer, detonating the earth within feet all around. "Keep it moving. Don't give Fritz a sitting target."

The sound of something like a woman screaming pierced William's ears, drowning out the rat-a-tat machine guns. A silvery flare burst at his feet, cleaving into his skull. Burning metal tore into his flesh, lifting him off his feet and charring him from the inside out. He hurtled through the air, higher and higher until the dead weight of his arms and legs pulled him down. Slamming into the ground, dizzying red dots whirled in his head. And then blackness.

CHAPTER 26

Gwyn rolled the mug of hot chocolate between her hands as she stared past the open flap of her tent. A light drizzle had turned the afternoon sky to dull gray and the ground to a muddy mess. Though she'd patched every hole and tear in the tent, the tiny drops managed to slip under the thin floorboards and warp the wood until nails poked out, catching her shoe more than once when she forgot to light the lantern after an all-night drive. Like last night's.

They'd lost seven men on the way back, suffered two blown tires, a missing first aid kit, and a busted crankshaft. And, of course, rain. What the summer offered in heat and sweat, late September matched in cold wetness.

Gwyn inhaled the delicious brew and took a deep sip. It coated her throat with its velvety texture, slipping down to curl into her belly. But all too soon the rich scent disappeared behind the mustiness of her tent. If not for the chocolate to keep her occupied, she might claw through the thin walls that seemed ever ready to close in on her. She needed to occupy her hands and thoughts before they turned against her. Again. Buried memories found stillness the perfect stage to emerge with their terror on full display, and she their sole audience. Around and around the performers went, all staring at her with lifeless eyes. Except Eugenie, who pointed a skeletal finger at Gwyn.

Raising her cup, she swallowed too fast. Hot liquid scalded the back of her throat. She choked and sputtered, wiping the burning dribble from her lip. The taste buds were gone from the tip of her tongue, but she'd lost the nightmarish images.

Slamming the cup down on the folding table, Gwyn grabbed her leather cap off the bed and stuffed her frizzing hair underneath it. Flinging the oil skin trench over her shoulders, she sloshed into the rain.

Her feet took her straight to the garage, or what they considered a garage, as it was once home to pigs and cows.

"You're supposed to be sleeping." Alice didn't look up from the tire she was patching.

Gwyn stamped the mud from her boots and peeled off her wet coat. The familiar scent of grease calmed her headache. "How did you know it was me?"

"Who else would be in here when they're not on shift? Why aren't you sleeping?"

"Too restless. That itchy cot doesn't help." Gwyn selected one of the empty field kits and sat down on a low stool near the supply box. "Don't mind the company, do you?"

"As long as you're not one of those Yanks. I'm tired of them asking me to repeat words just so they can hear what a Blimey girl sounds like. A Blimey girl. Have you ever been called that?"

Gwyn shook her head and reached into the box for ointment. "Can't say that I have, though I've gotten 'grease monkey' a time or two. Any proposals?"

Alice snorted. "They save those for the nurses. Not that I'm complaining, I've got more important things to do than worry about men batting their wandering eyes at me, unless one of them was handsome like that captain of yours. Then I might bat right back at him."

An ache twisted in Gwyn's heart. She hadn't heard from William since she'd sent that letter about Eugenie over two weeks ago. No news was supposed to mean good news. People who touted that message needed a slap upside the head.

"I'm sure he's safe." Alice's voice softened.

Gwyn wrestled what she hoped was a smile to her lips. "I'm sure you're right, but the worrier in me has a hard time going down without a fight."

"Maybe you should inform him that our boys are nearly untouchable now with those newfangled dragon machines they got."

"The tanks?"

"Dragon machine is more accurate. Metal bodies with dragging bellies rolling around on chains and belching smoke." Alice shuddered. "I'd hate to be Fritz and see one of those coming over the hill."

The first time Gwyn had seen one was three days ago on her way to a field station. The monstrous beasts chugged over a wooden bridge. She watched with mouth open as the simple structure wobbled under the massive weight. A honk from behind had swerved her back onto the road and away from plunging into the river.

She fingered the edge of the box, recalling the tremble of the earth as they roared by, their metal snouts glinting deadly in the sun. They plowed over ruts and mud as easily as gliding over glass. "I wonder if they're difficult to drive."

Alice rolled her eyes and turned back to the tire. "You would think of that."

"Why not? If those things are as invincible as the boys claim, then the driver must be snug as lug nut in there. Why not give one of us a go and free up a muscled man to shoulder a rifle?"

"Because they're the newest toys. Don't waste your breath trying to convince a man to give it up. They're just now getting used to the idea of us driving at all, and you want to jump right back into all that mess."

"But you love driving."

"Yes, and I'm finally able to shift gears without a single stall. Eugenie taught me a trick to—oh, I'm sorry. I didn't mean to bring her up."

Heaviness dropped on Gwyn's shoulders and wound around her in cruel knots. "Eugenie had a lot of tricks. We're all better drivers for it. Remember the time she lifted the back wheels on her car and tied a rope around them to spin that fan around? It worked for about fifteen seconds."

"Until she pressed the pedal too hard and the rope broke. Lady Dowling almost suffered the fate of Marie Antoinette."

Cecelia flew through the door, face red and chest heaving. "There you are, G! Do you know how long I've been looking for you?"

Alice frowned. She hated nurses in the workshop. "Was the garage really that mystifying a guess?"

Ignoring her, Cecelia grabbed Gwyn's arm and yanked her up. Supplies spilled from Gwyn's lap to all over the floor. "You have to come with me. Now."

"Do you know how long it's going to take to reroll all these bandages?" Gwyn started to bend over but stopped when she saw Cecelia's filthy backside. "Have you been playing in the mud?"

"I skidded on a patch just outside your tent because I was running like a deranged woman. Come on." She shoved Gwyn from behind.

"Wait. My coat." Gwyn barely had a second to grab it before Cecelia had her out the door. "I'll be back soon, Alice."

"No, she won't."

Her hat deserted in the haste, Gwyn flung the coat over her head. "The garage is the last place you need to get high and mighty in."

"I don't care what people think."

"Well, I'm the one who has to continue working in there, so please—for my sake—the next time don't come storming in like it's your private parlor."

"This is for your sake." Cecelia's lips flattened into a colorless line.

A shiver ran across Gwyn's skin. "What's happened?"

"Lady Dowling received a telegram."

"And?"

"And I don't know. She wouldn't say."

The shiver sharpened to icicles, stabbing Gwyn with each step she took.

Lady Dowling waited for them in the tiny church office. She stood with her back to the large-paned window, her tall figure erect against the gray sky. The only crisp color was a small white envelope in her hand. "I won't say this any way but the plain truth. Captain Crawford has been injured. It's bad, I'm afraid."

Gwyn's knees gave out. Cecelia caught her elbow and guided her into the room's spare chair. Gwyn dropped her head into her hands, willing the words to say something different, but they pounded loud and clear. "How? Is he ...?" The words stuck on the sandpaper in her throat.

"An explosion during the assistance of another unit in the field. Almost two weeks ago. Lieutenant MacDonald has outlined a few more details in his letter." Lady Dowling held out the envelope. "He was assured that I would deliver it to you."

Gwyn took the letter in her shaking fingers. Desire to know warred with the safety of ignorance. Black scrawled letters shone through the water spoiled envelope, taunting her. "I wonder why it was not Captain Morrison to write you." The catch in Lady Dowling's breath brought Gwyn's head up. "He's dead, isn't he?"

"Yes."

Numbness seeped over Gwyn's body until all emotion ceased. A clock ticking somewhere in the room noted the passing of minutes, but it was a lie. The entire world seemed to have stopped spinning. Gwyn knew without a doubt that William had been with Roland.

"It's all in the letter." Lady Dowling walked around to the front of her desk. Her heavy taffeta skirt rustled with each step. "Would you like some privacy to read it?"

Gwyn shook her head. No point in hiding her terror behind a closed door. Pulling the single sheet from its envelope, she scanned the scratched contents. Once, then twice to make sure she understood each word. Summoning courage she didn't quite feel, she stood. "I'm going."

Lady Dowling nodded. "I thought you might. Pack a light bag, and I'll have one of the drivers take you to the nearest clearing station. You should reach Calais before night tomorrow if the trains are running."

"I'm going too." Cecelia sniffed, tucking her hand into Gwyn's arm.

"You'll stay here." Lady Dowling's sharp eyes glinted, calling a paleness to Cecelia's cheek. "There's work to be done, and the men need you. Captain Crawford and Miss Ruthers will manage on their own."

"But what if there aren't enough nurses in Calais? What if Gwyn can't do it alone? She needs a shoulder at a time like this." Tears streaked down Cecelia's face and plopped onto her lacy blouse.

Sighing, Lady Dowling pulled a starched handkerchief from her belt and handed it to Cecelia. "There, there, my girl. No need to get in a tizzy. Miss Ruthers is perfectly capable, but you have a job to do here."

"Oh, G!"

Gwyn stumbled back as a sobbing Cecelia launched herself at her. As Cecelia continued to cry, Gwyn patted her back. "It'll be all right." Her calm words belied the sickening throb in her chest. Would it truly be all right? The tragedy waiting for her stole the breath from her body, but William didn't need a quivering woman right now.

Her mind reeled with the items needed for the trip, should the hospital have limited supplies. "If I need anything, I shall write to you immediately."

"Yes, and then Mother can send over extra supplies."

"This came for you as well." Lady Dowling picked up a worn envelope from the corner of her desk and handed it to Gwyn, this one—forwarded from Great Malvern—featured Papa's firm print.

Pulling away from Cecelia, Gwyn ran a light finger over her father's writing and flipped the envelope over for the return address.

Stinson School of Flying, San Antonio, Texas. A jumble of emotion passed through her. She creased the envelope to steady her shaking fingers as she slid the long-awaited letter into her pocket. There would be time to think of all that later. She had a train to catch.

CHAPTER 27

The port of Calais was flooded with a sea of khaki and stained white. The wounded had arrived any way they could—train, auto, wagon, stretcher, and walking—to take over every inch of space as they awaited their turns to be loaded and shipped home.

Stepping off the train platform, Gwyn stretched her aching legs. Two long days crammed into a cattle car loaded wall-to-wall with crying and moaning wounded had left more than just her bones hurting.

A massive dockside warehouse with a large red cross painted on its side stood in the center of chaos with smaller tents sprouting around it. All over the country, the most unusual buildings were being converted into hospitals and operating rooms. And somewhere, in one of them, lay William.

A cold vise squeezed around her heart. Had he regained consciousness? Had the burns destroyed ... She pressed a hand over her mouth. It didn't matter what had been destroyed. She wasn't one of those women who screamed and ran the other way. This was William.

"Excuse me," she said, stopping a stretcher bearer. "Can you tell me where the burn unit is?"

The man shook his head. "Head over to that tent, and the nurses can point you."

Gwyn found the tent and marched up to a nurse sitting at a desk with a clipboard and stack of papers in front of her. "Name and rank." The nurse didn't bother looking up.

"Gwyn Ruthers, an ambulance driver for Lady Dowling."

The nurse's head lifted. She took in Gwyn's rumpled clothes in one long sweep. "A driver, you say?

"Yes, for Lady Dowling's private unit, but I'm here in regards to a patient."

"We don't allow family members, friends, or *special* friends in to see the patients. Hospital rules."

Dropping her bag, Gwyn leaned both hands on the desk, casting a shadow over the neat marks on the nurse's clipboard. "I am the lead driver for the Marchioness of Dowling's private ambulance fleet, and I have received first aid training from the Sisters of the Holy Mercy, which I used extensively on the Front and behind enemy lines as a POW. By the looks of your neat nails and pretty white hat, you've never been. I'm looking for Captain William Crawford of the Oxfordshire and Buckinghamshire Light Infantry. Where might I find him?"

The nurse's pale lips parted. Pink darted up her neck. "I'm sorry, we just get so many different types of ladies at the port. I just thought—"

"I'm sure you did. Captain Crawford?"

"We don't keep an entire roster here. There are too many going in and out, which I'm sure you know from your post on the Front. Inside the hospital, ask for Sister Paulette. She should be able to help you."

"Thank you."

Gwyn forced her feet into a steady march to calm her heart as each step took her closer to William and the unknown. Inside, she was directed down a long hall and up a flight of stairs. Stopping at a door with a frosted glass window, she smoothed her hair. Loose tangles caught between her fingers. No wonder that nurse confused her for some dockside doxie. *Why didn't I bother with a mirror?* Pulling the small canteen from her bag, she poured a few drops of water on her fingers and smoothed down the wild hairs as best she could, tucking the rest into the braided twist at the back of her head. She took a fortifying breath and knocked on the door.

"Come in."

Gwyn stepped in the office and fixed her eyes on the white habit sitting erectly behind the center desk. The sister laid down her pen and laced her thick fingers together on top of her desk. Soft laugh lines creased her round face, but the glint in her eye suggested intolerance for nonsense. "May I help you?"

"I'm Gwyn Ruthers. I received a letter that Captain William Crawford is here, and I've come to see him."

"Your relation to Captain Crawford?"

"An acquaintance from Great Malvern. We've also served together on the Front."

The sister's eyebrows lifted. "I did not realize women were allowed on the front lines."

Gwyn grinned. "They're not, ma'am, but drivers don't adhere to lines."

"A female driver? How astonishing. And good for you, but I'm sorry to inform you that you've come a long way for nothing. We simply do not allow visitors to come in and out of hospital. I'm sure you understand."

"I'm not here to visit. I've been in country long enough to know that the medics have their hands full, and there aren't enough nurses to spread between patients. I have training, and I'd like to offer it."

The sister rose from her desk and moved to a file cabinet, her long habit floating behind her stout frame. Pulling the second drawer up, she rifled through the brown folders. "Captain Crawford, you said?"

"Of the Oxfordshire and Buckinghamshire Light Infantry."

Passing a few more folders, she plucked one out and scanned the contents before closing it again. Serious gray eyes pinned Gwyn to the floor. "What do you know of Captain Crawford's injuries?"

"Only that he was caught in an explosion and suffered a head injury and burns." Gwyn swallowed the lump in her throat. If she cracked now, then she'd never be allowed through any door except the exit. "At the time the letter was written, he had not gained consciousness."

The sister nodded, and for one agonizing moment, Gwyn feared the letter still held true. Or worse. "You will be happy to know that Captain Crawford has awakened," the sister said. "Though brief, it is a good sign."

"Thank God." Joy rushed through Gwyn's veins. "And the rest of his injuries?"

The soft lines around the sister's mouth eased. She tapped the corner of William's file against her robed leg. "How well is your acquaintance with the captain?"

The gray eyes penetrated to find Gwyn's crack like a blacksmith testing the worth of his metal in the fire. Gwyn's back stiffened at the challenge. "Well enough that I left my own post to come to him. Well enough that I cannot breathe again until I see him."

"Are you certain he wishes to see you?"

"Not entirely. In fact, I wouldn't be surprised if he put up a fight, but I'm not leaving. I've been told no before, and if I'd listened to it then, I'd still be stuck over my father's garage and not here in France pulling men from out of the rubble. The men here need help." She spread her hands wide. "Here I am."

"Quite a determined thing, aren't you?"

"Driving a Rolls Royce in the middle of no man's land, you have to be."

Studying her for several long minutes, the sister replaced William's folder in the file cabinet. "Under ordinary circumstances, I would never allow this, but I have a feeling that if I said no, you'd find a way back in somehow."

"You're probably right, ma'am."

"Sister Paulette. I trust you know how to cleanse and wrap a bandage? In bed bath? Check for infection and hemorrhaging?"

"Yes, ma'am, I mean, Sister Paulette."

"Good. I don't have time to teach the basics. They send us so many girls who've never seen a splinter in the finger." Her brow creased in frustration then smoothed back. "You should know that

Captain Crawford's wounds are extensive. How much experience have you had with close range shell explosions?"

"More than enough to fill my nightmares."

"Your nightmares have been tame compared to what some of these men come in with. The atrocities that human beings can inflict upon each other … Captain Crawford is blessed that he still draws breath."

Gwyn gripped her hands behind her back, her fingertips tingling. "Please tell me. I'd rather not wait until I see him."

"Burns cover the entire left side of his body. The MO was able to remove most of the shrapnel, but some of the openings may never heal properly because of where they pierced. He has several fractures and bruises from when he was launched into the air and landed on his back, which—blessedly—did not break. Miss Ruthers, I caution you. It is a miracle of our Lord that he is still alive."

William was alive. God had answered her prayer. "May I see him?"

Sister Paulette led Gwyn down curtained-off sections of the ground floor. The stench of battle, festering wounds, and disinfectant assault Gwyn in one quick punch. She'd smelled it before in the field, but here it collided with molding wood and stale sea air.

"This was once a storage warehouse," said Sister Paulette. "We are fortunate to have secured such a large facility for a hospital. My sisters in the field tell me they often have to operate in dugout shelters of earth and tent. We aren't sufficiently prepared for the amount of wounded coming in daily. Especially after the Somme. I fear we shall see the remnants of that offense for some time to come.

"To your left are our operating rooms, and just past is our immediate recovery room. Everything to the rear of the building is for special cases. Every man here is a special case, Miss Ruthers, make no mistake, but there are some who need a little more care."

She didn't need to go on. Gwyn knew exactly who she meant. Hushed tones echoed off the bare walls, punctuated with whimpers of pain so lonely one might fear the heart was torn in two. For some, it was.

Pulling back the curtain, they entered the back corner section. Three nurses moved between the double row of beds, tucking a blanket in here, pouring a glass of water there, checking bandages, and offering a cool cloth to burning foreheads of the nearly motionless patients. Gwyn's eyes roved among the beds, desperate for a familiar glimpse, but the swath of bandages made it impossible to tell them apart from a distance. Her legs ached to race from one bed to the next until she found him. Only Sister Paulette's whispered greetings to each man kept her sedate.

She smiled at each man they passed, but hollow eyes stared back. She wiped her clammy hands on her skirt as nerves collided in her stomach. Unwilling to restrain her frantic heart any longer, Gwyn scanned the remaining beds. There, next to the last cot, she found him. Stripped to the waist and wrapped in wet gauze, she saw no part of his face, but it was him. It was William. Motionless and scorched.

"William? William, it's me. It's Gwyn."

"He can't hear you, my dear." Sister Paulette. "He's slipped back to sleep."

But William heard. Her lovely voice, so near, made him want to weep. How many nights had he dreamed of hearing her, of feeling the warmth of her presence, of smelling the sweet scent of flowers blooming through all the death? But how many days had brought the harshness that she would never want him now? And yet, she was here. How had she found him? Why did she come to see him when he was nothing more than a butchered piece of meat?

He forced his breathing to remain even despite the burn

clawing up his side. He wasn't ready to see her, not yet. Not when he could still imagine her in his perfect dream. If he dared to open his eyes now, the illusion would be shattered. He would see the horror on her face as she took in his mangled body, seared from the outside and flayed open with shrapnel. He wasn't ready for that yet. Tomorrow. Tomorrow he would summon the strength to face her terror and the loneliness it would seal for him.

"It's best to let him rest when he can." The soft rustling folds of Sister Paulette's robe scratched his ears like nails on metal. "Perhaps tomorrow he'll feel more like entertaining visitors."

"Sister, I told you I'm here to help," Gwyn said. Something heavy settled on the floor. "I won't leave his side even if he takes all month to wake up."

William's heart pounded, stretching the bandages over his chest which burned him like flaming serpents. A cool hand touched his bruised right cheek, killing the serpents of pain.

"He's having nightmares," Gwyn whispered, moving her feathery touch to the unharmed area of his forehead. "The burns, they torment the mind as much as the body."

Torment. Night and day to day and night, lashing him to a body that he no longer controlled. It burned as if scratched by the devil himself. His fingers longed to claw at the skin and tear it from his bones, to rid himself of the blistering pain, but even the slightest twitch ignited white-hot sparks. He could do nothing but lie still during the torture.

"Sleep now, my dear William. Nothing will harm you tonight, and I shall be here when you wake."

Wetness slipped from the corner of his closed eye and swerved down his cheek. A kiss, softer than air, brushed the corner of his mouth where the tear pooled. "Rest in peace now."

CHAPTER 28

A wheezing cough snapped Gwyn's head up. Fuzziness swirled through her sleepy mind as she glanced around the ward and found the source of the noise. A soldier in one of the first beds. A nurse rushed to his side, water pitcher in hand, and wetted his lips and brow.

Gwyn rubbed the back of her hand over her bleary eyes and looked to the window high against the wall. Darkness with pinpricks of stars. How long had she been asleep? Standing, she stretched her arms over her head, letting all the kinks work out from her fingers to her toes. It might take weeks to ease the ache from sitting on that hard, wooden chair for so long. A cup of hot chocolate would do wonders for the late-night pains.

With warm thoughts of rich chocolate on her lips, she leaned over to check William's forehead. Two eyes stared back at her.

"Hello, Will." Heart tripping over itself, she pulled her chair close and sat back down, chocolate forgotten.

He blinked, catching the low lantern light in the center of his eyes.

Gwyn shifted in her chair. She'd waited all day for him to awaken, had ridden miles and miles just to see him, and now that the time was there, a sudden bout of nerves sprang within her stomach. "Are you thirsty?"

At his slight nod, she grabbed the pitcher from the stand and poured a small amount into a glass. Slipping her hand behind his head, she cradled him and lifted the glass to his lips. The water trickled over his lips and down his chin. She lowered him to the pillow and wiped the water running down his neck. Air hissed through his teeth.

"I'm sorry. I know that hurts, but the flesh is pink. A good sign. We don't want to see black, green, blue, purple, or angry red. I'm not sure if there's a proper color called angry red. Probably something a doctor invented. They're always giving things a funny name, or one that ordinary people can't pronounce. I suppose people may say the same thing about mechanics." The nerves prattled her tongue. Golly molly, if she didn't get a hold of herself, she'd drive him right back to unconsciousness. "Are you cold? Hot?"

He shook his head, his eyes never leaving her face.

"Were you watching me sleep?" She raised a hand to her mouth, praying not to find remnants of drool. "What a pretty sight that must have been."

"It was."

The rust in his voice threatened her undoing. She smiled, straightening the side of his dog hair-blanket with shaking fingers. "I bet you say that to all the nurses."

"What are you doing here?"

"I've come for you."

"But how?"

"MacDonald wrote me. At the time, you had yet to regain consciousness."

"He told you of Roland."

"I'm so sorry, William." She wished she had thought to sit on the other side of his bed. She needed to hold his hand, to press comfort into his mind, but the bandages covering his left side from the ear down prevented it. As soon as he fell asleep again, she would rearrange.

A tear slipped down his scarred cheek. "I lost too many men that day, yet I survived."

"God watched over you."

"And now He's sent an angel to watch over me."

She shook her head. "No. Just a simple girl who prayed for you every day."

"You're hardly a simple girl, Gwynevere Ruthers."

Heat rushed over her cheeks. "A few wounds and bandages and you've turned into quite the flatterer. Perhaps I should have knocked you over the head a long time ago."

"Perhaps if you had, it would have saved me the experience of getting blown apart by a kaiser shell." Another hiss rushed over his lips as his eyes pinched closed. His whole body seized.

Gwyn reached for her bag. "I have morphine."

"No," he gasped. "It's not that bad."

"You're about to grind your teeth into dust. Let me give you something."

"No. I need to feel it."

Feel the martyrdom, more like it. She'd seen it time and time again. Men needed to feel the rush of pain as a sacrifice to their survival while their mates lay buried in the mud. Survivor's guilt. Yes, she knew a little about that.

"Here." She pulled up the Pekinese blanket that had slipped to expose the raw skin of his chest. "Don't want you catching cold in this drafty warehouse. Who would have thought combed dog hair makes the softest cover for sensitive skin?"

"Seems to work well for the dogs." His body eased, relaxing his face. "I see the irony in that."

"No irony in wanting to keep our brave boys warm and taken care of."

The corners of his mouth dipped. He ran his good hand over his bandaged one, picking at the edge. "Haven't you been in the field long enough to see that bravery isn't always there? Most of the time it's stupidity and blind orders."

"Two things you'll never be accused of because bravery and loyalty run too deep in your veins to allow for anything else." She leaned forward, combing her fingers into the fine hairs around his temple. Heat leaped from the darkness of his eyes and seared into her pulse. "If you were any other kind of man, William, I wouldn't be sitting here."

He cupped her cheek with his good hand. So warm, so strong, his touch reached down and plucked the shards of loneliness from her soul. "I didn't think I'd see you again," he rasped.

She turned her face, pressing a kiss into his palm. "All those nights lying awake wondering and waiting. It was the worst fear I've ever known."

"Even worse than being forced to stay in one place your entire life? Chained to monotony?"

She smiled. "Yes, even worse than that."

"Horses are anything but monotonous."

"I suppose if I had a strong, handsome man around to chase after me, should one of the ponies gallop away, then I could be convinced to give them a try."

"You're too big for a pony."

"Why, William. How outrageous you talk. Don't you know you're never supposed to call a girl big?"

His thumb stroked over her cheek, tingling her skin to a rosy warmth. "I learned from the second I found you under Lizzie's motor that the rules of what one is supposed to do and not do don't apply to you. I wouldn't want you any other way."

"Not going by the rules. How out of character for you. You must've hit your head harder than I thought." His hand stilled, the tease gone from his eyes. A perfect moment, and she had ruined it. "I'm sorry. I don't know why I said that." She reached for his hand and held it between her own, desperate to rekindle the warmth from a moment ago. "My mouth just opens sometimes without thinking."

"At least it was the truth. Most of the nurses and doctors here put on brave faces and tell us how well we look. How well indeed. We know what we look like. That's why they have us in this back room."

"They have you in this back room so you can rest and recover in peace. Up front, they have a table tennis match going. Think you can sleep with that noise?"

"Darling, I've slept with shells exploding over my head for the past two years. A tiny ball bouncing around won't disturb me in the least."

But he wasn't sleeping well. Sister Paulette had told her of the violent thrashings and crying when he was first brought in. The outbursts had quieted, but he still trembled.

He yawned, grunting as the muscles in his neck stretched. Slipping a finger into the bandages, he tugged them away from the raw skin.

"Are they too tight? Shall I loosen them for you?"

"No. There's a safety pin in here rubbing off what's left of my skin. Some new nurse with shaking fingers stuck me trying to put it in."

Gwyn bit back the urge to demand her name and training station. She'd find out first thing in the morning and give a demonstration on how to properly secure wrappings. "I think it's time you got some rest. We can talk more in the morning."

"You'll still be here?"

She brushed back a damp bit of hair from his brow. Despite the uniform and commanding presence, the shadow of a nervous little boy hid deep within. "Where else do you think I have to go?"

"The men need drivers, and I didn't think Lady Dowling would want to lose her best."

"You need me more. Or at least, I hope you do. If not, you owe me a train ticket."

He caught her hand and pressed a gentle kiss to her fingertips. "I think I've always needed you."

A heavy breath swelled his chest. His eyelids drooped as he released a sigh. Gwyn sat perfectly still until the deep, even breathing of sleep rolled in his lungs. Slipping her hand from his, she rose and kissed his scarred cheek.

"Sweet dreams, my brave love."

He loved her. Of that he was certain. Sweeping into his orderly life like a string-pulled top, she'd spun everything upside down, leaving him breathless and out of sorts. Embodying everything he'd been told to steer clear of, her passion for life and its possibilities beyond his boundaries was enough to make the yearnings deep within spring to life.

Struggling to sit up against the thin pillow behind him, William watched as Gwyn stood across the ward instructing a group of curious nurses on how to make a field sling using a belt and puttee. Cheeks pink with excitement, her hands flew about the task with precision. She'd done it a hundred times with a hundred different objects, and the challenge thrilled her to no end.

And now she was stuck inside four walls. She needed fresh air, the wind caressing her cheeks, the sun sparking red and gold in her dark hair, a new adventure just beyond the horizon. Yet she rushed to this festering place. To him.

A dull ache throbbed down his spine and legs as the metal framed bed dug into the bruises covering his back. He shifted to adjust the pillow, but his sore arm cried in protest. Defeated by pain, he slumped back. Little good he was. An invalid with half of his body resembling spitted meat after a camp roast. Just what a beautiful vivacious woman shouldn't tie herself to.

She glanced up from her demonstration and flashed him a smile bright enough to shame the sun. His heart swelled with desire to hold her close and kiss her soft lips until the world no longer mattered.

It was for that reason he had to let her go.

His scarred existence would only bring her wandering dreams to a halt. Stinson would never accept her with him limping behind, and all those places on her list would forever remain out of reach. She'd resent him for it, and her disappointment would be enough to make him wish that shell had landed right on him. He should never have permitted his guard to falter with her. He had allowed sentiments to rule duty. It was not a mistake he could allow to continue.

"I think they got it." Gwyn tossed her supplies into the box next to his bed. "How some of these women ever passed the training course without learning field first aid is beyond me. A few more lessons, and they'll have Florence Nightingale smiling."

"It wastes time and energy to train women for practices that they'll never engage in."

She bent over the box in search of who-knows-what to teach the next session. "It wasn't a waste of time for me."

"Because you refused to obey the rules and stay back where you belonged."

Straightening with a limp roll of linen in her hand, a frown puckered her brow. "If I had stayed where I belonged, men would have died without a chance of rescue or survival. If I had stayed where I belonged, you would have endured an alcohol bath this morning by some green-nosed nurse from Darby instead of the proper Lysol swab your chart instructs."

With a flick of her wrist, the linen unraveled down to her knees. She wrapped it around and around her two fingers until it was rolled into a tight ball. Her chest rose with several deep breaths that softened the pressed line of her lips. "Are you feeling all right? A nap would do you good after sitting for so long."

"All I do is lay down," he said. "And when they sit me up, my body feels like it's covered in heaping coals."

She replaced the linen in the box and touched his forehead. He pulled away, unable to stand her velvet-like smoothness.

Pulling up her chair, she sat and opened the worn Bible from her luggage. Her mother's, she had told him once, longing tingeing her voice. "Another story can help take your mind off the bed confines. How about Samson? He was a bit of a stubborn fellow. You can relate."

"No more stories." He noticed a folded piece of stationery

peeking out from the middle of the book. "What's that?"

Excitement lit her eyes. "My acceptance letter to the flying school. I'm to start in October. I wrote them yesterday to say how thrilled I am, but that I'd like to push back my start date until after the war is over. My duty is here. Once you're back on your feet, I'm sure we can find a way. It's only a four-week course, but I asked to learn repairs and rebuilds, which pushes it closer to ten months. Just long enough for you to miss me terribly. Once I have that license in my pocket, we can start planning which we'd like to visit first—the horse farm in the Shetlands you want to see or white sandy beaches in the South Pacific where we can finally warm ourselves."

Her words—her altered dreams—flayed him like a bayonet. "No."

"No, you won't miss me? Perhaps I can drag out the lessons to ensure—"

"No 'we.' No crossing off anything. No nothing. My burns are punishment enough for me. I won't inflict them on you too." He took a deep breath that ached throughout his chest. "Go for your ten months and start your exploring. Leave me out of it."

Her excitement sputtered like a flame in a harsh wind. "Your injuries aren't punishment. It took bravery to lead those men when hell was falling all around you."

"I led those men into a slaughter. If I were you, I'd take notice and steer clear."

"Well, you're not me, and I have no intention of steering clear." She closed the book and reached for his hand. "William, you cannot blame yourself for what happened to Roland. Or to Tindall and Farrow. Or to any other man who fell when it was his time. I'm still learning that lesson myself."

"You don't understand. You never will."

"I understand better than you think I do."

He scoffed and pulled his hand away. "You think so? Wearing petticoats and having a few doors slammed in your face is hardly an experience in the injustices of the world."

The pink of her cheeks blanched white. "Did you get up on the wrong side of the bed this morning?"

"How am I supposed to get up?" He flung the dog blanket aside revealing his normal leg—pink with health—and his burned leg, too shredded and swollen with holes of extracted shrapnel to get a proper bandage around. "Perhaps if you could find me a leather strap to bite on so I can swing this foot over without collapsing, then I might be able to wake up on the correct side."

"Most of your injuries are only skin deep. Dr. Carlington says that in time and with a little therapy—"

"Skin deep." He laughed, the coldness of it raking down his spine like a rusty saber. "I have no skin left, Gwyn, or did that escape your notice?"

"My notice of you goes much further than skin." Her eyes sparked with steeled intensity. "I see to who you are inside your soul."

"You should take another look because everything inside me was burned to ash. There's nothing in there for you."

She pushed to the edge of her chair, tipping it forward on its front legs. "I don't believe that. Last night you told me you needed me."

"I may have said a great many things under the flicker of lanterns, but this morning, the harsh light of reality has dawned on me as it should you. Go home, Gwyn. Go back to your ambulance and hospital, or back to your father. Go to the people who really need you. I'm not one of them."

The back legs of her chair hit the floor. "I don't believe you."

"Believe me or not, but there's nothing I can give you. Not now, not ever."

Ignoring the blinding pain engulfing his chest, he dropped onto the pillow and turned his face to the wall. Her chair scraped the floor as a sob strangled in her throat. Her running footsteps pounded into his head like a hammer.

He squeezed his eyes shut. It was done. But the pain had only just begun.

Redness gone. Swelling down. All visible evidence from the past hour of crying wiped away. Gwyn attempted a smile at herself in the small hand mirror. Hollowness stared back. Taking a deep breath, she emerged from her hiding place behind the storage shelves. And ran directly into Susan Yarling, the busiest mouth in the hospital.

Susan startled, but the surprise expertly dropped to feigned sadness. "I'm sure he didn't mean it." She laid a hand on Gwyn's shoulder in the way all those frilly VADs did to calm the frightened boys. "Sometimes the pain and fear make them say things they wouldn't otherwise."

"Pardon?"

Scandal gleamed in Susan's eager eyes. "Captain Crawford. Everyone knows."

Thanks to you, no doubt. "The only thing that everyone knows is Captain Crawford has been seriously injured and needs as much care as every other man here."

"But none of the other men have a personal nurse they declare love to one day and banish from sight the next. It's for the best, I'm sure. Your type is better suited for driving through the mud."

Gwyn clutched the sides of her skirt to keep from swiping the smirk from the rich girl's face. "Was there something in particular you needed back here?"

"What? Oh, yes." Glancing back to the shelves, Susan tapped her fingers over boxes. "Sister sent me back here for new linens to remake the beds."

"I believe the orderlies did that only an hour ago."

"For the old patients. They're being shipped back to England to make room for the new boys coming in."

Gwyn's pulse zipped. "When?"

"Why, right now." Susan's eyebrows lifted. "Didn't you know? Oh, poor dear. Perhaps that's what Sister wanted to talk to you about after you disappeared."

The hand mirror smashed to the floor as Gwyn knocked past Susan and flew through the hospital. Orderlies jumped back, and nurses shouted warnings as she dodged trolleys of surgical instruments and towering stacks of wash basins.

Sister Paulette stood at the curtain of Ward D—William's ward—directing the outgoing traffic. "Ah, Gwyn. There you are. I tried to find you earlier."

"Where is he?"

"Take a breath, my child. Your face is red and eyes wild."

"Where is he?" Gwyn side-stepped, but the round little woman blocked her.

The lines around Sister's eyes softened. "Please understand—"

Gwyn brushed past her and ran to William's empty bed. Stripped clean, no folded uniform at the foot. No blanket. Only her bag and Bible sitting on the floor. *No, no. This isn't real. I'm imagining he left without telling me.*

"I'm sorry, my dear." Sister Paulette stood behind her, her voice quiet and sorrowful. "We received the order less than an hour ago. I wanted to find you, but Captain Crawford said no. I try to respect the wishes of my patients, but sometimes I find exceptions to my own rules."

A ton of bricks slammed into Gwyn's chest. "Where are they taking him?"

"To England, on the next boat." Sister folded her hands in front of her long white robe. "He's in pain. Much more than we realized. The medics can tend his physical wounds, but it's the internal ones that I worry about. Don't give up on him."

Grabbing her Bible, Gwyn ran out of the warehouse and straight to the docks. She scanned the crowd of white bandages and khakis waiting to board one of the Red Cross ships. Her heart plummeted to her feet. How was she to find him in all this?

"William? William!" Curious eyes turned to stare. She didn't care. She'd scream herself hoarse before letting that ship sail away. "William!"

Her ears strained for his voice, but the caw of seagulls and thumping of heavy feet drowned out any reply she hoped to hear. Spinning in a circle to examine the faces around her, panic raced down her veins and squeezed her heart. *Oh, God. Please help me.*

"*Mademoiselle!*" A French orderly weaved his way through the stretchers. Despite the chilling breeze, a sheen of sweat popped across his sunburned forehead. "*Ma'amselle,* what are you doing here?"

"I'm looking for someone. A soldier. They told me he's being loaded for transport back to England."

"There are many soldiers here today. We are having trouble keeping the incoming separated from those cleared to leave."

"His name is Captain William Crawford. He was in Ward D."

The orderly tapped a calloused finger to his chin. "Ward D. That is the burn unit, yes?"

Gwyn nodded, hope flaring. "Yes, yes. The entire ward was taken."

"They loaded the overflow of wounded first to avoid the glare of the sun in the decks below. Any hospital patients are loaded last onto the available top deck." He shrugged. "I do not know for sure, but that is how I have seen them loaded before. Good luck."

"Thank you." She raced down the wharf. Her heels thumped against the planks as the waves licked through the cracks and pooled into slippery puddles.

"Hey, miss! Slow down!" A sailor holding one of the ship's ropes leaped back as she sailed past. "Hey! Hey! You're not allowed on board. Stop!"

Her feet didn't stop as she barreled up the gangway. "I'm a nurse. Official business." The ship rolled beneath her feet as she landed on the top deck. Rows of stretchers covered the top deck while others leaned against the foam-slimed rails. She gulped a breath into her burning lungs. "William!"

"I'm a William," said a man three stretchers down. He was missing both arms.

"Sorry." She walked past him. "Not the one I'm looking for."

She hurried to the front of the ship, calling his name and scanning each face. Several replied that they could be a William if she wanted him to, a few offers of marriage, and one rather rude suggestion concerning her ankles in boots.

"It might help if you tell us which William you're looking for, miss," came a thin voice near her elbow. A man with a wiry mustache leaned heavily against the rail while his unwrapped arm tipped his missing hat. "Might make your search go quicker."

"Captain William Crawford." She shielded her eyes against the bright sun flashing off the top of waves. "Of the Ox and Bucks. He was in Ward D."

"Oh, them fellows all bandaged up like mummies? Back there on the port side." He pointed around the smokestack to the left.

Ward D was laid out like sardines in a can along the port side. William lay at the end of the row, his heard turned from the rest of the men as he gazed blankly out to the foaming sea.

"Trying to sneak off?"

He flinched at her voice but didn't turn. "You shouldn't be here."

"Too late for that." She knelt beside him, casting a shadow over his smooth unblemished cheek. "How could you leave without telling me?"

"Within minutes of the order, we moved out. There wasn't time to even buckle my belt if I had one."

"You had time to talk to Sister Paulette. Why, William?"

"Because there's no reason for you to be here."

"You are my reason." She touched his shoulder. "Please look at me."

His head swiveled to her. Bright blue eyes stared coldly into hers. "Stop wasting yourself on some cripple. You'll only find disappointment. Go back to driving, go back to planning your life of adventure. You won't find it with me."

The boat trembled, its vibrations shaking deep into Gwyn's bones. One prick, and she was sure they would shatter from the agony splintering deep in their core. "You're so very wrong."

A whistle pierced the air. Beads of water on the deck began to roll backward.

"You better get ashore," William said. "This isn't your ride."

The flat hollowness of his voice cut into her like glass. "Please don't send me away."

"Everything between us was a mistake. I never should have allowed it to happen." He turned his head back to the water. A vein throbbed in his neck. "Go. Forget me. Forget all of this."

"It was never a mistake. Not when I love you, and I know that you I—"

"Lieutenant, please escort this lady to shore." William signaled to a sailor with a clipboard in his hand. "She has no right to be on this ship."

"Come with me, miss." The officer tugged her to her feet. "All unregistered passengers must go ashore."

"William, please." Tears crowded her throat.

The officer's fingers curled around her elbow, pulling her along. "Ashore, miss."

"Take this, if you'll have nothing else of me." She pushed the Bible towards William. It thumped against his uninjured leg.

Staggering down the gangway, she stood on the dock until the ship faded to nothing against the churning deep blue waves. The wind chapped the tears streaming down her face, but she didn't lift a finger to dry them. Let them burn. Their sting was the only thing left of him.

Another love. Gone. First her mother, then Eugenie, and now him. She should have fought harder. Should have forced him to … to what? To want her? To need her?

Blackness caved her insides, stealing the shred of hope that she had tried to cling to. She stared across the empty waters. The world, once wide and open, disappeared in a void as deep and cold as the one plunging in her heart.

CHAPTER 29

Throwing Rosie into park, Gwyn scrambled around to the back and flung open the doors. "I've got two head cases, trench fever, and a leg," she announced to the orderlies as they unloaded her wounded and carried them inside the hospital.

"Got some potatoes on the fire and a fresh mix of coffee," one of them told her before hooking a sturdy arm around the leg patient. "Get it while it's hot and steal the chill from your bones."

"I'll do a cleaning first." Gwyn's stomach rumbled traitorously. She couldn't leave a dirtied transport in case a new request came in. The cold was misery enough. The men didn't need to sit in a previous man's filth just because she decided to get coffee.

The orderly's face soured in disapproval, but Gwyn grabbed a bucket and marched off to the water pump. They all looked at her that way. Never approving of the tasks she took on, the extra shifts she picked up when one of the other drivers didn't feel well, or the amount of time she took sweeping the workshop. If she didn't do it, who would?

She filled the bucket with icy water before grabbing a broom, sand pail, and disinfectant. She trudged back to Rosie for a thorough scouring.

"What are you doing out here?" Bundled in a dark gray fur coat and matching hat, Cecelia glared at Gwyn from Rosie's open back doors.

Inside the ambulance, Gwyn threw another handful of sand to soak up the foulness in the corner. "What does it look like?"

"Like you're making a mess." Cecelia stamped her feet in the slush. No matter how much gunk surrounded her, she managed to stay spotless. "You've been out in the cold too long. Let someone else do that while you come inside and get warm. It's starting to snow again."

"I'm not asking someone else to do this for me because the last time—"

"The last time they did it wrong, and you had to start over from the beginning. Yes, I know. All the drivers know, the town knows, all of France knows." Cecelia rolled her eyes. "Who is supposed to meet your standards when you set them at impossible?"

"They're not impossible. I just like them done a certain way."

"A certain way? The old Gwyn I knew cared not a snap for standard practices."

A sudden pang pinched Gwyn's heart. "The old Gwyn you knew lived in a dream."

"That's it. Bruce, take her bucket away."

Bruce, their part-time driver and handyman, jumped into the ambulance and snatched the bucket from Gwyn's hand. "Sorry, Miss Ruthers. I don't make the rules."

Gwyn pointed an accusing finger at Cecelia. "And she does?"

"When she sneaks me an extra slice of pumpkin bread she does."

"This is ridiculous." Gwyn reached for the bucket. Bruce's long arms held it out of her reach.

"Stop being difficult, and come down from there. I've got a slice for you too." Cecelia stamped her feet again. "Hurry up. My feet are turning to ice blocks."

Gwyn debated arguing, but it wasn't worth it. Bruce was stronger, and Cecelia could outlast her in stubbornness. With a heavy sigh, Gwyn climbed down and patted Rosie's fender. "I'll be back, old girl."

"Not for a while." Cecelia hooked an arm through Gwyn's, dragging her across the slushy car park and straight into the kitchen.

Gwyn balked at the doorway. "I can't go in there. I've been stomping around the field all day. Look at my shoes."

Cecelia didn't bat an eyelash as she slipped off her fur coat and hung it on a peg by the door, then peeled Gwyn out of hers and added it to the collection. Reaching back into her coat pocket, Cecelia extracted a silk bag and handed it to Gwyn.

"Cecelia, these are house slippers." Gwyn held up the thin-soled dainty bits of satin.

Cecelia beamed as she took off her hat and patted her hair. "Aren't they darling?"

Gwyn sighed. It was no use. Wear the frippery or slide around an infected hospital in her stocking-clad feet.

They slipped into the kitchen for two hot mugs of coffee and settled in the far corner next to the fireplace, its heat filling the space with toasty comfort.

"I thought you were off duty this morning." Cecelia sipped her warm brew. "You drove last night, as well."

Gwyn shrugged and took a nip of her drink. Without sugar to aid the taste, the bitterness sliced down her throat in one horrible rush. At least it was warm. "I like to stay busy."

"Staying busy won't bring him back."

The cup slipped in Gwyn's hand. She caught it before it spilled to the floor. "I stay busy for myself and the men."

"The men on both sides of the line are quiet. It's too cold for them to bang away at one another, especially with Christmas only a few weeks away." Lowering her cup, Cecelia grasped Gwyn's hand and leaned close. "It's all right to miss him."

Gwyn stared into the orange flames crackling against the back of the fireplace. The pang from earlier wedged into her like a splinter. "He didn't want me."

"So you give up? Where's the pluck and backbone?"

"I'm not giving up, but I'm not chasing after someone who wants nothing to do with me. There are more important things calling for my attention right now."

Wildfire leaped in Cecelia's eyes. "You're hiding, G. And it doesn't become you."

Gwyn surged from her chair. Hot coffee splatted across her

knee. "What do you know about it?"

"I see you throwing yourself into everything except the one thing you should be doing. Fighting for William!"

Tears speared the backs of Gwyn's eyelids. "I did fight for him, but it's a losing battle when you're left standing on a dock holding the broken pieces of your heart in your hand."

"What is this shouting?" Lady Dowling appeared in the doorway. "You two. Come with me, please."

Like naughty schoolchildren, Gwyn and Cecelia followed her upstairs to the small office. Ice frosted the edges of the window, the cold tendrils slipping through the cracks and curling around the room. Gwyn rubbed the gooseflesh on her arms and stepped closer to the potbellied stove.

Lady Dowling stood at the window, her pointed chin held high and long fingers clasped behind her back. "Is there a reason for raised voices in hospital?"

Cecelia stiffened. "We were only having a discussion, m'lady."

"A rather loud one, wouldn't you say?"

"Only because Gwyn tries to keep her ears closed."

Turning from the window, Lady Dowling arched a thin eyebrow. "You were on duty last night. And then again this morning."

"Yes, m'lady. I got up early and volunteered to take another shift."

"We do have other drivers. More than enough, I find myself at odds to admit, with the action suffering under winter's strain."

"Most of the injuries we have coming in are from trench fever and frostbite," said Gwyn. "Not even the Germans feel like wriggling from their safe holes to battle the icicles."

Lady Dowling's fingers tapped against the edge of her desk. "And yet you still try to take on the other drivers' shifts. Where do you find the energy?"

Her tone seeped into Gwyn's bones faster than the frigid air. "If the men are in need, then I'll do whatever it takes to get to them."

"Interesting choice of words." Lady Dowling continued to

tap as her eyes remained fixed like a bird of prey. "But, as we just mentioned, the action has slowed. Why your sudden burst of exertion?"

"I like to stay busy. It helps ease the days."

Cecelia huffed with impatience. "It's time."

Lady Dowling blinked, breaking the tension. "I'm afraid you're right. I hate to do it, but I see no other course."

Uneasiness pricked Gwyn's palms. "Time for what?"

Lady Dowling sighed, rustling the taffeta across her bosom. "I'm sending you home."

"What?" Gwyn's outburst ricocheted off the stone walls. "No. I can't leave."

"You can, and you will."

Disbelief surged, knocking the breath from Gwyn's lungs. "Have I done something wrong?"

"You are the best driver I have, the best I've known, in fact. Reliable, quick, and dutiful past the point of exhaustion. That's why you have to leave. And the sooner, the better."

"But the men—"

"Will go on without you. You are not the only person standing between them and death."

"Lady Dowling, I beg you to reconsider."

"This is not a negotiation."

Gwyn grabbed a chair and dropped onto it before her knees gave out. Leave France? Leave the men with one less driver? Certainly, they needed ambulances in England, but here she felt most useful. To take that away now … she'd feel like a failure. As if the pressure had become too much. Her grand adventure would come to a grinding halt, at least until Stinson offered her another chance. If they ever would again now that she'd put herself back on the waiting list.

She dropped her head to her hands to ease the blood pounding in her temples. "Why?"

"My dear, as old as I am, I can still see when a person is trying to hide by throwing herself into her work." Taffeta rustled as Lady Dowling walked around her desk and pried open a drawer. Something flat and bulky smacked the desk's surface. "This is why."

A leather-bound journal, small with worn pages. With trembling fingers, Gwyn touched the smooth cover. She'd seen it before. Flipping it open, she discovered a fantastical world of sketched horses, buildings, countryside, and soldiers slogging through mud. At the last page, her breath caught in her throat.

Soft pencil strokes etched a wide field with horses grazing among the tall grass. A woman stood on the edge of the field dressed in a long gown that caressed the tops of her bare feet. Her long dark hair danced on a breeze, soft tendrils teasing her neck. Her face was turned towards the hills, but Gwyn knew. He had drawn her as part of his dream.

She traced the curved lines, running a thumb over the shaded areas he had captured with the perfect dimensions of light and dark. His fingers had created this. Each brush of his pencil an extension of his mind and the emotion he kept locked away from the world.

The world faded away as her eyes blurred above the drawing. *Oh, William. This is where I belong.* Closing the journal, she cradled it to her heart. "When do I leave?"

CHAPTER 30

Gwyn flung out her folded pairs of drawers and stockings for the third time until her fingers hit the bottom of her bag. "Papa! Where did you put that extra box of ointment? I can't find it anywhere."

Her father slouched in the doorway of her bedroom, wiping his blackened hands on a cloth. "In the bag, already packed and waiting by the door."

"The extra bandages, chamomile, oil silk, and carbolic lotion?"

"In the same bag, though I'm more than sure the hospital has plenty in supply."

Gwyn refolded the discarded garments and stuffed them back into the suitcase. "We didn't in the field. We had to have our own stock in case."

"This isn't the field. It's London."

"And London is overflowing with soldiers, so the better prepared I am, the smoother things will go."

"You think they'll just allow you to march in and take over a patient? A severely injured officer with an actively retired general father?"

Gwyn snapped the locks closed and cinched the buckle of her bag before looking at him. "I'll get in."

Papa tucked the cloth into his back pocket and eased himself onto the room's only chair with a bone-weary grunt.

"Are you all right, Papa?"

He waved her off with a smile. "Long day under the bonnet with a pair of loosened bolts. Wrenched them into submission, though."

Guilt pricked her heart. In her time away, gray had streaked its way through her father's hair and deep lines carved around his eyes. She sat on the edge of her bed and took his calloused hand. "You work too hard."

"Ah, I wondered where you got it." He smiled. "That, and the stubbornness to keep going when logic tells you to stop."

Her gaze dropped to his hands. So large and warm, they had cradled her when she'd scraped a knee and helped her change her first tire. They were as adept at installing new gear shifts as folding in prayer. "You don't think I should go?"

"I think you have to do what you believe is right." He lifted her chin with his thumb. "The boy is hurting, in body and pride. It'll take stubbornness to pull him from it. And as much love as you can give him."

"He sent me away once. He'll try to do it again. I know he will."

"I tried to make the same mistake once with your mother. Mind you, once. She never let me do it again, and I praise God for it every day because I wouldn't have you if I'd let my pride stand in the way."

"What do you mean?"

Standing, her father walked to the tiny window that peered across the gravel drive. "She was the most beautiful woman I had ever seen. Thick hair, a touch of auburn lighter than yours, and a quick laugh. Her dream was to travel the world and see the places she'd only read about in all her stacks of books. For some reason, she fell in love with me."

"Mama was smart."

Papa's sad smile reflected in the glass. "Aye, I thought so, too, until she decided to give up her dreams and become a poor mechanic's wife."

Gwyn's fingers curled into the coverlet folded at the foot of her bed, longing for a mother's touch that she hadn't felt in years.

"I told her to leave," he continued, "that I never wanted to see her again, never letting on that my heart was breaking with each word. Tears clouded those beautiful green eyes of hers, the same ones she gave to you, baby girl. 'Bernard Ruthers,' she said to me, 'you are the stupidest man I've ever met, but I love you still. Order me away if you like, but I'm not leaving. Marry me now, or I'll tell everyone you stall in second gear and cheat at cards.' What could I say to that?"

Crossing to her nightstand, he took the silver-framed picture of her and Mum and extracted the black and white photograph. Gwyn, not more than a year old, sat on her mother's knee while staring up at the woman who she now looked so much like. Stroking a loving finger over his wife's hair, Papa flipped the photograph over and handed it to Gwyn. Her mother's delicate script scrawled across the back in a message she'd never seen.

New List
Take Gwyn to feed the swans on the Thames.
Learn to drive.
Picnic with Bernard under the stars.
Family trip to the seashore.
Watch Gwyn run barefoot on the sand.
Listen to Lina Cavalieri perform at the Crystal Palace.

Many of the items were crossed off with only a few remaining, including the very last one. *Never part from the ones I love.*

"All this time. I thought …" Gwyn shook her head as disbelief rocked her settled notions.

"You thought I made her give her life up. That her dreams of doing great things skidded to an end when she gave into love and wasted away into a quiet life above a garage. Dreams often change to include the ones we love." He smiled sadly. "I knew I could never explain that to you and have you truly believe me. Oh, I know you would want to, but some things must be experienced before true understanding takes place. When you met William … well, I prayed you would discover it for yourself."

Gwyn hung her head in shame. "I'm so sorry, Papa."

"There's no one to say sorry to, my girl. Only yourself." He turned away from the window and sat next to her on the bed. "I've watched you throw yourself into the same hopes as your mother did. I've watched you push down boundaries that threaten to keep you from running, but with all this running you've limited yourself from enjoying all of life's possibilities." He reached out and grazed his fingertips across her cheek. "William is your possibility."

Tears scalded the corners of her eyes. Her mother had never been forced to choose which life she wanted. Love hadn't blocked her path. It gave her a new one. Lightness flooded her heart. She didn't have to choose either. William was what she wanted. Not one day with him had been boring, and they never would be. But … "He'll fight me."

"Of course he will, but when have you ever backed down from one of those?"

"Never." She grinned with anticipation at the coming challenge. "I could threaten to tell everyone he's a lousy shot and sits a horse like a girl."

Papa laughed and threw his arm around her shoulders, holding her close. "Aye, you could, my girl. Worked for me."

A burst of sniffles filled the pristine waiting room. A girl around fifteen dug into her handbag, pulled out a crinkled handkerchief, and thrust it under her mother's red nose. A loud honk and the sniffles continued.

Gwyn shifted in her seat to ease the ache in her backside and to shift her view of the pale, bloated faces of the crying family next to her. The heavy double doors swung open as a starched nurse with a headpiece billowing behind her like wings stopped just inside the room. "Mr. and Mrs. Phelps?"

A man and woman jumped to their feet. "Mr. and Mrs. Phelps." The husband slipped his hand under his wife's elbow. "That's us."

The nurse didn't blink. "Follow me, please."

The door swung shut behind them with a *thump*. Silence weighed like a blanket thick enough to suffocate the room. Gwyn stared at her lap. What was taking so long? The woman next to her began her sniffling again, each nose whistle grating down Gwyn's nerves.

Shooting from her chair, Gwyn stalked to the bay window at the far end of the room. Outside, rain pinged off the pavement, glittering among the cobblestones like tiny diamonds. People shuffled by on the slushy footpaths, their collars pulled tight and hats angled low to keep the freezing drizzle out. Two weeks to Christmas and not one person carried a shiny package under their arms or a warm smile on their faces. Gloom and destruction had stripped the joy of the season from them.

The door thumped open again. "Miss Ruthers."

Gwyn's heart lurched into her throat. This was it.

"Come with me," the nurse said without emotion.

An unadorned hallway stretched for miles beyond the double doors. The nurse's flat-soled shoes squeaked over the green and white checked linoleum floor. The overpowering smell of sterilization clogged Gwyn's throat. How was anyone expected to recover without suffocating first? "Do the men receive time outside? For fresh air?"

"Don't you think they had enough fresh air over there?"

"I know that some of their lungs, particularly the gassed ones, need air away from the chemical scents of medical supplies."

"Unlike your field tents, St. Matthews cares for its patients with the best instruments and practices available. Most visitors do not come in waving letters of acquaintances from Earls and Marchionesses. Our visitors must be family." The nurse stopped at a door and glanced down at Gwyn's bare left hand. A thick eyebrow arched in contempt. "But with Lady Dowling as a great patron of ours and a third cousin to the Duke of Kent, I see that our sacred rules do not apply to all."

Any nerves Gwyn had burned away in a flare. "I didn't outdrive the Germans to come under attack on home soil. Am I allowed to see Captain Crawford or not?"

"These men deserve better than having titles thrown around just so anyone off the street can traipse through here. They deserve respect and quiet."

The flare inside Gwyn died at the woman's heart to protect the boys beyond the door. "My friends and I pulled many of these men from the trenches. We're on the same side, Sister."

The woman stared at Gwyn long and hard. With a deep breath, she turned on her heel and pushed into the ward. "This way, please."

It was like any other ward Gwyn had been in, only nothing shook. Each bed was filled with occupants dressed in white cotton bandages and light blue pajamas. They watched with open curiosity as the women passed. Gwyn had heard that female visitors never came to the burn ward—too many of them ran out screaming in hysterics at the sight of the men.

The nurse stopped at an empty bed and frowned. She turned to the man in the next bed. "Where is Captain Crawford?"

"Left about ten minutes ago." He nodded his burned chin towards a door at the back of the room. "I can figure where he went."

"Where does that lead?" Gwyn asked.

The nurse sighed. Apparently, this wasn't his first absence. "To the garden. He's been warned not to go out there alone."

She started for the exit, but Gwyn caught her arm. "Please let me."

"He won't come." The man peered at her through half-hooded lids. "I think he's trying to drown his sorrows in pneumonia."

Gwyn grinned, buttoning the top buttons of her overcoat. "Lucky for me, I have a talent for dealing with stubborn men."

"Doesn't sound too lucky for the captain."

"Not a chance."

Rain dribbled through his hair, wetting his pajama top as it slipped down his neck. William shivered. He should have brought a blanket, but the only ones they kept in the ward were those itchy dog creations. If he asked for anything else, the nurses got suspicious. How could they expect him to stay inside, suffocating under the stench of death and rotting skin all day?

William shoved away from the pole and skimmed his hand over the porch rail, dashing raindrops onto the bricked courtyard. The water plopped into the collected puddles, fanning into tiny rings.

Stinging from the icy specks, he buried his hands deep in his pockets. Was it raining in France? How many of his men had the fortune of a roof over their heads, such as he did now? No shelter, no food, and barely enough material to cover their backs. He gazed across the courtyard, bleak and piled with gray slush. His own no man's land. Except this one wasn't dotted with purple and blue bodies buried in the frozen ground.

His stomach churned with helplessness. *Why me, God? Why take me away from my men when they need me? What good can I do from here? Part of Your master plan, is it? If she hadn't left me that Bible—*

No. He wouldn't think about her. The hole in his heart was too singed. Every peal of feminine laughter, every light touch to his forehead, every ambulance that drove by was like dousing his insides with kerosene.

The door creaked open behind him. Delicate footsteps picked their way over the ice.

"Ten more minutes," he said. "I needed fresh air."

"Ten more minutes and your lungs will freeze out here."

The hole in his heart blazed to life. He gripped the rail until it shook, ready to splinter under his fingers. "What are you doing here?"

"Someone needs to drag you out of the rain when you don't have sense enough to do it yourself."

The desire to turn and face her assailed him like a mass of bullets targeting his heart. He grit his teeth against the urge. "I mean here, in London. At St. Matthews."

"Did you think I wouldn't come after you?" Her voice, so soft and low, caressed the weary flames around his heart. "Or did you actually assume your stubbornness would deter me?"

"Clearly, I underestimated your desire for disappointment."

"William."

The sweet plea shattered his control. He turned to face his doom. She was even more beautiful than his dreams recalled. Dressed in deep green that turned her eyes to emeralds, and her lustrous mahogany hair tucked up under a daintily propped hat, she was the image of a Christmas angel.

Sand coated his throat. "What are you doing here, Gwyn?"

She stepped towards him. Oh, how he wished she hadn't. The red of her lips begged him to forget swearing her off. Despite the cold, he knew how warm they would feel.

"I came to take you home," she said.

"My family is not in residence for the time being, and the nurses won't allow me to discharge into my own hands. Seems they think we're all incapable of taking care of ourselves."

"You've been discharged into my care for transport to the hospital in Great Malvern. You don't need specialized treatment anymore, just rest away from all the big city commotion."

Heat gnawed up the back of his neck. The last person he expected to make decisions for him was Gwyn. She knew the sense of helplessness and worthlessness of having someone else dictate your next move. "You did all this behind my back? I assume you pulled a few strings to arrange this. Throw in a marchioness's name, perhaps a baron's?"

"Lady Dowling and Lord Somerset were most eager to help. Lord Somerset has even offered his home for convalescence until you're fit to return to your own."

"I have no intention of returning to Great Malvern or depending upon the pity or charity of others."

Hurt flickered in her eyes despite the brave smile. "The country air can do wonders, you'll see."

"Can it give me back the skin shredded down my body?"

Her smile flattened to a sheet of ice. "So that's it, is it? You want to rot away here and feel sorry for yourself." She shook her head, catching mist in the burnished curl grazing her jaw. "I've known you to be many things, William Crawford, but a pathetic coward was never one of them."

"You expect me to trot along behind you like some obedient pup after you went behind my back?"

"I came prepared for the fight I knew you were going to pick with me."

"If you'd stayed away like I said, there wouldn't be a fight."

"You were wrong to order me away, and deep down you know it. You're using these surface wounds to cover the true hurt inside."

He laughed. As harsh as nails against metal. "Hurt? What could I possibly hurt for inside?"

"Your lost friend. Your men. Your duty cut short. The need to prove yourself worthy." She moved closer, the glint in her eye softening. "I fought the same battle, and it turned out useless. Every day over there, I was trying to prove myself, but God had a different adventure in mind for me."

"You think God tore me up and ripped away the only life I know because He'd rather me skulk away to the country?"

"Perhaps He needed to get your attention."

"And this is how He does it?" William ran a hand over the roughly patched skin along his cheek and neck. "So much for mercy."

"Our definition varies widely from His."

"Like tossing that man in the belly of a fish?"

She smiled faintly. "Would you rather that have happened to you?"

"I'd rather none of it happen."

"But it did happen. Terrible as it was. I came too close to losing you."

He turned away, ashamed that the longing in her voice echoed the longing in his heart. Snow began to fall. The lacy bits of fluff drifted down from the gray sky, dusting the roof and stone benches. He was amazed that something so simple could cover such ugliness. If only it covered all things. "You don't need me. You shouldn't want me. Not like this."

"But I do need you. And I want you exactly like this." She cupped his scarred cheek, pulling his face around to hers. "Makes you look more dashing. I'll have to beat off the other girls with a stick."

"Don't count on any takers. Women may want a war hero, but not one who resembles a hunk of meat prematurely thrown off the fire."

Gwyn rolled her eyes. "If you keep talking like that, I'll take a stick after *you*."

He pulled away. The warmth of her touch evaporated on a puff of frigid air. "I admire your devotion, as misguided as it is, but you're wrong to think I can give you what you deserve. What happened to traveling the world without fetters? You think living the quiet life in the country is going to make you happy? You'd be miserable, and worse, regret that you never broke free when you had the chance. I won't sentence you to that kind of life."

"And shoving me away won't do the same for you?"

"It's a chance I'm willing to take."

"Well, it's the wrong one." She balled her hands on her hips. "These past few months have been the most miserable and lonely of my life. All the hopes and dreams I have for life mean nothing without you to share them with. I'm half a shell. I need you to make me whole again."

William gripped the rail as her words battered his defenses. His entire life had been devoted to duty, but after seeing his shrapnel-marked and battered body, the fighting forces no longer saw his worth. He'd believed the lies feasting on his misery, never imagining he'd commissioned Gwyn to the same fate. When he'd found those poppy petals in her Bible, he'd nearly ground them to dust for the hope they'd once represented. What a selfish fool he was.

Fresh snow swirled in the air and kissed the tops of his hands, blanketing the uneven backs with pristine whiteness. He could no longer tell the scarred from the smooth.

"Did you mean this?"

He turned and stared at the leather-bound journal in Gwyn's hand. All this time, he thought it lost somewhere in France. "Where did you get that?"

"Sister Paulette found it under your bed after you left. She thought I might know how to get it back to you. Did you mean it?"

How many nights had he lain awake with ghostly images marching before him, the whites of his enemy's eyes stark against the darkness? His only relief had been putting pen to paper and capturing every curve of Gwyn's face and strand of dark hair. It kept him sane in the midst of uncertainty, and she was offering it to him again.

"You didn't really want me away, did you?"

The pain in her soft words unraveled the last bit of string holding his tightly-bound control together. "I never wished to be away from you. I'd rather stand in front of a firing squad than lose you because of my stubborn pride." He held his hands out in a helpless gesture. "I refused to become a millstone around your neck."

"How could your heart ever be a burden to me?"

Her green eyes blazed into his soul, shattering past his shield wall and scorching the wretchedness he'd wallowed in for months. Months without her. Could her sweet words be true? Did he dare to hope for happiness reaching out to him after an absence so long? His pulse galloped, and he sucked in a steadying breath. "Is that what you truly wish for? My heart in all its mangled brokenness."

"It is more precious to me now than ever before."

"You laid claim to it a long time ago. You and no one else."

"Good. I have no intention of sharing." She cocked her head to the side. "You don't plan on running out on me again, do you? Because with those flimsy slippers, you won't get far."

"Who else would take me?"

"You're only giving into me because you don't have any other prospects? With that kind of declaration, I think I'll leave you to Sister What's-Her-Name and her squeaky shoes."

With a toss of her head, Gwyn turned for the door. William grabbed her elbow and pulled her around, locking her against his chest. The feel of her against his still-tender injuries rippled pain down his body, but it was a pain he was willing to suffer for all eternity to have her so close.

"I don't want squeaky shoes." He pulled the pins from her hat and tossed them to the ground. He dug his fingers deep into the hair curled at the nape of her neck. Her warm skin pulsed against his hand. "I want you, running barefoot in the field with the sun in your hair and the wind at your back. I want to hold you every night knowing you belong only to me, and—someday—when we're old and gray, and after I've taken you to every little dot on the map you wish to see, I want you to tell me that there's no place on earth you'd rather be than in my arms."

A slow smile tilted her full lips as she wrapped one arm around his neck and cupped his scarred cheek with the other hand. "I can tell you that now."

"You're going to that flight school. I don't care how long I have to wait. No arguing."

"Yes, William." Her fingers glided over his marred skin, tingling it to life. For the first time since waking up in hospital, hope flared within him. He could live again. With this woman, he could do anything.

He touched his forehead to hers. She closed her eyes and sighed. The hope flared to desire as his lips caressed her eyelids, silky cheeks, the curve of her jaw, and the outside of her lips. "I think I've loved you since the day I saw you buried under that rusty old car."

The sigh rumbling up her throat caught. Her eyes flashed open. "You think?"

"Well, I had to do a little recalculation when I discovered you aren't overly fond of horses."

She moved to speak, but he cut off her outcry with a kiss filled with all the passion he'd locked away. Curling his fingers around the back of her neck, he slanted his mouth to capture the exquisiteness of her. She pressed into him, responding with the same eagerness that set his heart galloping. He clung tight, afraid to let go should she slip away and steal the peace of love flooding his soul.

"*Ahem.*"

William jerked back, cracking the moment like a pick to ice. Sister Squeaky Shoes glared at them from the open door.

"I wanted to make sure the snow didn't swallow you." Her eyes narrowed. "I can see now the two of you would melt anything before it had a chance to take you captive."

Unfazed, Gwyn nuzzled her head under his chin. "I'm quite happy with my current captor."

"So I see." Sister notched her chin. "Perhaps he might release you to allow the doctor a quick exam before he signs the discharge papers. And inside if you don't mind. We don't need the good doctor catching pneumonia."

With a queenly sweep of her flowing white habit, the good sister made her leave to the elegant cadence of *squeak squeak squeak.*

CHAPTER 31

1918 November

Gwyn ground Lizzie to a sputtering halt and vaulted out, the morning's newspaper clenched in her gloved fist. Sprinting across the front lawn, she threw open the cottage door and gasped for air. "William!"

Silence. She darted into the kitchen. "Will?"

A stack of freshly washed breakfast plates and his cup of cold coffee sat next to the sink. She burst through the back door, her thick-heeled boots crunching across the dead grass tinged with early morning frost as she raced past the whitewashed paddock and training circle.

She threw open the stable door and stepped inside. The musty scent of hay and horse curled under her nose. "William!"

Straw rustled from the far stall. William's head popped around the gate, a pitchfork in one hand and a look of panic on his sweat-sheened brow. "What's wrong? Did you have an accident?"

"No. No accident."

He set the pitchfork's tines into the ground and swiped a hand over his mouth, easing the lines of alarm. "I told your father you had no business driving that rust bucket all over town delivering the paper when the roads are slick with ice. Why he insisted you take Lizzie is beyond me."

Gwyn ignored his tirade as she sailed past the stalls of horses poking their heads out to see their owners' latest commotion. "It's over!" She waved the paper in William's face. "It's all over. The war. They've signed an armistice."

Leaning his tool against the wall, William took the crinkled paper from her hands and read the bold headline. "The Great War ends. Germany surrenders." The muscles in his neck constricted. "Armistice to begin at eleven o'clock Paris time. Terms of agreement follow on page two."

Gwyn laughed as the years of anxiety melted away. "It's finally over. They can come home. We don't have to fight anymore. Isn't it wonderful?"

He dropped the paper and swept her into his arms, spinning in wide circles. "Wonderful," he murmured into her ear. Clenching tight, his arms threatened to break her ribs and squeeze the air from her lungs.

Gwyn didn't care as she pressed kisses over his cheeks, jaw, and every inch of exposed skin she could find. The countless hours of prayer had finally come to pass. Cecelia and her dear Doctor Bennett could finalize their engagement, and Rosie would find her new home right next to Lizzie, thanks to Lady Dowling.

Too excited to stay put, Gwyn wiggled out of William's arms and grabbed his scarred hand. The wounds had healed well, but his body would carry the scars for the rest of his life. "Let's go into town and celebrate with everyone. The mucking can wait for today."

"Tell that to the horses." Despite his weak protest, William allowed her to pull him along.

"More than glad to because not even their long faces can bring me down today."

"Long faces?" William rolled his eyes. "Did you really just make that crack?"

She laughed, stepping out of the barn. Brilliant morning sun sparkled through the icy branches of the apple orchard surrounding their cottage. Tonight she would make a special batch of apple cider to toast the glorious day.

"I need to send a telegram while we're in town. To Johnny Philson," William said.

"The man you bunked next to at St. Matthews?"

William nodded and looked to the sky, shielding his eyes against the bright glare of blue and white. "Was part of a flying squadron, but got shot down over Belgium. Managed to walk away from his burning aircraft. Now, he delivers air post near his farm in Norwich. High time he took on a pupil."

Gwyn's feet stopped. If possible, her excitement doubled over. "A pupil?"

"The Stinson school closed when the Yanks joined the war, and there's no word on whether it'll reopen. You'll simply have to obtain your pilot license here in dear ol' Blighty." He raised her hand to his lips and kissed the simple band wrapped around her fourth finger. "That way, I can come watch you do those loopty-loop circles while making sure Phil keeps his curious hands to himself."

"Oh, Will! How wonderful. You'll come fly with me, won't you?"

"My feet are perfectly happy here on the ground, but I'll wave every time you rush by on a gust of wind, my darling."

She bounced on the balls of her feet as the future spread wide with awaiting possibilities. William and their horses. Her pilot's license. And now… "You know what the best part of this war news is?"

He brushed a wild curl from her cheek, tucking it behind her ear. "What?"

She grinned, kissing his hand. "It's over before Christmas."

AUTHOR NOTES

I remember the day I entered the world of *Downton Abbey*. On Christmas morning, a costume drama period piece that had somehow escaped my knowledge waited for me under the tree. Thankfully, my husband knows how to cover my blind spots. That night, with a box of fudge on my lap, a world of silk, jewels, witty repartee, manners, and sprawling aristocracy swept me away to a beautiful dream. As the exquisiteness of Season One rolled into the Great War, I began to contemplate the relationship between the rich young daughter in her nurse's uniform and the handsome chauffeur. And when I heard "If You Were the Only Girl in the World" being sung to a returning soldier, *A Rolls Royce in No Man's Land* was born—only you may know it by its more romantic title, *Among the Poppies*.

Diving into the struggles of the Tommies, women on the homefront, trench layouts, and all manner of medical duties, I experienced the great struggle of all historical writers: wanting to include every ounce of detail possible. But readers aren't often interested in the different types of trenches, artillery shell sizes, and the various problems an ambulance can rack up during one night shift on the Front. Whatever detail I do decide to include, I do my utmost to provide the most historically accurate account I possibly can. But where to start? I decided early on that I didn't want a militarized unit like the FANYs, VADs, or Red Cross so I settled on a private ambulance fleet run by a private hospital which would allow the freedom to move outside the strict guidelines enforced by rank and regulations. Many wealthy ladies turned their English estates and French chateaus into much needed convalescent homes and hospitals, such as the Countess of Carnarvon and the fictional Lady Dowling. Much to the Marchioness's chagrin, the Duchess of Westminster and her friends truly did dress in their finest diamonds and silks to meet the wounded at her villa-turned-hospital in Le Touquet. It was the least they could do to boost the soldiers' morale, the Duchess would say.

While Gwyn is part of a private ambulance fleet, she did take the same first-aid classes a VAD would have. And she was required to pass a driving test like the FANY, whose headquarters was indeed located at 192 Earls Court Road in London. She and her fellow drivers also wore large fur coats in the winter that were donated to them by wealthy ladies, again just like the FANY. There was a "Gutless Gert", but she was a Rover Sunbeam who saw service in France and I felt it appropriate to christen Gwyn's infamous jack with the moniker. After a long hard day and night of driving, these brave women of the driving fleet would finally sit back with a steaming cup of hot chocolate—a decadent juxtaposition between the juggling of life and death they faced at every turn. It was one of the few ways they could hope to find a sense of normalcy. Many people who had yet to make their mark on the world drove ambulances, such as Ernest Hemingway, Gertrude Stein, and Walt Disney. Disney served as a Red Cross Ambulance Corps driver in France. He even managed to decorate his own ambulance, but he never saw action since his unit didn't ship out until the day after the armistice was signed. I simply couldn't resist having him make an appearance earlier in the war.

The Great War raged for four uncompromising years, filling history with some of the bloodiest battles ever recorded and wiping out an entire generation of young men. Soldiers returned home broken and shattered, oftentimes burned so badly that only combed Pekinese dog hair woven into light garments could cover their fragile skin. Perhaps these brave men are remembered best in John McCrea's immortal poem *In Flanders Fields* where the poppy flower, crimson red against a field of green and white crosses, has come to symbolize the Lost Generation. I hope in some small way that I've managed to pay tribute to these courageous men and women who gave their all not only to their country, but to their brothers and sisters who stood beside them among the ravages of No Man's Land.

GLOSSARY

- alcohol bath – Used to decrease body temperature.
- banger – Sausage.
- beef tea – Boiled rump meat and strained to drink. Used especially for the sick.
- Blighty – Soldier's slang for England. A Blighty wound was the most Desirous as it was just serious enough to send a soldier home but not bad enough to maim or kill.
- bonnet – Hood.
- bottled chicken – Jellied skin and bone of chicken.
- brollie – Umbrella.
- bully beef – Finely minced beef in a small amount of gelatin and used as a main field ration for the British army. Commonly known as corned beef.
- chatts – Lice.
- clearing station – A military medical facility behind the front lines for treating soldiers out of range of enemy artillery. Not intended for long-term stay.
- CO – Commanding officer.
- COMMS – Communications.
- dressing station – First aid post close to a combat area.
- duck board – A platform built over muddy ground to form a dry passageway.

- FANY – First Aid Nursing Yeomanry. Founded in 1907 and provided nurses, ambulance drivers, and general volunteer aid.

- fire step – Built into each trench two or three feet from the floor to enable soldiers to peer over the side of the trench through the parapet into No Man's Land and across to the enemy line.

- firestorm – Heavy shooting.

- Fritz – Germans.

- Front – The main theater of war where the battles took place.

- hardtack – An inexpensive and long-lasting biscuit made from water, flour, and sometimes salt. Commonly used during long sea voyages and military campaigns.

- Jack Johnsons – A black German 15 cm artillery shell, the heaviest used by the German army to create a crater twenty feet deep. Nicknamed after Jack Johnson, the US world heavyweight boxing champion.

- Jerries – Germans.

- Kaiser – Wilhelm II the German Emperor.

- lorry – Truck.

- lysol swabs – Used to clean wounds.

- mape – Slang for a Canadian derived from maple.

- MO – Medical officer.

- No Man's Land – Area of ground between the two opposing armies.

- over the top – An idiom dating back to WWI meaning excessiveness. Chiefly used by the British, it's the process where infantrymen emerged from their trenches and scrambled into No Man's Land to attack the enemy.

- POW – Prisoner of war.

- puttees – A long, narrow piece of cloth wound tightly around the leg from ankle to knee to provide support and protection.

- quartermaster – A senior soldier responsible for quartering, rations, clothing, and other supplies.

- RAMC – Royal Army Medical Corps.

- reserve line – Backup trench for the second line trench should the enemy break through the lines. Contained extra supplies, cooks, medics, and new recruits.

- Sam Browne Belt – A wide belt, usually leather, supported by a narrow strap passing diagonally over the right shoulder of an officer's military uniform.

- Sister – A position of authority within the nursing hierarchy who is registered and can administer drugs. As nursing used to be province of religious orders, especially orders of nuns, the term 'Sister' was used.

- Stahlhelme – German helmet.

- tincture of iodine – antiseptic.

- Tommy – British soldier.

- VAD – Voluntary Aid Detachment. A volunteer unit providing field nursing services. Cheekily referred to as Very Adorable Darlings with noted members Vera Brittain, Agatha Christie, and Amelia Earhart.

- Yank – American.

Made in the USA
Middletown, DE
05 July 2021